THE JERUSALEM PUZZLE

Laurence O'Bryan has worked in IT marketing for many years, ten of them in London, until he was made redundant. He then returned to Dublin where he has lived since.

To find out more about Laurence, find him on Twitter @LPOBryan, follow him on Facebook at www.facebook.com/laurence.obryan and visit his blog www.lpobryan.wordpress.com.

By the same author:

The Istanbul Puzzle

LAURENCE O'BRYAN

The Jerusalem Puzzle

AVON

AVON
A division of HarperCollins*Publishers*
77–85 Fulham Palace Road,
London W6 8JB

www.harpercollins.co.uk

A Paperback Original 2013
1

First published in Great Britain by
HarperCollins*Publishers* 2013

A catalogue record for this book is
available from the British Library

ISBN 978-1-84756-289-0

Set in Sabon LT Std by Palimpsest Book Production Limited,
Falkirk, Stirlingshire

Printed and bound in Great Britain by
Clays Ltd, St Ives plc

MIX
Paper from
responsible sources
FSC
www.fsc.org
FSC® C007454

FSC™ is a non-profit international organisation established to promote
the responsible management of the world's forests. Products carrying the
FSC label are independently certified to assure consumers that they come
from forests that are managed to meet the social, economic and
ecological needs of present and future generations,
and other controlled sources.

Find out more about HarperCollins and the environment at
www.harpercollins.co.uk/green

'When the blast of war blows in our ears, then imitate the action of the tiger.'

Henry V Act 3, Sc. 1, Wm Shakespeare.

The best part of this story is true.

1

Flames burst into life with a whoosh. It was an unusually cold night for late February in Jerusalem. Lead-coloured clouds had been rolling in from the Dead Sea, east of the city, since midday. By ten o'clock that night the streets of the Old City's Muslim quarter were deserted. Smells of cardamom coffee and kofta drifted from shuttered windows.

At one minute past ten, the stepped passage of Aqabat at-Takiya echoed loudly with the sound of footsteps. Two men dressed in dusty suits and chequered keffiyehs were hurrying down the wide steps.

The high masonry walls on each side gave the alley the appearance of a gap between prisons. As the men approached the arched entrance to Lady Tunshuq's Palace they saw orange flames coming from the recessed doorway.

They stopped, waited a few seconds pressed against the wall, then moved slowly forward, craning their necks until they could see what was burning. Whoever had set the fire was long gone into the warren of narrow alleys all around.

As a gust of wind blew the flames up, they saw the body burning fiercely in front of the double-height, green steel doors. Then a throat-clogging smell of burning flesh hit them.

The man who'd seen the flames first was already talking on his phone. He could feel the heat from the fire on his face, though they were fifteen feet away. He coughed, backed away. The acrid smell was getting stronger.

They watched as the flames rose. The wail of an ambulance seemed far away as blackened skin slipped from the man's face. Tendons and muscle glistened in the flames. A white cheekbone poked out.

Above the head, paler smoke was drifting where hair should have been. The sickly smell was all around now. A man shouted from a half-shuttered window high up. A woman wailed to God.

A spurt of hissing flames reflected on the alternating light and dark bands of Mamluk masonry and the stone stalactites hanging above the doorway. The sound echoed down the long passage.

2

I turned the radio down. Verdi's 'Chorus of the Hebrew Slaves' had passed its climax.

'This website says Abingdon is the oldest continuously occupied town in Britain.' I looked up. A squall of rain hit the side of the car.

'It says people have lived there for 6,000 years. That's got to make for one hell of a long list of mayors at the town council.' It was hard reading while Isabel was driving, not just because it was a rainy morning in February, but also because the road we were on, the A415 from Dorchester, twisted and turned at that point under a high canopy of trees.

'In 1084 William the Conqueror celebrated Easter here.' I looked at Isabel.

She kept her attention on the road ahead. 'It is St Helen's Church we're looking for, isn't it?'

'Yes,' I said.

'It was the first monastery to be established in England,' she said. 'It's even older than Glastonbury. You could get four years out of purgatory for visiting it. Sounds like a good deal, doesn't it?'

She was smiling. Her long black hair was tied up at the back. She looked good.

'The church is still looking at all sorts of schemes to get people in the door. Did Lizzie tell you they had to go on a marriage preparation course before they used the church for their wedding?' I said.

'She doesn't tell me things like that.' She sniffed. It was barely audible, but its meaning was clear.

I didn't reply. I wasn't going to go there. Lizzie worked at the Institute of Applied Research in Oxford in the office next to mine. We'd always been friendly, though it had never led to anything. Her husband-to-be, Alex Wincly, had followed her around like a day-old puppy for years.

'They spent three Wednesday evenings talking about their relationship,' I said. 'What a nightmare. How did they find enough to talk about?'

'It sounds like a good idea to me.' Isabel kept her attention on the traffic, but her eyebrow on my side was up half an inch, at least.

'I reckon she's pregnant,' I said. 'Why else would they get married in February?'

'There's a lot of reasons people get married in winter, aside from being pregnant.'

The car radio buzzed as we swept under electricity cables strung between giant pylons. 'This is the eleven o'clock news from Radio Three,' said the announcer.

There was another loud buzz. I missed a few seconds of the next sentence.

'. . . the badly burnt body discovered in the Old City of Jerusalem early this morning was that of an American archaeologist named Max Kaiser, according to local sources. His death is being blamed on Islamic extremists. In other news . . .'

Isabel slowed the car. A car behind, tailgating us, blew its horn.

'Kaiser's dead,' she whispered.

She gripped the wheel. The car sped up again.

I got that out-of-body feeling you get when you discover someone you've heard of has died, as if all your senses have become heightened as you realise how fortunate you are to be alive.

We didn't know Max Kaiser well. We'd only met him once in Istanbul when he'd helped us out of the water in the middle of the night, and allowed us to dry out on his yacht, but we were involved with him. He'd staked a very public claim to a manuscript we'd found in Istanbul so he wasn't ever going to get my vote for person of the year, but he didn't deserve to die like that.

'Poor bastard,' I said.

'It's hard to believe,' she said.

'Do you think he told Susan Hunter the truth?'

Isabel shrugged. She looked pale. 'Susan wouldn't have fallen for his bullshit,' she said. She glanced at me. 'They did say he was burnt to death?'

'Yeah.'

She went silent.

Dr Susan Hunter was the Cambridge archaeologist who was producing a report for the Turkish government on the ancient manuscript we'd found in an aqueduct tunnel deep under Istanbul. It was the arrangement that had been agreed soon after the manuscript was found.

Dr Hunter was the leading expert on early Byzantine manuscripts in the world. The promise of her personal involvement had probably secured the agreement of the Turkish archaeological authorities for the manuscript to be studied in England.

'I read that book she wrote on Byzantine superstitions. They believed some totally crazy stuff,' said Isabel. She shook her head, as if shaking something off.

7

'Looks like this storm is getting worse,' I said, leaning forward to look out the window.

By the time the wedding reception was over we'd experienced the best that Abingdon had to offer. It rained for most of the afternoon, but the bride and groom managed to get wedding pictures by the hotel's private mooring on the Thames. We enjoyed the reception, especially the all-girl band from Windsor, all mates of Carol's apparently. We danced non-stop and thanks to Isabel not drinking we were able to drive back to London late that night.

On the journey I checked my email, scoured the online news sites to see if they were saying anything about Max Kaiser's death. They weren't. I reread the last email I'd received from Dr Hunter earlier that week. In it she'd said there was no definite delivery date on her final report yet. I'd replied, thanking her for keeping me informed, asking to be put on the circulation list as soon as the report was available. She hadn't replied.

It was six months since our return from Istanbul. I'd expected Dr Hunter to say her report would be ready in another year or more. At least she hadn't done that. We all despaired at the institute at some of the reasons academics gave for taking so long to do things. It was a running joke for us.

'Do you think Kaiser's death will make any difference to her report, Sean?'

I shrugged. 'No idea,' I replied.

After we got home I composed an email to Dr Hunter, asking whether she had heard about Kaiser. I also asked about his level of cooperation. It was probably a bit over the top, poking my nose in, but I couldn't stop myself.

I needed to know whether she knew how important her report was to us. It had become a talisman. Alek, a colleague and a friend who'd worked with me at the institute and had

8

gone out to Istanbul ahead of me, had been murdered there. The manuscript we'd found was something good that had come out of his death. It felt almost as if he'd given up his life for it. I had to know what was in it, what Dr Hunter's translation would uncover.

My boss, Dr Beresford-Ellis, had postponed our final project review meeting on what had happened in Istanbul because of the report. My job was now tied up with it all. That was my mistake.

But I knew I was right not to let it go.

We'd stopped a plot to infect thousands with a deadly plague virus at a Muslim demonstration in London after investigating what had happened to Alek. But some of the people who'd been behind that plot had escaped.

That was the unsettling part. My friend Alek had died out there because of these people. Isabel and I had almost died too. And whoever had been digging under Istanbul, looking for that plague virus, were clearly people with substantial resources, whose reasons for going to all that trouble were still unclear.

The best thing that had happened, out of everything that had gone on, was that Isabel and I were getting on so well. She had taken an early retirement package at the Foreign Office. She wanted to leave her old life behind. She didn't tell me all the details, but she told me enough for me to understand why she wanted out.

The rest of that weekend was uneventful. But on Monday morning I got another shock. I was checking the BBC News website before heading to Oxford for a meeting at the institute, when I spotted an article about a fire in Cambridge in which one person had died. The article didn't name the person, but the fire had taken place in Elliot Way, a fact that made something twist inside me.

A conversation I'd had with Dr Hunter came back to

me, in which she'd mentioned she wanted to move out of her house in Elliot Way, as it was too big for her needs now.

It had to be a coincidence. Was I getting paranoid?

Maybe my GP was right. It was going to take a long time to settle back into a normal life. He was the Zen master of common sense. I'd only gone to him because of Isabel's pestering. Having your sleep disturbed week after week was the sort of problem I usually tried to solve myself. That's a male thing, isn't it? We think we should be able to fix everything, even ourselves.

I checked my email.

My mind was put to rest. There was an email from Dr Hunter. I opened it quickly. 'Sean, I'm in Jerusalem. I'll be back in London on Friday. Will call you then. There's something we need to talk about. SH.' It had been sent on Sunday afternoon.

I thought about replying, asking her what was so important, but I decided not to. I would find out soon enough. And I had to work on being patient.

I kept my mobile at hand all day on Friday, even though Isabel said I was losing the plot. I even left it on vibrate in a management meeting. Finances have been the main issue in these meetings for the past year, and we've all taken a pay cut. Our survival is not in question but what we spend our money on is. That evening I checked my junk mail to see if a new email from Dr Hunter had ended up in the wrong place. It hadn't. I wasn't overly concerned, but I looked up Dr Hunter on the internet. What I found out disturbed me.

10

3

Five minutes' walk from Amsterdam's flea market in Waterlooplein there is a side street with a bricked-up end wall. The red brick building at the end of the street had been a squat for a long time. Recently it had been converted into small apartments, rooms really, and let out by the week.

The two young men who had taken the top floor room ten days before had the appearance of derelicts. They were unshaven and dressed in dirty jeans, t-shirts and thin jackets when they arrived, though the sun in February in Amsterdam is a cool affair.

The fact that they didn't appear out of their room for a week attracted no notice. It was only when the manager of the building, a big mousy-haired woman, knocked on their door that their existence came into question. That was because of the pungent smell that filled the tiny area between the door and the rickety stairs. When she opened the narrow door using her key the sight that greeted her was one she had never seen in all her sixty-six years. And she'd seen a lot, especially in the old days in the red-light district.

Both young men were tied to the bedstead. The mattress

had been stripped from it and the iron frame had been upended. Both were naked. That wasn't what upset her.

Their skin was black and shrivelled to the point where they resembled burnt wooden sculptures rather than humans. The window behind them was open and the room was freezing.

The Amsterdam Medical Office would later determine that local pigeons must have spent many hours feasting on the bodies, particularly the faces, before they were found. The cause of death was obvious. Both of them had suffered one hundred percent burns. But not in one go.

They had been burnt by a blowtorch or some other flammable device on each part of their body, without damaging the room, except for scorch marks on the bedstead. The cloth that had been stuffed into their mouths to keep them quiet must have caught alight, as in each case all that remained of it was a black mulch.

The coroner confirmed that one of the men had died five days before, the other four days before. It was likely that the torture of one of these men was used to encourage the other to talk. Whether he did or not is hard to know. He certainly didn't benefit.

It would be another twenty-four hours before the National Criminal Database in the United Kingdom would tell the authorities who these men were and what they had been involved in.

4

Dr Hunter's house had burnt down and her husband had died in the fire.

Even worse, Dr Susan Hunter had gone missing from where she was staying in Jerusalem. It was only a small article, an interview with an Israeli policeman looking for anyone who might have seen her. But the article said she hadn't been seen since Sunday night, just about when she'd contacted me. And the police were now looking for her.

I sent an email to Beresford-Ellis. Things had been tricky between us for a while, but I knew what I had to do. I wasn't going to let the rumours about the collapse of our project in Istanbul impact on what I'd decided, even for a second.

I checked the visa requirements for visiting Israel and booked a flight. I heard Isabel calling me from the kitchen as I was staring at my itinerary. 'I'm coming,' I shouted.

Over dinner we discussed what I'd found.

I told her about my flight plans.

'You really think it's a good idea to go to Jerusalem?' she said. Her right eyebrow was raised.

'Yes.' I said it softly.

13

'You are crazy. You know that, don't you?' She leaned towards me. She had her serious expression on.

'Getting burnt to death is an especially bad way to go,' she said. 'Way too many people have died that way.' Her eyes gave away how worried she was. 'Bloody hell, even God does it to the Innocents in the Bible.'

I put my knife and fork down. I'd been eating slowly. Rain was lashing at the door out to the balcony. I stared into the darkness, my appetite gone.

'I feel responsible,' I said. 'That manuscript we found in Istanbul, it's like a bloody curse. Now Kaiser's dead. And Susan's missing. I don't like coincidences.'

She put her knife and fork down too. 'It's not your fault Alek died,' she said. Her powers of perception were one of the things I liked about her, even when they made me uncomfortable.

'I could have gone with him.' I said it forcefully.

'You told me he insisted on going alone.'

She was right of course, but I could have stayed in contact with him more. He might have told me that he'd found that cavern under Hagia Sophia. I could have gone out there, intervened. He might be alive if I had.

'You're not going to wait and see if they find her?'

I shook my head. 'I can't.'

'I have to go out there.' I spoke fast. 'Waiting's not an option. Nobody in Jerusalem will know anything about what Susan might be caught up in, her connection to the book.'

'Well, I'm coming too,' said Isabel. 'It'll be fun.'

I looked at her. Her loyalty impressed me, and if I was to be honest I was pleased she wanted to come. Her intelligence and wit were an asset – she'd already saved me from being kidnapped in Istanbul. 'You need me, Sean. Admit it.' She smiled.

I leaned and reached for her. She pulled away.

14

'Have I ever denied it?' I pushed the plates aside, leaned further and pulled her gently to me.

The following day I called Beresford-Ellis.

'The authorities can do this a lot better than you, Sean,' he said.

'I want to see what's going on for myself.'

He snorted. 'This is not your business.'

'It is my business. She's been translating the book we found. Now she's missing and her husband is dead.'

He made a honking noise, like a startled pig. 'Have you gone stark raving mad, Ryan? You're a research director, not a private investigator. This sort of stuff is not in your job description. Not in it at all.' Mr Nice was long gone now. 'Do you know anything about the situation out there?' He didn't wait for me to answer.

'It's a bloody powder keg waiting to go off. Think about it, Ryan. This is crazy. You're crazy even talking about it.'

That made me more determined than ever.

'Crazy or not, I'm going. And I'm doing it on my own time too, so it doesn't have to be in my job description.' I breathed deeply, working on keeping cool.

Now there was a bonus to going. I could enjoy Beresford-Ellis's discomfort.

'I've quite a lot of holiday time coming up and I can't think of a better way to spend it. You told me yourself that I hadn't taken off enough time after Istanbul.' Check, mate.

'Your contract is something we need to talk about, actually.' The frustration in his voice told me everything I needed to know about what he thought of my contract.

'Sure, when I get back.'

He hummed loudly. 'Make sure to tell the authorities everything you get up to. I don't want any policemen ringing me. Every department is having its budget revised this year, Ryan, particularly the wasteful ones. I was planning to tell you in a few days, but I think you should bear it in mind. We may need to make further cuts. That may include staff numbers too.'

It was as veiled a threat as a knife poked in your face. If he could persuade the management committee that I was wasting the institute's funds, my chances of continuing Alek's work and of buying new equipment for other projects, would rapidly approach zero. I was angry, but with myself now too. I should have expected this.

'Keep me informed,' he said.

I cut the call.

On the way to the airport Isabel showed me an online article about people being burnt to death. It listed the thousands killed by fire and brimstone in Soddom and Gomorrah, the people burnt to death for making the wrong offerings, and lots of other weirdness.

We stuck out among the corporate types on the train. Isabel was in her trademark tight indigo denims. I was in my thin suede jacket and black jeans. We both had black Berghaus backpacks. We might as well have put up a sign saying ON HOLIDAY over our heads.

This was my first time visiting Israel, but not for political reasons. If I was honest, I'd have to say I was glad I had a good reason to go now.

The queue for the flight was moving like a film being downloaded over a slow connection. We went through three separate security checks. Given the daily media reports about Israel, I wasn't too surprised.

'Do you think it's going to kick off out there?' said Isabel, pointing at a headline in a newspaper about Israel denouncing Iran.

I shrugged. The man ahead of her turned the page.

'We certainly got our timing right,' she said. 'To get there for the start of the third world war.'

5

Henry Mowlam, a senior desk-based Security Services operative, threw the bottle of water towards the blue plastic recycling bin next to the back wall of MI5's underground control room in Whitehall, central London.

It missed the bin and burst open. A shower of water sprayed over the pale industrial-yellow wall.

'Bugger,' said Henry, loudly.

Sergeant Finch was at the end of the row of monitoring desks. She looked up, then walked towards him.

'You all right today, Henry? Working weekends not suit you?'

Her starched white shirt was the brightest thing in the room.

'They do, ma'am.' He saluted her abruptly.

She went over, pushed the plastic bottle towards the bin with her foot. It looked as if she was checking what the bottle was at the same time. Then she came back to him. The simulated outdoor lighting hummed above her head.

'Are you sure you're okay?'

'Yes, ma'am.' He was staring at his screen.

She walked away.

The report on the screen, which was the latest summary of the electronic monitoring of Lord Bidoner, a former member of the House of Lords only because of a title his father had inherited, had given him nothing new to go on. Lord Bidoner was one of those lords who didn't apply himself to his responsibilities, and whose shady connections and wheeler-dealing made sure he'd never get an invitation to Buckingham Palace for a garden party.

But they still had nothing definite on Lord Bidoner. Taking a phone call from someone two steps removed from a plot to spread a plague virus in London was enough to put you on a watch list and get you investigated, but it was not enough to get you arrested.

'We have new threats, Henry. We checked him out. You know there's been a flood of suspects coming in from Pakistan and Egypt. We have to put Lord Bidoner on the back burner,' was what Seageant Finch had said to him a week before.

But Henry wasn't convinced.

He'd mentioned it again at their Monday morning meeting. The head of the unit had brought up Bidoner's file on the large screen and had reeled off the details of the vetting he'd been subject to over the past six months.

'He's passed every check. His father was well respected, a pillar of the house. I know his mother was Austrian, but we don't hold that against people anymore, Henry.' There had been titters around the room. Henry hadn't replied.

It wasn't having an Austrian mother that made Henry suspicious. It was Bidoner's use of encrypted telephone and email systems, his endless profits on the stock market from defence industry shares he picked with an uncanny prescience, and his political speeches at fringe meetings about population changes in Europe and the rise of Islam. Taken one by one they were all legitimate, but together they made Henry's nose twitch.

He stared at his screen. He had other work to do. His hand hovered over the Bidoner report. He should delete it. And he should request that the Electronic Surveillance Unit discontinue the project.

He clicked another part of the screen. He would ask for the surveillance reports to be cancelled later. He had to review an incident in Amsterdam.

The victims of a bizarre double burning had been identified. They were a brother and a cousin of the men who had been arrested in London as part of the virus plot the previous August. The men arrested had known nothing about what they were doing that day. They had been dupes. But they were still in prison on remand.

It looked very much like whoever was behind that plot had just disposed of some people who could betray them.

There was another fact about this incident that concerned Henry. All these dupes were exiled Palestinians, from a village south of Jerusalem. A village where some sickening incidents had taken place.

6

In front of us in the queue there was a bald-headed giant of a man and his stony-faced partner. He must have been six foot eight. I was six one and he towered over me. I overheard a few words in Russian between them.

'They look like they're auditioning for the Organizatsiya,' whispered Isabel.

I shook my head.

'The Russian Jewish mob,' she said.

'That's a bit harsh,' I said. 'What does that make us?'

'Generation Z dropouts.'

'Speak for yourself. I haven't retired at thirty-six like some people I know.'

She gave me one of her smiles, then glanced away, as if she was looking for someone. I turned. There were too many people behind to work out who she'd been staring at.

'Expecting a friend?'

'No, it's not that.' She leaned toward me. 'I thought I saw someone I know.' She shook her head. 'But it wasn't him.'

On the plane I spent most of the time reading a guide-book about Israel. About halfway through the flight a small group of skull-capped men went to the front of the cabin and swayed back and forth, their heads down. They were praying.

Later, I looked out of the window when I heard someone say they could see the island of Mykonos. It was barely visible through a blue haze near the horizon. There wouldn't be many people on the beaches there now.

As we began the descent and the seatbelt sign turned on again, I saw a plume of smoke spreading across the sky.

'It's a forest fire on Mount Carmel,' said Isabel.

'How the hell do you know that?'

'There was an article about it on the *Jerusalem Post* website this morning.'

When we landed at the airport near Tel Aviv I felt the buzz of excitement around me. We reached immigration by passing along a wide elevated sunlit passage. There was a big queue for passport control in the area beyond, but it was moving quickly. Isabel's 'Russian mob friends' allowed us to pass in front of them. I nudged her. There was a rosary in the woman's hand.

Isabel made a face at me, as if to say, okay you were right.

We passed through immigration quickly. Outside the building there were young soldiers to the left and right in brown, slightly oversized uniforms with machine guns hanging from their shoulders and watchful looks in their eyes.

We took a taxi to Jerusalem, to the Hebron Road not far from the Old City. Coming towards the city on a modern motorway, with large green signs in Hebrew, Arabic and English was a surreal experience. We passed dark green tanks on dark green transporters going the other way. There must have been ten of them. As we neared the city, a glint of gold sparkled near the horizon, set against low hills and a crust of buildings.

'That must be the Dome of the Rock,' I said, pointing out the window. 'Where Solomon built his famous temple.'

Isabel held my hand. 'I've always wanted to come here,' she said.

The highway turned. The spark of gold was gone. Pale cream, modern two and three-storey apartment buildings filled the low hills around us. As we got close to the city there were older buildings, and long tree-lined boulevards of apartments.

There was a lot of traffic too. Sunday's the start of the week here, our driver said.

He had given us a running commentary on the latest news from Egypt and on the situation in Israel almost all the way from the airport. Our hotel, the Zion Palace, was a four-star, but it didn't look it from the outside. The entrance was down a set of wide steps, like descending into a cave, but inside, the lobby was wide and marble-floored. There were brass coffee tables at the back, surrounded by chocolate-brown leather high-backed chairs. Huge blue ceramic pots sat in the corners of the lobby and paintings of Old Jerusalem hung on the walls.

The view from the small balcony in our room made me want to hold my breath. We stared out at the city. To our right were the pale gold sandstone walls of the Old City.

The hill of Mount Zion, crowned by the high upturned-funnel style roof of the Dormiton Abbey with its dome-capped tower was just visible to the far right.

There was an ancient magic to this view. There was history and religion in every glance, and something older overlaying it all. Countless wars had been fought over this patch of land and its fate was still in bitter dispute.

The hum of traffic, honking car horns and occasional shouts came up from the road below. Leaden clouds rolled slowly overhead.

I pointed at the Old City walls.

'Just a bit further up that way is the Jaffa Gate,' I said.

'Do you see the valley to the right of the walls?' Isabel nodded. 'That's where the followers of Ba'al and Moloch sacrificed their children by fire, while priests beat drums to hide the screams.'

'Yeuch, that's too sick.'

'They call that place Gehenna, the valley of hell.' I went to the edge of the balcony, as if drawn forward. The start of the valley, the part we could see, looked dried out, rocky, its low trees withered and dusty.

'That's where the entrance to hell is for a lot of Jews, and for some Christians and followers of Islam too. They think that's where the wicked will line up to be punished at the end of the world.'

'And now you can find it on a map,' said Isabel.

Famished by the time we reached the hotel, we sat down immediately for dinner, eating in near silence, the fatigue of the journey capturing our thoughts. Back at our room I scoured Israeli websites for any news about Dr Hunter. There was nothing about her disappearance mentioned anywhere in the last few days. The only thing I found were the original articles about her going missing.

The main story on the Haaretz website was about a Jewish family that had been burnt to death in an arson attack the night before in a settlement near Hebron. The horror of it leapt off the screen. Pictures of a small blackened house with an ambulance in front of it, surrounded by Israeli soldiers, filled the news page. Isabel looked over my shoulder as I read it.

'They're blaming some local Palestinians,' I said.

'How many more people are going to get burnt to death?' said Isabel.

'You can get shot out here too,' I said. I pointed at another article. It was about a funeral of a Palestinian youth who'd been shot in the back after being part of a demonstration in

23

a village sandwiched between Jewish settlements. A Jewish settler was being blamed for that death.

'It's all sickening,' said Isabel.

'There's a vicious fight going on here, unbending hatred,' I replied. Opening my email, there was the usual array of special offers from every hotel, airline and social network I'd ever used and some I hadn't. I spotted an email from Dr Beresford-Ellis. It had an attachment. I clicked on it. The message wouldn't open. The screen just froze.

Had the internet stopped completely? I went to another tab and tried to download a page. It wouldn't work either. Nothing would. I waited another minute.

'I'll go down and see if they can do anything about the signal; find out if it's better in the lobby,' said Isabel.

'Can you see if you can get some fruit, I'm still hungry?' I said.

The internet was still off ten minutes later and Isabel hadn't come back. I let the door bang as I left the room, pushing the old-fashioned key into my pocket as I waited for the lift. I was hoping it would open to Isabel's smiling face, but it was empty when it arrived.

In the lobby there was no sign of her either. I went to the reception. The dark-haired girl who'd checked us in was gone. In her place was an older guy with a bald spot he was trying to hide by brushing his hair over. He was standing in a corner of the reception area that was walled with blue and white Ottoman-era tiles.

'No, I haven't seen a lady in dark blue jeans with straight black hair,' he said, after I described Isabel. His expression was quizzical, as if he was wondering whether I was asking him to find me a date.

'Maybe she went to the shop. It's down the road. Not far.' He smiled, showed me his yellowing teeth.

'Is there a problem with the Wi-Fi?' I asked.

'No, sir. It's working perfectly.'

'Not for me. How far away is this shop?'

'Not far.' He pointed towards the front of the hotel, then to the left.

I walked to the glass front door, then up the steps to the road to see if Isabel was coming. I'd never been this protective of Irene, my wife, a doctor who'd volunteered and then been murdered in Afghanistan two years before, but after what had happened to her my urge to look after Isabel couldn't be ignored. Irene had been robbed of her life. I couldn't bear for anything like that to happen to anyone else.

It was dark outside.

I had to tell myself to stop being paranoid. I looked back down at the hotel doors.

A man's face was peering up at me through the glass door.

'What are you doing out here?' said a friendly voice behind me. 'Did you miss me?'

I turned. Isabel was coming towards me from the other direction to the shop. She had a brown paper bag in her arms. 'I got you your fruit.'

She held the bag forwards, smiled, then touched my arm as she passed. A ridiculous iron weight of fear lifted from my chest. When we got back to the room the Wi-Fi was working perfectly.

'I got a call from Mark while I was out,' she remarked. 'He's stationed in Cairo these days. Not a million miles from here.'

I spoke slowly. 'Why does he keep calling you? I thought you two were over.'

She'd dumped him a year ago.

'You are so jealous!' she said. There was a sympathetic note to her voice.

I gave her my best see-if-I-care smile.

'He wants to meet me again.' She shook her head as if the idea was outrageous.

'What?' This was getting annoying.

'I'm not going to, don't worry.'

I opened the balcony door and went outside, staring over the lights illuminating the Old City walls. Isabel didn't just have skeletons in her cupboard, she had live exhibits, waiting to be set free.

I felt a hand on my back and Isabel whispered in my ear. 'Come to bed, Sean. I want to prove to you that there is no one else.' Taking my hand she pulled me back inside. It was another hour before I got to sleep.

7

Arap Anach took the thick yellow candle from its holder. It burned with a blue-white flame and gave off a sweet scent; olive oil mixed with myrrh, the ancient incense Queen Esther had bathed in for six months to beautify herself for her Persian King.

Myrrh was used at times of sacrifice. Arap knew its scent from his childhood. One man in particular had smelled of it. A man who'd brought pain.

He closed his eyes, breathing the ancient smell in. Myrrh came from a thorny shrub which wept from the stem after it was cut. Some varieties are worth more than their weight in gold.

He put his left hand out and held it over the flame. The pain was familiar. The walls of the room danced around him as the shadows from the candle played on the walls. He wrenched his thoughts away from the flame, focusing on the wall hangings. The thick red one with the stylised flames embroidered on it was the one he liked most.

He bent his back. The searing pain in his hand grew in steps, as if ascending towards an ultimate crescendo. He threw his head back and opened his eyes. Not much longer. Seconds. One . . .

The low white roof, its plaster filled with tiny cracks, swam in his vision. The cracks were moving. It always amazed him what pain could do to your consciousness.

His need to take his hand away was making his arm tremble now. It was moving, rocking as muscle spasms from the pain were shooting up his nerves. He kept his hand to the flame.

He had to. It was the only way. He had to know the pain he would inflict on others, the better to enjoy inflicting it when the moment came.

He jerked his hand away, breathing in and out slowly. It was time to make the call.

He turned on the mobile phone, pressed at the numbers quickly, his hand trembling, the pain of the scorched skin pulsing in waves. As he put it to his ear he heard the ring tone at the other end of the line.

'Rehan,' said a voice.

'Father Rehan, I am so glad I found you. I am just checking that everything is in order.' Arap Anach forced himself to sound friendly. His breathless eagerness he didn't have to feign.

'Yes, yes, my son. Your donation has been received. We are all very grateful. Is there anything we can do for you?'

Arap Anach hesitated. 'No, not really, Father. I'm just happy to be able to help with the restoration of the church.' He coughed.

'Please, there must be some small thing we can do for you while you are here.'

Arap coughed again, then spoke. 'There is a small thing. It would make me so happy. I have prayed for it for a long time.'

8

I woke in the middle of the night. There was fear in my dream. Fear and flames. I wondered for long seconds where I was. My face was hot, sweaty.

The gray shape of the curtains and the yellow glimmer of street lights in the gap between them brought everything back. We had come to look for Dr Hunter, to find out what had happened to Max Kaiser.

For months after we got back from Istanbul I'd wanted to have a long conversation with Kaiser, to give him my honest opinion about him claiming that the book we'd found in Istanbul was his. He needed someone to puncture his ego. It would have ended up in a shouting match or worse, but I didn't care.

But now he was dead, and in such a horrible manner that my instinct for revenge had turned to pity. He'd reaped what he'd sown. God only knew how many people he'd enraged before me.

I was hoping the dream wouldn't come back when I fell asleep again, but it did, and the flames were nearer this time and hotter.

But this time I was woken by a voice.

'Sean, Sean, wake up.' Isabel's tone was concerned. I was breathing fast. I sat up.

'Was it the same as before?' she asked. She hugged me.

'Yeah.' I didn't have the heart to tell her about the flames. That part was new. The fear wasn't.

'Do you want to talk about it?'

'No, I'll be ok,' I said.

I lay down again. Isabel had spent a couple of nights asking me all about what had happened to Irene; how I felt about everything that had happened. It had been good to talk, but this felt different and after her speech about people being burnt to death before we came here, it didn't seem right to tell her what had got into my dreams.

It was light when I next woke. I'd slept a long time. Isabel was in the shower. The hum of cars, a distant car horn honking and the morning sounds of Jerusalem filled the air when I opened the balcony door. I was glad the night was over.

The traffic was heavy on the road outside. A bell tolled far away. I stared at the old walls of the city. They looked like props from a movie about Crusaders and Saracens. A rolling blanket of clouds filled the sky.

I looked up Max Kaiser on the internet. There were quite a few pieces about his body being found at the back of Lady Tunshuq's Palace. The police had questioned some local hardline Islamists. Others were being sought. It was clear who they thought had murdered him.

I found an older article about some work Kaiser had done with a scientist attached to the Hebrew University. His name was Simon Marcus. Had Kaiser met him again while he was out here?

I trawled the Hebrew University website looking for anyone I might know. I needed someone to introduce me to Simon Marcus, someone he would trust.

After almost giving up, I finally found what I was looking

for. A Dr Talli Miller in the Laser Research Unit. We had a tenuous connection, but it was better than nothing. She'd presented a paper at a conference I'd spoken at and we'd been at the same table for lunch. It was enough.

I found a contact number and picked up the hotel phone to call her. The number at the university rang and rang. I looked at my watch. It was just past 9.00 a.m. Surely they were open?

Finally a voice answered.

'University' was the only word I understood. It was a thin voice. She was speaking in Hebrew, the main language in Israel, the ancient language of Judaism. I knew only a few words of it. Easy words, like shalom: hello.

'Dr Talli Miller,' I said.

Normally I'd have spent time learning a language if I was visiting somewhere. My German wasn't bad following a project we'd worked on in the Black Forest, but a day and a half wasn't long enough to learn any language, no matter how dedicated you were.

The line sounded dead. Had she hung up?

Then it fizzed.

'Shalom,' said a woman's voice. Talli's voice.

'Hi, it's Sean Ryan. I'm in Jerusalem.'

There was a long silence.

'Who?'

It was nice to be recognised so quickly. 'Sean Ryan, I was on the panel when you gave a speech about high temperature lasers at the University of London.'

'Sean, Sean.' She repeated my name slowly. 'How are you?' Suddenly she was friendly and her voice returned to normal. We reminisced for a few minutes. Then I asked her if she knew Dr Simon Marcus. She did, but not well.

'That's a pity,' I said. 'I need to speak to him urgently.'

'I may be able to do something. I'll call you in a few minutes. What hotel are you in?'

I told her. My spirits lifted. I'd done it. My connections were going to get me to Simon Marcus.

We ate breakfast in a long high-ceilinged dining room. There were groups of people in the room speaking French, Polish and Spanish, all pilgrims visiting their Holy City.

The breakfast, a selection of cheeses, scrambled eggs, olives, jams and soft bread would have satisfied anyone.

One of the waiters, a black-haired, smiling man, came to our table with a wireless telephone handset as we were finishing.

'Dr Ryan?' he said.

I nodded. I never used my title in public, but Talli might have used it when she rang the reception. I took the phone. 'Hello.'

'I'll be at your hotel in one hour. Be ready.' The voice was Talli's, but the friendliness was gone. In its place was a distinct hardness, the sort of attitude she probably reserved for her most disrespectful students, the ones who insulted her in a lecture.

The line went dead.

'She's on her way,' I said.

An hour later we were in the hotel lobby. I went outside to see if she was coming. It was cool, but my suede jacket was enough to keep me warm. After a while I went back inside.

An hour and a half later we were still waiting.

By then it was nearly eleven. I called the Hebrew University. A receptionist answered. She checked, then came back and told me that Dr Talli Miller was not available.

By 11.30 a.m. I was properly pissed off. We took turns going back up to the room. God only knew what had happened to Talli. Had I misheard her about the time? No, I couldn't have. I even tried asking the hotel if they could bring up the number of the person who'd called me. They couldn't.

For something to do I looked up the main hospitals in Jerusalem and went to their websites on my phone using the hotel lobby Wi-Fi. I was thinking about calling them, asking them if a Dr Susan Hunter had been admitted. We might just get lucky. I took a note of their telephone numbers. I was about to start calling when Talli appeared through the revolving main door of the hotel. Her hair was a mess.

She came towards us, looking solemn. She wasn't the person I'd remembered from the last time we'd met. That had been someone who'd laughed a lot, poked at you, filled any room she was in with her energy. All that was gone.

After brief hellos, she said, 'Let's go.' She motioned for us to go with her.

'What happened to being here in an hour?' I said. I tried not to sound too irritated. I don't think I succeeded.

'Do you want my help or not?' Her cheeks were puffed up and bright pink, as if she'd been running.

'Where are we going?' Isabel was playing the part of the unruffled partner. She was smiling sweetly.

'To the Hebrew University. Simon Marcus is expecting you. He's waiting.'

'Let's go then,' I said.

It took only twenty minutes to reach the Edmund J. Safra Campus of the Hebrew University of Jerusalem. It was located on the spine of a hill a little to the west of the city centre. The buildings were modern concrete lecture and administration blocks. In between them was dry-looking grass, tall thin cypress trees, short pine trees, and the occasional palm tree.

Talli said Simon Marcus was holding a symposium that lunchtime in one of the teaching labs for his graduate students.

She drove us there in a pale blue beaten-up old Mercedes. She excused its appearance by telling us how badly academics were paid in Israel, and how high their taxes were these days.

We passed a sign for the Manchester teaching lab. Groups of students were hanging around outside the next building. Talli went straight up to the nearest person in one of the little groups and began talking. We waited a few feet away by a concrete bench. She was back with us in a minute.

She threw her hands up in the air. 'Simon's not here. It's not like him, they say. He hasn't even texted anyone.' Her eyes rolled.

'I spoke to him just before I met you. He told me he'd be here.' She sighed. 'Something must have happened.' She looked at me accusingly.

I stared back at her. If something had happened to him she couldn't blame it on me. On the way here I'd told her about Max Kaiser being burnt to death and about Susan Hunter disappearing. I was starting to regret having said anything.

'One of the students has gone to look for him. I don't know what to do after that.' She waved a hand through the air dismissively, then sat down heavily on the bench.

A few spots of rain fell. Then a downpour started. We all ran.

Talli had parked her car in an underground car park near the sports centre. Once inside the doorway we shook off the rain and walked, squelching, towards the lower floor. As we turned a corner I heard a voice call my name.

I turned.

A young woman with an earnest face and shoulder-length curly black hair, wearing a pink, rain-spotted t-shirt and pale blue jeans was walking fast towards me. She waved, as if she knew me. Isabel was a few paces ahead of me. Talli was even further on. Then she went up to the next floor, the floor the car was on.

'You're a long way from home,' the woman said.

'I am.'

'Don't you remember me?'

'When did we meet?' I had a vague memory of her, maybe

34

from the early days in Oxford. We used to get a lot of interns passing through when we first set up the institute.

She bent her head to one side, glancing over my shoulder.

I turned. Isabel was beside me. 'Hi,' she said, in a friendly manner. Talli's car started up with a roar on the floor below. The noise of the engine filled the air.

The girl was backing away. She looked as if she'd expected me to remember something else about her. 'I have to go,' she said. She turned and walked away fast.

'What was that all about?' said Isabel.

I shrugged. 'I think I met her in Oxford.'

'You don't remember her?' said Isabel.

'We get a lot of exchange students who intern at the institute. Some of them send long pleading emails. I stopped reading them. Beresford-Ellis does all that now. Maybe she was hoping for another job.'

Talli's car was right behind us. She beeped the horn. We got in.

As we drove off the campus I kept an eye out for the girl, but I didn't see her. Talli's phone rang. She pulled over to take the call. We were parked in a dangerous place, half blocking a side road leading back into the university.

Within a few seconds I had figured out who she was speaking to. It was Simon Marcus.

Talli spoke in Hebrew, looking at us, gesticulating. Then she went silent. She was listening.

'You don't remember that girl?' whispered Isabel.

'We used to have a party before the interns left each May. We used to hire a room at the Randolph in Oxford and drink all night. We were asked to leave the last time we did it. Someone let off a fire extinguisher in one of the stairwells. It was a nightmare.'

Isabel shook her head mock-disapprovingly. 'No wonder you don't remember people.'

That incident was the real reason we abandoned the intern parties, calming things down after our first years of successes. We'd been lucky no one had sent a picture of the foam on the stairs and people rolling in it to the media. We'd been applying for new research grants that year, and a picture of one of our researchers wielding an extinguisher would not have made good PR.

Talli was talking quickly on the phone. She sounded angry. Then she was listening again.

'What did Irene think of these parties?' Isabel asked quizzically.

'She enjoyed them,' I said. 'But that was ten years ago.'

Isabel looked away.

She'd told me early on that an old boyfriend used to drink himself into oblivion. She'd finished with him when he'd refused to give up.

She was very different to Irene. Irene and I had enjoyed occasional benders right up until she died.

After that, grief had taken away any desire to get drunk. Drinking brought back too many memories.

Talli had finished her call. She was putting the car back into gear.

'What did he say?' I asked.

'We're to meet him in half an hour at a cafe.'

'What happened to him?'

'I'll let him tell you himself.'

Twenty minutes later we were at a small Armenian cafe near the Jaffa Gate. The Jaffa Gate was history come to life. It had originally been built by Herod the Great in the early Roman era. Beside it was a gap in the old city wall, which cars could drive through. The gap had been made in 1898 to allow the German Emperor, Wilhelm II, to drive into the Old City.

On either side of the gate the crenulated city wall ran away left and right.

When General Allenby took Jerusalem in 1917, recovering the city from Islam after seven hundred years under its control, he entered the city on foot, through the original arched Jaffa Gate.

The gate is to the west of the warren of flat-roofed, sand-coloured buildings and alleys which make up the Old City. Once inside, to the right is the Armenian quarter, to the left the Christian quarter and straight on, the Muslim and Jewish quarters.

The road for cars curved to the right beyond the gate and there was a small paved area on the left lined with shops and cafes. These buildings were all three and four-storey high Ottoman-style shops with tall windows, rooftop balconies and arched entranceways. Plastic signs, canopies, and racks of postcards lined the pavement in front of the cafes, tourist offices and money changers.

'I'll have the lamb kebabs and a coke,' said Isabel to the white-shirted waiter who hovered over us. I ordered the same, with a coffee. Talli just ordered coffee.

'I hope he doesn't let us down again,' she said.

'Let's enjoy our lunch, whatever happens,' said Isabel. 'We don't get lunch in Jerusalem every week.'

'What do you do, Isabel?' Talli asked.

Isabel spent the next few minutes telling Talli about the low-level job she used to work at in the British Consulate in Istanbul. I think she overplays all that. I don't think I've ever met anyone else who makes their previous job out to be so lacklustre. Talli's eyebrows kept going up as Isabel described rescuing drunken businessmen from the wrong bars near Taksim Square.

Beyond the window of the cafe, I watched people walking up from the gap in the Old City wall. Three policemen were talking to each other by a set of concrete bollards near a taxi rank on the far side of the road.

All kinds of people were passing the window: priests in black habits, monks in brown, nuns with their hair covered, a group of Arab women similarly modest, American tourists, Chinese tourists, Israeli girls giggling.

A white police car drove slowly by.

The rain had stopped but the clouds hadn't gone away. They were stuck above us, like a lid over the city.

'My grandfather's brother died near this gate.' Talli turned, pointing out the window.

'When was that?' I thought she was going to tell me about some suicide bombing incident.

'In '48. He was in the Haganah. He fought against the British, then against the Jordanians. At this gate the fighting was fiercest. The Arabs wanted to kick us all out of Israel. I'm not kidding. He was shot in the head. He lay right there for four hours before his comrades could get to him.' She pointed at a spot halfway back to the gate.

'We didn't win the Old City that time, but he opened the way for Jerusalem to be free for Jews after fourteen hundred years of ill treatment and exile.' She paused and looked down at the red and white chequered tablecloth.

'His girlfriend, Sheila, she never married. I met her once. Her eyes were pools of sadness. She was so incredibly beautiful when she was young. But she was old and grey when I met her. And now she's dead.'

I glanced out the window. Two Orthodox Jews, seemingly pressed to each other for solidarity, moved fast past the window. Their long beards were black and thick, their shirts crisp and white.

Walking towards us was an older man in a faded cream suit. The girl who had approached me in the university car park was beside him. A vein thumped in my throat.

Why was she here?

38

9

The British Embassy in Cairo is in Ahmed Ragheb Street, in an affluent suburb called Garden City, on the eastern shore of the Nile, between the river and the city centre, just south of Tahrir Square. The cream, colonial-style building with its first floor balcony and lawns down to the river was in a style more suited to the days of the Raj. But behind its calm exterior a number of alterations had been made to the building to bring it into the twenty-first century.

The basement area had been extended. It now housed an intelligence suite, a situation monitoring station for the British Intelligence Service in Cairo.

That Monday afternoon it was 1.30 p.m. in Jerusalem, 12.30 p.m. in Cairo and 11.30 a.m. in London. Mark Headsell, seconded to the embassy after three and a half years in Iraq, was watching a large LCD screen on the far wall of the suite.

The screen was showing the border crossing from the Gaza strip to Egypt. The crossing was open and trucks were using it, a line of them heading slowly into Gaza. It appeared they weren't being searched.

The last time this had happened, an Israeli air raid had taken place. Two people had died. The Israelis had claimed they could prove rocket parts, destined for Hammas, were on those trucks. Whatever the UN said about Israel, there was no escaping the fact that the country would defend itself whenever it felt under threat.

Mark's worry at that moment was how far that defence would go. Since the post-Mubarak elections, things were unpredictable here. The players were changing and the military restive, eager to regain influence. The reaction of the Egyptian army to the next Israeli air strike could not be guaranteed.

Other things about Egypt worried him too. Some of them were displayed on other, smaller screens along the wall. One showed an anti-Israel demonstration in Tahrir Square. An army unit, from Zagazig, was stationed there that day and Mark's concern was about how they would react to the demonstration.

A report on the movement of an Iranian submarine near the southern entrance to the Suez Canal also disturbed him. A satellite image, courtesy of the United States NSA office, of the last known position of the submarine, was displayed on a different screen. A radar map of the area was overlaid on the image.

But the big screen on his own desk was showing what he was chiefly interested in that day. A high definition security camera feed from the main entrance to the hotel in Jerusalem where Dr Susan Hunter had stayed. The feed was paused. The Herod Citadel Hotel was one of the best in Jerusalem, but Susan Hunter hadn't chosen it for its five-star facilities.

She had chosen it because of its security arrangements. One of these, which she wasn't even aware of, nor were the security staff at the hotel, was the fact that the British Intelligence Services had tapped into the security camera system.

The ability to tap into private security systems, to relay images of diplomats and high-powered businessmen anywhere in the world, was not something the British Security Service wanted to advertise.

Dealing with public outrage about invasions of privacy would waste resources. Explaining that almost everyone would be better off with people watching their backs was unlikely to assuage true liberals. People who never had to deal with the threat of a gun attack or a suicide bomber intent on exterminating their kind were apt to be unaware of what was being done every day in their name.

And if corporate titans, religious leaders and government tsars were afraid that pictures of them with teenage escorts or coincidentally young and clearly gay personal assistants would end up in the media, they could always clean up their act.

Mark leaned forward. The woman in the centre of the screen – the reason the security camera had gone into frame-hold mode, as the facial recognition software had thrown her up as a *possible* – was similar in complexion and hair colour to Susan Hunter, but it was definitely not her. He pressed Ctrl-X on his keyboard. The screen jumped back to showing real time.

He turned to his secure instant messaging screen. The message he had highlighted a few minutes before was in the centre in a small pop-out screen. Other social media posts, Tweets and Facebook updates were flowing past it. He tagged the post as important, then closed the pop-up.

He turned to his secure email system and read his messages. A signal from Dr Susan Hunter's phone had been picked up. It had only lasted ten and a half seconds, and tracing the exact location of the transmission hadn't been completed, but the most interesting thing was that a signal had been picked up at all.

It could be a trick, of course, or a summons, but it could also be an amateur mistake on the part of her captors. The length of time the signal had been active made that a real possibility. Someone hoping to lure them would have left Susan Hunter's phone on for longer. It was well known that it took thirty seconds for a phone's location to be reliably established.

Few people knew about the latest, ultra-fast location tracking software the Israelis were using. It wasn't always right, but with a bit of luck they would soon be able to identify the location of Susan Hunter's phone and some other interesting information too.

The screen to his left was showing rolling news from the Nile News Channel, the state-owned Egyptian news service. He watched it for a few seconds, then turned up the sound.

The image on the screen was of the burnt-out house where a poor Jewish family had been found a few days before. The Arabic script flowing across the screen, from left to right, said that a 'no questions asked' reward of one million dollars had been offered by an American-Israeli group to anyone who could help them to arrest the perpetrators.

Whoever had blocked the doors and burnt that house would have to hope that everyone who knew they'd done it was as dedicated to the cause as they were.

And what would happen if someone pointed a finger at a terrorist who had recently crossed from Egypt?

What would the Israelis do then? Start bombing the crossings into Gaza?

10

The girl who had spoken to me peeled away from Simon Marcus just before he reached the cafe. Isabel was saying something to me now, but my mind was elsewhere, in the past.

'Earth to Sean. Come in, Sean.' She was waving her hand in front of my face.

'Very funny. Did you see who's coming?'

She turned fast, just in time to see Simon Marcus entering through the front door.

I leaned over the table, whispering to Isabel, 'We'll probably need your people skills with this guy.'

'I love a challenge,' she said.

Talli was halfway out of her seat already. 'Simon, good to see you.'

He sat beside me, facing Talli. 'Is this the man you told me about?' He turned to me and put his hand out.

I took it. His skin was rough, his grip hard. He shook hands with Isabel too.

He must have been six foot three. He was wearing faded jeans and a floppy navy corduroy jacket. He had a big face and his blonde hair was balding a little, but that didn't take away from the image he presented, which was of an ageing Viking.

'Who was that with you outside?' I gestured with my thumb.

'She's a graduate student. She's helping me with some important work I'm doing.' His smile was thin, his expression puzzled. 'Do you know her?'

'She may have worked briefly as an intern with my institute.'

'She was in England studying. She would have joined us, but her mother is sick. She had to go.' He shrugged.

Talli leaned over and began talking in Hebrew to Simon. She spoke fast. I had no idea what she was saying. It was disconcerting.

Finally, Simon put his hands up, turned to me and spoke in English. 'Is this about Dr Hunter?'

I nodded. 'We're trying to find her. She was doing some translation work on a book we found in Istanbul.' I pointed at Isabel, then back at myself.

Simon smiled at Isabel. It was a warm smile, as if he was keen to get to know her. Isabel smiled back.

My phone rang. It took me half a minute to get it out. That's what happens when you wear baggy chinos with voluminous pockets.

'Is that Mr Sean Ryan?' said a woman's voice with a Scottish accent.

'Yes.'

'This is a courtesy call, Mr Ryan. Your phone has been used in a country you have never previously visited. This call is simply to verify that it hasn't been stolen.'

'You're getting very security conscious.'

'We look out for our customers,' she said. 'Do you mind if I ask you a few questions?'

I agreed, after she told me they might have to restrict my

44

phone service if I didn't. She asked me my date of birth, and all the other usual questions that are asked at moments like this. I turned away from the table, dropped my voice as I answered.

When I was finished, Isabel and Simon were having a deep conversation about London.

'Did you see Dr Hunter when she was here?' I asked him, jumping in.

'No, I didn't.' He shook his head.

'Did you hear what happened to Max Kaiser?'

'Yes, yes, I did. It was terrible.' He looked me in the eye. 'You must be careful, Mr Ryan. These are dark days.'

'Why would anyone want to kill someone like that?'

He put his thumb and finger together in front of him, pressed them together. 'Some people enjoy being evil.' He spread his hands out on the table, as if he was holding it down. 'I pray they catch the terrorists who did it. Are you investigating his death?'

Isabel spoke. 'Kaiser may have met Susan Hunter. We're looking for her. If we find out where Kaiser was working, we might be able to track her down too.'

'He was working on a dig, I know that much. He used me for a reference to get onto it, but no one told me exactly where the dig is. Max was off in a world of his own,' Simon replied.

'That's true,' I said. 'What general area is the dig in?'

'In Jerusalem, somewhere.' He shrugged. 'Sorry, I know that's not much good.'

Talli joined the conversation. 'I'm sure you'll find Dr Hunter. Have you spoken to the police?'

'Not yet, but we will,' I said. I turned back to Simon. 'What happened to your meeting at lunchtime?'

He spoke slowly. 'We had a bomb scare in my apartment. There are a lot of idiots around. The police wouldn't let me take my car out. At the beginning they said I could. Then they changed their mind.' He put a hand to his forehead and rubbed it.

'Some people make me crazy. I'm a busy man.' He lowered his head. 'But I have to accept it. It's all in the name of security.' He put his palms together, bowing his head as if he was praying.

Then he looked up at me. 'What is your area of expertise?'

'Digital analysis, pattern recognition. I helped found the Institute of Applied Research. We have multidisciplinary research teams. We're academics who want advanced research to be used for practical purposes, and as soon as possible.'

He looked interested. 'Good, good. I believe I've heard of you. You would like what I'm working on. Perhaps we're ahead of even the great Oxford University.' He grinned. It was one of the grins I'd seen academics use before, when they thought they might have discovered something interesting or at least more interesting that what you were working on.

'What's the project?' I asked.

'It's not published yet, so I can't tell you.' His smile was enigmatic. 'But I will send you the article when it comes out.'

'What area is it in?' Isabel had her head to one side.

'The use of lasers for manipulation of molecules, cells and tissue. It's called biomedical optics. It's a whole new science. We got our own journal only in 2011.'

I joined the conversation. 'Two of our researchers have published papers in that journal this year. We're the only research institute in the world to have published that number in it so far.' If it had been a spitting contest, I'd have hit the far wall.

His cheeks reddened.

'Then you should see what we're doing. We're ahead of everyone.' He jabbed his finger at me.

The waiter was hovering. Simon ordered a coffee. We'd finished our kebabs. They'd been good; soft and spicy.

Isabel talked about how interesting Jerusalem was. Talli gave her some advice on where we should go while we were here. Simon's coffee came. I watched him stir it.

'A lot of people come here for their souls,' he said. He gestured toward the pedestrians passing beyond the window. 'They think they will find it in the old stones here. They look, and then they look some more, but a soul is not easy to find.'

'They need better maps,' said Talli, solemnly.

'You know about the show in the Tower of David?' Simon motioned over his head towards the museum and walled fortress on the far side of the road.

'It's not from King David's time though, is it?' said Isabel.

'It's a perfect illustration of the layers of misunderstanding in this wonderful city. The citadel is called the Tower of David because Byzantine Christians thought it was built by him. But it was built by Herod the Great.' His hands were in the air. 'A madman who murdered his family.'

Talli put her hand on his arm. 'Aren't you supposed to be somewhere?' she said. Simon looked at his watch.

'Yes, yes, what am I thinking?' He pointed at me and Isabel.

'You will come with me,' he said. 'You will see what we are working on. And you will tell all your friends in Oxford when you go back how advanced we are.' He stood.

We paid for our food.

'Where are we going?' I asked, as we headed towards the Jaffa Gate.

'To another citadel.' He gripped my arm. I put my hand on his, squeezed back, in a friendly, but determined way.

He leant towards me. 'I have a meeting this afternoon at the Herod Citadel hotel. I am presenting at 5.30. The meeting will be private, but I'd like you to see the presentation. I think you will be surprised at what we're doing. And a little jealous, perhaps!'

I didn't take the bait. I wanted to see what he was doing.

We crossed a busy highway, passed modern-looking apartments. The air was cool now, and heavy with the promise of rain.

The Herod Citadel Hotel, a five-star hotel was a step up from the one I had picked for me and Isabel.

The Old Terrace restaurant was on the roof of the hotel. It had stunning views of the Old City, to the golden Dome of the Rock and the hills beyond. And it had a glass roof that looked as if it would stay intact in a meteor shower.

We waited near the elevators. Simon went off walking through the restaurant.

He arrived back a minute later with a tall, ultra-thin, black-haired, regally attractive woman beside him. Many of the male heads in the restaurant turned to look at her as she passed.

'This is Rachel, my assistant,' said Simon. 'Come on. I have work to do.'

We went down to the meeting room. It had bright red and gold wallpaper and was set out for a presentation with rows of gold high-backed chairs and three tables lined up at the top of the room. There was a stack of brown cardboard boxes near the tables.

'You can help us,' said Simon. 'If you want. Take the reports out of these boxes. Put one on each chair.' He pointed at the chairs, then began opening boxes.

Isabel smiled at me. It was her let's-be-nice smile. Simon had to be the pushiest person I had met in years. I was tempted not to cooperate. But I had some more questions to ask him. It'd be worth a few minutes of helping him out to get some answers. I took a pile of light blue reports, put one on each chair. Then I stopped.

My telephone was buzzing. I took it out and saw the name 'Susan Hunter' flashing across the screen, but as I pushed the green button, the line went dead. My elation at seeing the call turned to frustration in a second.

11

Susan Hunter prayed. She prayed for her husband waiting for her back in Cambridge and she prayed for her sister. And at the end she prayed for herself. She wasn't used to praying. She hadn't done it since she was eight years old. And she'd never been into it that much back then either.

But she had every reason to start now.

The basement was perfectly dark. She knew how many steps away each wall was, fifteen one way, twenty the other, but some times it felt as if the dark was endless, no matter what her brain told her. Her hands were pressed tight into her stomach.

Pain was throbbing through her.

She was doing all she could to ignore it.

She wanted to cry, to wail, but she wasn't going to. He might be listening. And he'd enjoy it too much. That much she knew.

Where he had the microphone placed in the basement, she didn't know, but its existence was irrefutable.

He had come down after a period of her whimpering and played a recording of the noises she'd made to cheer her up. That was how he'd put it.

But the sounds hadn't cheered her up. They'd chilled her until her insides felt empty.

And then he'd taken her upstairs. The pain then had been horrific. And in the end he'd made her say things, which he recorded.

Then he told her he'd enjoy burning her again, if she didn't do exactly what she was told every time he asked.

The thought of how he'd said that, his certainty, was enough to set her praying again.

12

The call went straight to voicemail. My deflation was immediate. Isabel must have seen it on my face.

'Who was that?'

'Susan Hunter. Can you believe it? Now her phone is off. I didn't even get to speak to her!'

'So she's around somewhere?'

'I have no idea. I'll try her again in a few minutes.'

Simon was standing near me. 'I can put those ones out,' he said, putting his hand on the reports.

'It's okay,' I said. 'I'm doing them.'

He pulled his hand back. 'I'm trying to help you, Dr Ryan.'

'I know,' I said. 'I'm just a bit distracted.'

I turned, began putting the reports on the chairs again.

I tried Susan's phone twice in the following five minutes. The response was the same as every time I'd called her in the past six days, since I'd heard about Kaiser.

The number you are trying to reach is unavailable. Please try again later.' They must be the thirteen most frustrating words in the English language.

As I finished with the reports, Simon was putting a stack of leaflets on one of the tables at the top of the room.

On the other table a laptop had already been set up.

He sat in front of the laptop, turned and motioned me to him.

'This is what I wanted to show you.' He clicked at a file. It opened slowly.

'Who's coming to this meeting?' I asked, bending down.

'Some iron skull caps.' He didn't look up.

'Iron skull caps?'

'They're a type of Orthodox Jew,' said Isabel.

She was on the other side of the table. She looked good in her black shirt.

'You are right.' He pointed a finger at Isabel. 'But that doesn't mean I endorse their views.'

'What views?'

I was peering at what Simon had on his screen. It was a blown-up picture of a real DNA strand with lines and labels pointing to various features on the strand. We were looking at something 2.5 nanometres wide, a billionth of a metre wide. It's hard to even imagine something that thin.

'I'm not going to explain what they believe. But I'll tell you this. They were looking for someone who can do non-destructive DNA splicing, someone who can manipulate down to the molecular level. And they were willing to pay good money for the research to make it happen.'

'You're involved in a red heifer project, aren't you?' Isabel's eyes were wide.

He stared up at her, beaming.

'What's a red heifer project?' I said.

'It's a project to create one of the biblical symbols of the coming of the Messiah,' said Isabel.

'What?' I said.

'Apocalyptic Christians want to breed a perfect red cow, an act which would signify the time was right to build a new Temple,' Isabel explained.

If this was what Simon was working on, he was crazier than I thought.

Simon's head went from side to side, as if he was throwing off water.

'You haven't been in Jerusalem long, have you?' His expression was one of benign, irritating superiority.

'There are more crazies per square mile in this city than anywhere else in the world. Stop people in the street and try this: ask them about their religious views. You'll get predictions about the end of the world or about the Mahdi or about the Gates to Hell opening soon for non-believers.' He had a determined look on his face.

'Don't get me wrong. Everyone's entitled to their opinion, but where does it say I have to believe the same things my sponsors believe? You must understand this, the two of you. Don't tell me you don't.' He scrolled forward a few slides on his laptop, then back again.

'You don't think the Messiah is on his way?' said Isabel.

'My sponsors do. They run Bible studies classes here in Jerusalem. They've done it for years. They have a soup kitchen, and a matchmaking service. If someone like that is willing to cover the cost of a few years of our research, should I not take the money?' He put his head back and looked straight up at me.

I didn't answer. We had strict rules about who we would take money from. But we were lucky; we'd had major breakthroughs. And we were in Oxford. We could attract funding from many sources. And success spawns success in applied research, like in everything else.

'What do you believe in, Sean?' he asked.

'Apple pie, the moon landings, lots of things.'

'See, you can believe in anything you want. I didn't ask you to fill in a questionnaire before I brought you here, did I? We're all free to think what we want.' He twisted his shoulders, as if he had back pain he was trying to ease.

'What about your results,' said Isabel. 'Have you bred the perfect red heifer?'

He rubbed his chin. 'We've bred over a thousand red heifers. The question is, are any of them perfect? The standard is high, very high. Not one single hair can be black or brown or white, God forbid.'

'If you do breed one, a lot of people are going to claim the end of the world is nigh,' said Isabel.

'People are claiming that all the time. I don't think it will lead to a panic.'

Isabel had come around the table and was looking closely at the slide on the screen. She spoke in a low voice. 'Let's hope you're right.'

'Can you tell us anything else about Max Kaiser?' I said. It was time to get something out of all this.

'With all due respect, you are strangers here, Dr Ryan. Our police are the best people to look for your friend Susan Hunter. I think you must talk with them, for your own good.'

Talli was standing beside us now. 'Did you know Dr Ryan's organisation, the Institute of Applied Research, runs one of the best academic conferences in the UK these days? Many of the world's leading researchers attend. So I've heard.' She gave me a tentative smile. It crossed my mind that maybe she wanted to speak at one of our events.

'I wouldn't want to make an enemy of them, that's all I am saying, Simon,' she continued.

Her description of our conference would have been disputed by some, but many cutting-edge researchers would have agreed with it. We'd built a reputation for having fun too, and avoiding some of the boring stuff you'd expect at such conferences.

Simon looked at me with an interested expression. Was this the route to get him to help us, or should I press another button?

I peered at the laptop screen. 'You're laser splicing at the single nanometre level, aren't you? That's unprecedented. What's the damage threshold?'

'Lower than your dreams.'

'You'll be looking for Nobel prizes, if you can get the right people to promote your case.'

His expression bordered on conceit now. No wonder he wanted to show me what he was up to. Not a lot of people would understand the real breakthrough he'd achieved.

'How did you get to this point?' People like Simon usually yearn for an audience, people who will hear them out and understand how truly clever they are.

He looked pleased as he began to tell me the history of their project.

I let him talk. He loved listening to himself. His eyes grew wider, as if he was in the headlights of a truck, as he went through the ins and outs of his work: how he'd discovered the breakthrough himself, how a colleague had let him down in the early stages, had even disputed his findings. And how he'd been vindicated in the end. It was the usual academic front-and-back-stabbing stuff.

When he'd run out of steam, Isabel said. 'You should definitely be at the institute conference next year. Shouldn't he, Sean?'

She had an enthralled look on her face. I hadn't known she was so interested in optical science.

'I forgot to ask, do you remember where Kaiser was staying the last time he was here?' she said.

He smiled at her, answered quickly. 'Somewhere on Jabotinsky.'

'What number?' I said. I hadn't heard of the place, but I assumed you'd need more than a street name to find out where Kaiser had been staying. Jabotinsky could run all the way to Tel Aviv, for all I knew.

'I don't remember.' He shrugged dismissively.

He knew more. He had to.

Isabel was still looking at the screen. 'Did you meet him there?' Her tone was soft, friendly.

'I picked him up a couple of times, no more than that. He was, without doubt, the most arrogant archaeologist I've ever met.'

'How were you helping him?' asked Isabel.

'He used my name to get himself admitted to a dig. I got a call from someone checking up on him, to see if he was who he said he was. They didn't say where the dig was though. But they'd heard of me.'

'Do you even know what section of Jabotinsky he was staying on?' said Isabel.

'Somewhere near the middle. Honestly, I can't tell you any more. I was never in his apartment. I picked him up on the street, twice. Once at a bus stop near the middle. Another time at a coffee shop at the end. Maybe if you go door to door someone will remember him.' He gave Isabel a sympathetic look.

'It's a very long street,' said Talli, looking at me. 'There are lots of apartment buildings. If you go door to door you'll be days at it.'

'I can't help you any more,' said Simon. He looked at his watch. 'My meeting is starting soon and . . .' He didn't finish his sentence. It was clear he wanted us to get going. There was tightness around his eyes, as if he was about to miss the last train home for Yom Kippur.

'We're out of here,' I said. 'Thanks for showing me what you're working on. It was interesting.' I gripped his arm.

Seconds later we were standing by the lifts. There were two dark-suited men in the corridor outside the room we'd just come out of. One of them had cropped hair. The other had longer hair and was younger. Their eyes were watchful.

They looked as if they'd be suspicious of their own wives.

'Is that the local CIA?' I said, half jokingly, as the elevator went down.

'Shush,' said Talli. She glanced up at the small black dome of a security camera in a corner of the elevator.

When we got down below she turned to me. 'That was the Security Service. I'd bet my pension on it.'

'Simon is an important guy?' asked Isabel.

Talli shrugged.

That was when I spotted the knot of people, maybe six or seven, waiting by a table near the revolving glass doors leading from the outside. Two blue-shirted female police officers were waving two-foot-long wands over people, before letting them pass in or out. We joined the queue.

I'd never seen people being checked leaving a place as well as entering it.

Talli threw her gaze to the ceiling as she waited. She whispered, 'You never know what the Security Service is going to do next here.'

I was dealt with first. The older looking of the two officers held her hand out. 'ID?' She said. I gave her my passport.

She couldn't have been much older than me, maybe a year of two, no more than forty for sure, and she was attractive. She had thick brown hair, big soft eyes, glowing skin, and an authoritative manner. She stood with her legs wide apart and her head back, as if she might bellow a command at me at any point.

'What were you doing in this hotel?' Her accent was soft.

'We were visiting with a friend.'

'Someone staying here?' She was holding my passport, leafing through it slowly. She stopped on a page, brought it close to her face to examine it.

'No, someone having a meeting here.'

'Who?'

'Simon Marcus, he's upstairs.'

She snapped my passport shut and put it in the top pocket of her shirt.

'I need that,' I said.

'How do you know Simon Marcus?' The other policewoman was waving someone else through. Isabel was behind me.

'He's a professor. He knows a friend of mine. We were introduced a few hours ago.'

'You are here to help him with his work?' She was looking at me as if I was a conspirator, hiding something.

'No. I'm not here to help him.'

'Will you be staying in Jerusalem for much longer?' It crossed my mind that she was actually saying I should leave Israel.

'A few more days. We'll be here less than a week. Why do you ask?'

She stepped back, looked me up and down. It appeared as if she was debating whether to arrest me or answer my question.

'We have a lot of security troubles here in Jerusalem, Dr Ryan. We wouldn't want anything to happen to one of our distinguished guests.'

She pointed at some high-backed chairs nearby.

'Wait here. Do not go away.' She turned, strode out through the glass doors, heading towards a police jeep that was pulled up outside. I moved towards the chairs, but I didn't sit down. I stared after her. The jeep had darkened windows.

What the hell was she doing? I looked around. Two more men who looked like security guards were standing by the lifts. They were staring in my direction.

13

It was 5 p.m. in London. Henry was preparing to leave the office. He was back on normal hours, as his wife called them. He would be joining the crowds surging through Westminster Underground station in a few minutes.

Then a ping sounded from his workstation computer. It was a warning that a priority email had come in. He clicked through to the contents.

REQUEST: 3487686/TRTT
STATUS: CLOSED/EXCEPT: LEVEL 7
CASE: 87687658765-65436

No further information can be provided on the manuscript you requested.

He read the email twice. It gave nothing away. He knew from experience that no further response would be provided to any additional requests he made on the matter. Information on an item that was only available to Level 7 personnel would not be accessible to him. He was lucky he'd received even this response.

What intrigued him about it all was why an ancient manuscript, the one Sean Ryan and Isabel Sharp had discovered in Istanbul, would now be subject to such a restriction.

As he made his way out to the Underground platform heading north he thought about what could be in the document that was so important.

14

The policewoman had opened the back door of the police vehicle and climbed inside. I imagined her examining my passport in detail, photographing it maybe, or putting it through a computer check, but she could have been doing anything beyond those darkened windows.

'What did she say to you?' Isabel was beside me.

The other policewoman was checking people and keeping an eye on me. She needn't have bothered. I wasn't going to go anywhere without my passport.

'She wanted to know if I was helping Simon. I got the impression she knew all about him.'

Isabel stood with me.

And then the policewoman reappeared. She'd only been gone a few minutes. She handed me back my passport.

'Be careful in Israel, Dr Ryan,' she said. 'The situation here is difficult these days. We have to double-check everything. I am sorry for delaying you.'

I passed her by quickly. What she meant was clear. I'd been warned.

I watched as Isabel gave over her passport. The

policewoman examined it carefully, asked a few questions then gave it back.

I wondered why she hadn't asked us where we were staying. Maybe she didn't need to. Our hotel had copied our passports in front of us when we'd checked in. They'd probably used the copies to register us with the police. And with the number of security cameras around, they probably knew more about our movements than if we had a stalker.

We walked back towards the Jaffa Gate.

'What's Simon's phone number?' I asked Talli.

'He told you everything he knows. I'm sure of it,' she said, after she gave it to me. 'We have a good reputation for helping academics from other universities.' She held her hand out to bid me goodbye.

'Thanks, Talli. I appreciate all your help. It means a lot to me. Send me an email in a week or two about what you're working on. Maybe you can come and do a talk for us too.'

She beamed. Then she was gone, and Isabel and I were heading for a taxi that had pulled up. It was disgorging a family of American tourists.

I checked my phone again. Susan hadn't called back. I tapped her number. I must have dialled it ten times since she'd rung me. The number still wasn't available.

It was looking increasingly like the call had been an accident of some sort. Maybe her phone had been stolen. Maybe someone had turned it on briefly, pressed the redial button, before taking its SIM out.

'Can you take us to Jabotinski?' I said to the driver. He looked at me as if I was a piece of bait drifting on the top of a pool. Then he grinned. He was young, had a few days' growth of beard and a t-shirt with swirling red and green paint stains on it.

'You're tourists, right? Where on Jabotinsky are you going? It's a long stretch, my friend.'

'Near the middle,' I said. He moved off. Isabel traded pleasantries with him for a few minutes. I was trying to work out the significance of everything we'd heard from Simon. Was it relevant that he was involved in a red heifer project? Probably not. They were just another bunch of end-timers, weren't they?

Still, I felt uneasy.

The taxi pulled up a few minutes later on a long street heading up a hill with three-storey white apartment buildings on either side. The buildings were set back from the road. Palm trees, carob trees, eucalyptus and other shrubs separated the buildings from the street. There was a small roundabout at the top of the hill.

'This is the centre of Jabotinsky. You can walk either way from here, but there's not a lot to see.'

I was deflated. This wasn't going to be easy. I'd hoped for a busy street with shops, cafes maybe, people we could talk to, ask if they'd seen an American of Kaiser's description. He hadn't been a quiet guy who could escape attention. But this was a long street full of anonymous apartment buildings.

'What's your plan?' said Isabel.

'I thought we might have dinner? Look at all the restaurants,' I gestured around us.

She put her hands on her hips, turning on her heel. 'Yes, what a big choice.'

A pizza delivery motorbike went past. 'There is pizza somewhere,' I said.

'Wonderful, are you going to run after him?' The noise of the disappearing motorbike faded into the distance.

'Let's walk that way.' I pointed back down towards the Old City. 'He has to have stayed one side of this roundabout. That gives us a fifty percent chance of being right.' We walked onto the pavement.

The weather was getting even more gloomy. It was 3.30 p.m. and colder than I'd expected, like London in mid-March. All we needed was for it to start raining.

Up ahead, where the road curved, a red car was parked. As we watched, it pulled away. A group of young people were coming towards us. They were moving like a rolling party, the boys swirling around the outside of the group in long t-shirts mostly with the names of obscure bands on them. The girls were laughing, linking arms.

As they came near I approached one of the boys. He was tall, had Clark Kent glasses and a puzzled expression.

'Do you know an American archaeologist living around here?' I said.

His accent was all New York when he answered. 'Yeah right, half the professors in our university look like American archaeologists.'

One of the girls stopped in front of us. 'What are you people doing in Israel?' she said. She had a thick wave of curly brown hair and a friendly smile.

'We're looking for a friend of ours who got lost,' said Isabel.

They were all in their late teens or early twenties.

'Everybody's looking for somebody,' said the girl.

The guy was eyeing up Isabel; most men found her attractive I'd noticed. He was giving her a big grin. 'You wanna come with us for a few beers,' he said. He didn't even look at me. Isabel's straight black hair and dark tight jeans took at least five years off her age. She could have easily passed for someone in her late twenties.

'You can come too,' said the girl. She pushed her hair away from her face. 'We're all going to a party. Are you Jewish?'

I shook my head.

'It don't matter,' she said. 'I can hear an American accent under there.'

'I grew up in the States,' I said. 'Then my dad was stationed in England.'

'You poor thing,' she said. 'Having to listen to Oasis every day.'

'I like Oasis.'

Isabel was looking at me sceptically. I motioned for us to go along with them. We might be able to ask them a few questions about what went on in this neighbourhood.

As we walked, the girl turned to her friend. She was taller than the first girl. She was grinning at me. I looked away. The next time I looked at her she had a big joint in her mouth and there was a trail of blue smoke coming from it like a steaming power plant. This was not what I needed. Getting arrested was not in the plan.

'I think you better throw that away,' I said, turning back to the girl. 'There's a police car right behind us.' It was true. I'd just spotted it. They had to be trailing this group.

The girl turned her head fast, then looked back at me. 'Goddamn it,' she said.

The joint fell from her fingers.

'We'll catch up with you later,' I said. I took Isabel's arm.

'They're all going to get arrested any minute now.' Isabel waved goodbye as we peeled away from them. We headed for an entranceway, as if we were going into one of the apartment buildings.

'I don't think spending a night in the cells is going to help us.'

'They might have known something,' said Isabel.

I shook my head. 'There has to be a better way than this.'

I stopped, bent down to tie the laces on my trainers. I was facing back towards the road. The police car passed us at walking speed. The officer on our side, who had big glasses on, stared intently at us as they passed. I gave her a smile in return. What could they do to us, charge us with talking to someone?

'I have an idea,' I said.

'I hope it's better than your last one.'

'Come on.'

We walked to the bottom of the road. Ten minutes later we were at the nearest takeaway pizza place.

'No, I want to sit down and eat,' said Isabel. 'Not eat pizza at the side of the road.'

'You don't have to eat anything,' I said. 'Don't worry.'

I pulled two red two hundred shekel notes from my wallet. Then I went to the delivery guy by the big glass window of the pizza place. He was leaning against his motorbike and had big earphones on. I began talking. He took the earphones off.

'Hi, can you help us? I'm supposed to meet a friend of mine here for a party. He's an American, a guy called Max Kaiser. He's a big guy, with bushy black hair, a young-looking professor. He lives on Jabotinsky, but for the life of me I can't remember which number. If you can tell me where he lives, I'll give you this.' I pushed the two notes forward. 'I don't want to miss my chance with that one.' I nodded towards Isabel.

The boy, he seemed more Arab than Jewish, looked at me as if I was certifiable. He had patches of beard on his face and a collection of beaded necklaces hanging from his neck.

'Can't help,' he said. 'Don't know who you're talking about.' He turned away, making it clear that even if he did know something, he wasn't going to tell me anything useful.

'How many delivery guys does this place have?'

He glanced at me, then looked away, putting his phone to his ear as if he'd suddenly remembered he had an urgent phone call to make.

I went into the shop, asked the guy behind the counter how many delivery people they had. He looked at me as if he had no idea what language I was even speaking in. He pointed up at the plastic sign above his head. Another bigger guy was looking at us steadily, as if getting ready to pull a baseball bat out at the first sign of trouble. Though, considering what country we were in, he probably had a legally held UZI under the counter.

'Which pizza you want?' the first man said. He sounded as if he'd been smoking for a hundred years.

Isabel leaned over the counter. The man was staring at her.

'Have you got a guy called David doing deliveries?' she said.

They looked at each other, clearly trying to work out why a woman like Isabel would be trying to find a particular pizza delivery guy. You could almost see their brains grinding through the possibilities.

'We have no David here, sorry.' He shook his head.

'How many delivery guys do you have?'

'Two. There is the second one. And he's not a David.' He pointed.

I turned. A second delivery motorbike had pulled up outside. The guy on it was huge. The bike looked tiny under him. I went out, walked up to him.

'Your boss said you would help us.' I pointed back inside. The guy behind the counter waved at us. The delivery guy looked from him to me.

'We're looking for an American called Max. He's got bushy hair. We're supposed to be going to his place tonight, but I lost his number. I know he lives somewhere on Jabotinsky.'

I leaned towards him. 'Your boss said I can give you this.' I had the two notes in my hand. I pushed them forward.

He looked at them, then back up at me. 'Yeah, I know your American friend, but you're too late. His apartment's burnt out. He ain't been there in weeks. You can't miss the place if you walk up Jabotinsky. But you won't want to go there tonight. He won't be entertaining anyone.' He took the notes from my outstretched hand and went past me into the pizza shop.

Isabel was still talking to the man behind the counter. If Kaiser's apartment had been on fire, there'd be a good chance that would be visible from the street. We had to go back to Jabotinsky.

But a part of me didn't want to.

I didn't want to see what had happened to his apartment. His death had been a distant thing up until this point.

Now I couldn't escape thinking about what had happened to him. That made a queasy feeling rise up inside me.

I was imagining what it must have been like. The flames burning him. I couldn't imagine a worse torture. Soon, I wouldn't need to imagine it.

15

The screen on Mark Headsell's laptop was glowing blue. He'd dimed the lights in the suite on the fifteenth floor of the Cairo Marriot on El Gezira Street as soon as he'd entered it.

The hotel was a difficult landmark to miss if you were aiming to bring down a symbol of Western decadence, but as it had hardly been scratched in the Arab Spring that had overturned Mubarak and his family, it was probably as safe a place as any in this turbulent city.

Being only forty-five minutes from the airport helped too, as did the fact that it was built on an island in the Nile and that it had excellent room service and bars full of expatriates. You could even fool yourself for an hour in Harry's Pub that you were back in London.

What was keeping Mark out of Harry's Pub that night was a series of Twitter posts that an astute colleague had been tracking. The one that particularly interested him was one that had been sent an hour ago from an unknown location in Israel.

Whoever was sending the Tweets was covering their tracks well. The fake IP address they'd been using had been broken through, but it had only left them with a generic address for an Israeli internet service provider. Whoever was logging in to make the posts was being very careful. That alone ticked the warning boxes.

We are ready to hatch the brood, was the latest message. It was an innocent enough Tweet on its own, it could have been about pigeons, but the cryptic nature of the others in the stream from the same source gave more cause for concern, as did the trouble they were having locating where the messages were coming from.

The fact that Twitter could be monitored anywhere in the world meant that it could be used to receive signals as to when to commence a whole range of activities. Such things weren't unknown. The Portuguese Carnation coup of 1974 had been triggered by the singing of the nation's Eurovision song contest entry in that year's program.

And this was where things got interesting. His colleague had managed to uncover that over a hundred people across Egypt were following this particular series of messages.

And most of the people searching and watching the Twitter feed were registered to IP addresses on Egyptian military bases or air force bases. It was that final piece of news that prompted his colleague to pass the details of what they'd been tracking onto him and place URGENT in the subject line.

If the Egyptian air force were planning something, then a source inside Israel could be useful to them.

But what were they planning?

16

The apartment building on Jabotinsky had four floors and eight apartments, two on each floor. It had been easy to figure out which building was likely to be Kaiser's; there was a big black stain above the balcony at the front. We'd also walked all the way up to the roundabout and back. It was the only building with any smoke damage, never mind anything worse.

It looked like a giant bat had wiped itself out against the front wall, halfway up.

The windows of the apartment were smeared with soot, and the door to the small balcony was blackened as if smoke had streamed through it.

The entrance to the apartments was at the side of the building. The main door was wooden and painted black; secure and sturdy looking. After three failed attempts of pressing the buzzer on each apartment and saying we needed entry to a party, we got in.

We went up in a tiny metal elevator. The door to what had been Kaiser's apartment was locked. Nobody answered when I knocked lightly. There was blue and white tape barring to it, so I hadn't really expected anyone to come. The door was also a different colour to the other ones on the floor. The door to what had been Kaiser's apartment was unpainted.

It looked as if someone had battered the original door down and then replaced it. The people in the rest of the block had been lucky that the fire hadn't burnt the whole building down. Someone must have called the fire brigade pretty quickly.

'I bet one of the tenants calls the police because we pressed all those buzzers,' said Isabel. 'We shouldn't hang around. They'll think we're back to burn the rest of the building.'

'Ain't nothing like being an optimist,' I said.

'I wasn't being an optimist.'

'That's what I said.'

'You should get your own show.' She pressed the button beside the elevator.

I pushed at the door to Kaiser's apartment. We were out of luck. It didn't open. I checked the ledge above the door, another one above a small window nearby. Someone might have left a key behind. I even checked under a dusty aloe vera plant on the window ledge. No luck.

The elevator arrived. As we got in, Isabel said, 'Do you really think this will help us to find Susan?'

'I don't know.' The doors closed. There was a smell of cleaning fluid.

'You remind me of a Yorkshire terrier we once had. When he got something between his teeth he was a demon for hanging on.'

She was right, of course. We shouldn't be here, pushing our luck again. We should be back in London, especially after what we'd got ourselves into in Istanbul.

But a stubborn part of me said, to hell with all that; you sat back once, Sean, before Irene died. All that's over for you. You're not the guy who sits on his ass anymore.

And I didn't care what it brought down on me either.

73

'Maybe I'm just a sucker for drama,' I said.

We went outside.

'No, you're a sucker for trying to do the right thing.' Isabel's tone was soft. 'And you blame yourself for way too much.'

She was right. But it was like I needed someone saying it over and over for it to go in.

I touched her arm. 'Look, that's where they keep the garbage,' I said. I pointed at a row of black plastic bins in a corner under a wooden cover. They each had a number on them.

'Have fun,' she said.

I went to the bin marked three in white paint on its side. There was nothing inside it. The police must have taken the rubbish.

A door slammed, footsteps echoed. I felt like a criminal standing by the garbage cans. I started walking back to where Isabel was waiting near the road.

'Can I help you?' said a reedy voice.

I turned. There was an old man standing there. He had white hair and looked dishevelled. I made a split-second decision.

'We came to see what they did to Max's place.'

He turned and looked up at the front of the building.

'Yes, it was terrible,' he said. 'Mr Kaiser didn't deserve that. He was always so friendly when we met him.'

He started walking back to the house.

Isabel was beside me. 'Did he tell you where he was working in the city?' she asked.

He stopped, turned. 'Who are you?' he said.

'We worked with Max on a project in Istanbul,' I said. We were forced together briefly by circumstances was the truth, but I wasn't going to say that.

I pulled my wallet out, took out one of my cards and handed it to him.

He looked at it as if it was dirt.

'We're trying to work out what happened to Max.'

'He never told me where he worked. I can't help you. Good night.'

There was a woman by the door of the apartment block watching us. She had a black cat in her arms.

'Maybe he told your wife,' I said.

He shrugged. I went after him. He stopped at the door, turned.

'Sorry to bother you,' I said. The woman was staring at me with a suspicious expression. 'We're trying to find out what happened to Max Kaiser. Did he ever tell you where he was working here in Jerusalem?'

She looked at her husband. He shrugged.

'It was so terrible what happened to him,' she said. 'You know, you are the first people to come by here, to take an interest in him. How did you know him?'

'We met him in Istanbul. I used to work for the British Consulate there,' said Isabel.

The woman smiled. 'My mother fled to England during the war,' she said.

I wanted to press her again, but I decided to wait.

She put her hand to her cheek. 'We used to meet Mr Kaiser on the stairs. He was always covered in dust, always in a hurry.'

'Did he say where he was working?'

'No.'

I was about to turn and go when she said. 'But I heard him saying something about Our Lady's Church. Don't ask me where it is. I was looking for my little Fluffy over there and he was getting into a taxi with another man.' She patted her cat's head, then pointed at the bushes near the road.

'I didn't mean to eavesdrop.' She looked from me to Isabel.

'Thank you,' I said. I had no idea if the information was going to be helpful, but at least we'd gained something.

75

We walked back towards the roundabout. I expected to see the police car again. But they didn't come. Finally, we saw a taxi with its light on. We were back in the hotel fifteen minutes later.

'Can you tell me where Our Lady's Church is?' I said to the receptionist.

The man behind the desk shook his head. 'There's one somewhere in the Old City,' he said. 'That's all I know.'

Upstairs I looked it up on the internet. The Wi-Fi was working, slowly again, but at least it was up and running.

'Any luck?' said Isabel, as she came back into the room from the bathroom.

'The nearest to that name is an Our Lady's Chapel just off the Via Dolorosa.'

'That's the street where people carry the cross at Easter, right?' said Isabel.

'Not just at Easter, all year round.'

'Wonderful, we're getting into the thick of it.'

'Maybe Kaiser was just doing a bit of sightseeing,' I said.

'At some obscure chapel?'

'Let's go and take a look tomorrow.'

Seeing the Via Dolorosa was the kind of sightseeing most people do here. Irene had wanted to come to Jerusalem for a long time. She'd been interested in all this stuff. I'd always been too busy. I'd always thought there was going to be more time.

Irene had been brought up on High Church Sunday school stories of Jerusalem. I'd been brought up a Catholic, but there were one too many scandals, and all the outdated rules had put me off. But now I wanted to see the Via Dolorosa.

A memory of my dad going to mass came back to me. He'd never forced me to go with him, but I always knew he wanted me to.

After I left home I never went again. Irene had nagged me

about it, asking me what I believed in. I never had a good answer, unless you count being flippant as an acceptable retort. I was good at all that back then.

For Irene, it had all meant more. She wasn't a church goer, but she'd believed in helping people.

She'd volunteered to go out to Afghanistan. She didn't have to. She'd been managing an emergency room at a busy hospital. She'd been the youngest in her class to rise to that position. She had responsibilities, and a lot more besides. But she wanted to give back.

I could feel the old anger bubbling.

For a while, since I'd been around Isabel, the anger had dissipated. Being here in Jerusalem, looking for Susan, was bringing it up again.

We made love that night. Isabel looked so beautiful. But I felt distracted, in a way I hadn't before with her. Being in Jerusalem was unsettling me.

One of my problems was that I'd never wanted anyone else in the ten years I'd been with Irene. I know that doesn't sound real, but it was true. I'd closed my mind to other women. Sure, I found some attractive, but Irene had been everything I'd ever wanted.

And I found it difficult to open up to anyone else after she died.

Isabel was the first person I felt I could really trust. One of the comments she'd made had stuck in my mind. *You're strong, Sean, but it's not enough; you need love.*

It was the best part of being with Isabel. I felt cared for. I felt loved.

17

'There's something weird going on,' said Henry. He shook his head. The social media tracking screen in front of him was blinking with the amount of data scrolling down it.

Normally he'd have let the automated systems deal with the feeds. They hunted for genuinely suspicious posts among the billions of Twitter, Facebook and forum posts, and spam ads and emails that filled the web each day. The algorithms they used were as important to the service as their best code-breaking tools.

The volume of postings on one subject was cresting like a wave. There'd been a thousand posts an hour about it yesterday. Now there was ten thousand an hour. And the rate was climbing.

Sergeant Finch looked down at him. She adjusted her glasses so they were further down her nose. She looked like a schoolmistress. A large and commanding school-mistress.

'I hope this isn't another one of your hunches,' she said.

He smiled up at her. 'This is no hunch. It's a prophecy.'

'You're a prophet now?' The smile at the corner of her mouth was either conspiratorial or from her anticipation of how she would describe this exchange to her boss over a coffee.

Henry didn't care. 'Not me,' he said. 'This is about what's been trending on Twitter and Facebook in Egypt over the last twenty-four hours.'

'Are you going to tell me?' Her eyes had darted to another monitoring screen operator who had raised a hand. The room was responsible for real-time monitoring about a hundred current threats to the UK's national security.

'All these posts are about a claim that a letter from the first Caliph of Islam has been found. Apparently, it states that Jerusalem, once captured by Islam, will remain Islamic for all time.'

'Do we know if this letter is real?'

'It's being looked into.'

'Let me know what they find, Henry. Another religious prophecy is the last thing they need in the Middle East. The place is a tinderbox right now. It could burst into flames at any moment.'

18

The following morning we took a taxi to the Via Dolorosa. If you imagine the Old City of Jerusalem as a roughly drawn square, a warren of narrow lanes, then the hill of the Temple Mount, with the golden Dome of the Rock floating above it to the bottom right. And the Via Dolorosa runs almost right to left across the middle, east to west that is, just above the Temple Mount. I say almost advisedly, because there's a kink in the road as the two sides of it don't exactly line up in the middle.

The Via Dolorosa ends inside the Church of the Holy Sepulchre, the long venerated site of Jesus' crucifixion and his tomb. The Holy Sepulchre was founded by Helena, the mother of Constantine the Great in 326 AD, after her son became the first Christian Roman Emperor. Miraculously, she also found the cross Jesus had died on, despite the total physical destruction of Jerusalem carried out by Titus in 70 AD.

The Via Dolorosa was first venerated in Roman times, before the city fell to Islam in April 637 AD. Later, the Franciscans kept the Christian rituals alive whenever they could. They established many of the rites that surround the route to this day. Some misinterpretations of the route still happen though. An archway of Hadrian's lesser forum, for instance, constructed in the second century, is still believed by many pilgrims to be the place where Pilate presented Jesus to the crowd.

Myth, faith and bloody history come face to face in Jerusalem.

Our taxi let us out at the Jaffa Gate. We walked through the Old City towards the chapel of Our Lady. The streets were narrow, intense with souvenir shops and small cafes. The pavements were stone slabs. The first lane went downhill in small steps. Arches and canvas awnings blocked out the early morning sun. At the start of the Via Dolorosa we passed a group of Christian pilgrims following a tall Eastern-European man with a cross on his shoulders.

The closely packed shops were selling wooden crosses, icons, statues of the Virgin Mary, rosary beads, Bibles, pottery, glasses, t-shirts, mugs and a hundred other souvenirs. Some of them had Persian carpets and Turkish kilims hanging outside. Many had low wooden trestle tables jutting out in front.

It was 10.30 a.m. now and the street was busy. There were monks in long habits, mostly brown or black, Arabs in head-dresses, women with their heads covered, and tourists with cameras as well as, at the major intersections where one busy and narrow lane crossed another, sharp-eyed Israeli soldiers with guns, watching us all.

Finally we found the chapel. We almost missed it. There was a crowd gathered at the entrance to a lane directly opposite it. They had caught my eye. The Via Dolorosa was wider here, maybe twenty feet across, and the entrance to the chapel was between two high stone buildings in that distinctive Mamluk style, which features layers of alternating light and dark stone.

The crowd on the opposite side of the street was made up mostly of Arab men, bareheaded or in keffiyehs, which flowed loosely over their shoulders. There was a camera crew filming it all.

I approached the cameraman. 'What's going on?' I said.

He looked at me, spat on the ground and returned to his work.

We went over to the chapel. It had an ancient grey wooden door, which looked as if it had been new when the Crusaders were here. The door was closed and there was a plaque above it. The plaque was in Greek. Another plaque, in polished brass, simply said *Chapel of Our Lady*.

Was this the end of us chasing ghosts? I looked around. There was a group of blue-shirted policemen beyond the crowd. They were blocking the entrance to a laneway.

'What about getting coffee? Look, there's a place over there,' I said. I pointed at an old-fashioned looking cafe back the way we'd come. It had a red plastic sign above its door and a menu stuck to its window.

A few minutes later we were sipping thick black coffee in a quiet corner of the coffee shop. We couldn't get a table near the window. The rest of the tables were full of tourists looking at maps or locals huddled over tea in glass cups or yoghurt drinks. 'There's a police station back near the Jaffa Gate,' said Isabel. 'In some place called the Qishle building. Maybe we can ask them if they know anything about Susan Hunter? I'm not sure we're getting anywhere wandering around aimlessly.' She sounded worried.

'We're not wandering around aimlessly. We're seeing the sights.'

'What did you think we were going to find here? Kaiser's dead. He was probably just talking about this place.'

'So what are all those people here for?'

She looked at the menu.

A nun in a black habit had come into the cafe. She must have been in her eighties. Her skin was creased, translucent, like the cover of a book that was about to fall apart. There were blue veins around her eyes. Her habit was made of rough faded wool, and her back was bowed.

I overheard her ordering tea. Her accent was cut glass English. I stood up and went to her side.

'Sorry to disturb you,' I said. 'I couldn't help but overhear you.' I smiled. 'Do you speak English?'

She looked me up and down as if she was wondering what stupidity might come out of my mouth next.

I put my hands up. 'Don't worry, I don't want anything from you.' I hesitated deliberately, then went on. 'Well, not anything material.'

Her eyes narrowed. I imagined she was wondering if I was one of those people who suffer from the Jerusalem syndrome when they get here, imagining they're the Messiah, with the power to change the world.

'It's just that I was wondering what all those people were gathering for out there. Do you know?'

She breathed in through her nose. Her nostrils pinched together. 'Young man, I am not a news service.' She looked down at the ground, as if to avoid speaking anymore. A waiter put a lidded paper cup in front of her.

'Please,' I said. 'I need a little help.'

'You're a journalist, I suppose,' she said.

I opened my mouth to deny it, but decided not to.

'I expect you want to know about the djinn they all claim has been released at that dig.' She sniffed again, gazed piercingly into my eyes, as if she knew what I was thinking, even if I didn't.

'Well, I can offer you nothing about such superstitions.' She clutched her tea with a claw-like hand, and shot a glance over my shoulder as if checking out someone behind me.

'That poor man was found near here, you know.' She leaned towards me. 'He was burnt to death. They all think it was the work of a djinn.' She glanced out the window.

'I hope,' she crossed herself. 'You're not going to write about evil spirits on the Via Dolorosa, because there aren't any. It's all superstition.'

I shook my head. 'I definitely won't.'

'Bless you, I hope so. It's bad enough already here. We don't need stories about evil spirits.' She put her hand to her mouth, as if she'd said too much. Then she crossed herself.

'God be with you.' She turned away. I saw a gold cross glint at her neck. It was plain, heavy looking.

Back at the table Isabel whispered in my ear, 'I hope you weren't hassling her.'

'I've only found out there's a dig going on over there.' I pointed towards the crowd. 'And that people think a djinn has been dug up or disturbed or something. They think it has something to do with Max's death.'

'What the hell is a djinn?'

'It's a spirit, you know, a genie, if you believe in that sort of thing.'

'You think Kaiser was working over there?'

'Maybe.'

'What sort of dig is it?'

I shrugged. 'Let's ask around, discreetly, see if anyone knows.'

It seemed such a simple idea, but it took two hours for it to sink in that we were not going to get any answers. Nothing at all, not a whisper. Four shopkeepers asked us to leave their shops, with varying intensity, after I asked them about the dig opposite Our Lady's Chapel.

The only useful piece of information we gathered was from a policeman. After showing him my card, he said that I would have to put my request in through an Israeli university.

After we'd finished with him we went to a juice bar nearby.

'Let's call Simon Marcus,' I said.

Isabel sipped her fresh orange juice. She was looking out of the window. The Via Dolorosa was almost impassable. What had been a small group was now a crowded demonstration with cheers and jeers, and young soldiers in khaki and efficient-looking policemen in blue watching everything.

I called Simon on my phone. It took three tries to get a signal.

He did not sound pleased when he answered. 'Did you talk to the police in the lobby when you exited the hotel?' he said, before I even had a chance to go into why I'd called him.

'She asked where we'd been. I had to tell her.'

'Half the people who were supposed to come yesterday didn't turn up, Mr Ryan. I found out later that some of them were turned back at a security checkpoint in the lobby. Someone has been making stupid claims about what we're doing.'

'That wasn't me. I didn't make any claims about your work.' I paused. 'We need some help, Simon, please.' There was silence for a few seconds.

'What sort of help?' He did not sound keen.

'We're trying to find out about this dig Kaiser was working on. We're getting stonewalled.'

Isabel was motioning for me to give her the phone. 'Isabel wants to speak to you.' I gave the phone to her.

She spoke to him for a few minutes. It sounded as if they were getting on well. Too well.

'That's really nice of you to offer to meet us,' she said, after a long gap listening to him. 'We're at a juice bar on the Via Dolorosa near Our Lady's Chapel. We think this is where Kaiser was working. Do you know it?'

He said something. She thanked him again.

'You were laying it on thick,' I said when the call was over.

'Do you want his help or not?'

'Yeah, but he gets a quick put-down if he asks you for a date.' I pointed a finger at her.

'I'd say he's after something else.'

I thought about that for a second. 'You think he wants to work with the institute?'

'Wouldn't you? Your institute is leading the world in academic research in loads of areas. That's what your website says anyway. Is it a lie?'

'You were on our website?'

'Just making sure you weren't an imposter.'

'Very funny.'

But she was right. He'd probably looked us up after we'd left the hotel. And he hadn't put the phone down on me, even though he'd been angry.

I ordered another juice. We watched the people around us. There was a bunch of shaven-headed American men at a table nearby. It looked as if they were all praying. They had their eyes closed and one of them was whispering something I couldn't catch. There was a guy with a long beard with them. He looked like an Old Testament prophet. He was reading from a heavy gilt-edged book and muttering.

'Djinn is a word derived from the Arabic root meaning to hide,' said Simon an hour later, after he arrived and I'd told him what we'd learned so far.

'It's an interesting word,' said Isabel.

'It's interesting people still believe in such things,' I said.

Simon leant his head to one side and gave me his best condescending expression.

'But Max's death was evil, wasn't it? So evil is not dead, Sean. The other words derived from the word djinn are interesting too. They are majnūn – mad – and janin – an embryo.'

'What sort of dig's going on over there?' said Isabel. She

was giving him one of her super-friendly smiles. I kicked her under the table. Her smile became even warmer.

'I can do better than that,' he said. His chest puffed up as he spoke. 'I asked around after you told me Kaiser was probably working here. One of my archaeologist colleagues was involved in the early days of this dig. He told me all about what they claim they've found.' He paused, smiled.

'But best of all, if this is the site I gave Max his reference for, they should be willing to let me look around. I have every reason to see the site after what happened to him.'

'Why don't we go over there?' I half rose.

'Don't you want to know what I found out about the dig?' said Simon.

I sat back down. 'Go on.'

He looked around first, as if he had something important to say.

'First, I must warn you, as my colleague warned me.'

He must have registered the look on my face, as he then said, 'We must all be sceptical about wild claims for sites in this city. I strongly advise you do that.' He cut the air with his hand, emphasising the words *strongly advise*.

'So, what are these wild claims about the dig?' said Isabel.

'My friend said they'd found the basement of a first-century Roman villa.'

'That's it?' I said.

'No, no, that's not it.' He looked over his shoulder. The Americans were still praying. Simon moved his plastic chair forward, lowered his voice.

'They found a reference to Pontius Pilate.' He raised his eyebrows.

'You mean the guy who sentenced Jesus to death?' Isabel had a look of wonder in her eyes. She was a good actress.

'Yes, yes.'

'I thought there was no proof he even existed,' I said.

'That's not true.' Isabel shook her head. 'They found an inscription to Pilate in the city of Maritima a few years ago.'

Simon smiled at her.

'So what have they found here?'

'Something amazing,' he said. 'You're not going to believe it.'

19

The tile-covered trapdoor was heavy, even for Arap Anach. He knew Susan Hunter would be desperate by now. The light streaming in when he lifted it would probably half-blind her, if she was near it when he opened it. After twenty-four hours in darkness, your eyes can hurt when they see light again.

Her thirst would have weakened her too. She might even be unconscious and need a slap to wake her.

He pushed the lid to the side and waited. It was possible, of course, that she would come at him like a wildcat with a piece of brick in her hand.

Nothing happened.

He could see the stone stairs descending, part of the earth floor below. As he walked down, the light from the kitchen filled every corner of the basement room.

She was sitting, hugging her knees against the far wall. Her gaze was fixed on a point in front of her, as if she was trying to ignore him. No appeal came from her mouth, no despairing cry for mercy.

He was tempted to admire her for that. But the feeling didn't last.

He put the litre bottle of water down. 'This is for you. You are more useful to me alive than dead.'

Her head bobbed once, as if the thought of the water had brought an involuntary response from her which she'd controlled as soon as she could. She didn't speak.

'Here is some rice.' He held up a plastic tub of rice mixed with egg. 'And now you will do one more thing for me.'

Her eyes were on him. They were the eyes of a cat watching a predator many times its size.

He walked towards her, put a sheet of paper on the ground, a lead pencil beside it.

'You will write a few sentences as to why you came to Israel on this paper and then sign your name.'

He stepped back. The eyes followed him.

'I hope I can release you soon, Dr Hunter,' he said. 'You have suffered enough and I do not want to hold you any longer than is necessary. I am negotiating for your release right now. After you write what I say, I will send it to the people I am talking with.'

She didn't move.

He picked up the water bottle, held it in the crook of his arm with the container of rice, then turned, heading to the stairs.

'This is what they asked for, proof that you are still alive. Maybe you will be more cooperative tomorrow,' he said. 'When you are a bit weaker.'

'I'll do it.' Her voice was still strong. That was good.

It took her only a minute to write the few sentences he dictated, adding her signature. Then she drank greedily from the bottle. She didn't even reach for the plastic tub, but he left it with her anyway.

Upstairs, after he'd pushed the lid back and the floor tiles looked perfect again, he went out to the iron brazier on the patio. It stood four feet off the ground and had three legs.

Its bowl, hanging at the top from a thin iron chain, was blackened from use and age.

He'd bought it many years before from a man who claimed it was found in a temple to Ba'al discovered only a few hundred feet from where he was. It was the reason he'd rented the olive farm and the old Ottoman farmhouse. The bowl was in the shape of a pair of hands cupped together.

He'd performed the ceremony a few dozen times. It helped to remove all doubt. He hadn't suffered from the affliction for a long time, but it was important to still carry out the ceremony. It reminded him of what was important, that the end justifies the means.

The ancients knew how the human mind worked. When tribes vied for dominance they needed a ceremony to help their people enter into a mindset where it was enjoyable to kill another human, to vanquish your enemy, to watch someone suffer, then die and relish it.

It was a ceremony that harked back to a time before Mohammad, before Christ, before Moses even, with all their soft talk about compassion and loving thy neighbour.

He crumpled the paper Susan had written on, placing it in the bowl. Then he took the knife that hung from the top of one of the legs, put the tip in the candle flame, and pricked the back of his hand. A drop of blood welled. He tipped his hand so the drop fell onto the paper. It made a deep red stain.

He touched the beeswax candle burning nearby to the paper. In seconds it was gone. Only ash remained. He pinched it with his fingers, smearing it on his face. Everything was done now. Her hopes had been raised. It was time.

The end game could begin. Death was waiting for her starring role.

20

'Pontius Pilate was the Governor of the province of Judaea at the time of Jesus. Roman governors in the early Empire in eastern provinces kept all the records of their term of office, including records of executions, at their villa for security reasons.'

Simon stopped. The hubbub of the street outside washed over us. I looked up as a Japanese tourist and his wife entered the juice bar. They looked alarmed by the demonstration outside. Isabel nudged me.

'My colleague, after a little arm twisting, told me they'd found a reference to Pontius Pilate at this dig.' Simon was talking quietly, almost whispering.

'Amazing,' said Isabel. 'Pontius Pilate!'

'Shussh,' he said. He held his hand up and looked around quickly to see if anyone was listening.

'It's not confirmed yet.'

'What's not confirmed?' Mr Get-straight-to-the-point, that was me.

He leaned closer. He was whispering now. 'Apparently they've found a cache of scrolls under some Roman-era rubble. There's a layer of soot above the rubble, which means the site has most likely lain undisturbed since 70 AD, when this part of Jerusalem was destroyed, after Tacitus put down the great Jewish revolt. This was all well before Islam started. Getting access to such a cache would be a wonderful thing for an archaeologist.' He made a low humming noise.

'Do those people out there know anything about this?' I gestured towards the crowd outside. They were a little way up the street, but they were still close enough for us to hear the chanting they'd started.

'Don't know,' said Simon.

I had no idea what they were saying, but there was real tension in the air. Almost everyone in the juice bar was craning their neck every few seconds to see what was going on. Outside on the street people were hurrying past.

I leaned forward, stretching until I could see the demonstration. The crowd had grown since the last time I'd looked. It was totally blocking the Via Dolorosa now.

'What are they chanting?' said Isabel.

'They're saying that no one should be allowed to dig in this area,' said Simon. 'They're saying that there used to be a Mamluk madrasa over there, that it was burnt down during a revolt five hundred years ago with all its students in it. They say the dig is desecrating a gravesite.' He finished his juice noisily.

'Is it?' I said.

'There are bones under every house in this city,' he said. 'I'm surprised they got permission for this dig at all.'

'One thing's for sure,' I said. 'A hell of a lot of people will be interested in this site.'

He held his hand flat on the table. 'I have no idea what the site will prove. But you are right, there are people who will be worried about any records from Pontius Pilate's era, in case they might show that the truth of that time is any different to what the Bible says.'

'Maybe there'll be universal rejoicing,' I said.

'And you still think you can get us onto this dig?' said Isabel.

Simon looked from her to me, then back again. I glanced at Isabel. Her black hair was tied up in a bun, but it was still unruly looking with odd hairs sticking out. She looked good with it that way.

'Come on then, let's see if I can.' Simon stood.

We walked all the way around to the other end of the lane from where the crowd was demonstrating. The lanes behind the Via Dolorosa were only four to six feet wide in places. The high walls of the buildings, constructed mainly out of sandstone, made them seem even narrower too. As did the windows, which were barred as if we were walking beside a prison, and mostly too far up to reach no matter how high you could jump.

Many of them were shuttered anyway, with thick sand-coloured planks. Some had iron bars too. Most of the thin, half-width, wooden doorways had one or two worn sand-stone steps leading up to them. In some places canvas awnings and stone arches high up blocked the light out completely.

This wasn't a medieval warren like you'd find in European cities. It was a Biblical-era warren.

A group of young men pushed past us. Then three more followed. They were all in a hurry.

After making another turn, we found the building they had come from. It looked like a school of some sort. Young men were hurrying out of it with bags under their arms or backpacks on their backs.

After we passed the school there were less people about. The lane we turned into as we circled back to the Via Dolorosa was narrower than any of the others we'd passed through. It seemed as if we were being squeezed by the buildings rising up on either side. There wouldn't be much we could do if someone with a knife held us up here, demanding our valuables.

Finally we turned another corner and our way was blocked by a shoulder-high blue plastic barrier. There were Israeli soldiers in khaki behind it. Their black helmets had see-through plastic wrapped around them to cover their faces.

As we came up to the barrier, we were the only other people in the lane beside the soldiers. Simon waved an ID card in the air. One of the soldiers shouted something at him. Simon held the card over the barrier. Half a minute later the barrier moved back and to the side.

Beyond it, up against the wall behind the soldiers, was a stack of plastic shields. Two of the soldiers had what looked like black paintball guns in their hands. They were probably tasers or something worse. They looked as if they were prepared for almost anything.

Simon said something in Hebrew as one of the soldiers examined his ID card. It was passed to the oldest looking soldier, perhaps all of twenty-two or twenty-three years old, who pushed his helmet back and started talking fast in Hebrew.

Simon replied calmly. Then he turned to us.

'Have you got your passports with you?' he said.

I took mine out of the back pocket of my trousers. I held it in front of me with the photograph page open. The soldier took it from me, peered at it, looking at each page. Luckily it was a new one. It had no stamps that he wouldn't like.

Isabel took hers and a small bottle of water out of her bag. That action brought four guns to bear on us.

Simon threw up his hands, said something that ended in 'Ayyyyyeeeee.'

Isabel showed them her passport with one hand, drank

from the bottle of water with the other, then passed it to me.

The soldier took Isabel's passport, looked through it for what seemed like ages. Eventually he passed it back to her. Then they let us pass.

Seconds later we turned a corner and could see the high steel barrier blocking the other end of the lane. There was a group of helmeted Israeli soldiers between us and the barrier. I could hear the chanting in Arabic beyond it.

Suddenly a pair of hands appeared and a walnut brown face peered over the top of the barrier. The soldiers standing on this side banged near the hands with metal truncheons. The face dropped back, but a cry went up, as if the man had been injured, or maybe it was the sight of us beyond the barrier that had set him off.

Whatever the reason, the next thing a shower of stones came over the barrier raining in our direction.

I put my arm up to protect Isabel.

The door we were in front of, a narrow one with a sandstone step, was like the others in the lane, closed tight. It had a notice stuck to it with blue tape around the edges. Simon banged the door. Nothing happened. Stones were dropping around us.

Simon banged on the door again, harder this time. Then it opened and we were looking at a man who took up the whole width of the doorway. He had a freckly-gingery look, ginger eyebrows and ginger hair. His skin was pale pink. And his shirt, which he was bulging out of, had a faded red stripe around the middle.

'What do you want?' Mr Ginger said, in a most unfriendly manner. He sounded as if he was from deep in the American south. For a second I thought I might be able to call on a little empathy, seeing how I held a US passport. Then he opened his mouth again and almost snarled at us.

'No visitors,' he said. He closed the door, fast. Stones fell around us.

'Ow,' said Isabel. She clutched at her side.

I banged the door with my fist. It rocked on its hinges. 'Open up, for God's sake,' I shouted.

I banged the door again and again.

Then it opened. 'I told you, no visitors,' said the friendly Mr Ginger.

Simon held up his ID card. 'I am entitled to come in and inspect this dig. I'm a professor with the Hebrew University. I gave a reference to Max Kaiser to enable him to get on this dig. I need to see where he was working, because of what has happened. These people are my colleagues.' He gestured towards us.

Ginger threw his hands in the air. 'We've no time to give tours.'

'We won't be long. If I have to come back with my friend from the Antiquities Authority, it will take us a lot longer. He is a stickler for sites being run properly.'

Ginger frowned. 'You gave Max his reference?' he said. Simon nodded.

A look of recognition replaced the suspicion.

'Are you working on a red heifer project?' he said.

'Yes.'

'Max spoke about you.'

Simon smiled, thinly. 'I don't want to have to come back. You know who I am. Let us in.'

Ginger sighed. 'Okay, come in. But your visit will have to be quick.'

He stood aside.

I went in first. Isabel followed me. Ginger shouted at us not to touch anything.

'Be very careful,' he said. 'Visitors are not covered by

97

any insurance.' His words echoed through the building.

'And don't take any pictures. And I want a word with you.' I looked back. He'd put a hand up to stop Simon in the doorway.

'Have a look around,' called Simon. 'I'll be right behind you.'

We were inside. He'd done it. There was a muffled throbbing coming from somewhere below. A stairwell beckoned to us from the other side of the large dusty room we were in. One part of it led down. The other part led up. Describing the room as dusty would be a bit of an understatement.

It was dusty in the way a sandpit is dusty. There were drifts of sand and cobwebs in each corner, and a thick layer of it on the floor with boot marks and channels in it. There was a heap of dust near the stairs too, as if that section had been swept down from the upstairs rooms.

Had the house been abandoned for decades? It certainly looked like it. We headed down the stairs.

The room below was darker, full of cobwebs. It had no stairs going down, just a three-foot-wide hole in the floor. There was light streaming from the hole. The throbbing noise was coming from it. I looked down into it. Isabel was behind me. I couldn't hear Ginger and Simon talking anymore. I could hear other voices, European voices. Someone was speaking German down there. The replying voice was German too. Who the hell was on this dig?

A shiny steel ladder led down into the hole. I took hold of it and swung myself onto it.

'This is one time where I don't think "ladies first" holds.' I looked down.

I could see shiny equipment, a portable generator and some white airtight plastic boxes on the stone floor beneath. There was another hole of a similar size in the floor below us too.

'You don't have to come down if you don't want to.'

'Why don't you try to stop me?' said Isabel.

There was no polite answer to that.

At the bottom of the ladder the air felt heavy. The generator was running, and a red pipe, about an inch thick, ran out of it and down into the next hole. The inside of my mouth was coated in gritty dust. The walls on this level were ancient foot-square stone blocks. There was no plaster on them, as there was on the walls up above.

The voices had stopped talking. Whoever was down below had probably heard us coming.

I had a look around. There was a knee-high pile of broken, pale ancient wood in one corner. This room was a different shape to the ones above. It faced in a different direction, diagonal to those above, as if the building it had been part of had faced a different way. There was an oily scent coming from the pump too. And the noise from it was a lot louder now we were on the same floor as it.

The hole going down was in the far corner here. I could see the start of a proper stairway descending this time. We were far below street level now. There was a recessed door near the stairs, totally blocked by a pile of rubble. It looked as if it had been there a long time. Where did that door lead? Why had it been blocked up from the inside?

The temperature was high down here. I felt sweat run down my forehead. My shirt was getting damp at the small of my back too. Then a head appeared, poking up out of the unguarded stairwell. And wheover he was, he was angry.

21

Henry Mowlam took the teabag out of his thin white plastic cup and dropped it into the stained bin. Working for the Security Service was not as glamorous as TV shows made it out to be.

He took his mid-afternoon tea back to his desk. He had a report to read. It was on one of his two smaller side screens. The report was a secure PDF, an un-printable and un-saveable document, which his password had allowed him access to. It could only be read on screen and the length of time it remained opened, and by whom, was being recorded as part of the document metadata.

The report was the latest impact assessment for a war between Israel and the US, and Iran and possibly Egypt too, as well as others, depending on which Arab governments got embroiled to prove their Islamic credentials.

Its contents were stark.

The human and economic impact of such a war would be greater than any conflict since the Second World War. Iran was a regional power now and had a standing army of 545,000 as well as a reserve of 650,000 men. It would be the largest and most advanced military force Israel had ever engaged. Israel had an active defence force of 187,000 and a reserve of 565,000. Israel's population was 7.8 million. Iran's 78 million.

The casualty predictions were based on a number of possible war scenarios. Even the most optimistic prediction for the loss of life in the region would be unacceptable to the public in any of the participating countries, should the information ever get out.

The second half of the document detailed the levels of long-term human and physical destruction if a limited nuclear exchange took place. It included details of the Israeli nuclear arsenal and an estimate of the restricted Iranian nuclear capability, currently believed to lie within their military's reach.

Henry was allowed to see the document only because the new remote pursuit protocol allowed him to track high-value permanent UK citizens outside the country for short durations, rather than hand over monitoring to MI6, the branch of the British Security Service focused on external threats.

The situation relating to Dr Susan Hunter, one of the UK citizens he was tracking, and the tension in Israel, where she had last been seen, necessitated he be aware of the latest intelligence for that country for his level of security clearance.

What he had to do now was evaluate the intelligence and decide how they should proceed regarding the Susan Hunter situation.

The report he had read before the war scenario document was the item he would have to take an operational decision about.

It claimed to have traced the report of a letter from the first caliph of Islam, regarding the fate of Jerusalem, to a statement by a Max Kaiser, the archaeologist who had died a week before, soon after he had given an interview to a journalist working for an Egyptian newspaper.

The article had only appeared the day before in Cairo, written in Arabic, and it had taken the translation service this long to prioritise and translate it.

It hadn't even mentioned Max Kaiser's death. Presumably, the reporter had interviewed him before he died and hadn't bothered to update his story, if he had been made aware of Kaiser's death at all.

A link between this article and Kaiser's death was one question he had to consider. But why would any Islamists want to kill him? The letter was in their interests.

And how was all this related to Dr Hunter?

22

The man had slicked-back silvery grey hair and a big pale face. He wore gold-rimmed glasses, and looked fifty-something.

'Heh, who are you?' he asked, with a German accent.

'We're here to have a look at the dig. I was a colleague of Max Kaiser's. I'm Sean Ryan, from the Institute of Applied Research in Oxford. This is my colleague, Isabel Sharp. A professor from Hebrew University is on his way down. He was Max's reference to get on this dig.'

He rubbed his forehead. 'We were expecting visitors after what happened to Max. It shocked us all. I'm Dieter Mendhol from the University of Dusseldorf. My colleague, Walter Schleibell, is below.'

We followed him down the stairs. The floor below was a totally different scene. The walls were covered in yellowing plaster. One wall had faded wall paintings, the sort that you'd see at Pompeii, with toga clad people in stylised poses.

A tingle of excitement ran through me. This was the real thing; a room that had been used almost two thousand years ago. Contemporaries of Christ and Caesar might have been here.

There were niches in the walls, where you could put busts. And the floor was whiter than the one above, smoother too. It looked as if it was made out of a similar sandstone as used in other parts the building, but from a different source, from a higher quality quarry.

Another Germanic-looking man, of the same vintage as Dieter, and wearing the same type of pale sand-coloured trousers and matching shirt, was standing by the far wall with his hands on his hips. He nodded steadily as we came down.

Introductions were made. We all shook hands. I gave them my card. Each of them examined it. I told them their colleague up above had allowed us in for a quick visit and the reason why. They looked at each other, then shrugged their shoulders.

'This is really something down here,' I said.

'Ja, it certainly is. First century is what we think,' said Dieter. 'Late Herodian era. Everything points to it. We'll be presenting a paper on the discovery, of course, and we'll include carbon dating analysis to back up our judgement. That will prove it all, for sure.'

'The History Channel will give you a whole series.'

He shrugged, as if he didn't care.

'How many rooms have you found like this?'

'Just this one and the one below.'

There was another hole, a jagged one, right in the far corner. A blue plastic sheet and some rolls of wide black plastic tape lay near it. Were they covering the hole at times?

'You're afraid of contamination?'

'Ja, moisture in particular. The rooms have been airtight for a long time. The moisture gets in at night as the temperature in the air above us goes down. We seal the lower floor as tightly as we can. Come, have a look.' He sounded keen to show their find off.

Beside the hole there were two stacks of see-through plastic boxes. They were all about a foot wide and six inches tall. Some of them, the pile on the left, had something in them; scraps of parchment, pieces of wood, a piece of marble. Each box was numbered. I looked down into the hole. The site that confronted me was extraordinary.

It looked like an ancient rubbish pit into which people had thrown the contents of several buildings. There were pieces of wood sticking up out of the mess, like whitened bones in an ancient charnel house.

Some of the pieces of wood looked like boards from shelves, others were carved intricately. I could see a lot of scrolls too, some were crushed, some were just fragments, but many were whole. Among the debris were pieces of masonry, broken bits of furniture. The whole lot of it covered the floor below completely. I couldn't even make out how deep the pile of ancient rubbish was.

There was a shiny steel ladder leading down. I put my hand out to hold it.

'We don't want anyone else to go down there,' said Dieter, quickly. 'We had a problem a few weeks ago. We think our security was breached.' He moved towards me and put a wide hand on top of the pile of boxes.

'As a trained archaeologist you know we have to make sure everything that comes from this find is properly recorded; that each item is identified, photographed in its layer and in its original position, before it is moved.' He sounded as if he was giving me a lecture, and he was only on his first slide.

'How far have you got with all this?' said Isabel.

'We're selecting sample items for testing right now.' He looked at his colleague, then back at Isabel. 'We expect the Israeli Antiquities Authority will take over this site after we present our findings. They'll organise the removal of the artefacts in sections to preserve impressions and any organic remains. If the site is what we think it is, there will be many

years of work in this place. All we have done is open it up.'
He sounded pleased with that idea. His colleague did not
look so happy.

'We've put in for an extension to our licence, of course.
But it's hard to say what will happen, after Max being
murdered and everything that's going on up there.' He pointed
at the ceiling.

I didn't argue with him. I was distracted by the wealth of
ancient material below.

'Why do you think all that stuff is down there like that,
all jumbled up?' asked Simon. He had come down the stairs
as Dieter was talking.

'We have a theory, if you'd like to hear it,' said Walter.

'Sure.'

My forehead was hot, my skin tight. It was certainly warm
enough and dry enough down here to preserve anything. The
recommendation for preserving archaeological finds,
particularly organic compounds, is to allow a 3% fluctuation
in relative humidity from the conditions in which the item
was found.

It was a tiny amount, given daily fluctuations at ground
level here were probably as high as 30% at this time of year.
Preserving finds was one of Susan Hunter's areas of expertise.
Was that why she came out here?

'We think most of the material was in this room or nearby
before someone dumped it all down there. It's unusual to
find a room full of material like that, but we think we know
the reason. In 66 AD, a group of Zealots, extremists called
the Sicarii, took over this part of the city. They were a fun
lot. They used to go to the forum and stab Romans who
passed by. They were trying to drive them all out. In the end
though, all they did manage to drive out was Herod Agrippa's
troops. At the time, Roman officials might have taken refuge
in this house and others like it. They might have thrown

106

racks of scrolls down into that room to give themselves more living space as they waited for rescue.'

I could see the remnants of racks down there.

'Maybe they tried to escape by night afterwards. If they'd been caught by Zealot patrols, they'd have all had their throats cut, no questions asked. Things were bad in the autumn of '66.'

'So why wasn't all this stuff found afterwards?' said Simon.

'When this part of the city was eventually recaptured by Titus a few years later, as he suppressed the great Jewish revolt,' said Dieter, his tone growing more confident as he spoke, 'the building up above was probably destroyed and turned into rubble. Titus ordered every building in this city to be torn down to its foundations. They did it quickly too. No arch or roof was allowed to remain standing. Eventually, when later builders went to work, they would have used the rubble of the floor above as a foundation. They wouldn't have bothered to break through to find out what was below. They were Roman slaves most likely, with orders to construct new buildings to a new street plan.'

'That's all plausible,' said Isabel. 'But I'm amazed these rooms have never been uncovered in all the time since. We're talking nearly two thousand years.'

'Much of this city was abandoned and in rubble for decades after the great Jewish revolt, not just for a few years. That was the key event in Jewish history. The city was deliberately depopulated. It was rebuilt to a totally different design by Hadrian in 130 AD.' He motioned at the ceiling above us, his hand cupped and turning.

'This part of the city was abandoned for long periods after that as well. Building work was banned in Jewish sections of Jerusalem for centuries.'

'How did the people who were down here escape?' I said.

Dieter pointed at a small hole in one wall. Straight beyond

it there was a wall of dusty rubble, but the hole could have been used to escape into another building, before that building was razed too.

'What's your best find?' I asked. I moved towards the boxes, bent over, put my knee on the ground and looked at them.

'That's a good question,' said Walter. He hesitated, looking at Dieter.

'This is one of the better finds,' said Dieter, softly. He held out one of the plastic boxes set apart from the others. The only thing inside was a piece of triangular marble the size of a large chocolate bar. It looked like a notice that might have sat at the top of an ancient shelf. There was Roman lettering on it. The marble was broken, in half it looked, but the second part of the inscription was visible when I moved the box, so the yellow long-life light bulb strung up above our heads shone down directly on it.

It read . . . S PILATUS.

'You think this used to say Pontius Pilate?' I held it forward for Isabel to see it.

Walter nodded vigorously. 'The Latin is the same as they found on the inscription in Caesarea Maritima.'

'So, you've found material from Pontius Pilate's time,' said Simon. 'Who knows what else is down there, maybe the plans for Herod's Temple.'

'Or a receipt for the marriage feast at Cana,' I said.

A shout echoed from above.

'Who's down there?' Whoever was shouting, his accent was American.

The atmosphere in the room changed in a second, as if someone had shouted *fire*. Our two German friends looked at each other as if they'd been found out. Then a clattering noise filled the air.

Walter put his hand out, took the box from me and put it

back where it had been. I stood away from the hole and the ladder.

Someone was coming down. More than one person, by the noise of them. Then legs, clad in green army fatigues, came down the stairs. Two crew cut men appeared, both at least six foot six, and big enough to be running backs for the Jets. They stood near us, as if they were security guards who'd caught us trespassing.

A third American, an older guy with white hair and a bushy white beard came down after them. He had a big white handkerchief in his hand and was mopping his brow as he arrived.

'How the hell did you people get in here? You ain't supposed to be down here at all. This is a closed site.' He stood in front of me and poked a finger into my chest.

I swatted at it. He pulled his hand back.

'And who are you?' I said. His two friends came up, one on each side of him.

'That boy upstairs made a serious mistake letting you all down here just because of a reference. You're trespassing. You gotta leave now.' He turned to Dieter.

'You didn't let 'em go down below, did you?'

'No,' said Dieter. 'No way.' He sounded so deferential I assumed at once that the older American was his boss.

'Did I miss you telling us who you are?' I said. 'Are you going to give us some idea of why we should listen to you?' I wasn't one of his employees.

'You do not need to know who I am. What you need to do is leave this site immediately.' It looked as if a bunch of rats were gnawing at the inside of his face, it was so bunched up, even purple in places.

'You'll have a heart attack if you take everything so seriously,' said Isabel.

109

'This site is beyond your comprehension,' he said. 'It is divine providence that it has been found. You should not be here.'

'I hope the whole world gets to see what's down here,' said Isabel.

I could see he didn't appreciate her remark. His face became even more purple.

'Take them upstairs,' he said. Then he headed for the stairs.

'Who is this guy?' I said, turning to Dieter.

'Pastor Stevson. He sponsors this dig,' said Walter.

'Well, we were leaving anyway,' I said. 'We've finished our tour. We've seen everything we needed, thanks.' I emphasised the word *everything*.

The crew cut guy near Isabel put his hand up again, as if he was going to take hold of her. I took two steps towards him, raised my hand and swiped it between him and Isabel, as if I was sweeping away a cobweb.

'We're going,' I said. 'Don't put a goddamned hand on any of us, unless you want your ass thrown down that rubbish hole over there.' I nodded toward the hole in the floor, not that far away from where the guy was standing.

'Go then,' said the other young guy. 'And make it snappy.'

'Did no one teach you any manners yet?' I said.

His grin had a bit of a snarl in it.

We headed up the stairs. Isabel and Simon went first. We didn't move nearly as fast as they wanted us to; I was nudged in the back twice, but I swung my elbow violently to warn them off. It didn't happen again.

Upstairs, the guy who let us in was standing sheepishly to one side by the door to the lane.

He opened it. There weren't stones falling around us any more, there were rocks. Not that many, one every few seconds, but enough to make the lane a place you wouldn't want to hang around when discussing the weather.

110

'Ow,' shouted Isabel, as the door closed with a bang behind us.

A rock had struck her calf. Her jeans were torn. There was a splattering of blood on them. I held my hand up, to try to stop anything else hitting her.

'We've got to get around the corner,' said Simon. 'You should go to hospital, have that looked at.'

'Where's the nearest hospital?' I asked the policeman who opened the barrier to let us go past.

'Go to the Bikur Cholin,' he said. 'They have a good emergency room and they're near.' Then he looked away. His expressionless face seemed to indicate he'd seen a lot worse than the scratch Isabel had suffered.

We headed back towards the Jaffa Gate and ended up at the taxi rank. Simon bid us farewell there.

'Any taxi will take you to the hospital,' he said. 'Call me if you need any more help.'

Ten minutes later we were pulling up outside the hospital. It was 3.55 p.m., Tuesday afternoon. We'd been in the city only two days and we already needed a hospital.

The place was busy. The older part of the hospital was a Victorian/Ottoman wedding cake of a building made of pale icing-like sandstone. It had pointed arched windows and a first floor balcony at the front where visiting Edwardian-era royals could have waved at the crowds who had come to see them. It probably didn't get much call for that sort of thing any more.

I held Isabel's hand as the nurse cleaned her leg in the modern emergency ward. It had taken only twenty minutes for Isabel to be seen, despite the waiting room being busy, which says something for the Israeli health care system. The examination cubicle we were in was as modern as anything you'd find in London or anywhere else.

'I'm not going to let them keep me in,' said Isabel, as we

waited for the nurse to come back. She had a determined look on her face.

There was a loud hum coming from the blue and grey equipment around us and from the lighting, but what I noticed most was that the hospital was dealing with an amazing cross-section of people. There were Arabs, Orthodox Jews with ringleted hair, secular Jews, French tourists, two ultra-thin Ethiopian-looking women, and a big blonde Mitteleuropean.

And that was just what I could see in the area near us. I'm sure if I'd looked further I'd have found more. The place wasn't a melting pot, it was a simmering stew.

The nurse dealing with Isabel was a small pale lady with short blonde hair. She was attractive, though not in Isabel's league.

After the nurse came back Isabel was invited to receive a tetanus injection. She declined. She'd had one only six months before, she said.

The nurse left us again. She was going to get a doctor to look at Isabel before they released her. The examination table Isabel was sitting on was set high up. Its covering was a white paper sheet with big Hebrew letters in blue running all over it.

'You were lucky it wasn't worse,' I said.

'Do you always have to look on the bright side?' She rubbed at her forehead.

'You'd prefer it if I moaned?'

'Do you think Susan's disappearance is to do with that dig?' said Isabel.

'Could be. Kaiser was always involved in weird shit, from what I can gather.'

Isabel straightened her back. 'It wouldn't take a genius to inscribe Pontius Pilate's name on some piece of marble. I hope you're not taken in by it all,' she said.

'It could be real,' I said. 'I reckon Kaiser asked Susan to come here for her expert opinion on preserving what's in that building. He may even have taken her down there to see what they were doing.'

'He probably wanted her to verify that the place was as real as it looks.'

The level of background chatter rose suddenly. I looked up. Two Israeli policemen were marching toward us. I assumed, for a long moment, that they were heading for someone else, for some criminal who was about to get his comeuppance, but I was wrong.

That had us in their sights.

'Are you Sean Ryan?' said the larger of the two loudly, as they came up to us. Their gaze was fixed on us, as was the gaze of everybody nearby. The chatter in the room died away.

Everyone was waiting for my reply.

Even the equipment around us seemed to go silent. All I could hear was blood thumping in my ears. What the hell was going on?

23

The girl bowed low, she was on her knees and her forehead almost touched the cream marble floor. Her hair, and most of her face, was covered by a tightly bound black headdress, but he could see ridges under it, as if she wore it the way they do in parts of Sudan. His father's house used to have servants like this girl.

'Rise,' he said.

She did. She was very thin.

The imam smiled. It wasn't often he got a young woman visiting him on her own these days. His house, the best one on the street and in the whole area, was in a poor part of Cairo, but it wasn't that which put them off coming. It was his reputation.

'As-salāmu Aleikum, Ali Bilah, my teacher. I need your help. I have done wrong. I am so terribly frightened.' She bowed her head low.

He didn't ask her to sit on the cushions nearby. It wouldn't be right. He shifted his big bottom on the low couch, looked at her. This would be a good afternoon.

She took a step forward and glanced up for a moment.

Her green eyes, all he could see of her face, had a jewel-like intensity to them.

'What place are you from?'

'Juba.' She bowed her head under his gaze. It was a true sign of her respect.

He'd been right about her coming from Sudan. 'What wrong have you done?'

The room was warm. The window shutters were open and a square of dust-flecked sunlight lit up the floor between them. The early afternoon sun had meant there was no need to light the fire in the big black stove below in the kitchen. That also meant he was alone in the house. His wife was dead, cancer had taken her early, but her sister came and made his evening meal most days, except for the occasional sunny day at this time of year, like this one, when she took her own children to walk by the Nile first.

'May I show you?'

He nodded.

What she did next brought a gasp to his throat. She bent, grabbed the bottom of her long black dress, and pulled it up to her thigh. She held it up with one hand.

Her legs were brown, slim. There was a blue tattoo of a snake coiled around her thigh, where a garter might have been. Its scales were purple, dark brown. He'd never seen anything like it.

'Have I done wrong?' she said. There was tremble in her voice.

He closed his eyes. This one deserved, without any doubt, to have the evil beaten out of her. A few seconds later he opened them.

The last thing he saw was the flash of the blade.

And the last thing he heard was the gurgling of blood from his throat as his vocal chords flapped ineffectually.

24

'Yes, I'm Sean Ryan. What's going on?'

The larger of the two policemen was holding a pair of handcuffs. They were shiny, and bigger than I'd imagined such things would be. He was wearing a dark blue shirt with a shield emblem on each arm featuring a white Star of David.

Then he did something that I'd never seen done before, except on TV. He stepped in front of me, put his hand on my wrist, and had a handcuff on it before I could say a word.

'You are under arrest for trespassing on a restricted archaeological site and violating the terms of your visitor's visa.'

I think my mouth opened in shock at that point. They say your jaw drops when you're surprised, and it's true, it does.

The other policeman was talking to a male nurse who had appeared. The second policemen had receding hair and a wiry frame, as if he hardly ate.

Isabel moved to get off the examination table, on the other side to where he was. He didn't like that.

'Stop, Isabel Sharp, do not move,' he shouted. Oddly, the

sound in the ward went from a hush to a sudden buzz, as if swarms of bees had exited from the walls around us.

'I'm only getting off the bed,' said Isabel, politely.

The policeman who was nearest Isabel had his gun out. He was pointing it at her. My heart thudded. What were they expecting? That Isabel was going to blow herself up?

'There's no need for that,' I said loudly.

'You will follow our instructions,' said the policeman.

'There's no need for you to pull your gun.' I spoke slowly, hoping to calm things.

'We're tourists, that's all.'

I turned to Isabel.

'Let's do what they say. This must be some mistake. I'm sure we can sort it out.'

She held her wrists out in front of her. The policeman had his cuffs on Isabel a second later. His expression told me that maybe I was being optimistic.

'We understand your treatment is finished here, that you are fit to leave,' he said to Isabel.

'You got the news before I did,' she said.

I could have said something about the doctor not having told her himself, but the cut on her leg was relatively minor and it had been bandaged with an impressive looking skin-toned plaster.

And I was right about being optimistic. They'd made no mistake about who they'd arrested.

We were taken to a large concrete bunker-like police station. It was only ten minutes' drive from the hospital, but I had no idea what part of Jerusalem it was in. It was on a main road with low office blocks set behind trees.

We were taken to it in the back of a white police car with blue stripes, no door handles in the back, and tinted windows. It brought us into an underground car park beneath the station.

117

After being thoroughly body-searched in separate rooms and having passed through metal detectors, we were brought down a windowless corridor together. As I looked at a pale-faced Isabel I had a vision of a long period of incarceration without trial, of being stuck in an Israeli prison not knowing what would happen to us next.

Then we were split up. I had no idea why they brought us back together just to walk down a corridor, but they probably had a reason.

Maybe they hoped Isabel would plead with me about something we'd done as soon as she saw me, but she didn't. If anyone imagined her as someone who scared easily, they were wrong.

Judging from what she'd told me about some of her escapades in Istanbul before we met, and from her behaviour during incidents when we were there together, a period in police custody wasn't likely to faze her.

It took them two hours to get the basics straight about us; to verify that we were staying where we said, that we were who we said we were, that we had return airline tickets, that I was one of the founders of The Institute of Applied Research in Oxford and that we had a good reason for visiting that site in the Old City.

I wasn't too concerned during all this. We'd done nothing wrong, in my opinion. In fact, we were trying to help them by looking for Dr Hunter.

It took them only another thirty minutes to decide to deport us. There is something to be said about the speed of Israeli justice. It was the exact opposite of what I'd imagined.

Isabel and I met up again in a room at the back of the police station. We were also reunited with our belongings from the hotel. That was the next of the surprises for me that night. It seemed as if they knew what was going to happen to us from the moment they picked us up.

Our backpacks had been searched thoroughly too. They'd been turned inside out. It wasn't hard to figure this out. Every item that had been in them had been put back in a different place. Clearly they didn't care whether we knew what they'd done or not.

The good news was that everything from the hotel was in our bags. Nothing was missing. Not even the old newspaper from the bedside table, which had been stuffed into my bag.

What surprised me most though was their decision to deport us. Sure, we'd pushed our way into that dig, and maybe we had broken several important regulations about who's allowed onto archaeological sites, but I'd never imagined that someone trespassing at a dig would be treated this way.

It didn't matter to them that we'd been taken there by Simon either. They would deal with him separately, they said. And we were lucky not to be facing criminal charges.

'You cannot be unaware of the importance of archaeological laws in Israel,' was how the policeman put it, while explaining what was going to happen to us.

In the end I didn't believe all that. Someone high up had decided we weren't welcome and that was it. We were history.

My hopes of helping to find Susan were gone.

The next big surprise was that we were allowed to pick which city we'd be deported to. That was a decision we were asked to make on the drive to Ben Gurion International Airport.

They had the siren on whenever we met traffic, so the journey took only thirty minutes. The main thing of interest I saw on that drive was a long line of military vehicles, tanks on trailers and odd-looking trucks pulling sand-coloured containers, which we passed, all heading for Jerusalem. There must have been fifty of them. Something else was going on here.

119

We were told by the friendlier policeman in the car that there were flights to London, Istanbul, New York, Frankfurt and Athens in the next few hours.

Isabel nudged me with the side of her hand. Then she turned to me. There was just the two of us in the back of the police car. She spoke to the policemen in front as her eyes were on me.

'We'll take the flight to Athens,' she said. She granted me a thin smile. It said don't argue.

I decided to go along with her. I shouldn't have.

I was hoping Isabel might have a plan. I assumed she still had enough contacts in London in the Foreign Office to help us in some way.

When we reached the airport I got another shock. Standing right in front of the terminal building, talking on his telephone, was one of the old white-haired preacher's sidekicks from the dig in the Old City. It was a weird coincidence. So weird my alarm bells were ringing and dancing at the same time.

It looked very much as if our swift departure from Israel had been precipitated by a complaint from this guy's buddies. It wasn't just about us breaking a regulation.

But why the hell was it so important that we left Israel, that someone had to make sure it happened?

'Did you see your friend outside?' I said to Isabel, as we waited for our bags to be scanned.

Isabel didn't even turn her head. She just smiled. When we got past the security check she asked the policemen whether she could go to a news-stand nearby. They nodded their agreement. She bought a copy of *The Jerusalem Post*. The front page was about a military call up. All reservists had been told to report to their units.

Half an hour later, after buying expensive tickets and

120

getting fast-tracked through two further security checks, we were waiting in the departure area. Our policemen were sitting nearby, keeping an eye on us. Thankfully they hadn't insisted on handcuffing us. That was, they said, because we'd agreed to leave immediately, and hadn't challenged the deportation order.

They'd made it clear that if we hadn't agreed, it would have meant a few days in prison, or longer, maybe even ten days, as we waited for a hearing. And if we lost that we'd never be allowed back into Israel again. This way we could come back, if we applied to an Israeli embassy first.

'So why are we really going to Athens?' I said, leaning close to Isabel.

Our heads were almost touching. 'Simon Marcus told me something while you were in the bathroom in that juice bar in Jerusalem. It came back to me while I was in the police station.'

'What did he say?'

She spoke quickly. 'He said Kaiser was obsessed with Ibn Killis.'

'Who?'

'That's what I thought,' she said. 'Simon said he was a Grand Vizier in Cairo. He was Jewish apparently. He helped establish the Fatimid dynasty in the tenth century.' She said all this as if I was supposed to know why any of this had any relevance to today.

'So?'

'Apparently Kaiser was planning to go to Cairo this week, to visit the Museum of Antiquities.'

'You think we should go there?'

'Yes. And if we want to get to Cairo from Israel by plane, Athens is the place to go. There are no direct flights.'

Egypt has been so much in the news, not only in the last

few years with all the ousting Mubarak drama, but recently too, as some of the changes there had begun to have an impact. An hour later we were in the air.

It was after lunch on Wednesday before our Egypt Air flight took off from Athens, almost sixty minutes late. The flight only took one and a half hours, and there was another delay at Cairo Airport's Terminal 3 after we arrived.

We had to queue to buy a visa and then queue again at passport control. The process seemed endless. While we waited, Isabel gave me some facts about Cairo. It was, apparently, the largest city between the Americas and India, and that includes the rest of Africa and all of Europe.

Its eighteen million inhabitants lived in one of the most densely populated places on earth, three times the population density of London. The pyramids of Giza were in its western suburbs and most of its good hotels, on the opposite east bank of the Nile, particularly on their higher floors, had amazing views out to the pyramids and on to the desert.

The city had been Roman, Greek, and then Muslim under various caliphates including the Umayyads, the Fatimids and the Ottomans. Each had left a layer behind in the city.

Saint Peter had written his first epistle here too. Coptic Christians, a long protected minority in Egypt, had held onto much of the oldest teachings of the Christian Church.

The greatest library in the world had been located here too, in the tenth century, under Fatimid rule. The Fatimids had, according to legend, been among the most tolerant sects in Islam, allowing Christians and Jews to partake fully in the affairs of the state.

After the Fatimids came Saladin, the Grand Vizier of Cairo, the man who pushed the Crusaders out of Jerusalem.

Finally, we were through the queue. We headed straight for the taxi rank. We ended up in a new, air-conditioned taxi, and had a slow, but uneventful journey to the Rameses Hilton on the east bank of the Nile, a ten minute walk from the famous, or infamous, Tahrir Square, where demonstrators had toppled Mubarak and still gathered regularly. The Museum of Antiquities, Cairo's must-see attraction, with its permanent exhibition of ancient mummies and Pharaonic-era gold, was even closer.

'You can see the Mediterranean from up there,' said the taxi driver in hesitant English, as he dropped us off. He was pointing to the top of the hotel tower. It certainly was tall enough. I found out later it had thirty-six storeys.

The hotel was at a busy intersection and there was a constant honking of horns as traffic sped by. There was a faint smell of burning in the air too, as if fires were somewhere not far away.

We checked in and were given a double room with, much to my displeasure, two single beds. Isabel claimed we were given that room because we weren't married. I asked for another room with a double bed to prove her wrong. I was told there were none available, as there was a convention on and all the rooms were booked.

We'd been lucky to get a room at all – so the unsmiling man said.

I pushed the twin beds together. Isabel showered first, coming out of the bathroom in a fluffy white bathrobe.

'You look good,' I said.

'I don't feel it. My stomach is acting up.' She stood by the window looking out over the city. It was dark, 6.30 p.m., and the evening rush hour was filling the streets below us with bright streams of headlights.

She looked pensive, as if being here was troubling her.

123

'If you want to go back to London, let me know,' I said. She turned to me, held her hand out. I took it.

'No, we're in this together. You have your demons to vanquish and I'm going to help you.'

'This feels more like following a thread than vanquishing demons,' I said.

She pulled me to her. 'I think we're following the right thread,' she said.

We held each other, staring out at the endless streams of headlights. It felt as if we were at the centre of an illuminated cobweb.

While I was showering she set up a meeting with Mark Headsell, her ex-husband. I can't say I was delighted with the fact that we were going to meet him again.

It crossed my mind to say something to him about the way he'd treated her. He'd done some stupid things, not the least of which was leaving her behind in a house, while it was being shot up by gunmen in Iraq. I wondered why she'd stayed with him after that.

When I came out of the shower Isabel had put a black skirt on. It wasn't short – it came to just above her knee – but it was a totally different look to the black or blue jeans she normally wore. She was applying make-up at the mirror.

'You look good,' I said, as I towelled my hair dry. 'Is this for Mark?'

'Don't be crazy. Mark Headsell is an idiot, but he can help us.'

She looked me up and down. 'Can you be ready in ten?'

'That quick?'

'There's some event going on here which Mark's attending tonight. If we want to see him we'll have to be quick.' She went back to fixing her make-up.

We were in the Sherlock Holmes pub, one of the features

of the hotel, ten minutes later. My hair was still damp and I was tired from the journey. Thirty minutes after that, when Mark still hadn't turned up, I was feeling for Isabel.

'Did you ever want to kill him?' I said, turning from the door again, after someone came in who wasn't him.

'Lots of times. Do you want another beer?'

My bottle of Egyptian Stella was finished. I was tempted by the thought of another cool one.

Suddenly, an alarm sounded from the foyer outside the bar. At first it was only a single alarm, then a klaxon joined in. I stood, looking around for the exits. The barman was around the front of his bar, pulling down the shutters. The waiter who'd served us was hurrying around the tables.

'Everybody must go,' he said, as he reached us.

We went out to the foyer. People were streaming out of the hotel. It wasn't a panic, but it wasn't far off. Isabel stopped, opened her bag, took out her phone and tapped at the screen. Someone was calling her.

She put her hand up to stop me heading for the main door, then when she'd finished the call, she said, 'We're to go up to the Terrace Restaurant. He's up there waiting for us.' She put her phone back in her bag.

'What about the evacuation?' I gestured at the people streaming towards the front door.

'He said we're to ignore it.'

'You reckon we should?'

'He was always like this,' she said, sighing. 'He probably set that stupid alarm off himself. I wouldn't put it past him.'

We headed for the elevators.

Two hotel employees were standing in front of them, blocking people from using them. Isabel went up to the nearest employee, leaned towards him and said something.

125

He waved us brusquely towards the only open elevator, which was right behind him. He smiled at me as I passed.

'What did you say to him?' I asked, as the elevator went up.

'I told him a security manager had requested us up on the terrace immediately.' She flicked a strand of hair from her forehead. 'The truth sets you free.'

The Terrace Restaurant was on the second floor. It overlooked the Nile and a wide concrete bridge carrying streams of cars going each way over the river.

The restaurant was empty except for an older waiter in a black suit who was tidying up the buffet, covering huge silver platters with their lids.

In the far corner of the low ceilinged room, with his back to the wall, was Mark Headsell. He waved us over. The waiter didn't even look at us.

'You guys have a great sense of timing,' said Mark as we sat down. He shook hands with me. He hugged Isabel. She raised her eyes to heaven as he squeezed her.

'You two are an item now, right?' he said, after we'd told him we'd flown in from Athens.

'You know we are,' said Isabel. She sounded surprised that he was asking.

'Since Istanbul,' I added. I gave him a fake smile.

'How is it being out of the service?' he said, turning to Isabel.

'It's good. I like being back in London.'

'You got out very young,' he said. There was a note of admonition in his voice.

'I should have done it earlier.' There was a distinct edge to their exchange.

'You would have got what you wanted, in the end,' he said.

She didn't reply. He turned to me. 'Would you like some water?'

He gestured towards a water jug with a silver lid that was in the middle of the table. I poured a glass for Isabel, then one for myself. He already had one.

'Did you get anywhere with what I asked you about?' said Isabel.

Mark looked at me, smiled. He was enjoying being needed.

'This is a big favour.'

'We appreciate it.' She smiled back at him.

He returned it. I wanted to go. We didn't need this asshole.

He turned to me. 'I could never say no to Isabel.'

'What did you find out?' she asked, very matter-of-factly.

He stared at her. 'There is no record of a Max Kaiser or a Susan Hunter coming into Egypt in the past month. If they did come in directly, it could only have been through the Taba border crossing, up by the Red Sea. But they've had a few glitches there recently.' He made a soft snorting sound. 'Actually, more than a few glitches.'

'You do know she's disappeared?' I said.

'It's unfortunate,' he said.

'Do you think the Israelis might have a record of her leaving?' said Isabel.

'I can ask.'

'You used to have connections in the Israeli Immigration service, didn't you?' she said.

'You have a very good memory,' he said, sounding surprised.

She turned to me. 'One of Mark's best friends from Bristol University is high up in the Israeli Immigration service. And I mean high up.' She raised her hand in the air, than rose it some more.

His expression gave nothing away.

'What area does he cover these days?' said Isabel.

He didn't reply.

'He's still friendly with you, isn't he?' She had a mock shocked look on her face.

'I'm still friendly with lots of people, Isabel.'

The sound of a low thud filled the room.

I rose out of my seat. Two alarms started.

'What the hell's going on?' I said.

'Don't go near the windows,' said Mark. 'Unless you want to die.'

25

Arap Anach closed his laptop. The villa was in darkness. The only noise he could hear was a car, far away, coming up the valley road. He listened as it passed. He'd employed two local women to clean the villa over the previous few months, but he'd let them go two weeks before.

This was his second chance to go down in history. He wasn't going to make any mistakes this time. There might not be a next.

Few people had the determination and the willingness to act as he had. He knew that. The vast majority of humans sit like frogs in water as it's boiled around them. They won't do anything to save themselves from being slowly cooked to death.

And being cooked to death was what was happening.

Islam was the fastest growing religion in Europe. What they hadn't conquered by the sword they would conquer in the next hundred years through the flaw in the theory of multiculturalism and comparative birth rates.

How long would they let Islam grow in Europe? Until all those *let's-get-along* liberal values were a minority again, and those who espoused Sharia Law began to dictate?

Because dictate they would. Islam was a religion that sought to govern, to impose. And once they were a majority they would use democracy against itself. Allowing Islam to grow rapidly in Europe was suicidal for Western values.

But he, and a few others, would be the antibiotic. They would jump-start the Western immune system. And if people had to die on the way, so be it. The end justified the means. There had to be sacrifices.

He was glad now that his senses had been dulled when he was young. It was a blessing. The priest who'd done it had even called it that, before he'd hurt him so badly he couldn't walk for days, making the other boys laugh at him.

But the old priest had been right. There were few blessings more powerful. Arap Anach's heart had been sliced up that winter, his first in boarding school. The final, deepest cut had come the night he'd cried pathetically on the phone to his father after they'd caught him when he ran away.

The policeman who'd brought him back had held him by the ear and had told him to be quiet when he'd tried to explain what the priest had done.

His father had cut off the call as Arap Anach had rushed to tell him what had happened.

The head priest had ordered him to pray for forgiveness on his knees, by the side of his bed. Later that night the old priest had come back with a thick leather belt. He'd pulled him from the dormitory, down the icy corridor to the chapel. The first thing he did there was to punch Arap Anach, hard, in the side of his head. So hard his skull shook like a bell rattling.

'That's for causing trouble,' he'd said. Then he'd punched him again. Arap Anach's head had snapped to the other side. A tooth had dislodged. Blood had filled his mouth until he had to swallow it. After that the priest used the belt freely. It flew snapping through the air as if possessed.

That had been the first of the real beatings. Beatings which left him shattered inside, as if his bones and his brain had turned to jelly.

The strap felt like burning coals being thrown at his skin. He'd measured their number by the gasps he let out as the scorching pain rose and fell.

As he'd hit him with the strap the priest had shouted, 'Evil boy. You get what you deserve. Nobody will comfort you but me.'

When the beating was over the priest had forced him to do other things. Worse things than he'd ever done before. His father's disinterest had made it obvious that he could do whatever he wanted with the boy.

Arap Anach had stopped crying later that night. He'd never cried since. Not for himself, and especially not for anyone else. He rarely slept properly since then too. He was always on tenterhooks, waiting, half-sleeping, for someone to arrive, to wake him.

But it had all made him strong.

And now he would be remembered too. As the one who had acted to save the West from its self-defeating liberal weaknesses.

26

'It's probably a controlled explosion. They found a device in a suspect car, parked on the highway out there,' said Mark.

He pointed toward the windows at the other end of the room. Heavy curtains covered them almost completely. The waiter who'd been tidying up was standing by them. He pulled them together the last few feet, then peered through the gap his fingers were making.

'There are a lot of fanatics who aren't happy with what's going on in Egypt. This place is an ideal target if you hate foreigners.'

'I didn't think things were that bad.'

'They are. Just because you don't see Egypt on the six o'clock news anymore doesn't mean everything's hunky-dory here.'

'So it's getting worse?' said Isabel.

Mark shrugged. 'There's a whole bunch of new players coming up.' He leaned over the table, lowering his voice. 'One new lot have been making big waves, the Wael Al Qahira, the Protectors of the Victorious, of Cairo. Al Qahira is Cairo's original name.'

'Never heard of them,' I said.

'You will. They assassinated an imam who's been preaching tolerance in some of the big mosques in Cairo. They blew him up in front of his mosque.'

'Lovely,' said Isabel.

'Indeed, then someone went and retaliated yesterday and murdered one of their imams, a chap called Ali Bilah.'

'Not good,' I said.

He leaned closer, speaking quickly. 'Except Ali Bilah deserved it. He had a nasty reputation. He was found with his throat cut almost right through. He'd been stirring things up like you wouldn't believe, calling for war against Israel.'

Suddenly, a series of firecracker noises echoed through the room. My insides jumped. Whatever was going on out there was getting a lot more serious.

The waiter at the curtains turned and waved at us. When Mark put his hand up the man did a thumbs down gesture.

'We should leave,' said Mark.

As he finished speaking, more firecrackers sounded and the window behind the waiter shattered. An explosion of glass showered into the curtain, blowing straight through it at the centre. I reached over to pull Isabel down.

Mark stood up, reaching over to protect her too. The shower of glass was tinkling on the floor. His reaction almost surprised me more than the window being shattered.

Cool air was rushing into the room. The waiter was crawling over the glass sprayed carpet towards us. Mark had his phone out now, pressing it.

Isabel stood. She walked towards the waiter. I followed her. When we got close to him our shoes were crackling on glass with each step. We'd been lucky to be at the back of the room. The heavy curtains had caught most of the shards. They were shredded in places now, but mostly still intact. A gust of wind shook the tattered curtains.

They swayed, as if they were about to come down. A smell of cordite and smoke hit me as a chorus of car alarms started up.

Mark was speaking into his phone. He was right behind us. 'Two minutes at the kitchen exit,' I heard him say.

We reached the waiter. Isabel bent down. He was kneeling. His eyes were wide, his face a mass of small cuts and blood.

I bent down. I couldn't see any other injuries, just the cuts on his face. 'Can you move?' I asked him.

I know you're supposed to leave people in the recovery position after they've been injured, but the window was open to the sky and I could hear shouts from down below, as if someone was calling out to a gunman.

The waiter nodded. His eyes were wide. His gaze moved from my face to Isabel's. He must have seen our shock at his appearance, because he touched his face. His fingers came away wet and red, as if covered in paint.

Mark said something to him in Arabic. The man nodded. Then, with Isabel and myself on either side of him, he stood. He wasn't steady on his feet, and he kept turning his head as shouts echoed from below, but slowly, as we crossed the room, his confidence grew and by the time we reached the door he was walking almost unaided. Mark had picked up a white napkin from somewhere. He handed it to him.

The sight of the blood on it when the waiter wiped his hands made him stare, his eyes bulging even more. When we reached the elevators he pushed us away.

'You go. I am good,' he said.

'You're coming with us,' said Mark. 'We'll drop you at the hospital.' His tone was stern. He wasn't going to take any arguments.

We rode down to the basement. Arab music was still playing in the elevator. We headed down a wide corridor with blue tiled walls, and turned into a shiny kitchen. At the back of the kitchen there was a thick steel door. It slammed closed behind us. The only people we'd seen were a few white outfitted kitchen workers who seemed scared of us.

There was a black four wheel drive waiting outside. It had dark windows. The engine was running as we got in. An African woman, Sudanese or Ethiopian, her hair in ridges and her green eyes sparkling when she turned to look at me, was in the driving seat. She was thin and had a black veil around her neck. It went up a little over her hair at the back, but it was no more than a token gesture toward the full hair covering you find in a lot of Muslim countries these days.

The car had a Speranza logo on the steering wheel. It looked like a copy of a BMW.

'This is Xena,' said Mark, as we settled in the back.

Xena turned, looking at us gravely. Her face was elegant, but it had a hardness to it too. She stared at me for a moment longer than was polite, then looked away. Isabel pushed into my side. The waiter was on the other side of her.

'Are you a friend of Mark's?' Isabel said, leaning towards Xena.

Xena didn't reply.

Mark said something in Arabic. Xena swung the car out and headed for a gate in the clean white wall that ran around the small courtyard at the back of the hotel. There were four security guards by the gate, peering out. They were all dressed in black, had black helmets and bulletproof vests on and were carrying machine pistols. They turned as we came up, raising their guns to us.

Mark opened his window, waved at them and said something to the guard who came to our window. He pressed at something in his hand. The gate rolled open. The guards took up positions behind us, as if they were expecting an attack.

Mark said something to Xena. We stayed still for a minute, with the gate open in front of us and cars moving past on the street outside.

What was he waiting for?

'Things are changing too bloody fast here,' he said. 'That's the second attack on a major hotel. If they don't get a grip here soon this place will be in a lot of trouble. They're throwing away a hundred years of progress.' He leaned towards Xena. He spoke in English this time.

'Just poke the nose out. We can reverse if anyone takes a shot at us.'

Xena squeezed the accelerator. We crawled forward until the front of the vehicle was outside the gate. Then we stopped. A dirty green Hyundai car and two black and white taxis sped by. One of them honked at us.

'Okay, let's go,' said Mark.

We moved slowly through the city. There were queues of cars everywhere.

About ten minutes after leaving the hotel, we dropped the waiter at the emergency room of a hospital. Mark and Xena went in with him. They came out a few minutes later. He'd told us to stay in the car.

Mark was smiling when they came back. 'He's going to be ok,' he said, as he got into the car. 'The embassy will take care of his medical bills. His wife is on the way. It'll be better for him if we don't hang around. That's the way it is here.'

'You haven't lost your knack for attracting trouble,' said Isabel.

Ten minutes after that we were in Tahrir Square. The square had no demonstrators in it. It had six roads converging on it, and a large concrete central area with low bushes. There was a squad of perhaps twenty policemen standing in one corner and people walking around them.

'There's a demonstration planned for tomorrow against Israel, but it isn't expected to be as big as the one last Friday.' Mark turned to Xena. 'That's right, isn't it?'

She shook her head. 'No, it will be bigger,' she said.

Mark turned to us. 'There are people here who think they can unify this country again if there's a war with Israel,' he said. 'No matter what the outcome.'

Xena honked the car horn repeatedly at a taxi that cut across us. We were heading south, parallel with the Nile, which was to our right, along a street lined with tall palm trees. It was busy with trucks and cars.

As we stopped at a traffic light, I stared at the people streaming across the road. There was a mixture of Western-looking men, men in low white turbans, many of them bearded, and others with round white caps, as well as all types of women from those in jeans and short leather jackets to others dressed in so much billowing black that only their eyes could be seen.

A few minutes later we were in the Rithmo Bar in the Cairo Intercontinental. The bar was in the Arabian Nights style and featured heavy armchairs, low settees and a scattering of Bedouin print cushions. It was busy with expatriates, almost full in fact. We'd passed through a security check coming into the hotel that included being waved at with a blinking metal detecting wand.

'Isn't this place likely to be attacked too?' said Isabel.

Mark pointed at the frosted windows. 'Every one of those windows has a double layer of steel mesh embedded in the glass. You'd have to put a bomb on the window ledge outside to break it.'

He paused for a few seconds and looked around. 'Someone is trying to stir things up here. They hit the Hilton for a reason.'

'For what reason?' I said.

Mark didn't reply.

'You don't think the Egyptians would be stupid enough to attack Israel, do you?' said Isabel.

'I wouldn't bet either way,' said Mark. 'They've cancelled all army leave for the next few weeks here.'

'Isn't that just a reaction to the attacks?' said Isabel.

Instead of answering, Mark waved at a woman who had just come in. She was waving excitedly at him.

'With a bit of luck she won't come over,' he said.

But she did. She had black high heels, black tights and a tight white top on. Her hair was piled up on her head and she had a friendly expression.

'Hello, Mark,' she said, in a high-pitched voice. 'Found yourself some new friends?'

Mark gave her a mocking smile.

'What have you been up to, Kim? Revitalising international relationships all on your own again?' said Mark.

Kim sat down. Slumped would be more accurate. She dropped the two shopping bags she'd been carrying near to the table and smiled at me. Then she glanced at Isabel.

'Aren't you gonna introduce us?'

Mark did the introductions. Kim was here while her husband was working at the Cairo MIASA oil refinery. It was her first time in the Middle East.

We talked about the restaurant of the Hilton being shot up. Kim was shocked. Then she switched the subject to herself and began complaining about being left alone in Cairo. I didn't envy her trying to make a go of it here.

I looked at her shopping bags. One was black plastic and had a Khan el-Khalili logo in circular Arabic-style script on its side. The other was from the Museum of Antiquities and was made from thick brown paper.

'You've been shopping?' I said, when she stopped talking.

She nodded. 'That Khalili market is bloody amazing,' she

said. 'It's like something out of Ali Baba and the Forty Thieves. It's lovely, just lovely.'

Mark stared at her. He was giving off the impression that he was hoping she'd leave soon.

'What did you get at the museum?' I said.

'Bloody sore feet.' She laughed.

'There was only a one hour queue for the Tutankhamun exhibition.' She followed my gaze to the bag.

'My husband asked me to get him some guide books. I think I bought the wrong ones.' She shook her head.

'Mind if I have a look?' I asked. The Museum of Antiquities wasn't far away, back past Tahrir Square, near our hotel, and despite a new, more modern museum being opened in Cairo, it still contained an incredible collection of materials from the era of the Pharaohs, and also Roman, Greek and Islamic artefacts.

'Work away, love,' she said. Then she asked Isabel what we were doing here. While Isabel answered with a story about sightseeing I took out the large coffee table book which I'd spotted. It was called The Hidden Treasures of the Cairo Museum of Antiquities.

'I shouldn't have bought that big one,' said Kim, pointing at the book. I put it down on the table so we could all admire it.

'It looks incredible,' said Isabel. She reached over, turned a page, then another. We watched as Isabel flicked through the pages.

'I better go,' said Kim. She turned and waved at a man at the bar. He gestured back.

As the pages flicked by I had a strange experience.

'Stop,' I said.

'What?' said Isabel. She stopped flicking the pages.

'Let me have a look.' I put my hand out.

I turned back through the pages. I didn't find what I

was looking for. Had I imagined it? I was about to hand the book back to Kim when I reached a page with a number of photographs of ancient pieces of papyri. Most were just small jagged-edged fragments. Some were tiny. One of the larger ones had two interesting hieroglyphs on it.

The bottom hieroglyph was a symbol of a square with an arrow pointing upwards inside it. It was the same symbol that was in the book we'd discovered in Istanbul; the symbol there'd been so many questions about.

Above that was another symbol. It had two triangles facing each other and two more below them.

Kim put her hand out for me to pass the book back to her. I bent down, peered at the tiny inscription below the fragment. It read:

Papyrus fragment found 1984 in rubbish pit near the Black Pyramid (built King Amenemhat III, Middle Kingdom era, 2055–1650 BC). The lower hieroglyph represents the Queen of Darkness. The upper hieroglyph has not been deciphered. The only other example of these hieroglyphs is from a stone inscription at the Gihon Pool in Jerusalem, a Canaanite province of Egypt during the Middle Kingdom era.

'This is interesting,' I said. 'Do you mind if I take a picture?' Kim shook her head. I took out my phone and snapped the page with the papyrus fragments on it.

'What's it all about?' said Mark.

I hesitated, wondering whether I should explain what I'd seen. It was, after all, only a hieroglyph.

'It's just a papyrus fragment with some hieroglyphs Sean recognised.' Isabel pointed at the page. She ran her hand down the hieroglyphic as if they all interested me.

Mark peered closely at the page.

'We did some work on hieroglyphs a few years ago,' I

said. 'There's a new theory about their evolution I've been following.'

'Some of these glyphs are on inscriptions all over the Middle East,' said Isabel.

Mark pulled away from the page, raising his eyebrows. 'You do know the Canaanites were into human sacrifice, don't you?' He looked from my face to Isabel's.

'You bet,' said Isabel. 'They used to roast their own children to death. They were a cruel lot. They thought Ba'al, their demon god, spoke through the screams of the anguished victims as they died.'

Kim made a squeamish noise.

'They worshipped goddesses too,' Isabel added. Kim smiled, as if Isabel had just made a stand for all the females in the world.

'Maybe this Queen of Darkness too,' I said.

'I wouldn't put it past them,' said Isabel.

'How do they work out what these symbols mean?' said Kim.

'Some of it's about star signs,' said Isabel. 'The morning star is the Queen of Heaven, so the evening star is probably the Queen of Darkness. It's usually something simple like that.'

'I like all that astrology stuff,' said Kim. She put the book away.

A few minutes after she had gone, Mark suggested we move to one of the hotel restaurants upstairs. We agreed.

I wasn't entirely happy with going out with him for dinner, but we hadn't found out much from him yet.

As we waited for Mark's credit card to go through, he started talking about a Cairo football team he'd been following, Zamalek. I listened to him telling us all about their last match. I knew then there were more reasons than just being

141

abandoned in a firefight, for Isabel to have left him. He didn't want to allow anyone to fit a single word into his conversation flow.

I went to find the toilets. As I crossed the foyer, I was startled to see Xena sitting in one of the cream leather armchairs. Why hadn't she come into the bar with us? I'd thought she'd gone off.

I passed near her. She didn't seem to notice me until I was almost on top of her.

Then she looked up and motioned me to her with a curling finger and a beguiling smile.

27

Susan Hunter woke and sat up. The stone wall behind her back was hard, icy cold. She felt every day of her forty-nine years. The image that had filled her mind since the last time he'd been down came back. She tried again to push it away. It wasn't easy.

She started counting. Was it day or night?

She could smell congealing sweat and the stink in the tiny room from the Arab-style toilet, a hole in the ground, on the other side of the basement. She pressed her arms into her stomach. It ached, as if something had gone wrong inside her. Her teeth were sore too, and her head felt like a weight on her shoulders.

The pains in her body gave no indication as to how long she'd slept. All they told her was that she was still a prisoner, still living on bowls of rice and bottles of water.

She remembered how her husband used to bring her warm drinks if she was ever sick back in England, how he used to come up and ask after her every hour. A longing to be home, to see his face, flowed through her like a hunger.

Then a memory of her hotel, the smiling girls who'd served her breakfast a week before, came to her. One of them had asked her about Cambridge University.

How good it would have been to talk to her more, to find out what she wanted to study. They could have had lunch, been friends.

How could she have ended up like this, waiting for this evil man, for the brief light and the food and the water that his return meant?

She ran her hands around to check if anything had changed, as she did every time she woke now.

All she could feel was hard earth. The earth that extended to the basement walls around her, a space that was big, but felt small in the darkness.

She was slowly swaying again. Never before had she felt such malevolence around her. Even the stones in this place seemed to leak evil. And the air was alive with it. It wasn't because of the pain he'd already inflicted or what she'd seen; the image that wouldn't fade, that burn on the back of his hand. It was because she knew what such a mark meant.

Susan had studied many ancient documents. She'd dated them, interpreted them, classified them. She knew what some of them said about our ancestors.

She'd examined the only papyrus ever discovered recording a Canaanite human sacrifice from before the time of Abraham. The description in that oblong fragment of how the high priest would burn his own hand, to taste the flame that would consume his victims, to know better what they would feel, was something that had stuck in her mind since the day she'd read it.

But she'd never expected to encounter such a thing herself.

Who was this bastard? And why was he resurrecting an evil that should have died out thousands of years ago?

And then a bigger question loomed, what was he planning for her? Was it what she feared?

28

'Hi Xena, you didn't want to join us for a drink?' I asked.

She looked up at me. Her eyes seemed bigger than before. Her expression was friendly.

'I don't go to bars,' she said. She put her hand forward, as if she wanted to shake mine. But all she did was open her fingers, as if passing me a handful of air.

'What brings you to Cairo, effendi?' She said slowly, leaning forward.

She had a beautiful face, almost too perfect in its proportions. There was something unsettling about her.

'I'm looking for a friend.' It was the truth.

'If you find friends in Cairo,' she smiled, revealing sparkling teeth, 'you can die here. That is what they say.' Her smile hardened.

The way she said it, it was almost a threat. A tiny shiver ran up my back, as if a spider had walked there.

'Sean?' It was Isabel's voice. I turned. She was walking towards us. Her gaze was on Xena though, as if she was examining her.

'You get around,' she said to Xena.

Xena switched her attention to Isabel. She nodded at her.

145

'Do you know Cairo?' asked Xena.

'No,' said Isabel.

'I can show you some interesting places tonight,' she said. She was looking at me when she said that.

'Maybe another time,' said Isabel. She put her hand on my arm. 'Mark is waiting for us.'

'Gotta go,' I said to Xena.

Her smile had a condescending edge to it now.

'What the hell are you doing talking to her?' said Isabel as we got in the elevator.

I hadn't seen such a flash of anger from her before.

'I was just being friendly. Where are we going?'

She looked at me for a few seconds, then replied. 'To the third floor, to the Pane Vino Italian restaurant.'

We rode the rest of the way up in silence.

The restaurant was on a terrace overlooking the Nile. I could see why Mark liked it. It was busy, dark, and the tables were far enough apart that you wouldn't feel you were being overheard. Pale yellow candles in elaborate ironwork Ottoman lamps sat on the floor. The view over the Nile was spectacular. The far side of the river was lit up by strings of street lights and the glow from apartment blocks beyond.

As we walked through the restaurant, being led by a waiter to Mark's table, a section of the far river bank, to the north of where we were, went dark, as if a piece of the picture in front of us had been wiped out.

As soon as we sat down, I asked Mark what had happened across the river.

'There's been a lot of power cuts recently. It's no big deal.' He turned to look at the dark section of the river opposite. 'Some idiot probably tried to steal some power cables. Probably fried himself. We've had a bit of that recently.'

As if in response to what he'd just said, flashes of brilliant white light broke out in the darkened section. They were small, but they were reflected in the water and went on for seconds.

'Is that gunfire?' I said. 'This place is like the Wild West.'

Mark shrugged.

The flashes started up again. They were from two sources now. People in the restaurant were pointing. Over the rumble of traffic and the din of car horns, I could just about hear a distant snapping noise.

Then, just as suddenly as they'd started, the flashes stopped. The noise in the restaurant went up, as if a wave of relief had passed through us all. I saw a few men waving at waiters, as if they were determined to consume with a renewed vigour.

'Order the Mediterranean pasta,' said Mark. 'They get their fish from Alexandria every afternoon, fresh from the fishing boats, which come in in the morning.'

I ordered a pepperoni pizza.

Mark shook his head in horror. I was sitting beside Isabel, Mark opposite her. Over the next few minutes he began to irritate me, like a wasp does when it circles a picnic. Not only would he not stop talking, most of it was directed at Isabel.

Eventually I got a word in. 'What do the locals call Cairo? I read the name Cairo is a European invention,' I said.

'A lot of them call it Misr; the metropolis, the city. That's probably where the word misery comes from. Did you know that fifty percent of Cairo's population is on the poverty line?'

I shook my head.

He jabbed a finger into the white linen tablecloth. 'A lot of people here say things were better back in Mubarak's day. If you're at the bottom of the pile in Cairo, living in the Muqattam Hills south of here, you eke out a life from trash mountains and live eight to a room in temperatures like an oven in the summer.' He paused for a few seconds. 'While you wait for the hill behind your mud house to fall on top of you.'

'What part of the city is Xena from?' I was wondering why she was hanging around with Mark. Was she his girlfriend, his bodyguard?

'She lives in Zamalek, an island in the Nile near here. But she's originally from Sudan. She likes it in Zamalek. Rich people live there. It's full of fancy boutiques, businessmen and fortune tellers with gold-plated mobile phones. And it has two million people living in it.'

He waved a hand in the air to catch the attention of a waiter.

'There's a lot more to Cairo than shuffling past Tutankhamun's mask in a sweaty crowd of tourists, or getting stuck in a traffic jam of tourist buses at the Pyramids,' he said. He pointed his finger at me. 'The Qaytbay funerary complex alone is better than all of the sightseeing in Venice put together.'

'What does Xena do?' I asked. I was being pushy, but I didn't care.

'She helps me with a few things,' said Mark. He looked at me as if I'd spat on the floor between us.

'She told me if you find friends in Cairo, you can die in Cairo.'

Isabel sat forward. 'Is that what they say?' she said, looking at Mark.

'I never heard it,' he said.

'Is she . . . ?' Isabel paused, smiled. 'Close to you?'

He replied, quickly and emphatically. 'No.'

'I hope you're not getting sucked in, like you did in Iraq,' said Isabel.

He stared at her, his eyes wide, as if she'd just extolled the virtues of living with Jack the Ripper.

'What exactly do you want, Isabel?' he said. 'Why are you here?'

'We need a little help.'

He sighed, as if he'd heard such pleas far too often. 'What sort of help?'

'We want our deportation notice taken off the Israeli Immigration system.'

There was silence at the table.

'That's a big ask,' he said. 'A very big ask.'

Isabel's expression hardened. She tilted her head to one side. 'I'm your ex-wife, Mark. I don't think it will look good for you to have me barred from Israel.'

Mark stared at her for a minute before responding. 'I might be able to do what you're asking, but I won't guarantee it.' He paused, his hand at his mouth, as if thinking hard. Thinking hard what lie to tell us, most likely.

He leaned forward.

'I'm going to Taba tomorrow,' he said. 'To a meeting of border security officers. I'll see if I can do anything.'

Isabel looked sceptical. 'You can do it, Mark, if you want to. I know that. You know that. So don't bullshit me. Remember, we worked together. This is in your interests.' She spoke slowly, emphasising each word.

'Are you planning to go back to Israel?' he said.

'If you get our records changed maybe we should,' she said.

'Wouldn't you both be better off staying away for a while, perhaps a few years.'

I leaned towards him. 'We were that close to finding out what the hell happened to Kaiser. I could feel it.' I held my thumb and forefinger almost touching in front of his face. 'Before we were thrown out over some stupid bureaucratic nonsense.'

'Are you doing all this to help your institute or for personal reasons?' he said.

'Both.'

He'd probably think I was crazy if I told him I thought

149

there was a connection between Susan's kidnapping, her husband dying, and the book she was translating. It was all too much of a coincidence that she'd got involved, just as disaster struck.

He looked at me. 'Are you planning to give Isabel a job at your institute?' he said.

She pointed a finger at him. 'I'm not doing all this to get a job. I want that deportation off my record.'

He was staring at her. There was simmering admiration in his eyes. I didn't like the sight of it. 'I told you, I'll see what I can do,' he said. 'And I will. Seeing as we're old friends.' He smiled at her, as if I wasn't there.

'Tomorrow?' she said.

'What's your hurry?'

'We have a return flight booked for Sunday from Tel Aviv,' she said. 'I don't want to waste the tickets.'

I could have said I didn't care about the tickets. I had more money than I knew what to do with. I'd been piling up cash in my bank account since Irene had died, not going out much and not spending, but I didn't say anything. Maybe I should have. What blinded me to the danger of going back to Israel was a sharp urge to get out of Cairo.

'You're not going straight back to Israel?' he said. He stared at me, wide-eyed.

I shrugged.

'Why don't we come with you to Taba?' said Isabel. 'Once the Israeli computers are updated, you can drop us at the border. You go through that way, don't you?' She turned to me. 'Taba's near Sharm el-Sheikh. There are taxis on the Israeli side that can drive us to Jerusalem in a few hours, if we've a few hundred dollars with us.'

'Great,' I said.

Mark pursed his lips, tapping hard on the table. 'You can come with me,' he said. 'But I won't be responsible for what

happens if you go back into Israel. That'll be on your heads.'
He pointed at me, then at Isabel.

If I was the type to believe in omens, I'd probably have
interjected right there with a decision not to go through with
it all. But I don't believe in them, even the ones that are just
common sense.

After we'd eaten we arranged to meet at the Hilton the
next morning. We should be in front of the hotel when he
came, he said, as he'd be on a tight schedule. It would be a
four hour drive to Taba.

Then he rang the Hilton to see if it was reopened yet,
after the attack.

I assumed it had been evacuated, that we would have to
find other accommodation.

'That's not the way they do things here,' he said.

And he was right. Apparently they had closed the hotel
for all of two hours, while every room was searched, but as
only one restaurant had been shot up and a controlled explosion had gone off, they'd reopened the hotel. The main
restaurant would be closed only until the morning, he said.

We took a taxi back to the Hilton and went straight up
to our room. I poured some slightly odd-tasting orange juice
from the minibar for both of us. We stood at the window,
looking over the city. It was midnight. There were still car
horns honking. The traffic on the bridge in front of us made
it look like a pearl necklace of lights.

'I didn't realise you wanted to go back to Israel tomorrow,'
I said.

Isabel put her hand on the glass and leaned on it, looking
down. I moved a step closer to her, brushing against her bare
arm.

'I thought it was a good idea when I heard he was heading
for Taba,' she said. 'I know how responsible you feel for
Susan disappearing. We were getting close to finding out

something in Jerusalem. I could feel it in my bones. You said so too.'

'You're right.'

She kept staring down. 'I got this weird feeling when I saw Xena with you.'

'What feeling?'

'There's a lot of stuff going on here that we don't know anything about.'

'That's the truth.'

'No, no, not just in general.' Her brow furrowed. 'I mean about us getting thrown out of Israel like that. There's something strange going on. Maybe I'm crazy, but . . .' She shook her head, as if she didn't want to say any more.

'But what?'

'Nobody seems to care much about what happened to Susan Hunter. The Israeli police didn't even blink when we mentioned we were looking for her.'

'I'm sure the British Embassy in Tel Aviv is trying to find her.'

She shook her head, slowly. 'I've seen what happens. They'll make a few enquiries; talk to the police, the hotel she was staying in, contacts of hers that they know about, and that's it. They're too busy to do much more. That's the reality. They'll do their best, but there's so much to do.'

'Do you want vodka in that?' I said, pointing at the tall glass of orange juice I'd given her.

'No,' she said. 'I've got a thumping headache.' She looked me in the eyes. 'I need to go straight to sleep.'

'Sure.' I said. I wanted to ask her if seeing Mark had given her the headache, but I decided not to go there.

It was the third night in a row she'd wanted to go straight to sleep. I lay in the dark wondering what was happening to us.

I knew for sure that if I asked her whether she still had

feelings for Mark, she'd deny it. And that if I didn't like her smiling at him, I was just being jealous.

But maybe knowing her answer wasn't the real reason I wouldn't ask her.

Was I afraid that if she hesitated at all, I couldn't pretend that everything was okay between us? Because then I'd have to confront her. I couldn't avoid it. And who knew what would happen after that. Best to leave it all alone until we got back to England. I had my own feelings to figure out too. They couldn't be denied.

We had an early breakfast. I'd told her about my plan to go to the Antiquities Museum and be back by 10.30 a.m. I had to find out if I was right about why Kaiser had come here.

'Do you want to come?' I said, as I picked up a second croissant from the plate I'd brought over from the breakfast buffet. We were in the Hilton's other restaurant, the Desert Café, overlooking the Nile. The white tablecloths, cutlery and blue bone china were all sparkling in the early morning sunlight.

The only sign I could see of the attack the night before was a notice saying the main restaurant would be closed until lunchtime.

'No,' she said. 'I feel a bit sick this morning. You're well capable of taking pictures of a few papyri without me.'

'One papyrus.'

'But you want to see if there are others like it?'

'Yes,' I said. I looked around. There weren't many people staying in the hotel.

'Kaiser is the key to everything,' she said. She popped a piece of croissant with some quince jam on it into her mouth.

After breakfast I walked to the Antiquities Museum. It was only five minutes away. It was due to open at 9 a.m. The papyrus collection was on the ground floor. The golden

153

treasures of ancient Egypt, which were still in the museum, were on the upper floor.

I arrived outside the gates at five minutes to nine. I was dressed in cream chinos, a loose black t-shirt and nothing else. Some of the locals had jackets on, but it was as warm as a good summer's day in London, so I didn't need one. I thanked God that we hadn't arrived in the summer. The sweltering heat then, strong enough to melt tar, would not have been my idea of fun.

I wasn't alone waiting. There was a slowly growing queue of tourists, as well as many Egyptians. We were a small demonstration of our own. There was a lot of shuffling and mumbling about the delayed opening, until finally the gates of the garden courtyard in front of the museum swung open and we were allowed in.

I had to go through two security checks, one near the steps of the museum and a second inside the doors. There was no photography allowed, but they let me keep my phone.

The museum was amazing. It was a relic of another age, a long colonial-era red stone Victorian museum. Outside in the courtyard, there were ancient statues, mostly all pale pink, including a small sphinx, stone pharaohs, and some mythical Egyptian animals. In its monumental entrance hall there were awesome twenty foot high statues of pharaohs.

I picked up a plan of the building at the entrance, headed to the papyrus collection. Most of them hadn't yet been moved to the new museum. I passed through a long, double height hall, with tall pillars and a gallery level above. The hall had more stone pharaohs, mostly sitting down, with straight backs, and a collection of tombstones.

The papyrus room was full of flat oak and glass cases containing collections of papyri from all over Egypt, from almost the beginning of recorded human history. I hadn't realised they had papyri going that far back, to the early First Dynasty, about 3,000 BC.

Glass-fronted cases lined the walls while others stood on their own in front of them. There was a dusty smell. I asked a guard standing in a corner to look at the picture of the hieroglyph and tell me where in the room the papyrus was. He looked at me as if I was an alien with flashing antennae.

'It's from the Black Pyramid,' I said.

He grunted, walking towards a nearby case. There was a woman wearing a headscarf and a long blue smock dusting it. He motioned me close to him.

'This, this,' he said. 'Am I right?'

'Maybe,' I said. I peered at a black tray on its own.

'Yes, that's the one.' I looked closely at it.

He stood right beside me.

'Do you have anymore from that time?' I gestured at the cases all around us. There were visitors in the room, but not as many as I'd seen heading up to the more popular treasure rooms.

'You like the Black Pyramid?' he asked. He smiled. His teeth were yellow and there were a few missing.

'Yes,' I said. 'And symbols like this one.' I pointed at the papyrus fragment with the arrow in a square symbol. 'That symbol has been found in Jerusalem.'

His smile faded. 'I must go,' he said.

He walked fast from the room. I studied the papyri fragment, then the others in the surrounding cases. Then I looked in all the cases in the room to see if I could see the same symbol on any other papyri, but I couldn't. I looked at my watch.

It was 9.50 a.m. I had maybe twenty more minutes. It was just enough time to look at some of the other rooms. I followed in the wake of some Japanese tourists heading towards the stairs.

155

As we reached the staircase an alarm started. Two nearby guards in brown uniforms began waving their hands in the air. 'Everyone must go outside,' they shouted. 'Please, you must go.'

People were streaming toward the doors. I followed. Whatever was happening, a fire drill or a security alert, they were getting everyone out of the place fast. A twinge of anxiety passed through me. A bomb could be about to explode.

Outside, in the courtyard, guards ushered people towards a far corner, presumably to wait to go back inside. I glanced at my watch again.

I had no time for hanging around. I headed for the gate, then walked back to our hotel and went up to our room. It was still only twenty past ten. Isabel was packing toiletries. My backpack was waiting near the door where I'd left it.

'The museum was evacuated while I was there,' I said to Isabel, as I poured myself some water.

'Did you get to see what you wanted?'

'I did, but I was hoping to find other papyri with that symbol.'

'It doesn't matter, does it? It's just some symbol.'

'Yeah, you're probably right.'

We were at the front of the hotel by 10.31 a.m. It was a narrow entrance with cars dropping off regularly. Some of the windows of the hotel were boarded up, but there were men working already to replace the glass.

Mark arrived ten minutes late. He left his engine running as he got out to open the back for us.

As I put our backpacks in, he said, 'There's been a security alert at the museum. The traffic around here is going to make it a nightmare to get to Taba on time. That's why I'm late.'

Xena was not with him. He was driving himself. I sat in the front beside him. We inched our way through the traffic,

156

and then, after half an hour of shuffling forward through packed streets, he found an elevated highway. Sand-coloured apartment buildings and office blocks three and four storeys high stretched away to the horizon in all directions. A haze, like a sandstorm, hung over the city.

All the houses, except for neighbourhood mosques, had flat roofs out here in the suburbs. Most of them had skeletal poles sticking up into the sky at each corner of the roof to accommodate a new floor, when a son or relative needed somewhere to live. There were piles of building materials and clothes lines and sacks of God only knew what on most of the roofs. The traffic was a constant flow of vehicles around us, an endless stream of logs moving down the tributaries of a river.

I saw a sign for the ring road in English and Arabic. Ten minutes later we were moving a lot faster, leaving the smoky haze of Cairo behind. I looked out through the back window. There was so much I hadn't seen; the tourist sites mainly. I was determined to go back some day. The Nile, in particular, gave the place a grandeur as it flowed like a giant snake through the city.

We went through the Ahmed Hamdi Tunnel, under the Suez Canal. It was modern and not very busy. We passed a line of trucks festooned with lights, going the other way. Once we were through we headed south. Much of the landscape was scrub and semi-desert now, though there were occasional villages with tall palm trees, goats and low, flat-roofed mud-brick houses with television antennas or satellite dishes. Some had wooden verandas projecting from their upper floors.

We stopped at a modern Co-op petrol station. It had miniature palm trees in front of it. At the side of the station there was a donkey and cart and an old Bedouin in an off-white headdress. He didn't even glance at us. We all got out, stretched our legs. I bought French chocolate, Egyptian water and dates. Isabel found orange juice, but it didn't taste right again.

Four hours later, the road was twisting and turning as it headed towards red-tinted mountains, off to our right. As they came closer they looked like mountains of sand, solid-ified, like something you might see on a relay from Mars. Among them, said Mark, was Mount Sinai, where Moses was given the Ten Commandments. The scrub and desert to our left extended off into a haze, broken by low bushes and occasional hills of sand or rock.

As we skirted the Sinai Mountains the landscape became paler in the afternoon light. Finally, as we neared the Red Sea the hills became rounded, more like sand hills than mountains. There were few people on the road except for the occasional bus, army lorries and trucks. Twice we passed Bedouins on camels by the side of the road.

As we approached the Israeli border we were stopped at a military checkpoint by the Egyptian army. We were all asked to produce our passports. Getting through wasn't a difficulty. An officer spoke on a walkie talkie for a few minutes before letting us go on.

'You're lucky you're with me. A lot of independent tour-ists have been turned back in the last few weeks,' said Mark, after we got our passports back.

'Why's that?' I said.

'There was a roadside bomb on the Israeli side of the border last month. With everything that's going on because of the new elections, and all the stuff that's happening in Gaza, everyone's jittery,' he said.

I was tired at that point. My eyes were hurting after looking out at the sunbaked landscape for too long.

Luckily, Mark had tuned the radio to the BBC on a digital radio he had set up in the car. I couldn't have taken listening to him chattering for hours. But as we approached the Israeli border he turned the radio down and began talking.

'Taba was an Egyptian Bedouin village before '46,' he said. 'The Israelis didn't even want to return it after the Sinai Peninsula was handed back to Egypt in '79. It didn't actually become Egyptian again until 1988.'

Isabel groaned. 'I'm sure Sean doesn't want a history lesson, Mark,' she said.

Mark shook his head. 'You were always a bit touchy when you were tired, Isabel.' He kept his gaze on the road ahead.

'It only seems to happen when I'm around you,' she said.

I couldn't help but smile.

There was a long pause before Mark replied. 'If you want anything else after this, Isabel, make sure you lose my number.'

She didn't reply to that. We were coming up to what looked like the border post. We'd joined another highway and the Gulf of Aqaba was to our right now. It was a deep-looking, wave-flecked blue stretching away into a distant haze of land beyond it, which must have been Jordan.

Mark parked near a two-storey white concrete building with a glass entrance hall. The Egyptian flag was flying in front of the building. There were two sand-coloured military jeeps and four soldiers standing nearby cradling black machine guns. They were all staring in our direction.

'Wait here,' said Mark.

'We're not going anywhere,' said Isabel.

We waited, then waited some more. After half an hour I got out and had a walk around. There was a row of shops on the main road. I went and got water for Isabel. There was an English language Egyptian paper, *The Egypt Times* in the newspaper rack. I bought it, stopping to look at the front page before I went back.

The lead story was an interview with an unnamed Egyptian army spokesperson. The article claimed there was a possibility of an Israeli surprise attack on Egypt in the near future. It said the Egyptian army was making all necessary plans to defend the nation. The army, they claimed, was confident they could defeat the Israelis.

The article was accompanied by a photo of a group of Egyptian schoolgirls wearing gas masks. A list of the military units defending Egypt, including 205 F-16s ready for action, was given in a side box along with a picture of an air force pilot giving a thumbs up from his cockpit against a desert backdrop. Another article gave details of an anti-Israeli demonstration in Tahrir Square, planned for later that day, which a million people were expected to attend.

There was an article below that about an imam in Cairo who had been murdered. The headline had made reading it hard to resist: *Evil Spirits Kill Imam Say Locals*.

By the time I got back to the car Mark had returned.

'It's all done,' he said when I got in. 'You can go through. I'll drop you at the next checkpoint. But remember one thing.' He turned to Isabel. 'My friend won't do this again. If you get into anymore trouble or meet anyone who was involved in your deportation, you're on your own.' He looked at me. His eyes were as hard as blue marbles.

'We're washing our hands of both of you.'

He drove us to the next checkpoint. The area was a mess of lamp posts, low concrete buildings, security cameras and rolls of razor wire on top of high mesh fences. The traffic going through was light. He pulled up near a pedestrian crossing, where other cars had stopped. He turned to us as he killed the engine.

'I can drive you back to Cairo, Isabel. Why don't you forget all this? You shouldn't put yourself in anymore danger.'

'What happened to you?' she said. Her eyes narrowed. 'Someone knock you on the head?'

'No.' He turned further in his seat. 'I just don't like the idea of you going back into Israel, that's all.'

'Should we be worried about something?' she said. 'Is there something you're not telling us?'

His expression was troubled, as if he was struggling with himself.

'There's lots I'm not telling you,' he said.

She sighed. 'What about giving us a clue then? A hint as to why we shouldn't go back.'

His voice went down a notch and he looked out of the window as he spoke. 'Susan Hunter has been kidnapped. A brief signal from her phone was picked up west of Jerusalem a few days ago.'

The hairs on the back of my neck stood up. It was what I'd feared. She hadn't gone off into the desert somewhere, or into hiding.

'Has there been any contact with whoever's holding her?' asked Isabel.

'Not so far.'

This meant Susan could have been tortured or murdered grotesquely or she could be facing years in hellish captivity.

'I won't run back to London because of what's happened to Susan,' said Isabel.

'It's not just her being kidnapped that worries me,' said Mark flatly.

'What then?' I said.

He turned to me, as if he was hoping I might persuade Isabel to reconsider. 'You went to Max Kaiser's apartment in Jerusalem, didn't you?'

I nodded. Isabel must have told him.

'Did you go inside?'

'No.'

He let out his breath in a *I knew it* groan. 'Well, if you had, you might think twice about sticking your noses into all this.'

He pointed at me. 'I saw pictures of what happened there. We're not dealing with ordinary criminals or angry Palestinians. This is way beyond that.' He turned to Isabel and spoke slowly.

'Someone was strapped to a kitchen chair in that apartment. I can only assume it was Max Kaiser. Then they were tortured. From the residue found near the chair, his skin was melted with a blowtorch. There were chunks of human flesh in puddles on the floor.'

The hairs on the back of my neck were right up now. Poor bastard. No one deserved that.

'It's the sickest thing I've seen in a long time,' said Mark. 'And I have no idea if he was dead when they took his body and dumped it in the old city, but I hope so.'

'Do you have any idea why someone would do all that?' I said.

He shrugged. 'There's a lot of shit getting stirred up at the moment.' He paused. 'I don't know if it's all connected, but I don't like the smell right now.' He sniffed, as if a bad smell had come into the car.

'My God, Mark, can't you just tell us what else is going on?' Isabel sounded annoyed. She was usually a cool customer.

Mark looked out of the window. He spoke then, as if he was talking to himself. Maybe he wasn't supposed to tell us what he said next, but he found it easier if he did it this way? Or maybe I was just guessing at his motivation? He could just as easily have been leading us up the garden path.

'There are a lot of rumours going around,' he said. 'There was a firestorm of activity on Twitter the other day about a letter from the first caliph of Islam, Abu Bakr, that's supposedly been found.'

'What did it say?' I asked. I had a strange feeling, as if something about this was connected to us, to me.

'It claims that if Jerusalem fell to Islam, it would be a

162

Muslim city for all eternity. It claims that that is what the Christian Patriarch of Jerusalem agreed to, so that Christians could keep their churches open after Islam took over.' He turned to me.

'The implication is that those were the terms agreed to in 637 AD, when Jerusalem fell to Islam for the first time.'

I sat forward. 'Yeah, that's going to stand up in a court of law. If we kept to every agreement from fourteen hundred years ago, the Byzantine Empire would rule half of Europe and the rest of us would still be paying tributes to Constantinople,' I said.

'It's crazy, I know,' said Mark. 'I don't know why it's sparked things off, but people are using it to attack Israel's control of Jerusalem. It's like they've found a justification for their anger.'

'It'll blow over,' said Isabel. 'We used to get lots of mad rumours in Istanbul. They disappear like a snowstorm after a few days.'

Mark looked at me. He didn't seem convinced.

'Our flights are on Sunday,' said Isabel. Her voice sounded strong, unaffected by what we'd heard. 'We'll only be in Israel for three days, Mark. We're not running away because of a few rumours.'

I put my hand over the seat. She held it.

'I'm with Isabel on this,' I said.

The thought of those idiots at that dig winning was highly irritating. Susan being kidnapped and a Twitter storm about an old letter weren't enough not to go.

'Have a good trip then,' said Mark.

We got out of the car. I turned back to look at him as we walked away. He was watching us with a sullen look on his face, as if he regretted bringing us here.

The Egyptians let us through the border without difficulty. The Israelis were different.

163

But we had a story ready, that we were on our way back to Israel after having done the tourist thing in Cairo, and we were heading home to London in a few days. And it was all true, even if our itinerary was a bit odd. Why had we flown to Athens and then Cairo, not come through Taba, the guard wanted to know? He was holding my passport open at the page with the Egyptian visa in it, from Cairo airport.

I told him we'd heard the border was closed, that when we'd found out it was open again we'd already booked our flights.

'And one drive through the desert is enough for me, thanks,' I said, at that point.

The Israeli border guard, in his short-sleeved blue shirt, with his harried face, nodded, then asked me where we'd stayed in Cairo. He kept us waiting for ten more minutes, asking us questions about how we'd gone from Tel Aviv to Cairo and checking his computer constantly, to see if there was any reason for him to stop us, I suppose. A few German tourists behind us moved to another line, we were taking so long.

I kept calm. I reckoned we had a good chance to get past him, if the record about us on their database had been changed, as Mark had promised. And as we'd agreed voluntarily to leave Israel a few days before, they hadn't stamped our passports to say we'd been deported.

I could see now why Isabel had been so keen not to fight the request for us to leave Israel. It was one thing to have a record of what happened on a computer system. It was something very different to have a big DEPORTED stamp in your passport.

She told me while we were waiting in the line at Taba that they'd stopped stamping passports with a deportation notice in all but the most serious cases. Many Arabs, and even some Europeans, had started using Israeli deportation

164

stamps as a symbol of their resistance to Israel, she said. They had become a collector's item for some people.

Eventually, after examining our passports with his eye up close to each one, the guard let us pass.

On the Israeli side of the border everything looked more modern. There was an official taxi rank, a place to change money, big posters on the walls, maps. The first taxi driver in the rank didn't want to take us to Jerusalem. Neither did the second. The third one was willing to talk about it at least. His English was accented, but word perfect. He sounded Russian, and had a bald head and a thin face with deep wrinkles. His car was a modern Mercedes. It had air conditioning. I wanted to go in his taxi.

'If we go by the Dead Sea, if you want to see Masada, Qumran, that will take longer. There's been an incident at Tzofar. Someone's been shooting at cars on Highway 90. There's a diversion there. It's not a good road. The price will be different if we go that way,' he said.

'What's the alternative?'

'We go through Mitzpe Ramon and Be'er Sheva. It's highway all the way too. Seven hundred and fifty shekels will cover it, if we go that way. A thousand if you want the Dead Sea with the delays. That road will be six hours, maybe more. The other will be four, maybe less.'

'Is that the official fare?' said Isabel.

'If you don't trust me, you can try another one.' He pointed his thumb behind him. 'Just make sure their air conditioning is working. Mine is.'

'It's okay,' I said, as much to Isabel as to the driver. I wasn't going to spend four hours in a taxi with dodgy air conditioning.

'Let's do this,' I said to Isabel.

We got in. To drive past Masada would have been interesting, but it was four o'clock in the afternoon and if we wanted to find a hotel in Jerusalem without attracting too much attention we should get there before it got late. Daylight wasn't going to last much longer.

Not long after leaving Taba, the driver pointed towards the sand coloured hills to our left.

'Look, over there, the oldest copper mines in the world.' He pointed in the direction of a long escarpment. 'The Pharaoh's slaves worked those mines for generations. Families were born, they lived and then they died around them.' He shifted in his seat and turned the radio on low. It played slow jazz.

By 4.30 p.m. shadows were lengthening all around us. The scrubland and hills had turned orange in the setting sun. I stared out the window. I didn't want to talk. I didn't trust the driver not to relate everything he heard to his next passenger. And I wanted the journey over, to be in Jerusalem.

I was wondering what we might find there. There was definitely something odd going on at that archaeological dig. We had to be careful. Whoever had murdered Kaiser might well know that we were taking an interest now. The people who'd tortured and burnt Max to death might even know about us.

That thought put me on edge. I would have to make doubly sure that Isabel was kept away from any danger. If anything happened to her I would blame myself.

Rightly too.

Mark had given me ample opportunity to tell her we should abandon this trip. Had I done the right thing coming back?

And was it a coincidence that the person, Susan Hunter, who was compiling a report on the ancient book we'd found in Istanbul was now missing?

We passed a few camels and oil trucks, other taxis and tourist buses and a line of army trucks going the other way, and then Bedouins standing by the side of the road as it got dark, as if they were waiting for something.

We stopped only once on the journey, at Mitzpe Ramon, a town in the Negev about halfway to Jerusalem. The petrol station was called Yellow. The sign at the front was in Hebrew, English and Arabic. The houses in Mitzpe Ramon were low flat-roofed desert buildings one or two storeys high.

'My cousin lives here,' said the driver, as we neared Jerusalem on a fast highway that twisted and turned through low, steep hills. There were modern buildings, cream-coloured apartment and office blocks, going up the sides of some of the hills and there was a lot more traffic now.

'What will you do here?' he asked.

'Sightseeing,' I said.

'Where will you stay?'

'I don't know yet,' I said. 'We're going to look for a hotel.'

'You like a proper hotel?' said the driver. He turned to look at us.

'Sure,' I said.

'You will like this one,' he said. 'My cousin, he works there.'

I was expecting a small hotel, somewhere we'd have to say no to if the rooms were tiny, but I was wrong. The hotel he took us to was the famous King David, overlooking the Old City. Winston Churchill, Bill Clinton and Madonna had all stayed in the King David. The driver had worked out that we had money.

He dropped us under the stone entrance arch in front of the hotel. He had called ahead on his phone to tell his cousin we were coming. I paid the driver, gave him a tip.

The foyer of the King David was like the inside of an

167

Egyptian temple but through the lens of a Hollywood studio. It had a polished marble floor, white pillars and a blue ceiling with golden lotus designs. Thick red rugs and cane furniture added to the illusion. The thin, dark-suited manager who registered us welcomed us as if we'd just travelled on foot from Taba.

Ten minutes later we were in a double room with a proper double bed. We were asleep an hour after that.

In the morning, at ten minutes to five, I woke. I could hear, faintly, the Muslim call to prayer. I'm not sure if it had woken me or if being back in Jerusalem was making me jumpy. At seven I heard distant bells ringing from one of the Christian churches. They rang slowly, mournfully. We were definitely back in Jerusalem.

The breakfast terrace of the King David had a view of the hotel's beautiful garden. Beyond it were the sand-coloured walls of the Old City.

'I can't stop thinking about Susan,' said Isabel, after we'd brought our breakfast over from the buffet table. She still hadn't got her appetite back. All she was eating was a croissant.

'Maybe we can help them find her,' I said.

We sat in silence for a minute as we ate.

'I've been thinking about what we should do next,' she said.

'Me too,' I said.

She looked at me with a quizzical expression.

'I think we should find out more about that archaeological site. If they're willing to get us deported for the stupidest of reasons, they're up to something. Maybe Kaiser and Susan found out what it is. Who knows what you'd find in a collection of scrolls from Pontius Pilate's era.'

The waiter came, filled up our coffee cups.

'I'd like to get inside Max's apartment,' said Isabel, lowering her voice.

'I doubt if there's anything left to see. Won't the Israeli forensic teams have scrubbed the place clean?'

'True, but I'd still like to see it anyway.'

'You're crazy. You know that?'

Was she just being ghoulish? Was this a side to her I hadn't seen or was there something else going on? Then it came to me.

'You want to see if Mark was lying to us, right?'

She smiled. 'You are quick this morning.'

'You think he'd make something like that up?'

She put her coffee cup down. 'Mark is capable of a lot of things. But if he was telling the truth, whoever did it wanted something from Kaiser. We have to know the truth about his death.'

'What do you suggest we do, break that door down? Where do you buy a battering ram in Jerusalem?'

She leaned forward, tapping the table with her fingernail. 'I had a good look at the front of his building. All you'd have to do to get into his apartment is pull yourself up onto that first floor balcony. The glass door was broken. I saw it. You could get in very easily. Didn't you look?' She smiled.

'You want me to climb up the front of his building?'

'Yes, Tarzan. I know you can do it.'

I groaned. I was about to become a burglar in Jerusalem. 'I'm not going to do anything in broad daylight,' I said.

'Did I ask you to?'

'And you're going to be lookout.'

'That's a deal.' She put her coffee cup down. 'Why don't you give Simon a call, see if he's free to meet up?'

'You're very decisive today,' I said.

'We don't have much time.'

'Okay, I'm going along with all this,' I said. 'If you agree to one thing.'

'What's that?'

'That you stay well out of danger.'

She smiled, tilted her head. 'I will if you will,' she said.

29

Susan closed her eyes. She let her breath out. He was gone.
Thank God!

She crawled on her hands and knees to where he'd left
the bowl of rice. There had been fried egg mixed with it the
last time, a taste she normally didn't care for, but she loved
it now, craved it, after having had nothing to eat for endless
hours.

Hopefully the water wouldn't taste odd this time. Her
fingers were cold, they felt icy, but her face was boiling, as
if she had a fever. How many days had it been?

She felt for the bowl, took the rice with her fingers, put
it to her mouth and gobbled at it. It was dry, undercooked,
but there was a taste of egg and for a moment she was in
heaven. She started listing the streets in the centre of
Cambridge again. Doing it had helped her stay sane in the
last few days.

And then a tear slipped down her face.

She had finished the rice and she'd remembered how her
husband used to try to get her to make proper dinners, how
she'd been unable to do so because of her work commitments.
She held herself, pressed her back hard into the stone wall

171

behind her. Why hadn't she listened to him? He'd told her not to come out here. The muscles in her body tightened like ropes under strain.

No, she wasn't going to cry. She wasn't going to let him win as he listened to her whimpering.

The taste had stung her throat. That was all. Nothing else. She'd been down here too many days. But why was he keeping her? If he had something planned for her, why was he waiting to do it?

Was it all a way to torture her? She banged her fist against the stone, hurting herself, not caring. Banged it again. Was this all because of what she'd said to Kaiser about the book? Had he told her captors?

And was her captivity leading towards a main event?

She'd read about people being burnt at the stake in Europe; Cathars, witches, Jews. Sometimes they were kept in cells near where the burnings took place. Often they were forced to listen to the cries of those who went before them. That alone must have magnified their fears excruciatingly.

Was he planning such a death for her? She couldn't dismiss the thought. She knew how Kaiser had died. And she was now in the hands of the man who'd done that. It made her want to scream.

How could this be happening in the twenty-first century?

It can take such a long time to die, if you're being burnt. Your legs can literally melt, and you might not even fall unconscious. The endlessly searing pain keeps you awake.

She'd read about how thousands had been burnt in pogroms all across Europe in centuries past. She knew it was a tradition that went far back, to the Celts burning enemies in giant wicker men, to tales from Rome and Carthage and evidence about children being sacrificed by fire.

Could she escape this fate? Could she kill herself, before it happened? She shivered. Her head touched the cold of the rock behind her. That was a decision she could only make if she had a tool to carry it out.

And she didn't have one yet.

She'd tried to bend the plate she'd been given, to see if a sharp edge could be broken off, but she hadn't succeeded. She'd also searched for a hard sliver of rock from the stone around her in the darkness, but she'd failed to find that too.

She had to start looking again. Start thinking. At least it would keep her busy for the next few hours, until she fell asleep again and started dreaming about food and then about fires burning.

30

I had a shower before calling Simon Marcus. I could still feel a trace of the dust of the Negev on my skin. It had filtered into the taxi the day before. Breaking into Max's apartment would be risking a lot. If we were arrested we'd be thrown out of Israel, permanently most likely, after a spell in prison. And it might take months to get out of an Israeli jail.

While I was in the shower, Isabel popped her head into the bathroom to tell me she was on her way downstairs to look for something in the hotel shop. I asked her to join me.

'Maybe later,' she said. Then she disappeared. I didn't blame her. Being here was not conducive to romance. In London we spent a lot of time going to restaurants, meeting friends, showing things we liked about the city to each other.

After I got out of the shower I called Simon Marcus.

'Sean, where are you?' were his first words.

'It's good to hear your voice,' I said, avoiding his question.

'They told me you were deported. Is it true?'

'Yes. But can we talk about the site we visited?'

'Sure, yes, yes. Amazing, wasn't it?' There was scepticism in his voice.

'You're not sure about their claims, is that what I'm picking up?'

He sighed. 'Look, Sean. It would be wonderful if we found a treasure trove of manuscripts like that. There's a lot that could be confirmed if we had genuine documents from that era. I'm sure a lot of Christians would be overjoyed.' He paused.

'If what's down there supports the Bible,' I said.

'We have a long way to go before we know that. I'm sure everything will come out in due course.'

'Or maybe not.'

'Indeed, but there's not a lot I can do about it either way. Now, how can I help you, Sean?'

'Do you think that dig could be connected to Kaiser's murder?'

There was a guffaw from the other end.

'That's a reputable dig. How could they be involved in a murder?'

'I didn't say they did it. But anyone could be watching that site, monitoring who goes there, following them. All I'm saying is that there could be a connection. I think it's a weird way to run a hugely important excavation; to have found all those documents, yet keep it all secret. And then we got thrown out of the country for going there!'

He didn't answer. I was hoping he was thinking about it.

'You don't think it's odd,' I went on, 'that none of them seemed the least bit fazed that Kaiser was murdered, burnt to death?'

'You really want to poke around in all this, don't you?' said Simon. His preference for staying quiet and not waking any dragons, was clear.

Bells began pealing in the distance. Then a far-off muezzin call to prayer started up. An intake of breath came down the line.

175

'You're still in the Middle East. Where are you?' said Simon.

'It's best you don't know.'

'Don't even think about coming back to Israel,' he said, fast. 'They throw away the key when they lock people up who break the immigration laws here.'

'Think about what I said, Simon. There's something going on with that dig.'

There was silence at the other end of the line for fifteen, maybe twenty seconds. Then I dropped our latest bit of news on him.

'Kaiser was tortured before he died.'

'What?' His disbelief made the word come out odd, high-pitched.

The reality of what had happened to Kaiser was something I found difficult to accept myself. I hadn't wanted to dwell on it at all, but this might be the way to get through to Simon. I needed an insider. And he needed some motivation.

'They found melted flesh in the kitchen of his apartment. He wasn't just murdered and his body dumped.' I paused. He didn't say anything. I could hear him breathing.

'He was tied to a chair and his flesh was burnt off in chunks.' The idea of it made me sweat under my clothes.

'Can you think of any reason someone might have done that?'

'No.'

'They could do it again. You know that, don't you?' My voice cracked, I coughed, gripping the phone tight.

There was a long silence. The muezzin call to prayer had stopped. An ambulance went past in the street below. Its siren wailed, then stopped.

'Someone painted graffiti on our apartment building last night,' he said. His tone had changed. He was worried.

'What did it say?'

176

'Traitors will pay.'

'That's bizarre. You don't think it was directed at you, do you?'

'Honestly, I have no idea. It was at the main entrance.' He hesitated. 'My wife has locked all the windows in our apartment. She's never done that before. I told her about Kaiser, about you being thrown out of the country. She wants me to stay away from trouble.'

'Did anything else happen?' I was concerned now.

'No. And this is not like some of the other intimidation campaigns. It feels different.'

'Is there any reason why someone would target you?'

I heard a rustling before he answered, as if he was moving. When he spoke, his voice was lower, as if he was afraid of being overheard.

'You asked me did I know if there was a good reason that someone might torture Kaiser?'

'You didn't answer me.'

'You must know this.' His tone was full of anxiety. 'Ordinary Israeli criminals steal wallets. They shoot holes in their rivals. They don't torture people to death. And I don't think this is Palestinian work either. It's something different. Bombs and rockets and shootings are political.'

'You still haven't answered my question.'

'I'm getting to it. You know there's a history of people being burnt to death, don't you?'

'That stuff happened a long time ago.'

'Not really. All over Europe there are still festivals with effigies of people being burnt every year. Never mind what happened in the past, Jews being burnt to death. Europe has an obsession with bonfires and burning people in effigy. The sanctity of human life hasn't been part of Europe's culture for that long, despite what they tell you.'

'What crime do you think Kaiser was guilty of?'

177

'I honestly don't know. I just see a link with what's gone on in the past.' He spoke quickly, as if he wanted to end the conversation, as if even talking about these things made him uneasy.

'I have to go,' he said.

'I'll call back tomorrow, Simon. If you get any ideas about our friends from the dig, I'd really appreciate it if you could tell me, help us out.'

'I'll think about it,' he said. 'But that doesn't mean I can help you.' The line went dead.

I looked at it for a few seconds. What had he just done? He'd warned me and now he wanted to stay away from us.

I like getting warnings. It sets you up for a good day.

I checked my email and responded to three queries from the institute. I told Dr Beresford-Ellis's assistant that I would not have my department's budget in until the following week, reminding her that I was on holiday.

I checked the institute's blog, which I contributed to. No new articles had been posted.

I looked at a couple of other web pages. There were articles on all the major news sites about tensions between Israel and Egypt. I read half of a long article about the demonstration expected that day after Friday prayers in Egypt. Then I clicked away. I couldn't concentrate. What Simon had said about people being burnt to death was stalking around at the back of my mind.

I went down to the foyer to look for Isabel. I found her in the hotel shop going through books about Jerusalem. Some of them had stunning panoramic pictures showing the golden roofed Dome of the Rock, the Wailing Wall, and the Church of the Holy Sepulchre.

We went outside for a walk. It was a warm day, spring-like, almost perfect. The air was clean, still.

We went into a modern one-storey shopping arcade. Isabel

spent a lot of time in a leather shop. She ended up buying nothing.

I'd had enough of not-shopping. I waited for her in a coffee shop, people-watching for another thirty minutes while she finished looking around.

'Some of those shops are amazing,' I said. 'You didn't see anything you liked?'

'I'm just distracting myself,' she said. 'Let's go.'

We walked to the Jaffa Gate and then into the Old City, where we did a little sightseeing. Then we decided to go back to the hotel to rest. The Sabbath had started after lunch. Quite a few shops and the Tower of David Museum were all closed. And we had an interesting evening ahead.

There was a big group in the foyer of the King David, waiting to be checked in. They looked like pampered financiers from every corner of the planet. As I stood watching them, waiting for our elevator to come, I saw a small man in a dark suit watching me over the top of his newspaper. He was standing by one of the Egyptian pillars. There was nothing particularly memorable about the guy. He was youngish, dark-haired, looked like a businessman and had a plain face and expression, but I was on edge immediately. Had our return been discovered?

I didn't say anything to Isabel. I didn't want to spook her. And it was possible I was being paranoid. We decided to eat before going to Kaiser's apartment at ten. Ten would be late enough that most people would be long off the streets, but not too late to attract attention. I'd bought a screwdriver and a small torch in a little hardware shop in the Old City.

After an early dinner in the Oriental Bar, a quiet wooden-floored haven in the hotel, we went back up to our room and got ready for our little operation. That was what Isabel was calling it anyway.

We weren't as professional as we could have been, but we were probably better prepared than we had been when we went down under Hagia Sophia in Istanbul. That time we'd ended up in a water-filled tunnel and had to beat off giant eels. I didn't expect anything like that this time.

We walked about half a mile from the hotel before hailing a taxi. I didn't want to advertise where we were going to the taxi drivers in the rank outside the King David.

All the way there we stayed quiet. He let us off at the roundabout. He must have thought we were the quietest people ever.

When we arrived at what had been Max's apartment, all was quiet. The Sabbath in parts of Jerusalem was almost like Christmas Day in London for how silent it felt.

The street lights were humming gently as Isabel went to the door of the apartment block. She wasn't going to press the intercom this time, she was going to start coughing loudly, to warn me, if anyone came out. The last thing I needed was for a resident to see me climbing up their building.

As I stood at the front of the building the seriousness of what I'd committed to doing was becoming evident. But I wasn't going to back down. A deep shiver passed through me as I breathed in, calming myself.

Across the street, behind cypress trees and a row of thick bushes, there were other similar apartments. I examined each building. There wasn't anyone out on their balconies, thankfully, but plenty of the apartments had lights on and some you could even see right into the rooms. If they came out onto their balcony and looked across the street, they would see me doing my Spiderman impression.

I had to get this over with quickly.

Luckily, the apartment on the ground floor of Kaiser's building had its curtains closed tight. As I got near the balcony I could hear a TV inside. They were watching a movie. My heartbeat quickened. It wasn't at 170 bpm, but it was heading that way. I put on the thin plastic gloves that we'd picked up that afternoon.

A sudden swell of strings was followed by a deathly silence. I held my breath. Had someone heard me and turned the TV down?

I didn't move for a minute, my pulse beating fast in my ears, until another swell of music allowed me to take a breath, making the tiny noises I needed as I climbed up onto the wall of their balcony.

I reached over to the two inch thick black cable that ran up between the apartment buildings. The cable was set in an indentation in the wall, which would help me climb if I put my foot against it. I held the cable high up with my left hand to steady myself, then reached for the lower edge of the balcony above with my right.

It was out of reach.

There was a thin concrete ridge jutting out where the floor level of the balcony above must be. It wouldn't be enough to hold me for long, but it might be enough to allow me to move my left hand up the cable a few more inches.

My right hand should then reach the balcony up above.

It was a dangerous manoeuvre, but definitely doable. If I missed the balcony all that would happen would be that I'd end up sliding down the wall and onto my ass in the front garden of the apartment block.

My fingers touched the edge of the balcony.

I'd almost made it.

Then the concrete edge slipped through my fingers and I was falling. It was a jarring, painful, wind-knocking end to my effort when I hit the ground.

I landed on my side, my breath forced out of me. I didn't get up for a minute. My arm was tingling from the pain of landing on it, but I could still move it. I was convinced the occupants of the apartment would rush out onto the balcony at any second, and I was planning what to say.

But they didn't appear.

I waited some more. Perhaps they were engrossed in the movie? Or perhaps there was no one behind the curtain and the whole thing was some elaborate electronic charade to convince thieves that the place was occupied?

Isabel was at the side of the building as I pushed myself to my feet. She had her arms folded. I put a finger to my lips.

She put one to hers.

I waved her to go back, glancing around as a car passed.

My second attempt was more successful. I pushed up, got a grip on the ridge, pulled myself up with the cable fast, just as a creaking noise indicated that someone was coming out onto the balcony below me. The TV was suddenly much louder and a shout in a language that could have been Polish split the air.

I crouched on the cement floor of Kaiser's balcony. It was dirty. There was a mud-like sooty scum on the floor. My heart was over 170 bpm now. I didn't move. I imagined a face peering over the balcony having come up the way I did.

Then there was another shout from below. I could hear breathing, mine, and hear my heart thumping. I willed myself to calm down. I wasn't going to be any good like this.

And where was Isabel? Was whoever was down there going to give her a problem?

Then the noise of the TV went down abruptly. I crouched, listening, slowing my breathing, my heart returning to something like normality with each passing second. Another car went by. There were no other noises from below.

Whoever had come out had gone back in again. They must have. I got to my feet, tried the door to the apartment. It was locked, but the glass was broken, just as Isabel had said.

There was a big hole, right in the middle of the door. Someone had smashed it. I bent down. It was just about big enough to get through.

I pulled a jagged piece of glass out, the most likely one I would cut myself against. Then I went through, very slowly, imagining what would happen if I slipped and fell against one of the shards on either side. It wouldn't be nice.

Inside, the smell of burnt debris was sour and strong. The light from the street lamps outside was barely enough to see by. I saw chairs overturned, a TV on its side.

I stood. My stomach was not happy. It was wound tight.

At my feet there was a piece of burnt carpet. It looked as if it had been pulled from some other room.

There was a door at the far end of this room. I guessed it led into a hall from which I could find the kitchen and the front door to go out and let Isabel in. As I walked across the room towards the dark oblong of the door, glass crunched lightly under my shoes.

I slowed some more, touching the far wall as I reached it. Then I took my torch out. When I got into the hall I closed the door to the main room. As darkness engulfed me, I turned the torch on. The hall sprang into existence around me, its walls smudged all over with smoke. The floor was black with dirt, but it wasn't burnt, it was stained.

And the smell was even worse now.

As if there was something evil in the air.

31

Lord Bidoner was watching Sky News in his suite in the St George's Hotel in Mayfair, London. He was sitting up in the imperial-size bed watching the LCD screen that had lowered from the ceiling at his verbal command. The LCD was white-edged to match the décor in the rest of the room.

The images playing on the screen were of the Egyptian army and a vast mob of demonstrators clashing in Tahrir Square in Cairo. *Three dead in Egypt* ran the caption across the bottom of the screen.

Everything was proceeding perfectly. Their last attempt to stir up conflict had failed, but this time the wheels of hatred were moving faster. It would not be so easy for the authorities to clamp down. The change was coming.

He picked up the iPad from the marble-topped bedside table, and checked for incoming messages. The search team report was due. He scanned the list of emails. It still hadn't arrived. He clenched his fist, smashed it down into the mattress. This was not good at all.

If Arap Anach survived this operation in Israel he would get him to teach the search team a few lessons in motivation. Or Lord Bidoner would intervene himself. He closed his eyes, resting his head back on the padded silk headboard.

He had to stay calm. They were near to achieving their objective. After what was going to happen in Jerusalem things would be very different. Fear would become contagious.

32

My heart was back doing double-time again. I could handle it, but I wanted to get out as quickly as possible. I opened the door of the apartment, put a piece of burnt rolled-up mat in the bottom to hold the door open, then raced downstairs to let Isabel in. I didn't wait for the elevator. I found the stairwell.

When I opened the front door she was standing outside with her arms crossed.

'What the hell took you so long?' she hissed.

'Thank you for that vote of confidence,' I said.

I waved her in and closed the front door. We went up the stairs fast. As I closed Kaiser's door behind us I turned on my torch and she stood still in the hallway of Kaiser's apartment, clutching her arms around herself, as if she wasn't sure about going any further.

'Which door is the kitchen?' she said quickly.

There were two doors to our right as well as the door straight ahead that led into the living room. They were all closed.

'One of those.' I pointed to the right.

'Great.' She did not sound happy.

I stepped across the hall and put my hand on the nearest door. I have a tendency to jump in where I shouldn't. I'd got into a few stupid scrapes in the past and you'd think I'd have learnt my lesson, but some things never change.

I turned the steel handle and pushed the door open fast. A thick, sooty smell greeted me. It was on my lips, in my mouth. It made me want to throw up. There was a cold sweat on my forehead now.

On the far side of the room was a window. Starlight was coming in. A ragged curtain was hanging from a rail, as if there'd been a struggle. A mattress was half off the bed. Part of it was burnt. The walls were black with sooty fingers, as if they'd been painted by a demented Goth art student.

Isabel walked around the room and opened the built-in wardrobe door. There were a few clothes inside hanging up, two jackets, some shirts. She pulled all the drawers on a soot-stained chest out, looked intently into each one.

'What are you looking for?'

'I was wondering if there was anyone living with him.' She pointed at a bright silver pair of handcuffs in a bottom drawer.

'What do you think this tells us?' she said.

'He liked playing cops and robbers?'

She snorted. 'Why do you think the Israeli police left them here?'

'I don't think they take everything when they examine a crime scene.'

'Any sign of a girlfriend?' I looked around.

Isabel shook her head. 'Let's try the other door,' she said. She pushed the drawer back in slowly.

I went out into the hall and over to the next door. The smell that came out was similarly sooty to the odour in the other room, but there was something else mixed in with it too.

A faint smell of roasted meat.

It was odd, but it made this room smell more pleasant than the bedroom. The thought of what that meant was sickening.

There was a window on the far wall of this room too. In front of it was a sink. It was piled high with smoke-blackened dishes, an upturned toaster and cooking utensils. Someone had thrown the flotsam of the kitchen there.

Around the walls there were bare worktops and blackened cupboard doors. The fire in here had been worse than anywhere else in the apartment.

There was a fridge and a cooker, and a washing machine down one wall. They were all damaged in some way. But what made my blood beat loud in my ears was the chair in the centre of the room.

It was burnt to a metal skeleton. There wasn't a seat or a back, just a black skeletal shape.

I went forward, shone the torch on the remnants of the chair. The hairs on the back of my neck were way up.

There were marks on the floor around the chair. I pointed the torch down.

Two faint black marks in front of the chair were where someone's feet would have been if they were sitting in it. They were dark shadows on the large floor tiles. If there had been any residue of human flesh there it had been cleaned away, almost perfectly. All that was left were the dark stains that revealed everything.

'Mark wasn't lying,' said Isabel quietly. In the distance the wail of an ambulance grew. It was a high-pitched squeal, more like the thumping urgency of an American ambulance than a London one.

'Let's not stay here,' I said. I'd had a picture flash through my mind of Kaiser sitting in that chair, screaming into a gag and I wanted to throw up.

188

'Look,' said Isabel. She was pointing at the floor around the remnants of the chair.

I shone the torch there. At first I couldn't see anything, then I noticed the ghost-like traces of powder about a foot away from the chair. In a line. What the hell was that there for?

The traces were faint lines on the tiles around the chair.

I bent down to look and shone the torch on the line. It was rough, barely there, jagged, almost cleaned away. And there was something familiar about it. I peered closer. Yes, someone had poured powder in a shape, an H shape, around the chair. And it was barely visible.

'Let's get some pictures,' said Isabel. She sounded weary.

I took pictures of the floor around the chair. The H shape didn't come out very well, but a part of it was visible.

We listened at the front door for a minute, my pulse beating fast in my ears, then I opened it a crack and waited, listening before going out. As we exited the front door I heard a noise behind us, but I simply closed it. We kept walking, pulling off our gloves. I didn't look back.

A few minutes later we were in a taxi heading to the hotel. It took the whole journey to get my heart beating normally again.

'Before we go back to London I want to take pictures of everyone who comes and goes to that dig,' I said, as we walked under the stone arch entranceway.

And then I saw him, one of the immigration policemen who had driven us to the airport. He was sideways to us, standing at the reception desk. There was another man who I didn't know beside him. And I remembered the guy who'd been staring at us in the morning.

'We've got to leave,' I said.

I took Isabel's arm and turned her quickly back outside. There was a chance the immigration guy wasn't here for us, but there was a better chance he was.

'Stop, you're hurting me,' Isabel hissed as we went back out under the arch.

'Sorry, but we can't hang around.' I released my grip. We walked out onto the street, then around the nearest corner. I waved at a taxi. He came towards us. Before we got in I explained to Isabel why I'd steered her back out, who I'd seen.

'I hope you're not going to turn out to be into physical violence,' she said.

'Only when I'm trying to save your skin.'

'Call Simon Marcus,' she whispered. 'He'll know where we can stay without getting arrested.'

We got into the taxi. It was filled with Israeli pop music. I could almost recognise the tune, but the singing was in Hebrew. It didn't cross my mind to ask the driver to turn it down. I was looking out the back window to see if we were being followed. After a minute, with no police car zooming after us, I pulled my phone out of my jacket pocket.

As soon as Simon answered and I told him who it was, there was silence. Then he said softly, 'You're back in Israel.'

He must have heard the music.

'We need somewhere to stay. Do you know anywhere?' I was hoping not to attract too much suspicion from the taxi driver. There was more silence. I had no idea what he was going to do. Would he turn us in?

Then he said. 'Come to my place. I'm crazy, I know, but my mother taught me never to turn anyone away.' He gave me his address. It was near the central bus station.

'Leave the taxi at the bus station,' he said.

Fifteen minutes later we were outside a four-storey apartment block that looked as if it had been designed in the '60s by a determined modernist. There were little Stars of David on each plastic buzzer by the front door. Simon came down himself to let us in.

He put a finger to his lips to get us to stay silent as we went inside. Then he went outside to look around before showing us upstairs. His family was away, he said, but from the mugs still on the dining table I got the impression they had scarpered in the last few minutes.

He hadn't told me he had children.

'My wife and daughter, she's thirteen, went away a little while ago to stay with her mother in Tel Aviv,' he said, as if to explain the mugs.

'We shouldn't be here long,' I said.

'Is there anywhere people can stay in Jerusalem if they don't want their details to be seen by the Israeli police in a few hours?' I asked, as we sat down on a long brown sofa.

'You will stay here,' he said, matter-of-factly.

'We can't do that,' I said.

He was standing in front of the door to go back out.

'You must. You will.'

'You're very good,' said Isabel. 'Thank you.' She stood, walked over to him and put a hand on his arm. 'Is there somewhere I can lie down?'

'Are you okay?' I said.

She turned to me. She looked pale. It had crossed my mind that I should insist we leave, but now I was rethinking.

She shrugged. 'I'm just tired. And I have a terrible headache. That's all,' she said.

'This way,' said Simon. 'You can use my daughter's room.' He showed us to a room with a single bed. He got out clean sheets and soon Isabel was sleeping and I was in the front room of his apartment admiring the photographs on the walls. There was one of him and Yitzhak Rabin in dinner suits and another of him in military fatigues in the desert.

191

'You get around,' I said.

'I wouldn't put them there,' he said, 'but my wife likes them.'

'I hope we aren't bringing problems down on top of you.'

He put a hand out in front of him, as if he was appealing to me for something.

'So why did you come back? What do you hope to do here?' His tone was aggrieved.

'You know Susan Hunter is still missing?'

'And you are the investigating team now, is that it? Are you qualified for this?' He was clearly not going to give me any credit for coming back.

'Nobody in the Israeli police force seems to give a damn about finding her.'

'You seem very well-informed. Have you met all the officers working on her case?'

'No, and I'm sure you're right. Some of them will be doing their job properly, but that wasn't the impression I got when I talked to the police here.'

He raised his eyebrows.

'I know things that might help find her. Do you think we should go home and sit on our hands, maybe wait until we hear they've found her body?' I was getting annoyed now.

'Because I won't do that. You don't know what happened to my wife, do you? You don't know that she was murdered in a roadside bomb attack. That no one told me a goddamned thing about what really happened for a long time. You're talking to the wrong person if you think I'm going to sit at home and wait for someone to knock on my door or to read about her death on a web page.'

He put his hands up.

'Forgive me,' he said. 'I didn't know about your wife. Come on, sit down. I will make tea.' He paused. His expression had softened.

'My wife likes peppermint tea. Would you like to try some?'

I nodded, but I couldn't sit down. I paced and started looking at the books on his shelves. It was difficult to wind down after what I'd seen at Kaiser's and then having to run from our hotel.

When he came back with the teapot, a tall Ottoman-style silver thing, alongside delicate green cups and saucers, I sat opposite him. As we drank I told him about what we'd found out at Kaiser's. He didn't ask how I'd got in.

I told him about the stain on the floor and about the H shape. I showed him the picture of it.

There was silence in the room for a minute. Something had changed in his demeanour. If he seemed a little frightened before, it was amplified now. He went to the windows, pulled a thick brown curtain over, though it looked as if the curtain was never pulled given the trouble it took to get across.

When he was finished he went to a glass cabinet, took out a bottle of Russian vodka with a gold eagle on it and poured a good dollop into his tea.

He looked at me over the bottle.

'You want some?' His tone was querulous, as if he didn't really expect me to say yes.

'You bet. That's just what I need.' I held my cup out.

The tea tasted very different now, sharp, mucus-clearing. I could feel the vodka warming my insides up.

Simon went to the bookcase that lined one wall and took down a small green volume. He looked through it, opened it wide at a page, and held the page in front of me. It was covered in proto-alphabetic symbols. He pointed at an H symbol.

'This is a very old symbol,' he said. 'It is an H now, but this was Heth in the Canaanite alphabet, their eighth letter. It is used to signify laughter.' He sipped his tea.

'I thought it was just an H,' I said. 'Who the hell uses Heth these days? Are you sure it's not just an H?' I couldn't imagine Canaanites coming back to put their mark in a modern apartment.

'The upward angle on the middle line gives it away. As for who uses Heth now, that's a different question.' He drank from his cup, finished it and put it down on the long, rough wooden coffee table that looked like an ancient door.

'I've seen references to Heth in a book from the 1920s,' he went on. He moved forward in his chair.

'Jerusalem was going through a spiritualism fad then. This letter became a symbol for the parties that a German baron used to hold here. He and his mistress, an Austrian beauty, would invite all the expatriates who were hiding out here; ruined Russian counts, Armenian dilettantes, wealthy Lebanese apostates. Actually, they were more orgies than parties. The Mufti found out about them and the two of them were run out of town by a Muslim mob. It almost started a revolt against the British. You could say that was the seed for the Arab uprising in '29. The Mufti thought the British weren't clamping down hard enough on European hedonists.'

'So it's a symbol of hedonism?'

'Laughter and hedonism was what it was associated with, but it was used for other purposes before that.'

'Such as?'

'It was an ancient curse symbol. It might have been put there to jinx any investigation.'

There was something nagging me about the symbol. I turned my phone on again and looked at the picture. There was something familiar about it. But what? I turned the phone off.

'I'm worried about what's happened to your friend Susan Hunter. Seeing this sign makes me fear for her even more than before,' said Simon.

He settled back in his chair. It was my turn to move forward. I reached for the vodka bottle, poured myself an inch. I would need something strong to help me sleep after being at Kaiser's.

'That's gold standard vodka from Moscow. My friend in the apartment next door brings it back. Go slow with it.'

I nodded. 'Tell me, why does this Heth sign make you fearful for Susan?'

And then it came to me, where I'd seen the sign before. It was on the t-shirts of the young men who'd interrupted us at the dig. Underneath it had been the words *Heaven's Legion*. Was someone trying to implicate them? I couldn't imagine any reason why an organisation would put its own symbol at a murder site.

'I'll tell you, but pass me that bottle first.'

I passed him the bottle of vodka. He put it away in the glass cabinet, then turned to me. His skin looked white and sickly in the dim light from the lamp in the far corner of the room.

'It provides an explanation for Max Kaiser's death.' He was staring at me, as if I'd brought a smell into the room.

I opened my hands. 'Which is?'

'He was a sacrifice, a human sacrifice.'

I could feel my face changing. First I felt a warm flush, then a quick coldness spread through me. I'd heard about human sacrifice, of course, but that was hundreds of years ago, wasn't it? Such things didn't happen anymore, did they?

'What the hell would you sacrifice a human for?' I blurted out.

'There were three reasons in the early Canaanite tradition,' said Simon slowly. 'To ask the goddess to change the weather, for someone sick to be made whole, or for someone to be resurrected from the arms of the Queen of Darkness, and be brought back to life.'

'The Queen of Darkness? Are you serious?'

'Yes. She was the goddess who the Canaanites believed controlled the underworld, the land of Mot. It's all on clay tablets from Ras Shamra in Syria. They were translated a few years ago.'

'They believed in a Queen of Darkness?'

'Yes, I have a picture of her.' He went to his bookcase and took down a pile of academic papers. He spent the next few minutes leafing through them. Finally he pulled out a thin journal.

There was a black and white image of an oblong cuneiform tablet with an aluminium ruler beside it. The tablet had a series of marks on it surrounding a large image made from indented lines at its centre. The image was of a thin girl with prominent breasts. In her hands was a skull.

I handed him back the journal.

'I need to sleep,' I said. The day had caught up with me.

'There's a camp bed in the wardrobe, if you don't want to disturb Isabel,' he said.

'That sounds like a good idea,' I said. 'She needs a proper night's sleep.'

He told me how to open it and gave me some blankets. I set it up quietly in the darkness under the window. Isabel was sleeping soundly.

I woke at four in the morning. I wasn't sure what had woken me. Then I heard a rumbling noise. I looked out of the window. Below was a carriageway with two lanes on each side separated by a low concrete divider and scraggy bushes. The side of the carriageway heading for the centre of Jerusalem was filled with tank transporters moving forward purposefully.

I watched them go by. They were dark green. The tanks had their barrels pointed straight ahead. One of the transporter's windows was rolled down. In the half light from the street lamps a young, determined looking, female driver no more than twenty years of age was staring at the road ahead.

It looked as if a war was starting.

33

Arap Anach pressed the *encrypt call* app. A dial pad opened up and he pressed Lord Bidoner's contact number. Twenty seconds later he could hear the phone ringing.

'Do you know what time it is in London?' said Lord Bidoner.

'Two in the morning,' said Anach.

'Is this conversation secure?'

'Your encrypt call application is open on your phone, isn't it?' said Anach.

'Yes. What can I do for you?'

'There's been a general mobilisation of Israeli Defence Force units this morning. Everything is proceeding as planned.'

'Just make sure you do it right this time. That fiasco in London left me out in the cold.'

'No one from the Security Service has approached you, have they?'

'No, but they've been poking around.'

'The chances of anyone figuring out what's going on are close to zero.'

'Make sure you deal with that woman as we agreed, when the time comes.'

'I know what to do. She will wish she hadn't been born.'

34

The following morning I woke feeling hungover and groggy. I didn't think I'd drunk enough to feel that way.

Isabel was already up. Sunlight was streaming through the window. Simon's ramblings about human sacrifice and the Queen of Darkness were far away night time subjects. I lay in bed thinking about the tanks. Israel was in an almost permanent state of readiness for war, but I guessed what had happened last night was something more.

There'd been a hell of a lot of them.

One thing was clear; whatever was going on, those idiots working at that dig had to be investigated. Isabel's idea of getting pictures of them was good. She could probably get Mark to run the images through their database to see if he could attach names to them, establish backgrounds and look for dodgy characters.

I got up and went looking for her to see if that was what she'd been planning. She wasn't in the single bed.

Simon was in the main room. The curtains were pulled back and he had coffee and plates on the wooden dining table at the far end of the room.

'Where's Isabel?' I said. I wasn't worried at that point.

'She went across the road to get some fresh bread. She insisted on going. I told her I could do it, but you know what women are like.'

I opened my mouth to say something, then I stopped. Something didn't feel right.

'Don't worry. I watched her going into the shop only a few minutes ago.' He must have seen anxiety in my expression.

'It's over there, straight across the road.' He pointed at the door to the balcony. It looked down over the front of the building and the main road.

'Why don't you grab a coffee, go out onto on the balcony, and watch her coming back.'

I poured myself a cup and gulped some. Then I did as he'd suggested. The store's name above the door was in Hebrew. It was on the corner of a block.

I waited, expecting at any moment to see her come out of the shop. I still wasn't panicking. There was no way that anything could have happened to her. But the seconds ticked on.

And she didn't appear. I checked my watch.

After ten minutes with no sign of her, and with anxiety gathering fast inside me, I went back into the apartment. I rang her mobile phone. I heard it ringing from the bedroom. She'd left it behind.

'I'm going to see what's happened,' I said.

'She must have gone to the shop behind it. If they don't have fresh bread in, they tell people to go to the next shop.' He looked at his watch, seeming puzzled. 'They should have had their deliveries by now,' he said. Then he waved his hands in the air.

'Maybe the bakeries are slow today. What with everything that's been happening.'

When I exited Simon's building, I noticed remnants of the graffiti he'd spoken about. I hadn't seen it in the dark. Someone had painted over a section of the outside wall of the building already, but the colours didn't quite match. You couldn't exactly make out what the paint had covered, but you could see dark shapes, curved lines.

I didn't bother examining them. I walked fast. I didn't care what the shapes meant. I wanted to find Isabel. Simon's ramblings the night before were echoing in my brain. Alarm signals were jangling through my mind. But another part of me was saying, *stop, stay calm, she's okay.*

But she wasn't crossing the road, as I'd hoped she might be. And she wasn't outside the shop. A car beeped at me as I ran across.

And she wasn't inside the shop. I raced down its two aisles, almost knocking over an old man in a baggy black suit carrying a giant bottle of water. He eyed me suspiciously. I wanted to explain what I was doing, but I didn't have time.

Where the hell was she?

I spotted another exit. I ran out, started towards the next shop. It was fifty feet away down the side street. Then it came to me. I had to check if the first shop had fresh bread. If they hadn't, I could keep looking for a shop that had.

I went back, feeling stupid. My heart was beating tightly in my chest, as if something was binding it. I headed down to the back of the shop again.

Yes, there it was. There were two tiered sections with a dozen different varieties of loaves. A heavy weight was crushing against my chest.

Why wasn't she in the shop? I looked from left to right, wondering if my eyes were deceiving me. A small woman wearing all black was standing staring at me. She said something to me. It must have been in Hebrew. I couldn't understand any of it.

I waved a rude *no* at her and ran for the door.

Maybe Isabel was back in Simon's apartment waiting for

me. She'd smile at my distress, then hug me. We'd talk about it over breakfast. I'd laugh at their gentle ribbing. But she'd be there.

She had to be.

I rang Simon's doorbell and was buzzed into the building. I ran up the stairs, taking two at a time. My heart was thudding as I knocked on his door.

I heard him talking.

That meant there was someone with him. That meant Isabel was here. Thank God!

Simon swung open the door.

'Where's Isabel?' he said.

'She's not here?' My voice sounded odd, the words tumbling out too fast.

I stood there looking at him, fear spreading from my heart. My face felt odd, stiff.

'She didn't come back?'

'No.'

'Who were you talking to?' Was he playing a game with me?

'A rabbi friend of mine, Jeremiah. He dropped by. Come in, meet him.'

I walked inside in a daze. It felt as if someone had knocked me over the head. I was listening for the doorbell, for me to have made a stupid mistake in that shop, for Isabel to arrive back. Simon was saying something. I only caught the end of it.

'Jeremiah, you tell him,' was all I heard.

Jeremiah was wearing a black suit. He had a thick black beard and ringlets of black hair running past his ears down to his shoulders. On his head there was a black velvet yarmulke. He was about my age, mid-thirties, but his skin was rough, as if he had eczema once for a long time. His eyes were electric blue.

'We have watered the garden from a pool that is running dry,' he said. His voice was low.

Was this guy for real? I looked at Simon. I didn't need this.

'Jeremiah is the most persecuted rabbi in the whole of Israel,' said Simon, as if that explained everything.

'You look unwell,' said Jeremiah.

'I've lost my girlfriend,' I said. He smiled at me forgivingly.

'You checked if the bread had arrived?' said Simon.

I nodded. My throat was dry.

Simon shook his head. He looked worried now. Panic was rising inside me. I wanted to turn back time. Then I got an urge to run back to the shops, to check them again, properly.

No, maybe I should wait here a bit longer, stay calm. There had to be a rational explanation for this. I went out onto the balcony so I wouldn't have to talk, so I could see the road, the shop.

I stared at it.

Simon was standing beside me.

'I don't think anything's happened to her,' he said. His words were calming, but there was a definite note of worry in his tone.

I was staring at the shop. Every time its front door opened my heart opened with it. Then another voice spoke behind me.

'She was in that shop?' said Jeremiah.

'We think so,' said Simon.

That was it, I was going back to it. 'I'm going there,' I said.

'I was in that shop five minutes ago,' said Jeremiah.

'Did you see anything suspicious?' I said quickly.

Questions were spinning in my mind. Could she have gone off for some reason? Could she have been kidnapped? I felt ill. I wrapped my right fist in my left hand, made a conscious

203

effort to gain control of myself. I would be no use to Isabel if I panicked.

'No, no, nothing.' He shook his head.

'Did you see a European lady? Black hair, tall, slim?'

He paused. Come on, I wanted to shout, answer the question. I pressed my lips together.

'I do not look at women. I am sworn against such things.'

'Was there anyone in the shop?' I was almost shouting. No, I was shouting. I put a hand out, felt for the balcony door, gripped it.

'Yes, I am sure there was.' He rubbed his forehead.

'Do you remember who you saw?' I knew Jeremiah wasn't responsible for what was going on, but I was finding it hard to contain my frustration.

He looked sad as he looked at me. 'I remember an American. A big man with a white t-shirt with something on it. He pushed past me.'

'What was on his t-shirt?' I said.

'I don't remember.'

A crazy idea came to me. I took my phone out, went to the photo of the burnt H sign. 'Was it something like this?'

Jeremiah looked at my phone, his eyes were red-rimmed. Red veins ran through them as if he'd been up all night studying the Torah.

After what seemed like forever, he said, 'I don't remember.' He shook his head.

'But it could have been?' I said.

'Maybe. Maybe not.' I wanted to shake him. Instead I pushed past him and headed for the door.

'I heard her on the phone last night,' said Simon.

'What?' I stopped, turning back.

'I wasn't going to say it, but it was a little odd. She was in the bathroom. It was in the middle of the night. I heard her talking. That's all. Maybe it means nothing.'

But maybe it did mean something.

Who had she be calling like that, from somewhere I couldn't hear her? Was this why she'd disappeared? Had she made an appointment to meet someone? I felt disconnected from reality, as if I'd discovered her secret life.

'Did you hear what she was saying, anything at all?'

Simon shook his head. Then something else strange about last night came back to me.

'What were all those tanks I saw at 4 a.m.? There was a heck of a lot of them.'

Simon stared at me. It looked as if he knew exactly what was going on, but was struggling to find a way to phrase it.

'There's a storm coming,' said Jeremiah. 'They are its messengers.'

'What the hell does that mean?' I said.

Jeremiah recoiled from me, took a step back.

'I speak what I see.' His eyes were penetrating me, as if uncovering my faults. 'Would you prefer lies?'

'No, I just want to find Isabel.' I put my hand to my forehead. I had to stay calm. I had to find her. Quickly.

'Jerusalem is on the edge of a precipice, Sean,' said Simon.

35

It was 11.30 a.m. on Saturday morning in London. Henry Mowlam's weekend had got off to a bad start. And not just because of the monsoon-like rain. He'd been summoned.

The underground offices in Whitehall were relatively quiet on a Saturday, which was good, but the tea was still as bad as it had always been, and the reports from around the world didn't stop coming in just because it was the weekend.

Henry had promised his wife that they would go shopping that afternoon in Oxford Street. He was hoping to confirm what time he would meet her in the next hour, as soon as he finished the handover report for the weekend monitoring unit.

And that was taking longer than it should have. Mainly because he was worried about what might happen over the next day or so.

It wasn't that he had any doubts about the weekend unit's efficiency. No, it was the implications of what the rising tension in Egypt might mean. You couldn't watch as countries slid towards war without feeling apprehension. It was a very different thing watching war on TV at home. That was more like entertainment, war planes going out and coming back, politicians making rousing speeches.

But when you saw pictures of men, women and children mutilated by bombs, the type of images TV executives had long since considered too shocking for Western viewers, the entertainment value lessened.

Henry had seen the slide to war enough times to know that what was happening in Egypt was not good. All the noises were ominous. A bomb had exploded in Cairo. Policemen were dead. An Iranian submarine was reported to be nearing the entrance of the Suez Canal.

Reports of tension in the Egyptian air force had come through too. One informant had speculated that a rogue air force general was planning a pre-emptive strike against Israel, to secure his popular appeal amongst the Egyptian masses.

That report, circulated late the previous day, had led the Israeli high command to commence troop movements, to reinforce defensive positions, and to disperse armoured units.

Other reports, from inside Egypt, were worrying too. Despite most imams there warning against war in their Friday prayers, tension on the streets was still high. A demonstration near Rafah, where the Israel, Gaza and Egyptian borders met, was attracting a big crowd. Rumours were circulating on the internet. There'd been a report in the Egyptian press about Max Kaiser's death in Jerusalem.

The report implied that Israeli intelligence might have been behind Kaiser's horrific death, so that they could blame the Muslim population of the Old City. It also claimed, without evidence, that plans were afoot for arrests and house clearances in Jerusalem in response to the murder.

That section of the report was based on the fears of a few residents who had seen more Israeli policemen than usual patrolling Aqabat at-Takiya, but none of that mattered to the readers.

As Henry watched the newsfeed he feared he might not be seeing his wife for quite some time.

36

'What exactly does that mean?' I said.

Simon held the top of his head in his hands.

'There have been developments, Sean. There's a general mobilisation of the Tzahal, our army. The radio this morning said the armour division we call The Steel has been sent to Jericho, near the border with Jordan. It all seems to be connected to what happened in Cairo.'

'What happened in Cairo?' I said.

'You didn't watch the news last night?'

I shook my head.

'Seven policemen died in an explosion at the police head-quarters there. They are blaming us. Can you believe it!' He put his hands high in the air, as if gripping an invisible ball.

'They closed the pyramids and the border. Some people are calling for a general strike there. There is pressure for the Egyptian army to take action against us.'

'What has that got to do with Jordan?'

'Military units are being mobilised everywhere. That is the way things are here. We are surrounded. You must know that.'

'My worry is Isabel. I can't even think about anything else.'

I headed for the apartment door.

As I walked across to the shop I took it slower this time, trying to figure out if I was missing something. Was this really so out of character for her? Hadn't she disappeared for a day in Istanbul?

Sure, we'd been living together since we'd returned from Turkey, but during all that time she'd seemed reluctant to tell me much about her life before I came into it. That couldn't be denied.

I'd put it down to her training. She'd been a mid-level staffer at the British Consulate in Istanbul, which meant she'd had a grounding in what many called *the dark arts*. And from what little she'd told me about it, one of the key things she'd been trained in was how to talk about herself without giving away anything personal.

She'd left the Foreign Office on a generous redundancy package. She'd said she'd had enough of them. But it had crossed my mind that there was other stuff going on that she wasn't telling me about, or couldn't tell me about. My biggest suspicion was to do with Mark. Was there more going on between them that she wasn't telling me?

And there was another conversation I kept thinking about. One of our best researchers at the institute, Will Stone, who I got along well with, had joked that Isabel had probably just gone underground, when I told him about her resigning. He joked that she hadn't resigned at all, she'd just taken up deep cover. We'd laughed into our pints. That laughter echoed inside me now.

I was walking slowly around the outside of the shop as my mind wandered. Then I went inside. She still wasn't there.

I stood at the front of the building looking at the occasional car going by. It was the Sabbath, and the street was quiet, but I was still hoping she might arrive, jumping out of a taxi. I was taking big breaths and holding them in, dampening my panic down.

The thought that I should contact her family crossed my mind.

But I'd only met her family once. We'd had a dinner in London, at Aikens in Chelsea on New Year's Day. It had been a lovely meal, if a little formal.

But what was I going to tell them? Your daughter's been kidnapped?

She'd only been missing an hour.

I walked around the whole block of shops and apartments, and started looking at each doorway for a sign that she might have visited a nearby business. It was possible, wasn't it? Maybe she'd needed a doctor?

I checked for alleyways, coffee houses. There weren't any. Then I stood outside Simon's apartment block and considered the possibilities as they raced through my mind.

I felt totally dazed, as if my body wasn't connected to my head. Everything we'd come to Jerusalem to do seemed stupid now, ridiculous. What the hell had I been thinking putting Isabel in danger?

But I also knew that it would have taken a ridiculous effort to force her to stay in London without me. I took a long deep breath.

Was there any possibility she'd gone off somewhere?

There had to be, but it was a slim one. She would have told me if she had to go, wouldn't she?

No, I couldn't hide from it anymore. I had to accept there was a reasonable chance she'd been kidnapped.

The word buzzed in my head. Kidnapped! Like Susan had been! Like Kaiser had been! The drumming in my chest was faster now.

My legs wanted to move. I had a sudden desire to run up the street, shouting Isabel's name.

Then I thought of Susan; her body hadn't turned up, which meant that whoever was holding her probably hadn't murdered her. Yet.

And then I remembered how Kaiser had died; in a ball of flames after being cruelly tortured.

The thought of anything like that happening to Isabel made a trembling shudder pass through me, like a stuttering engine. There was acid in my mouth. I had to stop this.

'Are you okay?' It was Jeremiah's voice.

I straightened. He was standing a foot away, a concerned look on his face, his hand reaching out to me.

'I think my girlfriend's been kidnapped.'

He shook his head sympathetically. 'You must go to the police. You must go straight away. They are good at their job.' He bent towards me, his black curls dangling in front of him.

'I am sure you will find her.' He stretched out his hand further. I took it, gripped it, even though I knew he was just trying to placate me. His fingers were cold, but they had the strength of steel wire.

I nodded. Then he was gone.

Could I go to the police?

Could I expect proper help from them if I didn't tell them everything, in particular about the dig in the Old City and why I was suspicious of the Heaven's Legion? And they'd probably arrest me, throw me in a cell for God only knew how long.

I took another breath. Maybe none of that mattered. Maybe the police would be better at finding her. That had to be a possibility.

All that mattered was getting Isabel back.

My phone was ringing. My heart flipped. Blood rushed through me. Was it Isabel? As the phone came to my mouth, I saw it was a UK number.

Was this something to do with Isabel's disappearance?

'Hello?' The line crackled.

'Is that you, Sean?' It was her step-mother. My heart headed down.

'Yes,' I replied. A wave of dread washing up inside me. What was I going to tell her?

'Where's Isabel?' She said it cautiously.

I could sense the hope in her voice, that I'd say *hold on* and pass the phone to Isabel.

'I don't know.' There was a pause. I could sense it filling with expectation.

'What do you mean?' There was a shard of tension in her tone.

I'd felt echoes of it before, as if it was related to questions about who the hell I was, and why the hell had Isabel fixed on me for her attentions.

I explained, slowly, what had happened.

She repeated my words with added shock as if for the benefit of someone else listening in to the call at her end. There was a crack in her voice as she spoke. I stifled a rush of emotion.

Another voice came on the line. It was Isabel's father, Arthur. My face was heating up again. A bead of sweat ran down my cheek. I rubbed it away.

'This is not good, Sean,' said Arthur. His tone had a crack in it too.

'When did you last see her?' He said it fast, as if trying to take command of the situation.

I explained again about what had happened that morning. I spoke slowly, for myself too, as if my mind needed to hear it all again to take it in.

'Have you called the police?'

I hesitated, then said, 'I will.'

'You must tell them, straight away.' I'd rarely heard such quick anger.

213

In the background I heard Isabel's step-mother say, 'You're not well, Arthur. Don't upset yourself.'

I could tell he was holding himself back from the quiver in his voice as he spoke.

'If you don't call the Israeli police at once we will tell the Foreign Office what's going on. Actually, I will call them anyway. You are in Israel, that's right, isn't it? In Jerusalem?'

'Yes,' I said.

He coughed, as if he was ill. 'That was what Isabel told me last night, when she rang. She said there was something strange going on. What was she talking about?' He got it all out, then coughed again.

I felt guilty now and in shock. That explained who Isabel had been calling last night.

'Dr Susan Hunter is missing too,' I said.

He ignored what I'd said. 'Isabel doesn't call us often.' He hesitated. A stifled humming noise, as if he was holding his emotions back, came over the line.

'Not recently anyway,' he went on.

That was a dig at me living with Isabel.

'But we are very close, despite all that. If anything happens to her, you might as well come and kill me. Do you understand?' He sucked in his breath.

'I will do everything I can to find her. I will not leave here until I do. I promise you.'

'I know, dear.' It was her step-mother's voice again. It sounded firm this time, as if she was putting a brave face on things.

'When Isabel told us you had moved in with her, I knew you'd treat her well. She told me what had happened to you, about your wife dying in Afghanistan.' She stopped. I sensed it was almost from embarrassment; that she felt she was intruding.

'She wanted to get out of the Foreign Office, and if you helped her do that we are grateful.' She paused.

The phone felt heavy, hot, in my hand. I heard someone blowing their nose in the background.

'Please bring her back home. Please.'

'I would die for Isabel Mrs Sharp. She means the world to me. Everything.' My voice cracked. I pressed my lips together. My hand was in a fist. Anger and fear welled up inside me like poisons.

'Just find her.' She cut the line. No doubt they would call the Foreign Office and there'd be an investigation. It was what I would do. Would they call Mark too, to see if he knew anything about his ex-wife's disappearance? That had to be likely, didn't it?

I should call him.

I made it back to Simon's. My head was spinning. I willed myself to calm down, to think. He was all concern. He wanted me to call the police as well. I said I would. I went to the bedroom we'd used, looking for Isabel's phone. When I turned it on, it wanted a password. I tried to remember it. She'd told me it.

What the hell was it? I could feel it, like a shadow in my brain. Was it 1906? 1909? 1919! That was it.

I was in. I looked up Mark's number.

He answered the phone after two rings. It sounded as if he was expecting to hear Isabel's voice.

I explained quickly what had happened. He had to ask me twice what part of Jerusalem we were in. My brain had thoughts spinning around in it.

'I bloody well told you not to go back there,' he shouted when I was finished. 'Who's this guy you're staying with?'

I told him.

'I'll be in Jerusalem at six this evening. Don't do anything stupid.'

'Thanks for the advice, Einstein. I'll keep it in mind.'

'What are you going to do today?'

'We were going to go to that dig in the Old City, see if we could snap any of the people there, maybe show the pictures to you to see if you can find out anything about them.'

'You still think they're connected to what's going on?'

'Yes, and I think I should go there. Get as many pictures as I can. It's the only lead I have.'

'Well get clear ones, please. They are Christians on that dig, yes?'

'Yes,' I said.

'They may have a few people working today, especially if they're on a limited licence, but don't expect the full complement. It's definitely not in the Jewish quarter this dig, is it?'

'No, it's in the Christian quarter.'

'Some of that area will still be closed today.'

A gust of wind rattled the window. Something sparkled on the glass. Was it fine sand from the desert? Was this normal?

'How are you getting here? I thought the border was closed? There were a lot of tanks rumbling down the streets here last night.'

'They've closed the crossing, but embassy staff can still get through,' said Mark. 'I'll be there at six.'

'Okay.'

'Do you trust that man you're staying with?' he said.

'I do. He's helped us a lot.'

There was silence on the other end of the line. I could imagine a sceptical expression on Mark's face.

I heard a noise and turned around. Simon was standing behind me. He had a gun in his hand. It was pointing at me.

37

Susan Hunter opened her eyes. All she could see was a thin glimmer of light. It came from the side of the trapdoor at the top of the stairs. But it was a beacon. She'd positioned herself directly below the stairs the previous day, at least she thought it was yesterday. She wasn't a hundred percent sure of the passage of time anymore.

She could tell when he turned the lights off in the house up above, and whether it was day or night by the dimness of the thin glimmer, but that wasn't enough to tell if a full day had passed.

She couldn't hear any noises from up above. No distant TV or banging sounds. Could he have gone out? Fear tightened inside her. If something happened to him, if he died in a freak accident, would she starve to death down here?

She took the sliver of rock from her jeans pocket. They felt like a dirty dishrag around her.

The sliver was the size of half a thumbnail. She'd found it in the far corner of the stone-walled basement. It felt good between her fingers. It was her key to get out of the place. Her key to escape.

The big question was, when should she use it?

The last time he'd been down with her food, she'd asked, in as calm a voice as she could muster, why he was doing all this.

'The change is coming,' he'd shouted at her. Then he'd laughed.

Now she was on her knees. It was easier to crawl than to walk. And it was easier to be quiet too when she was on all fours. If he had a microphone in the room and was listening for any noises she might make, there would be almost none to pick up when she was on her knees.

She felt like an animal as she went slowly up the stairs. She could smell things now, like an animal, which she would never have smelt before. The wood of the stairs under her hands smelt resinous. The plaster on the wall near the top smelt like bread. She'd imagined eating it a couple of times, when he'd seemed late with the food, but she'd managed to resist, so far.

When she reached the platform at the top of the stairs she leaned up, put her eye to the crack in the edge of the trap-door. She could just about see into the kitchen of the house above. It wasn't a great view. She could see the thick legs of a wooden table, a red tiled wall stretching away, and the side of a brown sack. But it was enough. It was a view of the world.

She stuck her tongue out. She could taste normal air. And there was something on the breeze coming through to her too. A taste of food. A taste of eggs and something else, olives!

Her tongue darted out. She couldn't help it. She licked the trapdoor with the side of it. It tasted of sand.

Then there was a noise. A shout! An explosion of voices. She pushed back. She was only halfway down the stairs when the trapdoor above opened and a wall of light came crashing into her eyes. She put her hand up.

'You should have stayed down below!'

She waited, head down.

He'd hit her before she could think too much about what might be coming. Stars flew through her head. Then he pushed her and she fell down, stumbling, to the rough earth floor. Everything was spinning.

Then she heard it.

A groan. She opened her eyes, blinking. There was someone else here! A woman.

She looked up. He was standing on the stairs above them. He had a knife in his hands. It was long, shiny, as big as any she'd ever seen. He sliced it through the air, practising using it.

'Get ready,' he said, looking down at them. 'There's something I want you to do.'

She hadn't wished for death before, but now she did.

38

Simon's gun was old, a dull black. It had scratches along its top edge, but it looked as if it would do the business.

'What the hell?' I said loudly. I wasn't thinking about my own life at that point. I wanted to go back in time, just a few hours, and wake up again with Isabel near me this time. I wanted for all this not to be happening.

'We may need it,' said Simon. He pointed the gun downwards, as if he'd only just realised it had been pointing at me.

He put his other hand out in front of him. In it was a small cardboard box with a line drawing of bullets printed on top.

He put the bullets back in the pocket of his cargo pants. 'What's your plan?' he said.

Should I trust him? But who else had helped me here?

'I have to go into the Old City. I think the guys at that dig are involved in all of this.' I let my breath out slowly. 'I'm going to take pictures of the people, if there's anyone there today.'

'You're not going to the police.' It was a statement, rather than a question.

'I'm going to give it twenty-four hours. Most police forces don't even follow up on missing persons before that time.' I'd made a decision while I was talking to Mark. I had to follow up any leads I had myself, then, if there was no other choice, I would go to the police. It was unlikely they would start a major search for her today in any case. I had no evidence that she hadn't decided to just take a break from me.

He stared at me for a few seconds then said, 'I'll come with you.' He put the pistol into a battered leather holster under his arm. It had a faded Star of David in raised brown on its front.

'You were in the military?' I said.

He nodded. 'I was a fresh-faced paratrooper in '67. We stopped the dynamiting of the mosque on the Temple Mount when we took Jerusalem. What a thing we did that day.'

'I read about it,' I replied.

His face changed, as if he was angry. 'They say we made a big mistake.'

I was thinking about Isabel. Had she been threatened, tricked? 'You think we'll need the gun?'

'Maybe. I have a permit. I can take it anywhere I want.' He patted the leather holster.

'Do you want to borrow it?' he said softly. His smile was crooked.

I shook my head. My hands were shaking a little as I ran them through my hair. It wasn't fear. It was frustration. I wanted to do something.

'It's tempting. But if I get arrested with that, they'll probably throw away the key.'

He nodded.

We took a taxi from down the street. It dropped us at the Jaffa Gate. It was midday by the time we got to the cafe on the Via Dolorosa where we'd sat down with Isabel a few days earlier.

Before going in we stopped and looked behind us, to check if anyone was following us. I told Simon we were wasting our time. We'd never spot a professional tail. He kept going with the pretence, looking at his watch as if he was waiting for someone.

We'd left a message on the wall by the door to Simon's apartment, just in case Isabel went back there. It was a piece of paper behind a pipe, and it simply said *call me*. And it had my name and number on it.

I didn't care about releasing my number to potential strangers. Let them have it. But my phone didn't ring.

As soon as we were finished with our tail-evasion exercise we took up a position at the cafe not far from the narrow lane leading to the dig entrance. Some of the other cafes were closed. We ordered coffee. I couldn't eat anything. I felt sick, light-headed.

I was hoping that someone on the dig that day would come out for lunch, or for something they'd forgotten. They'd have to pass us if they did.

There hadn't been a demonstration on the Via Dolorosa, but the entrance to the lane at that side was still blocked by a now permanent-looking steel barrier. It must have been ten feet high, at least.

Walls of desert-tinged sandstone rose high above us. Only distant grilled windows broke the cliff face of the walls. This was the environment that secret Crusader organisations were born in, where Ottoman conspirators connived and where Franciscan monks pursued century-long agendas.

We were at the edge of the Christian quarter. On the other side of the Via Dolorosa, to the east, was the Muslim quarter. The only giveaway in the thin alley as to where we were was a rough wooden cross high up on a wall, far beyond the reach of prying hands. It was grey and ancient, as if it had been put up there hundreds of years ago.

It probably had. And its significance there was most likely a convoluted story involving pilgrims and suffering.

The cafe faced into the street. It didn't have one of the cream sun awnings that other shops on the marginally grander streets nearby had, but I suppose that was understandable, given the alley it faced onto was barely wide enough for three big men to walk abreast.

The cafe was more of a tourists' rest stop than a restaurant. A radio was playing in a corner and bursts of music and rapid talking could be heard from it. There were four old men in the back listening to the radio. They wore their hair cropped so tightly you could see the bumps on their heads mixed with the spiky grey of their hair.

'What language is that?' I asked Simon. 'It sounds familiar.'

'It's Greek,' said Simon. 'They have a special dialect here. There's a Greek Orthodox hospice nearby.'

The coffee was okay, if a little watery.

Isabel had me spoiled with a smooth coffee blend we bought in the Portobello Road. I thought about our recent Saturday morning shopping trips in that area of London. A pang of fear hit me. It was almost too much to bear, only two years after Irene had been murdered.

I shifted my chair, looking around, stupidly hopeful every moment that I might see her.

'Are you okay?' said Simon.

I nodded, shifted my chair. I had an excellent view of the entrance to the lane where the dig was happening now.

We were two rows back from the small plate glass window of the cafe.

Occasionally, someone exited or went into the alley opposite, but no one I recognised. And then, at 12:50 p.m., Dieter, one of the friendly Germans appeared.

He was hurrying directly towards us.

Attracted by a tombstone headline saying WAR in big black letters, I'd bought a Herald Tribune at a news-stand near the Jaffa gate. But I hadn't been able to read more than the first paragraph of the story. My mind was elsewhere.

I lifted the paper in front of my face now as Dieter walked towards us. For a stomach-turning moment I imagined him coming in and sitting near us. How long would I be able to keep up the charade of interest in this newspaper?

'He's gone,' said Simon. He'd been studying the menu, as if it was a map to the Holy Grail.

'I'm going to follow him, get a picture of his face,' I said. 'Wait here.' I raced out of the cafe, my heart pounding. Would he spot me?

I was twenty yards behind Dieter and had to slow down not to catch up with him. He turned a corner. I ran to get to it, then slowed again as I realised people were turning to stare at me. When I rounded the corner he'd disappeared. I was sweating, all clammy inside my clothes.

Had I lost him? Was this all a stupid distraction? Then I spotted the shop a little further along. It was down two steps from the road and had bottles of water piled at the door. Was he in there?

I took my phone out, kept it to my face as I neared the door of the shop. It would be better if he didn't see me, but I'd survive if he did. He wouldn't be able to hold me. I just had to be ready. I went onto the balls of my feet.

And there he was, at the counter at the far end of the shop. As he turned, his eyes down on his change, I snapped. It was enough. I walked on. There was another cross on the wall high above. I faced it, my back to the shop and snapped again. I kept taking pictures like an avid tourist, fascinated by the wall and the cross.

Actually, I was waiting for a hand on my shoulder. The

sweat was drying on my forehead and my back. And then something tap-tapped at my arm.

I jumped inside.

Was it the police, or Dieter?

But it wasn't either of them.

It was a boy no more than ten years old. His head was close shaven, brown from the sun. He shook it, motioned at the cross above us and wagged his finger. He looked worried.

'No photo,' he whispered, in a lilting accent.

A few feet away a small woman with a black shawl around her head and a black wooden cross dangling at her chest said something loudly I didn't understand. The boy turned and was gone. Dieter was nowhere to be seen. I guessed he'd got what he was looking for and had gone back to the dig. When I arrived back at the cafe Simon waved me over excitedly.

'You missed it,' he said. He put a hand out towards me as I sat down.

'Missed what?'

He pointed to the old men at the back. They were talking hurriedly and were in a sort of huddle, an angry huddle. You could tell from the grim faces that turned to me occasionally.

'Your friend, Dr Susan Hunter, she was on the radio. It came on in English! It was a recording of her talking. It's causing a sensation.' He waved towards the men at the back of the room.

'They all started shouting,' he said.

Just then a wailing broke out. It was the sound of an air raid warning. I'd heard something similar once on an RAF base in Essex but this one was wailing faster and the noise was coming from multiple directions.

Simon's eyes flickered one way then the other, then he bent towards me, beckoning me to lean close.

'This is not good,' he said. 'I haven't heard those sirens in a long time.'

39

It was three o'clock in London. Henry had phoned his wife to tell her to go shopping without him.

He was looking at a report on his screen. It was about Lord Bidoner.

He hadn't sent a notice to his colleagues in electronic data gathering to downgrade the surveillance on Bidoner. He planned to do that on Monday. And if anything threatening national security in the United Kingdom emerged regarding Bidoner between now and then, he wouldn't have to downgrade at all.

That would suit him just fine.

Could this report be enough? It was about Lord Bidoner's commercial interests. It noted that he sat on the board of The Ebony Dragon Hedge Fund. There was nothing illegal about that. Ebony Dragon was one of the largest hedge funds in the world.

What was worrying though, was the recent positions the fund had taken in a range of firms associated with Israel. The Israeli stock market was opening as usual on Sunday morning at 9 a.m. local time, 7 a.m. in London. The head of the Israeli Securities Authority had, the day before, placed a request to the financial directors of three major firms likely to do well in times of war, to explain why they had recently issued billions in new share capital.

An out-of-hours buy-up of defence stocks on Wall Street was underway too.

The Israeli Securities Authority email had been intercepted and the link with Ebony as the main new investor had been identified by the automated electronic data gathering system.

It looked very much, to an objective outsider, as if Ebony was building a position that would surge in value if a war took place involving Israel. Each of the firms identified would benefit from immediate major orders from the Israeli defence forces in the event of a conflict, and immediate stock market share spikes, which could be capitalised on.

Would Ebony sell out when their investment doubled? Would they make billions in days?

He closed the document and tagged it.

Proving what he'd just theorised was going to be the difficult part. The very difficult part. Exposing how investors could profit from war would create a scandal. Leaking the details of what he'd found out had to be considered. Henry looked up the contact details of a journalist who'd appreciate this sort of tip off. Then he phoned Sergeant Finch.

40

'I missed the beginning of what she said, but I heard the last bit clearly.' Simon shook his head, as if he still didn't believe it.

'What did she say? Where the hell has she been for the last ten days?' I said.

'The audio was from a YouTube video put up last night. That's what they said after it all played out. They didn't say where the recording was made. But they did say she was still missing.' He looked sorrowful.

I took a long deep breath. It was good Susan was alive; that she was sending out messages. It meant Isabel might well be alive too. One of the knots inside me loosened a little.

'What did she say?' I was talking slowly.

'She said she'd translated a letter from the first caliph. She said it claimed the transfer of Jerusalem for all eternity into the hands of Islam.'

He raised his eyes to heaven, glanced at the old men. One of them was gesticulating, his hands sweeping through the air.

I sat back. Great. Publicising such a claim was just about the last thing anyone needed in a city on the edge of a cliff.

'Surely it won't be taken seriously, some ancient claim on Jerusalem from over a thousand years ago? No one will give a damn in a few days' time.' I was hoping he'd agree.

Simon shook his head vigorously. 'Every proof of legitimacy for one side or the other here is like winning the world series or the world cup for whoever finds it. If us Jews say an ancient scroll talks about us in Jerusalem, it's taken as proof of our right to own this city. And the other side do the same for any evidence they find.'

He glanced up as a young woman came into the cafe. She was different to most people I'd seen in the city. She wore a leopard pattern coat and high heeled boots and her hair was long and bright yellow.

Simon turned back to me. 'You'd be surprised how people try to take our historical legitimacy away, to minimise how long Jews have lived here, or claim we were different back then to who we are now. The lies would amaze you.'

He leaned close again. 'All this madness about a letter looks like an attempt to stir up the Arab street to me. How come such a find has never been publicised before, eh? And how would such a document have survived? No, no, it's a forgery. It has to be. There's a long, evil tradition of this sort of thing.'

'What do the Palestinians make of it?'

His head went down. He stared at the table. 'They are celebrating in Ramallah and Nablus. There's talk of a march on Jerusalem.'

I sipped from the plastic bottle of water I'd ordered with my coffee. Was all this trouble brewing because of the manuscript Isabel and I had found under Hagia Sophia in Istanbul?

'I know where the letter came from,' I said.

I told him about the manuscript, how we'd found it in an underground tunnel in the old part of Istanbul.

'It could still be a fake,' he said. 'Or Susan Hunter could

be twisting the translation after getting her own arm twisted.' He gestured in the air, as if he was wringing a wet rag.

'They better not twist Isabel's arm,' I said.

'I hope not,' said Simon. He put a hand to his forehead and held it.

'You know, I don't believe they've found a room full of Pontius Pilate-era documents over there.' He pointed over his shoulder with his thumb. 'It's all far too good to be true.'

'They looked pretty authentic to me.'

'Looked is the right word. It wouldn't have taken a genius to tunnel under that building.' He made a forward sweeping motion with his hand. 'Then stuff it full of fake documents. Do you have any idea how much all that will be worth in research grants?'

I shook my head, looked over Simon's shoulder. There was still an animated conversation going on at the back of the cafe.

'It could all be a scam. It wouldn't be the first time such a thing has happened in this city.' He banged his palm on the table. I leaned back.

'Point your phone at the door,' he said. 'Take some pictures, but don't turn your head.'

My phone was on the table. I put my hand on it, turned it on its side edge, angling it towards the door. I moved it until I saw the door in the screen. Outside was a big man with a white beard and hair. It was Pastor Stevson. He was looking down the street. I pressed to start recording.

Was there any other way out of this place? I glanced towards the back of the cafe. As I did, the woman with the blonde hair brushed past me. She was heading for the front door.

Then I remembered Simon's gun. Maybe we could use it to force a getaway.

'Holy cow,' said Simon.

230

That was it. I couldn't resist. I had to turn my head. What I saw made my mouth open wide. Pastor Stevson had his arm around the blonde. He was leading her away. I watched, mesmerised, as they went out of view. He looked like an old man with a deficit in self-awareness entertaining a very young friend.

'Did you get him?' said Simon.

I turned the screen towards him. It was playing a recording of the good pastor side-on, then putting his arm around the woman when she came out. I had a picture of Dieter, and of the pastor now. I attached the files, one at a time, to text messages and texted both of them to Mark's number.

As the last message finished sending I got a text back almost instantly.

ARRIVED EARLY WHERE R U?

It was from Mark.

IN THE OLD CITY & U?, I replied

AT THE TAXI RANK BY JAFFA GATE MEET HERE 15.

'What's going on?' said Simon.

'I've got to go,' I said. 'I have to meet someone.'

'You don't need me anymore?'

'I'll need somewhere to stay tonight. Can I come back later? Our flight's booked for tomorrow evening. But I won't take it unless I find Isabel.'

'I hope you do.'

He tapped his left side. I couldn't see his holster, it was under a brown leather jacket, but I knew it was there. 'Do you want this?'

I shook my head. We stood, hugged.

When I got to the Jaffa Gate, three army Land Rovers were blocking the road completely. They were sand-coloured and had large black radiator grilles and orange lights flashing on their roofs. Pedestrians were being forced to go through a narrow gap to the right of the vehicles to get out of the Old City.

231

There was a queue of people waiting to go through the gap. In the middle of it the Israeli police were checking people. Standing in line in font of me was a monk in a rough brown robe. It was what you would have seen his ancestors wearing two thousand years ago. His face was impassive as he waited, as if he'd seen this sort of thing before, many times.

When it was my turn, I was confronted by a young female police officer. Beside her there was a male officer with close cropped black hair. There were policemen in helmets behind them.

I was asked why I was in the Old City and to show my identification. Then I was let through. It had all been relatively easy.

It was twenty minutes after Mark had text me when I finally arrived at the taxi rank. There were no taxis there and Mark wasn't there either. I walked around in the shadow of the Old City walls. It was half past twelve now. The sky above the city was filled with dirty grey clouds. It felt cooler and it seemed as if it might rain.

My phone buzzed. It was a message from Mark. I was to go through the gate and go down the road to the left.

I walked down to a set of traffic lights. Pulled up near them, half on the verge, was a white Range Rover. It reminded me of the one belonging to the British Embassy, which Isabel had been driving in Istanbul when we met.

As I came close to it a window at the front went down. 'Let's go, Sean,' Mark shouted at me.

I didn't like his attitude, but I got in the back. He was sitting next to a driver.

'Belt up,' he said. 'We've an idea where your friend Susan is or at least where her phone is.' The Range Rover engine started. We turned 180 degrees and merged with the traffic heading away from the Old City.

'Did you identify the people in those pictures?' I asked.

'We're working on it,' he said.

'Maybe whoever has Susan has Isabel as well?' I leaned forward between the seats.

He shrugged. 'Maybe.'

The driver turned, giving me a stern look.

'Sit back, sir, put your seat belt on.'

I got the impression he wasn't happy with me being there. Maybe it was because I was a civilian or maybe he just didn't like the look of me. I suppose I didn't look too smart with my creased clothes and messed up hair.

I didn't care.

'Why the hell didn't you keep an eye on her?' said Mark. He kept staring out the front, but it was obvious he was talking to me.

'Don't try to dump this on me.' I pointed a finger at him.

'I told you coming back here was a bad idea.'

I didn't bother to respond to that. I took deep breaths. I wasn't going to get his help by fighting with him.

He handed me a bottle of water. 'Have you eaten?' he said.

I shook my head. 'I'm not hungry. The only thing I'm interested in is finding Isabel.'

I sat back and looked out the side window. It had started raining. If we did find Isabel would she be okay? Visions of the worst nightmares you could imagine came to my mind. I gripped the edge of the leather seat until I was afraid I was going to tear it. I wanted to break something. Outside, rain had started coming down, as if it was Noah's time.

I saw a woman walking at the side of the road. She looked like the woman who had stopped me in the car park of the university a few days before. She was holding an umbrella. She glanced at me as she passed. A memory came back of Irene's funeral in Oxford. Was that where I'd seen that woman from the car park? So many people had turned up that day.

233

I remembered a group had come running up the gravel drive to St. Clements, where we'd held the service. It had been raining. Most people had been holding umbrellas. I'd been standing outside, sheltering under the porch. They'd all shaken my hand, offered me condolences. I'd been in a daze. I hadn't wanted to go in. I hadn't wanted it all to be real, for that day to exist. A stream of memories came rushing back.

A wave of emotion rose up inside me. I hadn't thought about Irene's funeral in a long time.

Would we be holding a funeral for Isabel too?

I closed my eyes, said a prayer. My sweat felt cold on my skin as I stared out into the rain.

Soon after, we were on a highway with signs in Hebrew, English and Arabic. We didn't stay on it long. We passed through a village with modern shops, bright plastic signs and old stone walls that looked straight out of the Bible.

We pulled into a petrol station. Mark had been on his phone for a while, listening mostly, but he'd also watched something on the screen of it. I couldn't see what it was.

'We're going to fill up,' he said without turning to me.

When we'd finished, the driver pulled our Land Rover into a parking bay beside a red Toyota Land Cruiser.

He parked so close you couldn't have put a hand between the two vehicles. The window of the Land Cruiser went down.

Xena was in the driving seat. Her hair was in ridges ending in tails with black beads at their ends, which hung at the side of her face. She was wearing a high-necked puffy black jacket. She scowled when she saw me and said something quickly to Mark that I didn't catch. He was in the seat that was nearest to her. His window was down too.

'What's going on?' I said.

Mark spoke without turning.

'We'll leave you here, Sean. Sorry about that. We'll be back

234

in a few hours.' He sounded calm, as if he knew what my reaction would be, but didn't care.

'No way,' I said, my voice rising quickly. 'You're not dumping me here. Forget it! Don't try that crap with me!' I was shouting. I didn't care.

41

There was a stone inside her chest. A stone made of fear. She was doing her best not to think about it.

It seemed as if Susan had been moaning for weeks, but it couldn't have been more than a day since Isabel had been ordered to the top of the stairs to collect her. The trap door had only opened for a few seconds and Susan had been pushed down, clutching her head, groaning as if she was dying.

Isabel could only surmise what the bastard had done from the faint smell of burnt flesh, Susan's moaning, and the way she held her head constantly.

She'd tried, by touch, to figure out the extent of Susan's injury, but all she had done was to make Susan scream when her hands went near Susan's eyes.

And then the word came out. 'George.'

'What about George?' said Isabel.

'They murdered him. The bastards. They murdered him.' There were more sobs.

Isabel held Susan close, soothing her. After another minute she spoke again, more clearly this time.

'He said my husband would be killed if I didn't cooperate.

He showed me a picture of George sleeping in our bed with a knife in front of his face. I did what I was asked! I did it all! I spoke the words he wanted. Everything. Then he told me George was already dead!' She sobbed.

'And then he came at me.' She wailed.

It was a sickening sound. The sound of a wounded animal.

'Shhhh,' said Isabel. 'Don't bring him down on us.'

'But I can't see!' wailed Susan.

'Why is he doing this?' Isabel's words came out in a sob.

'He is evil,' said Susan emphatically.

'You will survive,' said Isabel, trying to find some hope for them both. 'We're going to get out of this.'

Hope was not easy to conjure at that moment. From the second he'd grabbed her, pulling her into his white van as she'd fallen unconscious with that cloth over her mouth, her struggles quickly fading, everything had changed.

And now she was almost totally powerless. And that made her body shake. She couldn't believe what had happened. Come on, Sean, she thought. Don't leave me here.

Now it was Susan's turn to hug Isabel.

42

'Don't play silly buggers, Sean. You're staying here. There's a coffee shop in the petrol station.' Mark pointed at it.

'Kick me out here.' I waved at the petrol station, then pointed a finger at his face. 'And I'll call the police and report what you're up to. I don't care what they do to me.'

I scanned the cars around us. There weren't any police cars, but there was a private ambulance with a blue roof sign parked by the shop.

'I'm sure they've got a radio in that ambulance. They could probably get the police here in minutes. All I'll have to do is give them your number plate and your little plan goes up in smoke.'

Mark shook his head. 'You do know you'll end up in a cell for months for breaking Israeli immigration laws?'

I put my hand on the door. 'I told you, I don't care.'

Xena's voice interrupted from the other car. 'Let him come.'

Mark and the driver exchanged glances. I saw a look of resignation pass between them.

'Okay, but don't blame me if you get your todger shot

238

off,' said Mark. Then he turned to Xena, leaned towards her and said something.

The windows between the two cars rolled up. We reversed off.

Ten minutes later, we were driving down a narrow road with a steep gully on one side. Xena's car was following. We were in a valley. There was a long ridge on the left. It was covered with tall dark green cypress, pine and the occasional tall palm tree, interspersed between flat-roofed cream-coloured apartment buildings. It was still raining.

We turned, passing slowly through a rundown-looking village. One of the bare, cheap-looking cafes had a blue plastic sign above its door. It read *Abu Ghosh Café*.

One of the two shops in the village was closed. There were parked cars everywhere and thin metal pylons holding up wires that criss-crossed above us. There were half-built houses beyond the cafe and two dirty flatbed lorries parked outside.

We took a narrow twisting road out of the village and headed up a hill so steep I thought our vehicle wouldn't make it. The incline had to be sixty degrees or more. There were rough sandstone walls on either side with houses beyond them. Two dogs barked at us excitedly as we passed. There was no other traffic.

The road turned a corner and flattened out. In front of us were red and white striped barrels. We drove up slowly towards the road block. To the left there was a narrow lane. We turned into it. Xena's Land Cruiser was still behind us.

'The prophet Jeremiah was born in this area,' said Mark.

I didn't say anything. I didn't care if the Queen of Sheeba's family still lived here.

The road was no more than a lane now, with pine trees beyond.

'I looked this place up,' said Mark. 'This is where King David kept the Ark of the Covenant, before he moved it to the Temple Mount in Jerusalem.'

'Do we have far to go?' I said.

'No,' said Mark.

After another minute of slow driving we pulled over. The wall on our left was set back from the lane here, and there was a dusty area where we could park. Xena pulled up near us.

'What's the plan?' I said.

'We're going to pay somebody a friendly visit.'

Before we got out of the car, Mark pointed at the GPS screen and said something to the driver that I didn't catch. The driver didn't reply.

Five minutes later the four of us were walking along the lane. The sandstone walls were about head height on either side. I can only assume that we had left the vehicles so we wouldn't be heard approaching where we were going.

I wanted to walk faster, but Mark made a gesture for me to calm down. Their pace was agonisingly laid-back, almost as if we were all on a Sunday stroll.

We passed an old fashioned wooden gate, then a modern-looking one.

The rain had stopped, but the sky above was heavy with clouds. They had settled over the landscape like a blight. There was an earthy smell in the air too, as if the rain had exposed something.

Then, at a spot where the stone wall on the left was broken, our driver stepped over the wall and headed off, without any discussion. We walked on.

'Where's he gone?' I asked.

'He'll watch the back of the target house, just in case anyone tries to make a run for it.'

'Are you expecting trouble?'

'We're prepared for it, let's just say that.' Mark opened his jacket and turned to me. I saw a black holster. It was bigger than Simon's and more modern-looking.

'Do you think Susan and Isabel might be here?'

'Maybe. This is the best lead we have.'

'You have others?'

He shook his head. 'Not really. The Israelis have been checking security camera footage from the area Susan was taken, but they haven't come up with anything yet. This is our best bet.'

I was getting more anxious by the second. I wanted to rush to wherever we were going, break doors down, search for Isabel.

A minute later, we came to a gap in the lane to our left where the wall was set back. In the centre of the gap there was a tall set of gates with curls of barbed wire above them. The gates had animal heads, a goat and a snake and an eagle, embossed on them.

In front of the gate was a policeman in a navy blue uniform. Were we too late? Had the place already been raided?

As we neared the policeman Mark said, 'Sean, meet my old friend, Ariel, from the Israeli Immigration Police.' I held out my hand. Ariel shook it. He had a firm grip.

'We might as well do this now, Sean.' Mark pointed at Ariel. 'Tell my friend about your suspicion that an illegal immigrant is holed up here.' He pointed towards the gates.

I stared at him. 'What?'

Mark sighed. 'Come on, tell him you think Isabel is in here,' he said, in an exasperated tone.

I did as I was asked. The policeman took a black leather-covered notebook out of his pocket, checked his watch, a big old fashioned steel thing, and wrote something in the notebook.

'Under the powers invested in me by the Entry into Israel

Law 5763 I will now enter these premises,' said the policeman in a low voice, as he put his notebook back in his pocket. He went over to the wall beside the gate, it was five foot high, and pulled himself up onto it surprisingly quickly. From the top he looked back at us. 'I'll need some witnesses,' he said.

He grinned at us for a moment, as if he was enjoying himself, then he dropped down to the other side.

Xena and Mark followed him over the wall. I was right behind them. On the far side it looked as if we'd gone back in time. Stretching ahead of us was a stone path with palm trees on either side. Their trunks must have been five feet thick, at least. They looked ancient. Their crowns met about fifty feet above us.

The path curved away up the hill. We were walking fast, almost running. As we came to a bend the policeman turned and said, 'Go to the right, Mark. You others stay here, then follow me in twenty minutes if you haven't heard any gunfire.'

I knew all about taking orders. But I also knew about bending them. The policeman was gone only a minute when I walked slowly forward, following him. Xena, who was being very quiet, walked beside me.

As we turned the corner we came into a clearing. There was a two-storey building in front of us. Its walls were made of roughly shaped stones. Ariel was at the front door of the building.

The building had small windows with rusted iron bars in a grid protecting them. Its roof was flat. Wooden beams protruded on the left side. A veranda ran beneath them. Bushes and trees came close to the house, almost protectively.

A big white Toyota van sat in the driveway. It was covered in dust. We were in the right place. I could feel it. This was exactly the type of vehicle that could have been used to kidnap Isabel and Susan.

We were going to find them.

We were going to find Isabel.

Anticipation rose inside me. I walked forward quickly, half running.

I was going to find the bastard who'd taken her. If he'd done anything to her, anything at all, he was going to suffer.

A video of Isabel had been playing in my mind over and over since she'd disappeared. A memory of her smiling, laughing. I could feel the warmth from it, and a longing to see her. After the cold years grieving for Irene I wasn't going to give her up. Ever.

I came up towards Ariel at the front door of the building. The door was wooden and had iron rivets in a circular pattern in its centre. It looked a thousand years old at least. Ariel pressed a brass bell at the side of the door as I arrived.

Then he turned to us. He didn't look surprised. All he did was shake his head, as if only mildly disappointed.

'I told you to wait,' he said, softly.

'Isabel might be in there. You can't stop me coming.'

'If you get shot, Mr Ryan, it's your responsibility. Do you understand?'

I nodded. He turned back to the door. 'And we don't have time for any arguments.' He knocked on the door with his knuckles and stepped to the side.

'There's probably a back door,' said Xena. 'I'll have a look.'

Ariel had his pistol out of its holster. It was a small, black mini UZI. I waited on the other side of the door. There was a giant pot with a spiky cactus behind me.

'To hell with this,' I said.

I reached for the door handle, turned it, pushed at the door. It stayed closed.

'Shoot the bloody lock off,' I said. 'Go on. Shoot it. Or I'm going to find something to break it with. If there's anyone in there, they know we're out here. They might be cutting Isabel's throat right now, burning her.'

'Stand back,' he said.

I moved away from the door.

'Further.'

I moved again. He pointed his gun at the lock. He was on my side of the door now. Any ricochets would hopefully go off in a different direction.

There was a loud popping noise. It echoed in my ears.

I stepped around him. There was a jagged hole where the lock had been. I pushed at the door. I knew I was putting myself in the line of fire, but I didn't care. I tensed as the door swung open to reveal a narrow corridor. I walked straight in. Ariel was beside me, his gun pointing forward.

'Let's check upstairs first,' said Ariel. 'Stay with me, and don't touch anything.'

There were four rooms on the upper floor. We checked them all, even under the beds, then went downstairs. I knocked over two wooden chairs in my haste. There was no sign of Isabel or anything amiss, except for the fact that there were no clothes or personal items in any of the rooms.

A bed was unmade upstairs and the bathroom upstairs looked as if it had been used recently.

Xena was inside when we got back down. We went in and out of all the rooms. The furniture was dark and heavy and the floors were tiled in red. There was a large sitting room with two heavy sofas and a big LCD TV, a room with only a table in it, and a kitchen at the back of the house with another dining table.

By the time I had finished going in and out of each room the disappointment was sickening.

The only thing that was odd downstairs, which made me think we were in the right place, was a big steel bowl on a tripod at the back of the building. In the bowl, it must have been three feet across, there was a thick pile of ash. I could feel the heat coming from them when I put my hand an inch away from the top of the thick grey crust.

'Stay out here,' said Ariel. He disappeared back into the building.

There was a bad smell coming from the bowl, as if God only knew what had been burnt out here.

Mark had reappeared by this time. He said he'd seen nobody on his travels all around the building. He joined me as I was looking for something to poke the ashes in the bowl with. I found a long white stick, started poking away.

'Not our lucky day,' he said. He was looking through unopened letters, ripping each one, examining the bills inside.

'Who lives here?' I said.

'I don't know. All these bills are more than six months old. They look like they're from a previous occupant.' He put the bills beside a steel bin nearby.

'There are no recent letters at all?' I said.

He shook his head. 'Anything in there?' he said, nodding towards the ashes.

'No.' That was, of course, the moment the stick hit something.

'Maybe.' I poked some more, leaned forward, and pushed the hard thing I'd encountered towards the edge of the bowl.

The heat came up in waves off the ashes.

'What's that?' he said. The ashen, curled edges of what could have been a book had appeared in the bowl. I pushed at it. It was a notebook. The top and bottom of the notebook were clumps of ash, but right in the centre of it, a part of it still hadn't burnt.

'Hold on,' I said.

I put the stick under the notebook, pushed it out of the side of the bowl. It fell in a cloud of ash onto the rough red-tiled floor of the veranda.

'I was thinking we should wait for proper equipment,' said Mark.

'There'll only be a pile of ash soon,' I said.

'There's not much more than that now.'

I bent down and poked at the ragged, ash-edged remains of the notebook. I turned pages. Some were empty. Some had handwriting on them. Many of the words were scrawled out. Whoever had put it in there, hadn't gone long.

Mark bent forward, started sniffing. 'I know that smell,' he said.

He was right. There was a familiar, sickly smell in the air.

'That smells like burning flesh.' He pointed at the steel bowl.

'I remember it from Iraq. I was in a village where every house was burnt. Thirty-two people died. I'll never forget the smell.' His face was twisted, his head shaking from side to side as if he wanted to throw something off.

I held my nose, peered close at the pages, and rifled through them. Some of the writing wasn't in an alphabet I recognised. It was symbols; squares, circles, triangles, moon shapes, wavy lines.

'That looks like a lot of magic bullshit,' said Mark.

'Someone's into some weird stuff,' I said. I took my phone out and took a picture of the ashy remnants of the book. Mark had his phone out too.

He was right beside me. 'The Canaanites were overlords in this area after Nebuchadnezzar destroyed the first Jewish temple. They used symbolic magic to invoke their fire goddess.'

A shiver passed through me. 'I've got a bad feeling about this place.'

'This is a definite connection to what happened to Kaiser.'

'I'm not stupid. I can work things out,' I said.

The idea that Isabel was in the hands of some sick fire worshippers was almost worse than her being missing.

He stepped back. 'We have to find her,' he said, softly.

An edge of a page had caught my attention. I pushed it open quickly with my fingers, The paper was hot. A part of a hand-drawn map was still visible.

'Look.' The edges of the page were smouldering. As I watched, a piece of it burnt away. I took another picture.

It was a map of Jerusalem. I could make out the Tower of David and the Ottoman-era city walls encircling the Old City. There were two spots on the map. They had traces of a waxy substance on them, as if someone had spilled candle wax on the page.

'Those spots are where the Via Dolorosa and the Church of the Holy Sepulchre are.' Mark peered closer at the map. 'They're the most venerated Christian places in Jerusalem.'

'In the world,' I added.

I turned the other pages of the notebook. There were no other drawings or maps on any of them.

'I bet this map is some ceremonial thing,' said Mark. 'There are a lot of superstitions about fire, you know, like blowing out candles and wishing for things.'

'This wasn't used at a birthday party,' I said.

He shrugged, pulled the page with the remaining part of the map from the ashen notebook with one quick tug at its edge. He took a small see-through plastic bag from his pocket and slid the map page into it, sealing it and flattening it with one stroke. Half the Old City was burnt away now on the map.

'Did you see a basement in there?' I said.

'No.'

'What are you guys doing out here?' said Ariel. He had just arrived.

'Checking the barbecue out,' said Mark.

'You should get your forensics to go through all this.' He pointed at the bowl, and at the ashen remains of the notebook on the tiles. 'God only knows what's in there.'

Ariel bent down. His hands didn't stay still for long, I noticed. They were either out in the air, or at his face, or smoothing his hair, or picking dust from his jacket.

'You said you traced a call from here.' He looked at Mark.

'We did.'

'Who was it to?'

There was a tiny hesitation, then Mark said. 'We didn't get that far. The call was encrypted. All I can tell you is it was to someone in London.'

His expression was impassive. He'd have made a good poker player.

'Did you find a basement in there?' I said. I pointed at the villa.

'No,' said Ariel. He turned slowly on his heel taking the whole place in. 'Not yet anyway. But you're right. This sort of farmhouse should have a basement. Maybe the entrance is out here.'

'Why don't we have another look in the kitchen?' said Mark. 'That looked like a new floor in there.'

'Don't disturb anything,' said Ariel.

I walked fast into the kitchen, bent down and started examining the tiled floor. Mark was tapping the walls. I was relieved to be doing something. I was thinking about digging the floor up when I noticed that the floor in the storeroom, at the back of the kitchen, was different. The tiles looked older. Why hadn't they put new tiles in there as well?

There was a seam around the old ones. I bent down, followed the seam to where it ran up against the bare plaster wall. Dust along the wall had piled up recently or something had piled it up.

The seam was wider near the wall too. And it went on under a wooden bench. I moved the bench. The seam was wide enough now for me to see that there was empty space beneath the floor. There was a dark space down there.

This was it. I'd found the basement. My fingers scrabbled at the seam.

'Isabel,' I shouted into the floor. 'Are you down there?'

There was no reply.

I couldn't get a grip on anything. My hands seemed useless. The skin on the tips of my fingers was breaking as I followed the seam in the tiles with my fingers, pushing at it, just to see if there was any way I could get the trapdoor that had to be there open.

I looked around for something to use to lever the trapdoor up. There was nothing. With each passing second the anticipation and desperation I'd been suppressing flowed through me until my fingers were shaking. I pushed the wooden bench further along to see the whole of the seam in the floor.

Then I heard it.

The sound of scratching, as if someone or something was on the other side of the trapdoor, trying to get out.

'Isabel!' I shouted.

43

Sergeant Finch leaned forward, peering at the messages – Tweets, Facebook and blog posts – which were streaming down Henry's main monitor. They were all being translated into English in real time.

'Is the volume still rising?' she said.

'It's doubled in the past three hours,' Henry replied. 'And that's just the Egyptian feed. He pointed at the smaller screen to the right of the main screen.

'The Israeli feed has picked up a lot too.'

Sergeant Finch turned to take in messages flowing down the second screen.

'This is exactly the way things developed in Libya and in Syria before the fighting broke out. Are you getting updates on the operation to find Dr Hunter?'

Henry nodded. 'We're tracking them,' he said.

He pointed at a third screen on which a map showed a blinking dot, a red heartbeat.

'I'm going to come back later. I don't like the look of this,' said Sergeant Finch. 'Call me if anything kicks off.' She tapped the pocket of her puffy black jacket.

'My phone will be on,' she said.

44

I turned. Mark was right behind me. For a moment I thought he was going to interrupt. I was ready to roar at him if he did. I looked back at him only for a second. My hands were shaking as they went along the gap in the floor again. The gap that meant there was something down there.

We were in the right place. I could feel it.

'There's a basement down there,' I said, pointing at the crack in the floor. 'There has to be. I heard scratching.'

Mark leaned towards me. 'Did you see any tools, anything, when you were looking around?'

'No. Sorry. Wait. Maybe there were some garden tools under the stairs. I think I saw a spade.'

He was gone.

I shouted into the seam again. I hadn't heard anymore tapping. Had I imagined it? I ran my fingers all over the floor, the walls, looking for a catch, a button, something. I put my mouth to the gap.

'Isabel!'

There was no answer, and no obvious catch to get the trapdoor open.

Mark arrived with a flat-headed spade and a torch. He

pushed the head of the spade into the crack in the floor. It didn't make any difference. He tried again.

I peered closer at the gap. Then I saw it, a piece of flat steel was holding the trapdoor tight. I looked at the wall beyond it. There was a small tile there. I tried to move it. It came out. There was a catch. I pushed and pulled at the trap door, jamming it hard each way. It lifted. We were in!

'Isabel,' I shouted into the hole as it opened. I saw a wooden platform, stairs going down into dusty gloom.

As I stepped down, the smell hit me.

I'd been hoping that Isabel would be waiting for us on the other side of the trapdoor, perhaps too exhausted to respond to me, but I was wrong.

The agony of bitter disappointment sucked at me as I looked into the bare basement below.

It was big. It could have been as big as the whole floor we were on. And it had been used for holding people. There were plastic bowls and water bottles in a corner. But there was no one down there.

Mark was beside me. He flashed the torch quickly around, lingered on an open doorway that led to a small toilet, a hole in the ground.

There were no bodies here, which was some relief.

Then one of the steel bowls moved and a long shadow flitted across the floor.

A rat!

'Don't go any further.' Ariel's voice. I could feel him behind me. I didn't turn.

'If this place is booby-trapped we're dead already,' I said.

Ariel growled. 'If you told me you were going to bring this klutz with you Mark, I wouldn't have helped you at all.'

Before he had a chance to stop me I stepped onto the stairs, walked down slowly, taking the place in.

I saw things that made me put my fist to my mouth to

stop it shaking. My nostrils flared in and out as I breathed in the dead, stench-tinged air.

There was a trail of blood from the stairs leading to the centre of the rough stone wall on the far side of the basement. And there was pool of it caked there on the floor. Someone had suffered down here. Suffered badly.

A pounding started up deep in my forehead.

Where had they taken her?

I looked up. There was something painted on the wall behind the stain on the floor. It was painted in red.

It was a symbol. A symbol I recognised.

It was the square and arrow from that book we'd found in Istanbul. I was starting to wish I'd never picked it up in that water-filled drain. Maybe none of this would have happened if I hadn't.

'We get a lot of crackpots in Israel,' said Ariel, loudly. 'Some wackos become messianic when they come here. They start pulling all sorts of crazy shit.' He went up close to the wall, sniffed at it, jerked away from it.

'I don't like the smell down here,' he said.

'Jerk offs use this sort of stuff for belief reinforcement. It fires up their warped little brains.'

'What's that?' Mark was pointing at an ancient pillar. There was one at each end of the wall. There was only the base of the pillars visible, standing maybe six inches proud of the stone floor, but they were clearly carved with swirling leaf patterns.

They looked as if they'd been used to form part of the retaining wall of the building.

'There are pillars like those in the Church of the Holy Sepulchre,' said Ariel. 'That could be Crusader-era work.'

'They must have been here when this house was built,' said Mark.

I didn't care. I was examining the walls for a door, a passageway, anything, a clue.

'We'll test these blood stains, see if we can do DNA matching with any traces in your girlfriend's baggage, Mr Ryan. Will you permit us to do that?' said Ariel. He had a small plastic bag in his hand and was puling thin white plastic gloves on.

'Do not touch anything,' he said. His voice was stern.

I wasn't planning to touch anything.

I was finding it hard to breathe.

'Some idiots believe they can summon up demons with stuff like this,' said Ariel.

'Who believes all this garbage?' There was a tremble in my voice.

'This site could have real historical significance,' said Mark. 'The Crusaders picked sites that had been occupied before they took them over.'

He pointed above the symbol. 'Look, there are words up there.'

He was right. They were faint, small, and inscribed in a similar dark red material as the symbol. I walked up close, skirting the stain on the floor. Ariel and Mark had their flashlights pointed at the section of the wall between the top of the symbol and the old wooden beams of the roof.

I could just make out the words *fame ad mortem*. Latin. Familiar. Goddammit, they were the same words that were in that book we'd found.

'Latin was hated in the first century in these parts. It was the demonic language of the Roman oppressors,' said Ariel.

'That looks like an invocation,' said Mark. 'A magic spell.'

'I don't want to hear any of that,' I said. The basement felt cold. A chill was coming up through my feet.

I bent down to the stain on the floor. Maybe this was Isabel's blood. I swallowed some bile that came into my mouth. My hand was pressing into my side. I could feel my blood pounding.

Mark spoke softly. 'Some evil bastard has them, and he's moved them.'

'Evil is right,' I said, looking around.

'Dante had a phrase for this sort of place,' said Ariel. '*Lasciate ogne speranza, voi ch'entrate* – all hope abandon ye who enter here.'

'You must leave,' said a woman's voice from behind us. I turned. It was Xena. She was standing on the stairs. She'd stopped halfway down, as if she didn't want to come all the way.

'Yes, yes. We must go,' said Ariel. He walked quickly toward the stairs, his arms out wide, as if to sweep us all back up.

'Follow me, gentlemen, at once.' His tone made it clear he expected compliance.

I went. I'd been down there long enough.

'We should walk every inch of this farm, make sure we haven't missed anything,' said Mark, as we went back up the stairs.

I was thinking about what Xena had said. It had sounded as if she knew what the basement was used for.

When we reached the veranda I caught up with her. I felt lightheaded, after being in that hellhole.

'Do you know what went on in that basement?'

She shook her head, too fast. 'No.' She looked scared. She walked away, quickly.

Mark called out to me, 'Sean, this way.'

He was walking across the rough ground at the back of the house, heading towards an orchard of thin, bushy carob trees.

I followed him.

It was twenty minutes past six, and dark and cool among the trees. The sun had gone down while we were inside the house. There was no moon visible either, because of the clouds.

I took the torch from Mark and walked ahead of him, stumbling a few times in my rush to check everywhere. My need to find Isabel was pushing me like an arm in the back. My ankle turned at one point and I was in pain for the next few minutes, but I didn't care.

We went on through the trees for about half a mile before we came to a wall made from misshapen sandstone rocks. The wall was six feet high, and there was a dip on this side of it, which made it seem double that height. In the dip there were other bigger stones that would break your ankle if you dropped onto them.

'Oh my God,' said Mark, suddenly.

I turned. The villa was on fire. It was clearly outlined through the woods with a sheet of flame coming from its roof.

We ran back along a rough path we'd found. I was clammy with sweat by the time we reached the end of the trees.

Mark didn't say anything. He just stared. We both stared. I could smell wood and plaster burning. The flames were reaching higher now. I could feel their warmth from fifty feet away. Thick black pieces of soot drifted in the air.

Our driver, Xena and Ariel were standing to our right, like us transfixed by the sight, and well away from the building.

I expected to hear the sound of a fire engine in the distance at any moment. But I heard nothing, only the crackling hum of the fire as it reached its zenith. We walked around towards the others, moving slowly, in a daze.

Anxious thoughts ran through my mind. Were there clues in the house to where Isabel might be which we'd missed?

'What the hell happened?' I shouted. We'd reached the others.

Ariel shrugged. Xena was just staring. 'I didn't see anyone else,' said the driver. He put his hands up, as if he was going to restrain me. 'Don't go near the building, sir.'

'You must know what happened,' I said. I was standing between Ariel and the house.

'Maybe it was booby-trapped after all,' he said. He looked me in the eyes. 'If you hadn't gone rushing into the basement I might have had time to check it properly.' He was angry.

'That's bullshit. A booby trap goes off straight away.'

'Fires start from nothing in a place like that,' said Xena. I turned to her.

'Don't feed me superstitious crap,' I said. 'I'm allergic to it.'

'We have to go,' said Ariel. 'The local police will be here soon. I can't keep them away.'

Mark's phone buzzed. It had a weird ringtone, more like an alarm clock than a phone.

He walked off into the trees as he talked. Ariel made a call on his phone. A minute later Mark was back.

'We're going to Jerusalem,' he said. 'We've another lead.'

As we walked back to the front gate, the fire hissing loudly behind us, I questioned Mark, then Ariel. I didn't get much out of them. Nothing at all out of Ariel in fact. And all Mark told me about his lead was that a phone signal of interest had been picked up somewhere near the Church of the Holy Sepulchre.

'You think they've been taken back to Jerusalem?'

'Don't get ahead of yourself. The phone we've been tracking could have been stolen. It could be a waste of time.'

As we clambered over the wall and said goodbye to Ariel, I could still smell the fire on our clothes. A dark plume of smoke reached up to the sky behind us as we drove away.

There were no police cars though. I didn't see another policeman until we were back in Jerusalem.

A line of traffic, like an exodus, was heading out of the city as we approached it. There wasn't much talking in the car. Mark told the driver to speed up.

'Watch out!' he shouted at the driver as we came off the highway and had to slow down sharply for a bus. After that the tension in the car was almost poisonous.

I stared out the window wishing we'd got to that villa earlier. It felt as if something had slipped from my grasp.

45

At one minute to seven, every evening in the winter, the official custodian of the Church of the Holy Sepulchre in Jerusalem mounts the ladder which he has put up against the left hand door of the church.

This highly venerated basilica, a focus for millions of pilgrims down through the centuries, is Christianity's most contentious site. The first church here, one of the oldest, had been built by Constantine the Great in 330 AD.

No other Christian church has six, often sparring, Christian denominations in charge of it.

The custodian, a Muslim, is a direct descendant of an ancestor who'd been given the position by Saladin himself in 1187, after the Islamic recapture of Jerusalem, following the fall of the main Crusader state.

The custodian is well aware of the significance of his duties. The Church of the Holy Sepulchre contains what has long been believed to be the tomb of Jesus, the site of Golgotha, the Hill of Calvary where he was crucified, and the chapel of Adam, the place where Adam's skull was believed to have been buried.

The custodian inserts an ancient iron key and locks the

main door of the church. Then he folds the wooden steps he stood on and passes them through a hatch in the right hand door to the Armenian sexton, who, along with a Latin and a Greek sexton and other priests, will spend the night in the church praying and awaiting its reopening at four the following morning. The sextons are trained to stay awake to ensure that no one breaks the rules of the status quo, the system for governing the church set down by the Ottomans in 1853.

The only people remaining in the church that night are eight priests, a mixture of Orthodox, Latin and Armenians and a specially allowed visitor.

That evening, as the custodian removed the key from the lower lock he thought about the odd thing that had happened only a few hours before. The special visitor, a man who had arrived with Father Rehan, had turned up only minutes before the closing ceremony. He was planning to spend the night inside the church in prayer and contemplation, but he'd seemed a very stony-faced character to be carrying out such a penance.

The custodian shook his head, dismissing his fears. He had seen many stony-faced Christians and quite a few odd overnight visitors to the church.

And the letter the man had presented to him, and the telephone confirmation of its authenticity, were all the checks he needed to officially make.

The other odd thing that the custodian had noticed was the fact that the special visitor had a black rucksack with him, which looked bigger and heavier than was normal for just one man.

But he hadn't done anything about that.

The custodian was allowed to request a spot search of all visitors to the sacred site, but he'd never requested a search of a special visitor. The fights between monks and priests over such matters as the moving of a chair and the leaving of a door open in the church, meant he was unlikely to do so for just one visitor either, unless he did it for all special visitors for all the denominations. It had crossed his mind that this self-imposed restriction might one day prove to be a horrendous mistake.

As he walked away across the courtyard, now that the doors of the church were officially closed, with Christian pilgrims all around, he said a prayer to Allah that no mistake regarding the church would occur in his lifetime.

Inside the church, in the yellow light from dim bulbs inside a string of glass lanterns, Father Rehan was standing listening to the evening prayer roster being read aloud.

The sing-song voice filled the air.

Arap Anach's right hand was feeling for the clasp on his backpack, which he was holding in front of him. He pulled the opening wide and reached inside without looking down.

Then he turned his head. There were only four priests in the small side chapel with him.

He flipped the switch on the mobile phone service disruptor. It would cause all mobile phone signals within 250 metres to become garbled.

Then he opened, by touch alone, the slim metal case containing the MP5-NX version of the famous Heckler and Koch short barrel machine pistol, a favourite of Navy special forces around the world. This version was fitted with a short carbon fibre sound suppressor. He'd tested it himself only a few days before. It worked well, as it should.

It was the best available at disguising the noise of short bursts of automatic fire in confined spaces.

As Arap Anach pulled the MP5 from his bag, he swung the gun up to point it at the side of the head of Father Rehan. As he pulled the trigger and bullets pumped out, causing his arm to jerk, Arap felt a warm surge pour through him.

261

The power of life and death is addictive, if you've no qualms about using it.

The next sound, apart from the low whump of the special 9mm cartridges slicing into flesh and bone as he turned the pistol in an arc, were the astonished shouts of the other priests as he killed each man with two soft-point expanding bullets.

The Hague Convention had banned such bullets, but that didn't mean they weren't available, if you knew where to ask.

In any case, using them was the most appropriate thing to do. Better to kill a man at once, with a bullet that expanded and disintegrated inside his brain, rather than have to go round and finish him off, and let him see his own death approaching.

One of the priests got all of five feet away, he must have been highly attuned to self-preservation, and was running fast when the back of his body disintegrated. Arap Anach's training sessions with the MP5 were paying off.

Murdering these priests had taken only a few seconds. He knew their shouts would bring the Greeks shortly, and possibly the other priests too, though they were further away and conducting a noisy prayer service, but he knew none of that mattered.

Once you can kill in extravagant numbers without flinching there is little anyone without a weapon can do to stop you at close quarters. He looked down. The marble floor of the chapel was slick with blood already. Adrenaline was spiking inside him.

The hunt had started.

Soon he would be searching out any last priest who had decided to hide. After that he would have the church to himself.

At one time there had been a secret back door into the

Holy Sepulchre, used by the Orthodox priests, but it had been bricked up owing to the outcry its existence had caused, due to fears that Orthodox monks who sneaked in might attempt to make physical changes to the building, which the other denominations had not agreed to.

The underground tunnel that led away from the church to a thick wooden door in a basement on El Khanqa, a lane at the back of the church, which was locked for a similar reason, would provide no escape for the priests who remained alive either. Father Rehan had the key for that door in his pocket.

But it would provide an escape route for Arap Anach when the time came.

He held his gun at his side as he waited for the other priests to arrive. When none came he pulled a giant Victorian-era wooden painting off the wall. Then another. The noise would bring them out.

The accelerant he'd brought with him, a mixture of lighter fuel and ethanol, was capable of starting a conflagration in a wet woodpile. It would have no difficulties with the bodies, paintings, intricately carved woodwork, embroidered altar coverings and candles that he would pile up.

Noticing a jerk from one of the bodies, he bent to check if there was a pulse from the priest. He could smell blood as he leaned over. It always amazed him how you could smell the iron from blood, almost taste it on your lips, if you were near enough to a still pumping source.

There was a noise.

When he turned, a Greek priest in his black robes was only three feet away. He had a six foot silver candelabra in his hands.

It didn't matter.

Arap shot him in the face and the man crumpled with a hole the size of a milk bottle in his upper cheek, from which red blood pumped in an insistent fashion that spoke about the energy of the human body and its fragility too.

It was time to hunt the remaining priests. He set off.

The first one he found was trying to escape through the main door, though it was locked from the outside. He was banging frantically at it as he died. Another was at a window waving, but it was too dark in that upper corridor for anyone to see him. Arap Anach came up right beside that one, his heart beating fast with pleasure, before pulling the trigger.

When he was finished, he pulled the bodies to the main floor of the church in front of the staircase leading up to the chapel of Golgotha. It would be fitting indeed that the corpses of these priests would burn and be sacrificed at the place of the skull.

When he was finished he took out something from his backpack. It was a sealed plastic container with Palestinian scarves, a wiring controller, known to be used by suicide bombers, and a pair of slippers stolen from a well-known Palestinian terror cell organiser. There would be enough DNA on these items to convict the Pope.

It was this that would make the coming conflagration worthwhile. Only indisputable evidence that Palestinians had committed an act of global-scale religious terrorism would be enough to stir things up as was needed.

He put each item around the church to look as if they'd been discarded in haste. One or two of them might be consumed by the coming conflagration, but the most likely outcome was that some would be found in the trawl for evidence. The fire would damage the church and many of its greatest treasures, but it was unlikely to reduce the building to rubble.

There was one more task to do before he started spreading the accelerant. He took the phone out of his pocket and placed it on the carved stone half-altar by the stairs to Golgotha. Then he reached inside his backpack and turned the mobile phone disruptor off. Within seconds he heard phones ringing from the bodies of the dead priests.

He picked his phone up, tapped out the number. It had cost quite a bit to get the number of a leading Hamas player, but all he would have to do to establish another indisputable link to the Palestinians would be to keep the call open for a few seconds. This time he would speak slowly, so he would be understood.

Soon, the blame for all this could not be denied.

46

The sound of a telephone ringing broke the silence inside the Range Rover. For a moment I thought it was my phone ringing. Then I remembered my ringtone was different.

Xena, who was beside me in the back seat, slid her phone out of her pocket. She said, 'Halo.' Then she listened. After a few seconds she cut the call.

'What was that about,' said Mark, turning towards her.

'Just a man,' said Xena.

'There's always a few running after you, isn't there?' said Mark.

I looked out into the darkness. It suited my mood.

'They're getting more rain here then they've had for twenty years,' said Mark.

I didn't give a damn. I didn't care about anything but finding Isabel. And I was wondering why we were really going back to Jerusalem. Sure, there'd been a report that the phone they'd been tracking, which had led us to that farm, had been triangulated to the Church of the Holy Sepulchre, but all that meant was that someone had passed near the place and had turned the phone on.

This could so easily be a stupid bloody wild goose chase.

If it was, should I go back to that farm, ask some questions, look around? Some neighbour might know the person who was living there and where they were from.

I put my hand on the door and gripped it.

'We made a big mistake,' said Xena. Her tone was calm, but her hand, which was on her knee, was closing and unclosing, as if she was a little psychotic.

'What mistake?' said Mark. He sounded irritated.

'There are forces at work here that we know nothing about.' She started banging her forehead with her fist. At first it was a light tapping, but within seconds she was doing it rapidly, fast enough to hurt herself.

'Stop that,' said Mark.

I reached over, grabbed her arm. She was strong, wiry. I was lucky to be able to hold her. Her arm slid in my grip.

'Stop, Xena,' said Mark.

Suddenly she stopped and turned to look at me. Her eyes were wide, bloodshot, as if she was on something from the psych trolley.

'You think we're wasting our time,' she said.

A mind reader. That was just what I needed.

Mark was half-turned in his seat. The driver moved to the inside lane, as if he was getting ready to pull over. The traffic was busy. The Sabbath was finished now.

'You mustn't go there,' said Xena, looking at me.

'Go where?' I said.

'To the Church of the Holy Sepulchre. It is not safe for you.' Her tone became more insistent with each word.

'Make him listen, Mark.' She tapped Mark's shoulder, hard.

His gaze flickered to me. His mouth was half-open, as if he was about to say something.

'Don't bother,' I said, loudly. 'I'm not listening.' If Xena

267

wanted me not to go to the Holy Sepulchre, that was exactly where I wanted to go.

Twenty minutes later the driver dropped us at the Jaffa Gate. Xena disappeared immediately into a group of green-clad Israeli soldiers passing by.

Mark just let her go.

'She's free to do what she wants,' he said. There was a wistful look in his eye. Not for the first time I wondered if there was a relationship between them.

'Let's do this,' I said.

My mind was turning over sick images of the basement at that house. Had someone brought Isabel back to Jerusalem to murder her the way they'd murdered Kaiser? A bitter rage flowed inside me at the thought of that. It had been bad luck that we hadn't got to that farm quick enough.

If someone did that to Isabel I wouldn't be able to bear it.

We were walking fast. We reached Christian Quarter Road, turned left into it. The narrow street was lined with tourist shops selling carpets, crosses, icons, leather goods, antiques of dubious provenance, blue Hebron glass, silver work, Christian icons and jewellery.

Some of the shops were closed, but most had black-haired proprietors outside staring with the dead-eyed look of salesmen at the end of a rejection-filled day.

Mark was on his phone. I could hear his frustration.

'Is that all we have?' he said in an incredulous tone.

As we came to an even smaller lane on the right, he turned to me.

'There's an Israeli security operation going on up ahead. Keep your mouth shut, at all times. I'll answer their questions, explain why we're here. Unless I ask you, don't say anything. Is that clear?'

'As glass.'

We turned right. Up ahead was a small door in a high stone wall. Beyond it was the courtyard in front of the Church of the Holy Sepulchre.

Looming above us to our left was the sheer edifice of the most sacred church in Christendom. My body was tense, and my brain was running fast, too fast. Images of what might have happened to Isabel had forced their way into my mind again.

I pressed my hand to my forehead. And in that moment I offered my own life up, to any power that might be listening, if only Isabel could be found and was all right.

The entrance to the courtyard was barred by a modern-looking green steel door. It had a foot square grating in it. The grating was blocked by a steel plate on the far side. Mark knocked on the door. A second later the grating opened. There was a spy hole in the door.

On the other side of the grating were blue uniformed Israeli policemen.

Mark took out an ID pass. One policeman leaned forward to look at it. Then he opened the gate. I thought we were going to be let in, but instead two burly monks in brown robes with a white rope tied around their middle and pale complexions came rushing out.

'What's going on?' I said to the monks. I was in their path.

The taller of the two, who was well over six feet, answered me in a soft voice.

'We do not know anything. Peace be upon you. Please let us pass.' I stood back. They were gone.

'They looked worried,' said Mark.

'Can we go in?' I said loudly to the Israeli policeman. He was closing the gate.

'Stop,' said a woman's voice. I turned. It was Xena. She was standing maybe five feet behind us and staring at me.

'There is evil there,' she said.

'This is the holiest place in Christendom,' said Mark. He was almost shouting. He turned back to the door. It was closed now, but the grating was still open.

'Please get your superior officer.'

The policemen shook his head.

A surge of anger rose inside me.

'What the hell's going on? Why won't you listen? This man is from the British Embassy!' I said. The policeman was staring me in the eyes. Our gaze held for a few seconds. Then he took a step backwards and turned to an older officer behind him. That man was silver-haired, and had a commanding air. He came towards the gate.

'I'm with the British Embassy in Cairo,' said Mark.

'The church is closed,' said the older officer, in American-accented English.

Mark held his ID card up to the iron bars. The younger policeman had taken a step back. His hand was resting on a black machine pistol that could kill us all in seconds.

The senior officer moved forward, peered at the card, shook his head.

Mark took the ID back, pulled a second ID card from behind the first.

'I have Mossad clearance,' he said. 'This card has my code name. Check it. Call your headquarters.'

The older policeman looked closely at the card and walked away. He took a small black walkie talkie from another soldier, spoke into it. Then he listened with the walkie talkie at his ear.

After another minute of waiting he came back over and barked something to the younger policeman.

Seconds later we were all inside the courtyard. Bright lights on an aluminium tripod lit it up as if it was daylight.

There was a huddle of priests and monks of various denominations in the first raised part of the courtyard. In front of them, to our left, there were steps down to the main flagstoned open area in front of the church.

Some of the priests were wearing round black Orthodox hats and had large gold crosses on their chests. Two others had thick beards and odd looking pointed black hoods. You could barely see their faces. One ancient grey-haired monk was wearing a dark brown robe.

'I will find out what's going on,' said Xena.

'How the hell can she do that? Why is she even here?' I said to Mark, as I watched her head for the group of priests.

'Xena can be very useful. She was brought up in an Orthodox Ethiopian nunnery. She'll probably tell them she's an abbess or something.' He put a finger to his lips.

'Actually, I think she was an abbess for a while, in the Sudan.' He rubbed his forehead.

'And you have clearance from Mossad?' I said.

He shrugged.

Xena was coming back over to us.

'There is something bad going on in the church,' she said. 'I told you.' She stared at me, pressed her lips together, as if she was angry that I'd refused to believe her warning.

'We haven't got time for this,' said Mark. 'What else did they say?'

She looked from Mark to me. Her eyes narrowed.

'They said that the Greek Orthodox Patriarch's secretary gets a call every hour to tell him everything is okay in this church. They've been doing that since there was some fight in there in the middle of the night a few years ago.' She leaned forward.

'The last two calls tonight did not happen. And no one is answering their phone inside.' She had a resigned look on her face, as if she knew there was a lot worse to come out.

'Why don't they just go in, open the door?' I waved towards the two Romanesque pointed-arch doorways in the far corner of the courtyard. One of them had been bricked up long ago. The other was a double-leaved wooden door that looked as old as the Crusader-era stones around them.

'Don't they have keys?' I waved towards the group of priests.

'No, they don't,' said Xena.

'The rules about opening and closing this place were set out in an international treaty,' said Mark.

I didn't care about any of that.

'I'm sure they've torn up the rules before.'

'Not since 1853,' he said. 'This church is shared by six Christian denominations. And none of them have keys.'

'This church is the centre of the world,' said Xena. 'Not even the Pope breaks the rules here.'

'And what about that?' I pointed at the upper level windows. There were three large high-arched windows in the wall of the church above the doorways.

Reflected in the windows was a flickering light. It could have been from candles inside the church or it could have been from a fire.

Or it could have been from someone being burnt to death.

A few of the priests turned and looked up at the windows, following my pointed finger. I assumed there would be an immediate mad eruption, that people would race for the doors to break them down, open the church up and find out if there was any danger, never mind if someone was being murdered inside.

But I was wrong.

The priests who'd looked up simply returned to watching the monk who was talking in front of them. Or maybe he was praying. His bowed head certainly gave off that impression. Were they going to wait until flames were coming out of the roof?

Had they even seen what I'd seen?

To the right of the entrance arches there were steps leading up to a domed single storey sandstone entrance portal. It appeared to be blocked off, no longer in use. The structure had thin marble pillars and numerous ledges.

I groaned.

I knew what I was going to do.

Once, when I was drunk, I'd scaled the front of a mansion in Maida Vale, when Irene and I were in college. I'd been looking for her. I could have killed myself, but it had left me with a stupid belief that you can climb the outside of buildings, if there are enough ledges. And there were definitely enough ledges here.

All I would have to do was reach that wide first ledge. I walked slowly forward. No need to attract attention. I went down the steps into the main section of the courtyard.

From behind I heard a voice.

'The Crusaders built most of what's here in 1170, after they captured Jerusalem.' It was Mark talking. He was following me. 'The original early Byzantine church was twice the size of this one. It was destroyed by the Fatamids in 1009, if I remember rightly.' He paused.

'Where are you going, Sean?' His voice had risen an octave.

I didn't answer. I kept walking. When I reached the sandstone wall of the church I went up the steep stone stairs to the right of the main doors. At the top I put my foot on a ledge to the left, part of the main church wall.

I braced myself against an indentation in the wall, reached up to the wider ledge above. The sandstone was rough under my fingers. I could smell dust. And my own sweat.

'You are fucking crazy,' Mark said.

I looked up. The wall loomed above like a cliff. My heart was audibly pounding.

'Stop!' A shout echoed so loudly in the courtyard it made my fingers slip from the bottom of the ledge I was reaching for.

I didn't look around. I knew what was happening. I pushed up again, reached as far as I could. I wouldn't have much time. My fingers scrabbled at the bottom of the ledge.

To say my heart was in my mouth would be an understatement. It was trying to find a way out of it.

I wasn't going to be able to reach the next ledge.

'Jump up,' a voice said. Mark's voice.

I felt a push on my thigh, then on the calf of my other leg. I was going to get a lift. I would make it!

There was a clamour of shouts behind me, an echo of feet slapping on stone.

I lunged up. The hands pushed me, then let me go.

A raucous cry sounded from below, as if a herd of cranes were wheeling beneath me.

'Stay back.' Mark's voice was insistent.

A whistle sounded. A police whistle. It was a loud shriek. Shouts accompanied it.

'Get down, get down.' There were a chorus of voices. Some echoed in different languages. They all meant the same thing.

I was hanging by one hand from an upper ledge now, half dangling in space. But I'd reached the ledge. I put my other hand on it, right in the corner. If someone tugged at my feet right now I would be back on the ground in a second and in police custody within a few more.

But no one tugged at me, and I swung my leg to brace myself against a thin stone pillar and pushed myself up.

Below me, Mark was in handcuffs and Xena was remonstrating with a policeman who was holding her arm. The older policeman was nearby looking up at me. He gestured for me to get down.

I'm not sure exactly what Mark had done, but he'd stopped them from pulling me back. There was a priest right below me now, one of the round-hatted Orthodox Greek priests.

He was leaning up to reach my foot and pull me down onto my head, breaking it if he could, I'm sure.

Further along, the ledge widened. There was a sun-bleached wooden ladder leaning up against a window made of dull glass in large leaded sections. I headed towards it, touched the wooden ladder accidently as I looked in through the grimy glass. A gasp came up from below. The short ladder toppled, fell off the ledge and down onto the priests and monks. Outraged shouts echoed.

I reached up. There was a half-inch crack in the iron window frame, in its centre. I put my fingers into the crack. The upper part of the window opened. It creaked loudly as it did. I could see flames reflected in the glass as it moved. And I could smell burning too. It was a sweet smell.

The smell of burning flesh.

'Stop! We will shoot!' came another shout from below in the courtyard. Could they not see that the church was in danger?

I pulled myself head first through the window, falling about four feet onto a narrow red and white tiled upper floor. My shoulder jolted against the floor as it hit. Pain shot up my arm. I found myself in a heap on the floor, but I rose quickly to my feet. An acrid burning smell filled the air now that I was inside.

Was Isabel dead already?

I closed the window. The shouts from outside grew faint. I looked over the stone balcony.

I was looking into the famous Church of the Holy Sepulchre. It had two stone colonnaded levels below a high dome decorated with a golden sunburst. I was on the upper level. Below was a flagstone floor, the main part of the church. In the centre of the floor was a pillared stone aedicule with a cupola on top of it where millions believe Jesus' body lay after he died.

A shout echoed distantly from outside. 'Desecrate this holy place and your soul is doomed!'

I didn't have time for any desecrating. There was a column of black smoke coming up from below. And flames were being reflected off the marble pillars and even off the sandstone walls.

I had to get down there.

I didn't want to find out what the fire most likely meant, but I had no choice. I couldn't fail Isabel. I moved fast along the balcony. The stairs down were in darkness. I hugged the wall as I went, felt a breeze move past me. The sweet smell of burning flesh was strong.

I wanted to retch at the thought of what that smell meant. My shoulder scraped a part of the sandstone wall that jutted out into the stairwell. It felt as if someone had touched me. My heart was thumping as if I'd been running. I reached the door at the bottom of the stairs. It was open an inch and radiating a pillar of light. I wasn't going to make any sudden exits.

I moved my head to the gap and saw, to the right, the back of a man who had scrawniness written all over him. His shoulders were hunched and his skull was prominent. He was wearing a black suit.

The man was looking at something beneath his feet. I couldn't see what it was.

But I knew what I had to do. I pushed the door slowly open, dreading its creak. But it didn't make a sound.

I took a step forward. The door closed behind me with a sigh. I hadn't expected that. Would he turn? I kept walking.

Every second felt like a minute.

He was twenty feet away.

I could see where the smoke was coming from now. There was a mound of rags. No, it wasn't rags – *it was mostly black clothed bodies* – behind him, in front of a yellowing marble altar. The shiny stone and marble floor and a line of silver candelabras beyond reflected the flames coming from the mound.

How could bodies be burning?

Then I saw the frames of paintings among the bodies. The smoke, rising fast, had obscured them. I could hear a crackling hum from the flames too, but no shout from outside penetrated the thick walls.

The smell was almost choking. It stuck in my throat. I was ten feet from him.

My fists were up. Had he killed all these people himself?

A plan was forming in my head. I would . . .

My foot touched a ridge in the stone floor. The noise of it, slight, but real, made the man turn. And that was when I saw the gun in his hand, black, menacing.

He spun around to face me as the sound of bells ringing, from somewhere up above, pealed out.

Then a flash bloomed from his gun like a firework exploding.

47

The Bang & Olufsen 37-inch flat screen TV on the wall of the St. George's Hotel in London, came to life with a flash of colour. The hotel featured the latest technology, an integrated TV and internet experience, which allowed visitors to turn on all screens in each suite by gesture alone.

Lord Bidoner had gestured as he passed out of the bedroom. The 'escort' he'd left behind would have to content himself with the stack of magazines on the bedside table. The young man was a regular, so his discretion was assured, and being from India he knew that if he ever made a mistake, his whole family would most likely meet a bloody end, if not the whole village where he came from.

The fact that he didn't speak English was a bonus for Lord Bidoner. There was no need for the bullshit that most English speaking escorts liked to spin.

But he didn't want the boy to even see his facial expressions as he watched the drama unfolding in Jerusalem.

Arap Anach had a good chance to redeem himself. His attempt at infiltrating an Islamic rally in London and spreading a virus had been a disappointment. The incident had drawn a lot of attention from the Security Service to a variety of people which he'd had to be very careful not to aggravate.

But if he managed to get this operation done and some execution-by-fire videos uploaded to the internet there was every chance current events would ignite a very useful wave of revulsion and anti-Muslim feeling in Europe, which would help to spur on what was happening in Israel and the conflagration that was to come.

Never mind the pleasure such videos would give to connoisseurs of similar delicacies.

He smiled, clasping his hands together in front of himself as he watched the TV anchorwoman asking a Palestinian representative who was denying any knowledge of what had happened to the priests inside the church, why they weren't responding. The man was waving his arms hysterically in reaction to the possibility that was put to him that one of the Palestinian factions had taken over the church.

'There is no proof of such a thing,' he said.

Lord Bidoner closed his eyes for a moment. It was all going perfectly.

If the promised video of Isabel Sharp's death was as good as the video of Max Kaiser's final minutes he had something truly special to look forward to in the next few hours.

Perhaps he should ask the escort to stay another night.

Was there anything else he had to do?

Go over his security arrangements.

Lord Bidoner considered every aspect of his connection to Arap Anach again. A few encrypted phone calls were all that could be proved against him. No court of law could judge him based just on those.

There was a more obvious risk, clearly, if Arap were to be captured, but Lord Bidoner had made plans for that eventuality too.

The big question in that regard was whether his contact

would be able to intervene fast enough if Arap fell into the hands of the authorities.

The interview with the Palestinian was over. He turned the television up with a gesture. The situation in Jerusalem was developing fast.

Sky News HD was relaying images of the Church of the Holy Sepulchre from the corner of the Muristan, about thirty feet from the entrance to the church, and from a helicopter circling a hundred feet above.

Images from the helicopter were on the screen now. All that was visible was a group of priests and a cluster of police in the courtyard of the church. Then a trickle of smoke rose from the cupola of the building. The commentator didn't seem to notice it for a minute, than her tone went up at least three octaves.

Lord Bidoner passed his hand over the flame of the black candle burning on the coffee table. He turned his hand over and let the flame linger on the scar on the back. Pain seared through him.

He held his hand steady for a few seconds, then pulled it away. A taste was enough for him. It kept him grounded.

He thought about checking Ebony's portfolio of stocks. He knew what would be happening to it already on the Israeli future's market – they'd all be climbing fast – but he decided to wait until he saw which way the Jerusalem situation developed.

When to sell was going to be the next big decision. Their gains would be far higher if he waited until a war actually started, and everyone was rushing to move into the right stocks. The wave of stock increases might crest higher than a two hundred percent jump, if he got his timing right.

He stood. The commentator was talking with the blogger who had notified the media that the mobile phone system had been out in the area of the Church of the Holy Sepulchre.

He'd watched the Israeli police units arrive on a tourist webcam overlooking the entrance to the church.

There was still no sign of any fire brigade equipment. The commentator wondered loudly what was taking them so long. The smoke from the roof of the building was a thin column, but it was rising fast.

Lord Bidoner turned the sound down. It was time to make the phone call. If the Church of the Holy Sepulchre was badly damaged, the reaction in the United States would be critical.

Five star generals might already be updating their war scenarios. What mattered in the coming hours and days was ensuring the right people knew who to blame, who to hate.

Anders Breivik in Norway had proved how much pain one man can inflict, but he'd gone down the wrong path.

It was better to inspire hatred than to seek publicity.

And a hurricane of hatred was about to arrive.

48

Isabel cradled Susan's head. The rock beneath them was no place to lay it. She was desperate to prevent the worst of Susan's pain, to stop the harsh reality of where they were being all that Susan experienced in her last moments.

They were in pure darkness. It was the sensation of emptiness Isabel hated. Waves of paranoia and fear passed through her regularly.

Cold was seeping up from the rock she was sitting on, as if it was crawling up her. There was a sickly smell in the air too, a smell of infection and damp and death. She could taste it.

At times Isabel imagined she was back in her apartment in London, in bed with Sean, with her eyes closed. It helped. But at other times the blackness was a gloved hand around her head and she wanted to beat it away.

A few times she swung her arms all around when faint noises gave her the impression that something was moving close to her.

There wasn't much time left for Susan. She knew that.

Susan Hunter had given up. And Isabel couldn't blame her. They both knew that their captor had left them underground and might never return. And even if he did, it might only be to inflict some awful final torture on them.

He'd moved them earlier that day. She knew it was daytime, because of the daylight she'd seen before he'd covered her eyes. Isabel had wanted to lash out, to kick and scream, but there isn't much you can do when your hands are tied behind your back and you can't see what to kick.

She'd tried it just the same, had kicked out at what she thought was the source of the pushes she was receiving in her back, but she'd suffered a slap across the head and laughter for it, which had made her think hard before doing it again.

Whatever the reason he'd brought them to this new place, it was not for anything but evil. She was sure of that.

'Isabel.' The voice echoed.

Isabel shook from the suddenness of it. It was Susan Hunter speaking and her voice was more lucid than it had been for a day or more.

'Hush, save your strength,' said Isabel. 'We'll be out of here soon.'

'That's not true.' Susan's voice was flat, accepting.

'Stop that. It is true.'

'I don't have long. Listen to me.' A rasping noise, like a death rattle, or something near it came from Susan's throat.

'I'm listening.'

'There are dark forces. They want power.' The rattle came again.

'There are always dark forces,' said Isabel.

'No, no. You don't understand.' Isabel felt the weak grip of Susan's hand on her arm. It was like a baby's.

'Don't say any more. No more!' Isabel didn't want to hear about dark forces. This was not the time for such talk.

'They want compassion to die.' Her voice was small, like a child's.

283

'There have always been people like that.'

'They must be stopped. If you get away . . . you must stop them.'

'I will. I promise. Now stop talking.' She said it softly.

'I met Max . . . before he died. He knew.' Susan coughed again, weakly. Then her voice came back.

'I think we're going to be sacrificed, Isabel.'

'What?' The idea was numbing, incomprehensible.

Susan slumped in her arms. She could feel Susan's body fading, as if she was giving up the fight.

'Stay with me,' she whispered. 'We'll get through this. Don't even think about all that stuff.' She had no idea if they would survive, but she had to say it. She had to believe there was hope.

'There was a secret in that book you found in Istanbul, Isabel,' Susan coughed.

'What secret?' Isabel hadn't asked Susan about what was in the book.

'A secret that could change the world.' Susan shivered. 'I came here to see Max. You know that, don't you?'

'Yes,' said Isabel.

'I needed parchment . . . to do a carbon dating comparison.' Susan coughed and coughed. Each cough was weaker than the last.

Isabel held her. She wanted to ask about the secret, but Susan was fading and she didn't want to do anything that would hasten the end.

After another minute Susan's voice started up again in the darkness.

'I needed to check, you see . . . to see if it was a forgery,' she said.

Isabel waited. It was another minute before Susan spoke again.

'One part of that manuscript you found is a quire . . .

284

goatskin folded into leaves, like they used to use in the first century.'

'Is that what you wanted to carbon date?'

Isabel was holding her tight. She could feel Susan's head nodding. 'Max said they'd found quires. They sounded similar.'

Susan groaned, it was a wrenching sound. The sound of someone in pain, near the end.

She couldn't resist any longer. 'So what's this secret that could change the world?'

Susan spoke slowly when she responded. 'There's an official Roman transcript of the trial of Jesus in that book you found.'

'My God,' said Isabel. Could this be true? It would certainly be spectacular if it was. It would be a sensation. Sean would be amazed.

'But that's not all of it, Isabel.' Susan was shaking her head.

'What?'

'There's a secret in the symbol in that book. I don't know what it means. But it's referred to in the trial document. Right at the end.'

Susan talked on in the darkness, drew the arrow and square shape on the back of Isabel's hand. Isabel shrugged when Susan asked her if she knew what the symbol meant. At that moment she didn't care.

49

Smoke was streaming fast from the mound of bodies. The fire crackling must have covered my arrival for a vital few seconds.

I was on him as his gun went off.

I smashed my fist into the arm he was carrying the gun with. Rule number one, disable any weapon.

The force of my arrival propelled him back on his heels as he was trying to get up. I could smell his sweat. The undiluted adrenaline of the fight poured through me, tunnelling my vision. I had to subdue him!

I found his throat, gripped it with my right hand. He was moving his head violently from side to side. I grappled with his gun hand. He still had the gun. His arm was swinging around, trying to get free. I was surprised at how he squirmed.

'You can't stop me,' he screamed in a strangulated roar.

I squeezed his neck, hoping he would give up. I felt his blood vessels pumping, his windpipe and skin squelching like rubber as he shifted away from me.

'Where is she?' I screamed. He reared up, tried to push me off him. My breathing was in loud gasps.

'You will die like Kaiser, begging for the pain to stop!'

he screamed. His gun hand was coming towards my stomach. I jerked it away.

His blue eyes were neon lit. Hatred roared from them, as if I was the one who'd done some terrible wrong to him.

Warm spittle hit my face.

We rolled. I banged his skull against the grey stone floor. Heat from the fire seared my back.

My head hit stone with force. I heard a crack, hoped it was from something else.

Sparkling lights swirled in my vision. Move!

I pushed desperately to the left. He came with me. My hand was still squeezing his neck. I was going to kill the bastard!

He slammed a fist into my stomach. Pain surged in a boiling wave. But my grip on his neck didn't falter.

I pushed his head back hard, rolling away from the fire, over and over. If only I could . . .

A chest pummelling blast, and a roar of wind hit us. I was knocked backwards as if a hand had taken me. It took me a few seconds to realise I wasn't dead and to reach around in the clearing smoke and discover that he was gone. He'd slipped from my fingers! Bastard!

I stood, stumbled, then looked around, hearing shouts. I was shaking.

Other arms were grappling me. There were voices. I was being dragged away by policemen clad in blue bulletproof vests. What the hell?

They dragged me outside, pushed me up against a wall. The courtyard was empty of priests now. Three of the policemen held me with a cold gun barrel pressed into my chest, while a troop of men dressed in yellow jackets, carrying fire extinguishers, raced into the church.

That was the moment my stomach reacted. I put my hand to my mouth, bent forward. The police stepped back. I vomited. I'd been holding my stomach, but the punch and the smoke I'd inhaled had turned it. Two different policemen, without armour, arrived as I was straightening up, wiping my mouth. One of them spoke into a walkie talkie as the other started reciting the laws I'd broken by entering the church out of hours.

They said they were going to arrest me. I shouted, and started gesticulating at the church door.

'Are you mad? I fought the man who started that fire! I was trying to stop him! You can't arrest me!' I shouted.

There was smoke coming from the front door of the church. It was hanging from its hinges with a gaping hole in each leaf. That explained how the police had got in. Presumably whoever had the key hadn't turned up quickly enough.

I pointed a finger at the door.

'I need to go back in. Let me go!' I took a step forward. I wanted to see if Isabel was in there.

The policemen grabbed my arms, one on each side, twisting them backwards painfully. I was lifted an inch from the ground.

'You won't do that, sir.' The officer on my right spoke quickly, politely. 'Describe the man who started the fire.'

I did, there wasn't much to say, and as I glanced at the door of the church and watched people running in and out, it dawned on me that they hadn't found him.

'I had a hold on him, until you broke the bloody doors in! You have to check the whole building!' The only reply I got was a dismissive stare.

Seconds later I was being hurried out of the courtyard and down a back lane, accompanied by four riot-helmeted and bulletproof vest-clad policemen. We passed through a blue and white police line, where a crowd of Arabs in keffiyehs, black robed priests, brown and white clothed monks, sombre looking nuns and a mixture of tourists had gathered.

There were shouts. I heard the words, 'Bashokh aleek!' It sounded like an insult.

Questions were shouted at me in English as we passed too.

'What have you done, blasphemer?' was the most memorable of them. The voices were all angry.

Beyond the police line there were two ambulances with a white Star of David on them parked in front of King David's Tower, inside the Jaffa Gate.

My mind was racing. I'd nearly caught him. I should have smashed his head in. What more could I do? Had I blown my chance to rescue Isabel?

Rage at myself for not finishing the fight tightened my fists.

I thought I was being taken to the police station, so it was a pleasant surprise when I was led to the nearest ambulance.

I shouldn't have been surprised. My injuries weren't serious, but they were real. My head was bruised, ringing oddly, sounds were echoing, and my stomach was aching. A few minutes later Mark arrived. He waved to me, then showed his ID and spoke to the blue uniformed police officer with a concrete hard expression, who was standing near the back door of the ambulance keeping an eye on me.

After the officer had closely examined the ID and had spoken into his buzzing walkie talkie, he let Mark approach the vehicle.

Mark leaned in the door.

'They didn't arrest you?' I said.

He smiled. 'The Israeli authorities are back in cooperating mode.' He paused, leaned towards me, as if examining me for injuries. 'You almost got yourself killed in there.'

'Did they find Isabel?' I was dreading that her body might have been somewhere in that burning building.

He shook his head. 'I personally went through the whole church. She's definitely not there.'

I nodded. 'The bastard got away, didn't he?'

Mark nodded. 'He must have had a key to a back door that hasn't been used in years.'

I closed my eyes. 'I had him!' I gripped the crisp blue sheet under me. Our best chance of finding Isabel had slipped away through my fingers!

Then something else came to me. 'Do they know who he is?'

Mark climbed into the ambulance. That was when I noticed a cut on the side of his forehead.

'No,' he said.

I was propped up on one of the gurneys. My arms were still trembling from the exertion of the fight. The sickly sweet burning smell lingered in my nostrils. A medic, dressed all in green, had checked me over already and had disappeared. He reappeared now, climbing into the ambulance.

'Are you coming with us, sir?' he asked Mark.

'Yes, I need to get this cut checked,' said Mark, pointing to his face.

The medic examined Mark, and made him lie down on the other gurney. He strapped us both in. Then he knocked on the sliding window that separated us from the driver and with our siren blaring we moved away.

The medic was sitting on a little fold-down seat and was talking loudly on his mobile phone behind us.

Mark took his phone out of his pocket and checked something on it. Echoes of the questions and curses that had been shouted at me while I was being bundled away from the church were playing in my mind. They were a demented chorus to my despair at having let the bastard slip away.

I thought about my phone and ran my hands through my pockets, groaning as the realisation came over me that I'd lost it.

'The police will find it if it didn't get burnt or smashed up,' said Mark when I told him. 'You'll get it back eventually. They put that fire out very quickly. You saw what he was burning, didn't you?'

I didn't answer. I was thinking about Isabel.

I'd imagined, initially, as I broke into the building, that she might have been in that church somewhere, being tortured. When I saw that sick pile of bodies, I thought she might be among them but I'd quickly seen that none of them were her.

But if she wasn't there, where was she?

Mark and I were taken to adjoining cubicles in the emergency room at the hospital when we got there. There were two Israeli policemen on guard near us. One was sitting on a chair.

The other one was over six foot six tall and built like a quarterback I'd seen once at a New York Giants game. His circumference must have equalled his height and he had arms as thick as my thighs. He could block a double doorway just by standing near it.

Presumably he was the muscle in case we did anything funny. Actually, it was probably me they were worried about.

I refused any pain killers, I didn't want to feel woozy, and after they'd put a dressing on my forehead they probed at my side to determine if anything was wrong in there. They wanted to keep me in overnight for observation, a nurse told me.

I wanted out of the place.

She also told us she'd seen the fire at the Church of the Holy Sepulchre on TV, after I'd explained where we'd come from. Apparently the whole incident had been relayed live to the world.

'Do you have immunity from prosecution here?' I asked Mark, leaning out of my cot towards him. I still wasn't sure if I was going to be locked up for breaking into the church. I wouldn't be much good to Isabel in a cell.

'I do,' he said. 'But you don't.'

His phone rang.

I didn't hear the first part of his conversation, as he turned his head away from me, but I did hear the next bit.

'Good news at last,' he said. He smiled at me. 'Now all we have to do is get away from our friends.' He glanced at the policemen. They were both staring at us.

50

Susan was sleeping, but she might have been unconscious. She'd talked for a long time about what she'd figured out from the book.

She'd been whispering, mostly, and had ended up rambling about the early Greek miniscule script alphabet, why it had been used in Jerusalem by scribes in Herod's day, and how that style in the quire pages alone proved that the manuscript was genuine.

Isabel's thirst was nagging fiercely at her again. He'd given them a bottle of water and a tub of cooked rice when he'd left them here, but it was all gone and panic wasn't far away now.

The darkness didn't help. She'd got a good look at the cave they were in. She'd seen it was no more than twenty foot by thirty, and that there was no other way out, before he'd sealed the way they'd come in – a three foot wide hole in the roof above her – by pulling a rock over it.

She'd always hated confined spaces.

She'd managed to take her jacket off and drop it below the exit hole before the darkness had come, to mark that spot, enable her to keep her bearings, as she'd learnt in the

Foreign Office kidnap training course. But it had been years since she'd done the course and she couldn't remember a lot of it.

What she did remember was one important part, the critical section about keeping hope alive. Because that was what she was having trouble doing.

The endless darkness was beating her down like a physical force.

She'd dreaded being held without light again when he'd taken her blindfold off and she'd seen the hole, seconds before she'd been forced down the ladder into the cave. And for a long time now she'd been battling frightening thoughts that wouldn't go away.

Was this what he'd planned for them? A slow, lingering death, starving, dying of thirst? Was she going to sit here while Susan's body decomposed nearby and the worms started eating at it? Would that be her fate too?

There was, she had to admit, very little chance that they'd be discovered accidently. Where they were, in a tomb-like cave under a rock in a barren valley that was littered with many other rocks, made sure of that. Being an hour's drive from Jerusalem, as far as she could work out – time was difficult to calculate when you were petrified – meant they'd left civilisation far behind. And with it, almost all chance of being found by accident. It might as well have been the first century out here, not the twenty-first. Sean could walk these valleys for the rest of his life and not find her. Even if he knew what part of the country she was in it wouldn't help.

She'd seen only barren rocks – no houses anywhere near – when the bastard had taken their blindfolds off, just before he'd pushed them, while waving his gun around, down the ladder into the tomb they were now held in.

'When are you going to free us?' she'd shouted at him defiantly, as she went down. His reply, a promise of eventual freedom if they did what they were told, was worthless, she knew, even as he spoke it.

His leaving them here at least meant one thing, of that she was sure. He had gone off to do something. And he didn't want them dead yet.

The ladder had been a real problem for Susan. She'd swayed on it at the top, and Isabel had in the end half caught her when she fell the last few feet to the rough stone floor.

That had winded them both.

Then he'd thrown down the plastic bag with rice and water in it. And without another word, he'd pulled up the ladder and had pushed the rock slowly over the entrance hole. It was probably one of the rocks she'd seen nearby in the valley; irregular, several feet wide giant lozenges. There was no possible way anyone could know they were under this particular one.

She'd wondered if the rock presented him with a difficulty too, how to make sure he knew which one to move to find them.

Unless, of course, he didn't intend to come back.

Stop thinking that, she said to herself. Stay positive.

She'd tried to reach the entrance hole by jumping. It was only about five feet above her head, from what she remembered, but she'd failed to touch the roof at all. And it had been like jumping in a nightmare. And so, after a while, as she lost her determination in the blackness, and heard a hollowness under her that spooked her, she'd given up on it.

Then an idea came to her.

What if she could dig away at the rock walls and pile up rubble under where the entrance hole was? At least she knew where to pile up the rocks she dug up.

It was a chance. If she could dig out enough rocks from the walls and floor, she might be able to reach the roof.

After doing it for a long time – she wasn't exactly sure how long she'd spent trying to break stones free from the walls – she had accumulated only five large rocks and some loose rubble, which, all together, added barely two inches to her height.

And her thirst got worse from the exertion. It was nagging at her relentlessly now.

She heard a cough. For a second she was disoriented. The cough had sounded near, but its owner was invisible in the endless blackness.

Now a wheeze. It was Susan. But her voice sounded different when she spoke.

'I heard you, moving . . . Please, don't disturb them . . . don't disturb the scorpions . . . The yellow one's bite can kill you in a few minutes.' Her voice was reedy, changed.

Isabel's skin flushed cold.

What was that noise?

She listened, concentrating hard for even the tiniest of sounds. She knew that scorpion bites were painful as well as possibly being deadly if a poisonous bite went deep enough or you received more than one.

But all she could hear was her own breathing. It was coming fast.

Then she heard another sound.

A fevered rustling, as if a horde of insects had been released somewhere nearby. And it was getting louder by the second.

51

'Take this,' said Mark. He handed me a small laminated ID card. There was no picture on it. It just gave his name and title: SECURITY OFFICER – HER MAJESTY'S EMBASSY, CAIRO.

'We have to get out of here. Say you need to make a call. Flash this at the two policemen. I'll back you up if they ask. If they let you pass, find the main reception area. I'll follow you as soon as I can. I'll get someone from Mossad on the phone to tell the policemen to forget what happened.'

'Why don't you just go up to them now, and get your Mossad contact on the phone?'

'It's better to ask for forgiveness than permission. This way there isn't much point in them making a big deal of it.'

All I said in reply was 'Okay.' I didn't care about consequences. I wanted out of there. I buttoned up my shirt, rubbed at the scuff marks on my suede jacket, gave up, put it on.

A haughty expression was just what I needed now. I walked straight up to the quarterback, held the ID card out.

'I'll be back. Keep an eye on our guest.' I pointed my thumb in Mark's direction.

The quarterback put a hand up.

He hadn't fallen for it. His eyes narrowed as he took the ID card, examined it. My heart pumped.

'Where are you going?' he asked. His voice was gravelly, as if he'd been smoking since he was a child.

'I've got to make a call,' I said, as calmly as I could. My voice sounded odd, lower than normal, but there was no way he could tell that.

He handed me back the ID card and looked away.

I'd done it.

Two minutes later I was sitting in a busy modern reception area. Near me was a Palestinian family, at least ten of them. Beyond them was an Israeli couple with a young child. Behind me was an older Bedouin woman with a sad expression. The other rows of seats were similarly busy. I was asked, by a dark-haired, sweetly smiling girl, if I'd come in to have my bandage changed.

'My friend is coming.' I said. 'He won't be long.' She smiled at me.

The noise of a police siren poured in through the doors as someone exited. A surge of adrenaline flowed through me. I stood up, walked around, waiting for the police to rush in looking for me.

Should I run for it?

I was getting weird looks, but I couldn't sit down.

'You look a sight,' said a voice.

I spun around. It was Mark.

Ten minutes later we had exited via a side door and we were in a taxi. I could smell leather and a strong pine deodorant. It almost made me sick after the tension of the last few hours. American rock music was playing loudly on the radio.

'Where are we going?' I said.

Mark didn't look at me. He said something to the driver

in what I guessed was Hebrew. The driver shrugged. The taxi sped up.

Mark turned to me.

'You need new shoes,' he said.

I looked down at my feet. My shoes were stained and scuffed badly. The taxi pulled over on King David Street outside a small shoe shop.

'I don't give a damn about my shoes,' I said, after the taxi was gone.

'Neither do I,' said Mark.

'So where are we going?'

'We're meeting Ariel.'

He started walking quickly. We passed a group of children who were squabbling loudly. There were five of them, Arab and Jewish children. They were shouting at each other, fighting over a bright yellow football that one of them was holding.

'This way,' said Mark. A green Toyota Land Cruiser, different to the last one we'd been in, was pulled up half on the kerb near a bus stop. Mark climbed into the front beside Ariel.

'You two look like trouble,' said Ariel, as I got in.

'Don't blame me,' said Mark.

Ariel turned, looked me over, as if he was checking me.

'You are a lucky man,' he said 'Breaking into an historical monument is an offence punishable by up to five years in prison.'

'Thanks for pointing that out,' I said.

I leaned forward. 'Do you have any news about Isabel?' My tone was so sharp Ariel turned halfway round to me.

'Sit back, Mr Ryan. Don't ask too many questions, unless you want to go back to your hotel to calm down.'

I sat back.

Ariel inched the car out behind two white buses.

A phone rang. I put my hand to my pocket, then remembered my phone was lost. Ariel had his out and was talking fast in Hebrew a few seconds later. Then he finished the call.

'Look out the back window and you will see a column of smoke,' he said, softly.

I looked. He was right. It was coming from the Old City and rising up towards the lid of clouds above us.

'A house, just off the Via Dolorosa, is on fire.'

I watched the smoke rise. 'We visited that area,' I said.

'You went to the house where Max Kaiser worked,' said Ariel. 'Where that classified dig's been going on.' It was a statement, not a question.

'Yes.'

'That's the one that's on fire,' he said.

My mouth opened. Then I realised I didn't care. I had to find Isabel.

'Is there any news about that bastard I met in the church?'

My whole body felt bruised, but it didn't bother me.

Ariel glanced at me in the rear-view mirror. He had a grave look that did nothing to reassure me.

My anxiety ticked higher. Was he saying nothing because he knew something he didn't want to tell me?

'What kind of person burns people to death?' I said to no one in particular.

No answer came.

'Where's Isabel?!' I slammed my hand into the door.

Ariel looked at me in his mirror, but didn't change speed. 'You break anything, you pay for it,' he said.

'Can you tell me how you're picking up these phone signals you're tracking?'

'That's classified.'

'Jesus Christ,' I said. 'Just give me a bloody clue.'

There was silence for a minute, then Ariel spoke. 'When

300

we pick up a signal from someone's phone who's gone missing these days, we can identify all other phones used from that location in the last week or the last month or the last year. Clever, no?'

'Yes.'

'That's all he needs to know,' said Mark.

'What about Xena?' I said. 'What's happened to her?'

'She's busy,' said Mark.

Ariel manoeuvred the car into the outside lane of the two lane highway and put his foot down. We passed a line of military vehicles, mostly trucks, with a few jeeps. The road ran between steep hills, then curved to the left. I had no idea which way we were heading out of the city. Then a sign went by that pointed straight ahead for Bethlehem.

I looked at my watch. It was half past ten at night. The traffic was sparse. That sickly burning smell was in my nostrils again. The smell of those bodies. The smell of death.

'Sit back, Mr Ryan. We will be there soon,' said Ariel.

I couldn't. My right hand was pressed across my stomach, pushing the ache inside away. I took a deep, long breath and held it. I had to be calm, believe that Isabel was safe, that she was alive. I couldn't give up. I wouldn't.

The highway curved through low, tightly packed hills. We passed the lights of a town. They stretched up one hill, as if the houses were on stilts. I looked out the back window. The lights of the occasional cars behind us corkscrewed back into darkness.

Then we went through a tunnel.

When we came out there were more hills. We slowed. There was a wide, brilliantly lit military checkpoint up ahead. Young olive green-clad soldiers carrying guns waited, standing off on each side. Ariel opened the window, waved as we came up to the metal barrier. The barrier lifted. We were through.

Ariel's phone rang again. He put it to his ear, didn't speak for a minute, then said something rapid in Hebrew and cut the call.

'What's going on?' I said. 'Where are we going?'

'Your friend has made two calls. The first one was from this road. The second was from south of here. That's where we're going.'

'Can't we go faster?' I said.

Ariel increased our speed a little.

Headlights flashed past us in the opposite direction. The road wasn't a highway anymore. There wasn't even a dividing line.

As we rounded a curve, a packed yellow minibus passed us at a suicidal speed. The driver must have been certifiable. He'd been totally on the wrong side of the road, right on the bend, going as fast as he could.

I closed my eyes, said part of a prayer I'd learned in a boarding school in Briarwood, New York, that I'd been at for just one year. *A periculis cunctis libera nos simper.* From all danger deliver us always.

I'd repeated that Latin phrase over and over all that year in the school. I did it now too. Nobody paid attention to my muttering.

That had been the year my dad had been transferred to England for active duty. We followed him the next year.

I couldn't remember the rest of the prayer, but repeating that part now was enough. I would take help from any place I could get it.

The road twisted and turned. Signs in Arabic only flashed by. We passed a group of men standing at the side of the road beside a barrel that had a fire burning in it.

They all seemed to be dressed in black. Ariel accelerated

as we swept past them. Then we turned a corner and a sparkling cobweb of lights filled the steep rolling hills to our left, like a scene from a sci-fi movie set on an alien planet.

52

Henry Mowlam was still at his desk. He'd been on duty for twelve hours. If he stayed on duty for fifteen his presence would be flagged to the duty manager.

He didn't care.

Events in Jerusalem justified him staying late, never mind the fact that the operation to find Susan Hunter and Isabel Sharp was, he knew from experience, at a critical point.

The situation with the Israeli stock market, due to open Sunday morning, had been enough to get him to stay for the afternoon, but the search for the two women, to avoid them meeting the same fate as Max Kaiser, was now uppermost in his mind.

If they were still alive, the next move for whoever was holding them had to be to kill them in a horrific way. He'd seen it before. When a mission looks like it's failing, the principles lash out, killing captives and followers who might betray them.

That thought left Henry without any desire to go home. He was needed here.

The cooperation from the Israelis had been first class, access to second-by-second mobile phone data and clearance at the highest level for Mark Headsell to participate in operations alongside their Security Service had meant the search for Susan and Isabel had proceeded as quickly as could be hoped.

And because of that cooperation, they had another lead.

The rising tension, bombings, tit-for-tat military deployments and media frenzy in Egypt over that caliph's letter, and reports of dirty tricks by Mossad to hide the letter and its translator, were all unwelcome distractions.

An even more unwelcome distraction would be a war between Egypt and Israel. A war, precipitated by mistakes on both sides and political posturing, which seemed eminently possible now, when it had seemed an unlikely, distant possibility only a week before.

The situation had moved so suddenly up the international agenda that a meeting of the UN Security Council had been called for the following morning in New York. Twelve hours from now.

What a lot of people were worried about though, was what might happen in those twelve hours.

Israeli military units had been deployed to front line positions and the Egyptians had recently responded. Sorties by their air force had resulted in two incidents with Israeli F-16I Sufa fighters. Missile systems had locked on and pursuits had been initiated.

All it would take would be some jumpy pilot to stray into a military zone, rockets to be fired in retaliation, and the slide to war would accelerate down a cliff.

The news from Jerusalem was only making matters worse. Already there had been vociferous international condemnation of the mass murder of priests and the significant damage to Christianity's holiest site. Commentators were speculating that Christ's tomb had been destroyed in the fire. Other media channels, Twitter among them, had leaked that clues pointing to a Palestinian terror group's involvement had been found.

The US news networks were running interviews with Christian preachers who were talking about signs of the second coming, Armageddon.

An email message came into his inbox. He scanned it.

The message was an automatically generated report on Lord Bidoner. It had arrived in a secure PDF format.

The report showed the contents of an email Lord Bidoner had sent to a private US security company. The message, which had been intercepted by GCHQ, was a request for a global 'all archives' search for any current or past references to a symbol, a picture of which was attached.

The picture was, he was surprised to see when he opened it, of the square and arrow symbol that was in the manuscript Susan Hunter had been translating.

Henry put his head in his hands. He was tired. It was approaching 1 a.m.

Had he uncovered a connection between Lord Bidoner and what was going on in Israel?

And why was the good Lord recruiting a global security company to instigate an expensive search which would include internet, academic libraries, museum libraries and a hundred other non-internet enabled repositories of data?

And why had the search request specifically suggested an international search of graveyards, mausoleums and burial places?

What the hell was going on?

Was it time to call Sergeant Finch back in? He reached for the phone on his desk. Then his hand hesitated.

53

The cream, flat-roofed houses, rising up the sides of the hills, were lit up with strings of lights. The steep hills behind the houses went up, almost perpendicular into the air, the houses covering the hills layer upon layer, precipitously on top of each other.

We sped on, curving and twisting between hills. Two black flags flipped past at a turn-off. I heard a popping sound, a burst of gunfire. The Israeli army maybe, or Palestinian factions fighting each other.

Then the lights all disappeared and we were curving through empty rock-covered, twisting hills, visible as shades of grey beyond our headlights. Ten minutes after that we pulled off the main road. The road we turned onto had no lights and no sign posts.

A line of scrawny trees to the right petered out after a while, as did a bent and mostly broken mesh fence on one side. After a minute travelling, our headlights picking out the rough tarmac road ahead, we turned onto another side road.

Ariel turned all our lights off. We drove slowly forward, our eyes getting used to the near darkness. The only light in the car was a low blueish glow from a GPS by Ariel's knees. He adjusted it and the glow almost disappeared.

To our right and left all I could see was the outline of rocks nearby and a ridge of hills rising beyond. Occasionally I saw bushes near the car, like round spiky beach balls, and a stunted tree. Everything looked dried out. After a minute, Ariel increased his speed. His eyes must have gotten used to the dark, though we were still only travelling at ten miles an hour.

Then, as my own eyes adjusted, I saw we were driving on a single width track now, and that our wheels were sending dust up behind us.

There was a smell in the air, a mixture of something like cinnamon and something dead. The car stopped where another track crossed over it.

'This GPS is a total loss,' said Ariel.

'Are we far from where the signal was picked up?' said Mark.

'No, no, it was around here, within a hundred metres. I can't get it any more precise.' Ariel bent down, adjusting the GPS until the blueish glow came up briefly, then disappeared again.

'Let's take a look around,' I said. 'Do you have torches?'

'We're not advertising we're here,' said Ariel. 'And we won't be staying long. All we're doing is looking for a vehicle or bodies. I have three night vision goggles. They'll pick up heat sources.'

'Do we have back-up?' I asked. I turned in my seat to see if there were any cars behind us. There weren't.

Mark turned to me. 'There will only be back-up if we call it in. We're supposed to get the Palestinian police involved if we mount a major search out here. But that will take too long. The Palestinians cooperate on missing persons, but it will take hours to wake up the right people and explain everything. We can't wait.'

'We should have left him at his hotel,' said Ariel. 'He asks too many questions.'

'No, he's useful. It'll be good to have him with us if the Palestinian Authority turn up.' Mark opened his door.

'I told you not to worry about them,' said Ariel.

'And I told you what I think of that attitude,' said Mark.

I got out and walked around the vehicle. I could see bushes, the outline of rocks, black hills.

Ariel opened the back. He took out three sets of night vision goggles. They had one large, round eye facing forward and two eye pieces for your eyes at the back. They also had a large round adjusting screw on the right side. They were lighter than they looked.

'Make sure they're strapped on tight,' said Ariel. 'And don't lose them.'

The three of us must have looked like aliens after we put them on.

'We won't go far,' said Ariel. 'We'll work our way forward between each of the four tracks, head out maybe fifty metres. This is just an unofficial check to see if there is any evidence of your girlfriend being here, any leftover heat sources.'

I knew what he meant; *any bodies*.

I wanted to get going, get it over with. 'Why are we waiting? Let's do this.'

I walked off among the stones. I could see them and the trees and bushes clearly in shades of green, in front of me. I could also see the occasional flapping thing too, which could have been a giant moth or bat. The centre of the flapping thing was orange hued from the heat it was giving off.

'Are there any houses around here?' I asked as Ariel came up beside me. His face was also orange, as were his clothes.

'There was a settlement near here. But it was razed. We might find the foundations.'

309

It was deathly quiet. The distant traffic noises from the highway, like when we'd been at the villa, were all gone. Here, there was nothing but stars and scrub and a blanket-like hush. Suddenly, a distant shriek, sounding as if it was from some prehistoric bird, cut through the air.

I looked up. The stars were a green blanket, pinpricks of light. We were seeing everything because of starlight, I realised. The moon was behind some clouds, but I could see the scraggy bushes and the hills around us clearly. An orange flash passed overhead. A bird. It had to be.

The hills looked steep. They were covered in scree and got higher on our left, but I couldn't see much detail further than maybe fifty feet away. Beyond that it was all green gloom.

I kept walking. Mark and Ariel followed behind. Blocking our path occasionally were stones as big as dining room tables. Others, scattered pieces of white lava, as big as cars, were jumbled up and leaning against each other in places. We walked on.

'Shusshh,' said Ariel.

I hadn't realised we were making any noise.

We stopped. There was deep quiet for half a minute, then, a rustling off to our left. It stopped as quickly as it had started. I saw a tinge of orange behind some green bushes.

My head was hurting again. My stomach was aching too, but I was glad I hadn't taken any painkillers.

'It's an ibex,' said Ariel softly. 'This is ideal ground for them.'

'Let's keep going,' I said.

'We should turn back,' said Ariel nonchalantly, as if we'd been looking for a lost set of car keys.

I kept walking.

'Come on, Sean. You can't just walk off into the hills!' Mark's voice echoed oddly.

'We have to cover a lot of ground. Let's go back,' he said.

'I'm not just doing fifty metres in each direction,' I said calmly. 'I'm going as far as I think I should go, depending on what we find.'

'Okay,' he said. 'If you want to prove you love her more than anyone else, be my guest. But walking off isn't going to get you any brownie points from me.' He sounded bitter.

'I'm not looking for brownie points.'

He didn't get it at all.

I stopped. There was a wall of spiky bushes and taller rocks ahead. To our right the hill became way steeper, almost impossible to climb. To our left there was a patch of open ground. I went there, and walked in a circle. Mark was right beside me.

It was a good place to turn.

We got back to the car five minutes later. The next section of the desert we searched had even more rocks. We had to walk over or around them constantly. Some of the bushes between the rocks had white spikes two inches long, just to keep our attention from flagging.

The biggest rocks here were truck-sized. They looked out of place too, as if they'd been scattered by giants playing some weird game. I wondered if Isabel had seen these.

If you wanted to hide something, this area would be a great place to do it in. I walked on. After another few minutes, with Mark and Ariel distant behind me, and about to disappear, and the car lost far away, I headed back. This was not looking good. I was running out of luck. So was Isabel.

When I reached the others, Ariel was fuming. His face actually looked puffed out.

'If you get lost in these hills, I'm not calling out a search party. You stay behind me in the next section. We have to get out of here soon.'

I shook my head. If he thought I was going to follow his direction he had another thing coming.

311

'Maybe you don't understand, Mr Ryan. I can arrest you now and have you locked up for weeks, maybe months, if you keep this up. You are illegally in this country.'

I spoke slowly as I replied. 'We will do this search properly. And as for arresting me, which country am I in anyway? This is Palestinian territory, isn't it?'

'You two stop this crap,' said Mark. 'We'll do this search properly, and fast. Now both of you shut up.'

We headed off again into the third section. This part was similar to the last in having large boulders, if anything even bigger than in the other sections. We walked for two hundred metres or so, finding nothing but a torn blue plastic bag that looked as if it had been out here for decades.

This time Ariel didn't ask to turn back until the car had disappeared completely.

'There's nothing else for miles out here. Let's go! If we lose our way back we could walk around out here until morning.'

'We're not going to die,' I said.

'That's not the point, Sean,' said Mark. 'You know there's talk of a war starting. This is not the time to do this. Anyway, we could be doing something useful somewhere else, rather than spending the rest of this bloody night out here looking for our car.'

'Okay, okay.' I looked around. There was nothing. Not one single other heat source except for us.

We turned back, spreading out once we saw the car, all scanning the area around us. Then, as we neared the crossroads, I noticed clear car tracks heading off past me into the scrub. I hissed for the others.

'Someone's been here!' Hope flooded through my exhausted body. In seconds all the aches and pains I'd been feeling disappeared.

'Let's get the car.' I was half running already. The Toyota was glistening in the starlight just beyond some rocks.

312

'Okay,' said Ariel. 'But don't run. You'll knock yourself out in the dark.'

He was almost right. I stubbed my toe, nearly tripping over, but I kept going, adrenaline tingling through me. It was a long shot that we would find Isabel, even longer that we would find her alive, but it was better than walking around getting desperate.

Ariel had locked the car. I had to wait for him to reach me before I could get in. We set off with no headlights as we were still wearing our night vision goggles, and headed slowly along the valley following the tracks. Ariel seemed to be checking around for something as we went. His head kept swivelling. He was muttering to himself too. I was in the front seat beside him this time.

After half a minute I opened the window on my side. Mark did the same.

'I'm gonna stop now,' said Ariel, a minute later.

'Why?' I asked.

'Can you not see?' he shouted. He pointed ahead.

All I saw was a greenish hue, an open area in front of us, and beyond that a patch of small rocks and spiky dried up bushes.

'See what?'

'Someone came out here to hunt. Look at the marks in the dirt. Then they turned back. You can see where they turned!'

'We have to take a look,' I said.

'Yes, yes, we will look around.' He turned off the engine. 'But when we are finished we will do the last section quickly. We can't waste anymore time out here. We can't search all night.'

I didn't bother telling him that I would search until I dropped if I wanted to. Mark looked at me as if he was torn about what to do. He looked worn out. For all our exertions we had achieved nothing.

'We'll need some rest, Sean, if we're to be of any use tomorrow.'

'You get some rest,' I said.

I got out of the car. Ariel turned the engine off. We walked around looking at the car tracks. Ariel was right. There was a definite turning circle and a place where a fire had been lit. The earth there was still faintly orange. And the car tracks didn't go any further.

We were nearly back at the Toyota when I heard a rumbling. It sounded like a distant train. That couldn't be right. We stopped, looked around.

There was a mass of orange coming towards us. Then I heard neighing.

'Take off the goggles,' said Ariel. 'Pass them to me, quickly.'

I did as I was asked. He pushed them into a black shoulder bag he'd been carrying.

I looked up. My eyesight wasn't as bad as I'd expected. The detail was all gone, but I could still see dark shapes. And the moving shape of a group of riders coming fast towards us on large horses and mostly wearing dark hoods. One of them shouted something in Arabic at us.

I hadn't a clue what he was saying. But it didn't sound friendly.

'Don't make any sudden moves,' said Mark firmly.

The heavy breathing of the horses was filling my ears now, as they came near. And then I could smell them. The odour of horse sweat was almost enough to make me gag.

54

Isabel lifted her head. It had been a long time since the insects, whatever they were, had departed. But she hadn't dared move since they'd crawled over her trousered legs. They'd seemed to be following each other and had passed over her as if she was a rock.

What they would do if they came upon her bare arms or, God forbid, her face, if she slept, was another thing. She shuddered deeply as she thought of it, then moved Susan Hunter's head. It was hurting her shoulder, it was lying so awkwardly.

It was all she could do to keep Susan's head and face from the floor of the cave. All hope of building a cairn to try to reach the hole in the roof was gone now. She would have to wait until Susan Hunter was dead to do anymore scratching around for stones.

Isabel's ears heard everything now, even her own breathing. She'd heard the insects approaching and them going away into some crack, most likely. She'd heard distant faint rumblings in the earth too. And now, suddenly, as she held Susan tight she heard a new sound. Another rumbling, like the sound of a distant river.

Could that be it?

No. It was something else. It was a drumming, like the sound of horse's hooves. And then it stopped. She put Susan's head back against the wall and rose shakily to her feet. She shouted, 'Help! HELP!' She drummed her feet on the floor. The noise echoed hopelessly, then died.

55

The horses were right in front of me. Two of them were pawing the ground, no more than a foot away, as if they wanted to dig their hooves into me. I looked around slowly. There were at least ten riders surrounding us, their horses flexing their shoulders, jittering, snorting and neighing.

We wouldn't get away easily.

The riders were wearing dark hooded outfits, all except the man on the horse directly in front of me. He was bare headed, almost bald, his skin pitted, as if from a long-forgotten childhood disease.

He shouted something in Arabic. The horses inched closer to us, pawing the ground. Ariel responded in Arabic.

One of the riders laughed.

'You look like you speak English,' said the man on the horse in front of me. His accent was oddly familiar, part Middle Eastern, part north London.

I was relieved to hear a familiar accent. Then he said, 'I am warning you not to run.'

'Why would we?' said Mark.

'Well don't, if you value your lives.'

The starlight was barely enough to see by. It left detail

beyond a few feet away in shadow. How they were moving around in this light was amazing.

Most of the riders were holding rifles in their hands. There were at least four pointing directly at me.

The man above me made a loud hawking noise. Then he spat. I heard it, rather than saw it fall. I think it ended up near me, but I didn't look down. I kept staring up at him.

'You people have the smell of death on you,' said the man. There was a murmur from some of the other riders, as if he'd given a signal. The horses' shoulders shifted menacingly. Their manes were long, ragged, their skin mottled shades of brown. Two of the horses had big white patches. The smell of horse sweat was heavy, pungent.

'You are spies,' said the rider. 'On that there can be no argument.'

'We're not spies,' I said loudly.

'You are an American, and that one.' He pointed at Ariel. 'He is a Jew. Admit your falsehood and it will be easier on you.' His horse shifted again, inching aggressively forward, as if it knew what its master was saying.

I expected my toes to be crushed at any moment, that a bullet would land in me somewhere.

'I have every right to be here,' said Ariel. His tone was aggressive.

There was a rustle around us, a low growl. The tension could almost be touched.

'You have no right to be here.' The rider's tone was affronted. 'This is Palestinian territory. I should shoot you all for trespassing.' The rider above me leaned down precariously. He swung his fist through the air, shook it towards Ariel.

His hand was dirty. There were strap marks on the back, like lines of treacle, and his knuckles were scuffed with dust that glistened in the starlight.

'You won't do that,' I said. If they wanted us dead they would have killed us already. No, there was a reason we were still alive.

He leaned down towards me. 'I should give you over to our friends in Hamas. They're always looking for spies.'

He spat. Spittle hit my face. I didn't move. He leaned closer. I could smell sharp spiciness on his breath.

'They'll keep you locked in an underground room without sun for a year, maybe more. Then they'll tell your family to raise a million dollars to get you released, or they'll start sending body parts. Would you like that?' His teeth glistened in the torchlight that was reflecting off the rocks.

I didn't answer. If that was what was going to happen, I had to look for my chance to make a run for it.

The first hour after a kidnap presents some of the best possibilities for escape, before they hide you away.

One of the other riders said something fast in Arabic. The man above me responded equally fast. The first one slipped off his horse, came to me, patted me down roughly. Then he moved to Ariel. There were words exchanged. Then the sound of rifles being cocked around us. The Palestinian continued his search. He held a black pistol and the goggles in the air a few moments later. He passed them to the guy above me.

'What do you need a gun for, if you are not spies?' he said, as he examined Ariel's pistol. He spoke softly, as if he was even more sure of what he was saying now.

'I am an officer in the Israeli Immigration service,' said Ariel. 'These men are not Israelis. And they are not spies.' It sounded brave. He had no idea if the next thing that was going to happen was that he was going to get a bullet in the head.

'I am an official with the British Consular service in Egypt,' said Mark. 'You have no reason to hold me. I am looking for a British subject, this man's girlfriend.' He pointed towards me.

319

'No lies,' said the rider, kicking his leather boot tip in my direction. 'Which government do you work for?'

'I don't work for any government. I'm looking for someone, like he said. These men are helping me. We have no quarrel with you'

The laugh that emanated from him spread like an infection through the other riders. Then a shout echoed from somewhere to the right. The leader said something to the rider beside him. Then he bent down, gripped my shoulder.

'What is your name?' he said.

'Sean Ryan.'

'Well, Mr Sean Ryan, if you want to see home again, on this side of the curtain of death, you will go with my friends without making trouble.'

He turned his horse and went quickly back the way he had come. About half the riders followed him. The others remained. There were six of them left. Each had a rifle trained on us.

'Walk this way,' said one of them. 'Follow that horse.' The accent sounded French, and it was a woman's voice.

I looked at Mark. He shrugged. We were going with them. We walked through the rocks. One of the riders led the way. After a few minutes I realised we were following a path that wound down the centre of the valley. Its sides were getting steeper, rockier.

I was walking near Mark. 'Do you think we should make a break for it?' I whispered when our heads came close, as I came up beside him.

He shook his head.

'Do nothing to make them start shooting,' he said. 'That's how you'll make all this go bad, very, very bad.'

The woman rider moved her horse up close and leaned down towards me. Her face was brown, her forehead high, her eyes dark and wide. She wore a thin black cloth, like something out of Laurence of Arabia, around her mouth.

'Don't be stupid,' she said. 'We may not be the best shots, but you are very big targets, and when the sun comes up you will not be able to hide anywhere. We will find you and use you for target practice.'

'Where are you taking us?' said Ariel. 'We have every right to be here. When I report this, there will be trouble for you and your whole village.'

'Shut up,' said the woman. 'My brother is dead. We will not let it pass. You will come with us.' She spat on the ground.

'What happened to him?' I said.

'That is not your business.' She moved her horse further away, then said something in Arabic to the rider in front of us. He began moving faster. We had to hurry to keep up. The clip clop of the horses reverberated among the rocks as we went.

As we reached a low point in the valley the rider ahead turned to the right. A row of silver bracelets, mostly thin, but one was at least two inches wide, glistened in the starlight as she turned.

The starlight was a fierce, almost neon glow above us now. The moon had come out from behind some clouds and was high in the sky. I scanned the horizon. There was a buzzing far off in the distance. It grew as we walked. The riders didn't miss a step.

The helicopter must have been Israeli.

It went over us fast. And it had no lights. All that gave it away was the noise and finally, a rapidly moving shadow in the sky. I imagined all types of radar and infrared washing over us. I expected the helicopter to turn and pass back over us again, but it didn't. It swept over the next ridge and was gone, buzzing into the distance as quickly as it had come.

We passed a giant house-sized lump of cracked white rock and I saw where we were headed. There was a fire in front of a building with empty sockets for windows. The two floors

321

of the building had been constructed against the side of a steep hillock, which went on another twenty feet higher, and then ended in a jagged spine.

The spine, a spur of the Judean hills, circled around us.

At the fire there were more Palestinians. A woman with a hunched body, wearing a black chador, was stirring a giant cooking pot set over the fire. Children huddled together in the shadows near a wooden cart with solid wheels.

Long knives were hanging in a bunch from a tripod. I thought of how Alek had been beheaded in Istanbul.

As we came towards the light of the fire all conversation stopped. Everyone stared. It seemed as though the air itself was waiting for something to happen. Some of the men did more than stare, they put hands on their guns, raised them. We were obviously not a welcome sight.

The woman rode ahead and slipped off her horse as she neared the fire. She passed its reins to a young boy no more than eight years old. He was wearing a Spiderman t-shirt.

People were sitting around the fire. Most had hoods on, like the riders, and some were bent over, as if praying. Others had turned to look at us.

We stopped. I had a bad feeling. These people did not look happy. They looked as if they were getting ready for a funeral.

The woman rider strode towards me. She was a little shorter than me, but she didn't lack confidence. Her eyes glared as she spoke.

'Your woman is missing, yes?'

'Yes.'

'What will you do to find her?' she asked.

'Whatever I have to.'

'What does that mean, American?'

'What I said.'

She leaned closer to me. Her eyes were bloodshot. As she

came within inches of me, she pulled the cloth covering her chin down.

Her neck and chin were pock marked, the skin broken, scaly, all the way up to her lips. She was suffering from a rare skin disease, a relative of leprosy.

'Would you kiss me?'

'Whatever I have to do.'

A wave of revulsion rose up from somewhere deep inside me and passed through my whole body. I did my best to keep my expression impassive. I wasn't sure if I succeeded.

She leaned closer. I could smell a sourness on her breath.

'We shall see your lies,' she said. 'And then you will see what we do to spies and people who insult us.'

She dragged a finger across her throat, pushing her scaly skin hard until it went purple and flaky. A piece of it slipped off. The purple skin underneath grew darker, as if blood was about to leak out.

56

Isabel listened. The rumble had passed far into the distance. The only sound she could hear was her own breathing.

And it seemed to be getting louder.

She couldn't tell whether that was because everything she heard seemed progressively louder anyway, the longer she was down here enveloped in blackness, or whether her throaty rasping was a sign of how her thirst was becoming more demanding, affecting her body as well as her mind.

She'd urinated into her cupped hands a few hours before and despite the awful acidy taste, had relished the liquid in her mouth and down her throat. But her throat was burning now with dryness and from the effects of drinking it. She wanted to scratch at it, pull it from her.

Where the hell was Sean?

Where the hell was this bastard?

She said another prayer for his return. It was ironic, she knew, that she was hoping for him to come back, the man who was treating her so cruelly, but he was her most realistic saviour right now.

Who else was going to rescue her? Sean was far away in Jerusalem. There was no way he could work out where she was. And any chance of rescue was highly improbable.

Then she heard it.

A faint hissing, a hundred thousand legs rubbing against each other. It grew louder and she could hear the rustling rise and fall, as if there was a conversation going on.

She reached in front of her for a rock to beat them away. As she felt through the stones, then raised the biggest one and held it to her chest like a sword, an idea came to her.

Yes, that was what she would do.

It would be better to be dead than to be eaten alive.

57

'I'm not a spy and I haven't insulted anyone.' I pushed my face toward hers. I wasn't going to be intimidated.

'You are as innocent as driving snow. Isn't that what you people say?'

'What do you want us for?' I wasn't going to bother correcting her.

She knocked her hand against her head, then banged her knuckles hard into the side of her skull, as if she was tapping on wood. Her bracelets jangled, sparkled.

'You think we're all stupid. My brother was right.'

She leaned forward, pointing a dirty finger into my face. 'You are a Westerner who has been softened by sitting down too long. Your legs have stopped working, and your brain too and the rest of you.' She poked a finger towards my chest.

I swiped fast and caught her hand as she pulled it away. I held it, crushing it lightly.

'You're wasting your time insulting me. Kill me, if that's what you plan to do, but I'm not a spy.' I pushed her hand down and let her go.

Her expression hardened.

'Allah will not save the likes of you.' She said something fast and loud in Arabic, turned from me, raised her hands together as if in prayer, then started ululating. Her bracelets sparkled in the amber light of the fire.

I was a thousand miles out of my comfort zone. There was a cultural gap of a hundred traditions and fervent beliefs between us.

I looked around and saw the other Palestinians staring at us. It looked as if they were deciding whether to kill us or not.

There was some other tension in their expressions too. They looked as if they were running from something.

'Ignore her,' said Ariel loudly. I turned. He and Mark were right behind me. They both looked pale in the moonlight.

The woman pointed at Ariel. 'And you, Ibn il-Homaar, son of a donkey,' she said. 'I bet you sent your mother to strangers to look after her, when she got old.'

'Watch your tongue,' he said. He pointed back at her. His finger was shaking.

She laughed.

A voice called out in Arabic.

I turned. It was Xena.

She was walking towards the fire, wearing a black scarf around her neck. It was wound tightly over the top of her head too, but her thin frame and face were unmistakable. Two men were with her. They both had rifles in their hands. I wasn't sure if they were her bodyguards or her captors.

'Welcome to the party,' said Mark.

'Who is your friend?' said Xena.

The woman who had led us here shrieked in Arabic.

Ten rifles went to shoulders. Some of them looked ancient, but others were modern enough to blow big holes in us.

'Don't do anything sudden,' said Xena.

Then she spoke in Arabic to the woman. She started softly. Then she turned to the men pointing their guns at us. She raised her hands as if to show they were empty. The guns pointing at us came down.

Then there was silence.

The rider with the skin disease waved her hand through the air, as if swatting a fly, said something in Arabic that sounded like a curse, spat on the ground, turned on her heel and walked away.

'Let us sit by the fire and warm ourselves,' said Xena.

'What the hell are you doing here?' I said.

'Looking for you, until your friends found me.'

It was cold and the night air was still. We had been warm while we were walking, but I could feel the cold now.

We went to the fire. I sat near Xena. Mark sat on the other side of her. Ariel sat beyond him. I raised my hands, taking in the welcome warmth. The fire glowed an orangey-red and was built with thicker branches and dry brush. A burnt pine smell filled the air near the fire. The smoke from it was thin. It drifted slowly up towards the stars.

'You took your time,' said Mark, as he sat down.

Xena shrugged.

The woman who was tending the pot hanging over the fire stood back and to one side and stared at us with suspicion.

'What the hell's up with these people?' I said. 'Why have they brought us here?'

Xena leaned towards me. 'They call this the valley of the evil eye.' She waved around her. 'They say everything here is cursed.'

'Did you tell them I'm looking for Isabel?'

'I told them I'm your translator, that you treat me like an insect and that I hate you all.' She spat into the fire, turned to me, smiled. Her teeth were very white. One of them had a gold filling.

'They do not believe any part of your story,' she continued.

'Why are they roaming around in the middle of the night?' I said.

'They are looking for someone, like we are.'

'Who?'

'A slave of evil.'

'They told you this?' I said.

She turned to me. 'I am their sister. I speak their tongue. Why wouldn't they?'

'How can we get away from them?' I said. 'I need to look for Isabel.'

Our eyes met. She leaned forward. 'They can help us,' she whispered.

'How?' I wanted to believe her, but I was sceptical.

Xena reached down to the earth between us, wiping away small loose stones and pieces of dried bush. Then she drew a symbol I recognised in the dirt. It was the arrow in a square symbol.

'They found this symbol,' she said. 'Near where your Toyota is.' She nodded back in the direction we had come.

'There are many caves in that area. They say a marker like this could be used to help someone find their way back to a cave. They have gone back there to wait and see if the person they are looking for returns.'

My heart was beating faster. They had found a connection to the book, and to Susan, and maybe Isabel too. I wanted to get up, race back to the car, find the symbol, and figure out where the cave it pointed to was. My hands pushed down into the dirt. I made a fist with sandy earth in it, let it trickle through my fingers. I had to go.

'Do not make any false moves,' said Xena. 'They are watching us.' She patted the earth, dusted the sign away from where she'd drawn it.

'How can we convince them we're the good guys?' I glanced over my shoulder. There were at least five sets of eyes on me. What would we have to do to be free from these people?

'Do what I say. I will find a way.'

Mark coughed, tapped her arm. She turned to him. They spoke for a few minutes, their heads close together. I looked around, trying to work out what the best way to run would be if I got a chance to make a dash for freedom.

Xena turned back to me. 'Mark thinks you and me can convince them we are on their side,' she said. 'He wants us to talk to them.'

'So who are they out here looking for and what did he do?' I said.

She leaned towards me. 'A man recruited that woman's brother, and his friend.' She nodded towards the woman watching over us, who had ridden in front.

'The man came to their village early last year. He spoke perfect Arabic, claimed he wanted to help them. Her brother was living in England at the time, in London. She gave the man his phone number. A few months later her brother sent a lot of money home. That was last spring. Last week her brother was found dead in Amsterdam. His body was burnt, terribly. They believe these things are connected.'

'So why are they out here in the middle of the night?'

'The man has returned. He was seen by someone out looking for lost sheep yesterday evening. They've been riding these hills since, searching for him. There are caves all over this valley. They are perfect for hiding things, because people avoid this area. They think the man may have found out about this from her brother.'

That would explain a lot. Isabel and Susan could have been moved to a cave in this area yesterday. It all sounded right.

Relief rose up inside me. Isabel might be alive. I'd been right to have hope. I closed my eyes, said a prayer.

330

Let it be true.

I'd imagined her dying horribly, many times, but I'd pushed those thoughts away each time. I looked around. I had to convince these people we weren't their enemy.

A noise, a soft drone, startled me. I looked up. It was still dark. It had to be the darkest part of the night. The stars were a glittering carpet of lights, the Milky Way visible like a path you could follow. The sound was coming from somewhere over the horizon. It was getting louder. It wasn't like the sound of that helicopter either. This was something on a much larger scale.

All eyes went to the heavens.

Then we saw them. Dark shadows. It wasn't just one plane flying over. It was lots of them. Nothing else could make such a noise. I'd heard the rumble of bombers and fighter jets crossing the sky before, at the air force base my dad was stationed at in England. And I knew that exercises with lots of aircraft over population zones was unheard off. There was only one possible explanation.

Why else do lots of planes fly together in the night, if it isn't for war?

Was this the Israeli Air Force heading away on a mission?

They had a few hundred F15s and F16s that could raid almost anywhere in the region. But where might they be going? To Iran? To Egypt? Had some General there crossed the border, launched an attack on Israel?

Was this the start of the big regional war that was going to drag us all into World War III?

The wind picked up. It whistled through the low bushes around the camp. It was a throaty howl. It sounded as if a wolf was echoing the thrumming noises fading in the sky.

Then something hissed.

Then hissed again.

331

There was a smell, as if the fire was spitting. Mark was the first to react. He looked around.

The bullet hit him in the back of the head.

It exploded in a shower of sticky grey matter, blood and spiky bone.

Part of it hit my face like a wet branch slapping into it.

A sense of total disbelief came over me. Something had happened that was more like a dream than reality. Seconds slowed, as if braking.

There was another hiss, a disturbance in the air near me.

'Down,' shouted Xena.

She was already at ground level, pressing into the earth. Ariel was leaning up looking the other way, out into the darkness. His jacket was speckled with pieces of Mark's brain.

The thumping of blood in my ears was loud and insistent.

And then a bullet hit Ariel exploding a large red hole below his shoulder. He slumped forward with hardly a sound. No one could survive that.

Shots rang out from nearby. I heard running feet. There were two more hisses. They were further away this time. I scanned around, turning my head slowly. I couldn't see who was shooting.

A shriek echoed. The woman who'd been watching over us went running into the darkness, a rifle held in front of her. Her shriek was cut off a few seconds later. I heard a thump as her body hit the dirt.

I was stretched out, my hands near my face. My head was up an inch and I was looking around, and hoping fervently that I wasn't going to get a hole in my head for not burying myself in the dirt.

Every muscle in my body was tense, from my feet to my neck.

A Palestinian man who'd been nearby, ran crouching, half jumping in the same direction as the woman. A burst of

332

hissing gunfire sent him reeling backwards, then falling face down. After a few twitches his body went still.

My heart was thumping faster. My mouth was paper dry. I inched forward. I could smell dust and blood. I reached for Mark's arm. I'd seen him twitch a few times after he fell. Was he dead?

More shots rang out from somewhere to our left. A flurry of single shots. Then a groan echoed into the unfeeling sky. It was followed by another long burst of gunfire. The sound of every bullet echoed through my body.

A scream put my nerves onto another level.

And then all the shooting stopped. The sound of my own breathing filled the air.

I looked around. I couldn't see anyone. Whoever was firing had either killed everyone or had sent them running into the darkness.

I looked around for a weapon. There was nothing nearby.

Whoever had been firing could easily be getting ready to come and see the results of their handiwork. That had to be what you would do after shooting up a camp site.

But was it a rival Palestinian group or some Bedouin doing this? Or was it my evil friend from the church out there?

'You again,' said a voice above me. I recognised it with a sickening feeling.

'Death and you are friends, aren't they?'

I turned my head, fast.

He was standing over me. How the hell had he done that? He was like a ghost.

I felt cold, then hot, then oddly calm. I stared up at him, assessing my chances. He had a dangerous looking black machine pistol in the crook of his arm. His face was puffed up, bruised, all yellow and purple down one side and at his throat. Then I remembered; that was where I'd punched him, held him.

'Do not get up,' he said. His accent was clipped. He pointed his gun at my face.

'Or you will die like all the others.'

Xena was half on her knees. She didn't move as he walked quickly towards her, his gun still pointing at me. She looked ready to pounce. He backed away, transferred the gun from his right arm to his left as he walked, then put his right hand to his belt.

A moment later I saw a silver pistol in his right hand.

He was on the other side of her now, facing me, ten feet or so beyond her. She had her back to him at this point. Her head turned, as he walked slowly behind her. Her neck extended.

I thought about getting up, making a run for him. I might be able to distract him enough to let Xena escape.

He stepped closer to Xena and said, 'Traitor.'

The pistol in his right hand fired. Then there was blood pouring from her chest, pumping, all shiny and red and splattering the dust.

'No!' I moved to get up, bile rising in my throat.

Thump. Thump. Thump.

Bullets hit the earth in front of me, banging one after the other like giant fists boxing into the ground.

I stopped my rise, looked at their path.

I was going to die.

The iron smell of blood caught in my throat. I could feel splatters of it on my face, taste it on my lips. The ground felt hot under my hands, as if the temperature had gone up.

The bullets stopped.

Xena had jerked upwards, as if she'd been interrupted in getting up. Now she slumped forward soundlessly, her gaze fixed on me, unblinking, her blood flowing, pumping fast into the dirt.

He walked towards me, the hole at the end of his silver

334

pistol pointing right at my eye. I could see the black emptiness of death. A wisp of smoke was coming from the end of the barrel.

'I will kill you, Sean Ryan. You should not have come here, sticking your nose in once again.'

He moved his gun hand, pointed it down my body, as if deciding what part of me to shoot.

'How do you know me?' I said.

'You disrupted us in London.' His eyes narrowed. 'A friend of mine died because of you. I remembered it after we met in the Church of the Holy Sepulchre.'

'You won't get away with this,' I said.

He laughed. 'But I have. Though unfortunately you will not live to see how true that is. Now turn over!'

I stared up at him. 'Go to hell.' If I was going to die it would be while spitting into his face.

His boot struck somewhere on my cheek.

The side of my face blazed with pain.

Then another blow landed on the other side of my head. Darkness engulfed me. The next thing I saw was a face floating in a deep ocean.

It was Isabel's face. It was floating away from me.

I struggled. But I was far from the surface. My hands and legs wouldn't move. I had to kick but I couldn't.

I willed my eyes to open.

They wouldn't. In the distance, through a fog of pain, I heard a voice.

'It is time for you to learn your lesson, Sean Ryan.'

The laugh that followed was the laugh of someone who had won.

58

The coffee machine was empty, but its service light wasn't on. Henry Mowlem shook his head and put his one pound coin into the big confectionary machine instead. A Diet Coke rattled to the bottom exit. He put his hand in.

On his way back to his desk he drank more than half the can. He needed it. He needed to stay awake. He looked at the text and video feeds, then his eye went back to the satellite image. It showed a huge circle of white cloud. It looked benign, but Henry knew what it had done. On its travels down from the Caucasus it had killed five in Armenia and twelve in Syria. There hadn't been a storm like it in a hundred years, so the Israeli weather service was saying.

And in the middle of all this, an air raid warning had sounded in Tel Aviv. The Israelis were getting twitchy. A rumour had gone around that the storm would be the ideal cover for Israel's enemies to mount an airborne attack.

Henry looked through the text feed from Mossad. It was sparse, infuriatingly so. The last update had been fifteen minutes ago.

He downed the rest of the Diet Coke. It had been a big mistake letting Mark Headsell do a minimum personnel operation to investigate that Dr Susan Hunter lead. The very least he should have done was order him to wait until an Israeli commando unit was available.

Henry threw the empty Diet Coke can in the bin. It rattled as it went in. It was totally frustrating knowing all he could do now was wait and wait some more.

A sheet of paper slapped onto the desk by his right hand, missing it by an inch.

'It's a good thing I came back in,' said Sergeant Finch.

Henry turned, looked up at her, his eyebrows raised. 'Your friend, Lord Bidoner,' Sergeant Finch paused, leaned down towards him, 'has just been identified as the financial backer of a TV station which has released a news video that's going viral in twelve Muslim countries.'

Henry looked at the paper on his desk. It was a row of alarming YouTube statistics for a list of countries. He turned and looked up at Sergeant Finch. She had that irritating, superior look on her face. No doubt she would soon claim that keeping an eye on Bidoner had been her idea.

'A YouTube news video?' he said.

She leaned further down towards him. 'Yes, Henry. A video, which further justifies our little leak this afternoon.' She glanced to her left and right, then leaned closer. He could smell her lemony shampoo.

'The video claims new evidence has been found to prove that Israel is using this crisis to suppress Islam's claims on Jerusalem.'

'What evidence?'

Sergeant Finch straightened up, took a step back.

'They claim that Israel is behind the murders in the Church of the Holy Sepulchre,' she said. She looked at the screens on Henry's desk.

'Are we on top of the Susan Hunter operation? There are a lot of people trying to stir things up out there.'

'We were,' said Henry. 'Until this bloody storm knocked out our live tracking system. I've been trying to get it back online. Let me have another look.' He turned back to his screen.

'Frigging hell,' he said.

59

A splash of water on my face woke me with a start. A burning sensation in my throat made me gag. I tried to sit up. I couldn't.

There was smoke all around me. My skin prickled hot. A taste of burnt wood filled my mouth. Something was cutting into my chest and my outstretched arms, as I tried to rise. I turned my head.

I knew what he'd done.

I was on the wooden cart, tied down. There was smoke rising all around the sides of the cart. He had pushed it over the fire. It would burn in the next few minutes and so would I.

The pain from the heat coming through the wood was making my body twist. Smoke was in my lungs, and swirling demonically above me.

I was on a bed of pain. I hadn't long left to live. As soon as the wood caught fire I was cooked.

I heard a laugh.

I tried to rise again, pushing against my bindings. It was no good. He had tied me down with wire. All I could do was arch my back away from the hot wood, move my knees from it.

I heard a voice.

'You will die slowly, Sean Ryan. And when you are roasted I will slice you open.'

'Go to hell,' I shouted. 'That's where you come from.' I coughed. I wasn't going to scream with pain and give him that victory.

'I'm not from hell.' The bastard laughed. 'Your one true God burns those who displease him.'

Pain flowed through me.

Suddenly I needed to urinate. I let the water pass out. I didn't want it boiling inside me. A cloud of acidic smoke rose up around me.

'Your lungs will liquefy soon,' said the voice. 'You will cough them up before you die. You cannot be saved. You should not have interfered.'

My chest hurt, felt constricted, as if his prediction was beginning. The pain in my wrists was biting at me. I twisted them. They were bent at a weird angle now and hurt excruciatingly. But I had no choice. I had to test how far I could move them.

And still I didn't scream.

I tried to shake, to move the cart under me, but all that did was dig the wires into my skin. And they were getting hot, transferring the heat from below the cart as if conducting electricity. And still I didn't scream.

But in that moment I knew that hope was gone.

Time slowed.

Every sense was overwhelmed by crackling, the thick smoke, the carbon taste of it, the rising waves of heat on my skin, the terrifying knowledge that I would die soon.

I closed my eyes. I may be dead, but Isabel still had a chance. Maybe my death would help save her, give the Palestinians time to come and get this bastard.

It was a small hope as the heat rose around me. And at least his mocking voice was gone.

340

And then a great shuddering whoosh sounded all around me.

The smoke cleared for a wonderful second and a huge wind blew beautiful, wonderful cold air against my skin, as if the wings of an angel were beating down on me.

Was this a trick of my mind?

Was this the approach of death?

But it wasn't. Shouts echoed. And I was coughing as the smoke swirled violently. And then I felt myself moving.

I was off the fire and something was at my wrists and ankles whilst someone was screaming something in Hebrew in my ear.

I recognised one word. 'Medic!'

I was still coughing as they peeled me off the cart. I expected I would leave half my skin on it, could almost feel it happening, but aside from my clothes being charred all down my back and my hands being red and raw from burns I was lucky.

Every part of my body was brown from the smoke or pink from heat, puckered in places and sore, but I was lightly barbecued, not blackened.

The Israeli Air Force helicopter that had dropped onto the camp had scattered the fire and smoke from underneath me.

I had been at the burning gate of death and it had opened to take me, but I was still here.

Intense elation and relief ran through me like ice roaring through my veins.

'Was there anyone else in your party?' someone kept saying. She was a female Israeli commando, dressed all in black, and attractive, with curly black hair and shiny brown skin.

Where was Isabel?

'Was there anyone else in your party?'

I didn't understand what she was saying. I was alive. I had a future again. I'd cheated death.

Seconds later they had stood me up, my smouldering clothes were gone, and they'd put me in a navy blue jumpsuit made from some strange elasticated nylon. It felt as if it had thick greasy cream on the inside. I didn't care. It was cooling my skin like water.

'Lie down,' someone shouted. I bent down, staggered, sat down by a stretcher, overcome with a series of shudders that passed through me, as my muscles reacted to the tension they'd been through.

'Was there anyone else with you?'

Finally, I understood. 'Isabel. She's still out there.'

I pointed out at the rocky valley.

I tried to get up. Another shudder passed through me. I sat down. I would stand again once it had passed. The helicopter was near. Its blades were rotating slowly. They were sending the nearby bushes flailing.

'Where?' she said. She was on her knees beside me.

I felt a great surge of hope.

'How did you find me?'

She looked up. There was another Israeli. He looked like an officer. He was wearing a cap with a red badge. His epaulettes had pale blue bars on them. His face was sun beaten.

He stared down at me.

'Our reconnaissance team was looking for your group. They spotted a fire.'

Ariel must have warned his superiors where he was going. A real dread for most senior Israeli officers was that they would be responsible for one of their soldiers getting kidnapped.

'Did you see anyone?' I asked.

'There was someone here when we started our descent, but they were long gone when we pulled you off that fire,' he said.

He'd run away.

'Do you know where your friend is?' She was leaning towards me. She sounded exasperated, as if she'd been asking me over and over and I hadn't replied.

I pushed myself up with my hand. I was halfway to my feet before she reacted.

'Sit down. You're going to the hospital.' She sounded shocked.

'I'm not. I'm good. I'm just covered in soot, that's all.' I rubbed some from my hands. It stuck stubbornly. My skin felt raw, but the searing pain had been replaced by a dull throbbing, so much better than when the fire had been near, it was almost welcome.

'I know where she is, but I can't explain it to you.' I shook my head.

She shrugged. 'Then show us. On a map.'

'No, no. I'm coming with you.' I shook my head again and again. 'There can't be any mistakes. I don't care what happens to me. Do you understand?' I pointed my finger at her.

The pain in my hands was considerable, but I could make a fist and bend my fingers fully, and the skin wasn't broken.

I pointed at her again, my lips clamped together, my eyes blinking like an idiot. I wasn't going to be whisked away. I was alive, but I had no idea what was happening to Isabel. That bastard could do anything.

She shook her head with exasperation. 'We get people like you now and again. If you last an hour I'll be surprised.' She took a silver pot of some salve from a pouch on her belt and took a big dollop out and held it in front of her.

'Rub this into your hands and your wrists,' she said. 'If you can do that you'll get by for a while.'

The first sensation when I put the salve on was icy heat, then a horrible crinkly pain rushed up my arms as I rubbed the cream in. It took a lot to keep my expression still.

343

'Did you find anyone else alive?' A sliver of hope was still hiding inside me that Mark, or Ariel or Xena might have survived; that I'd been wrong about their injuries.

'A Palestinian woman and an African woman are alive, but injured. My colleagues are tending to them. Five people are dead.'

I swallowed. There was a foul slime of soot in my mouth.

'I'm ready.' This wasn't the time for sentimentality.

'You're going to show us where your friend is?'

'Yes.'

She looked at the older officer who was standing near us. He nodded, looked at his watch, made some sign with his fingers. She pointed her finger into my chest.

'Now you listen to me. We will do our best to find your friend. But if we meet local resistance we have to pull out. And you will come with us, okay?'

'Why the hell will we pull out?'

'We're a snatch squad. We didn't come here to search these hills. We'll send a ground team in as soon as it gets light. They'll coordinate a search with the local Palestinians. You have minutes to find your friend. That's all we can give you. We have to get out of here soon.'

There was no point in arguing.

A stretcher was being placed in the helicopter as we walked out into the darkness. Its blades hadn't stopped spinning. They were ready for a swift take-off. How long would they wait?

Beyond, the darkness was thick. There were four of us walking through the valley away from the helicopter and the remnants of the camp. Another soldier in black had joined us. I'd expected there to be more of them.

The older guy spoke into a mouthpiece as we walked back fast along the path we'd come along with the riders. I looked back towards the helicopter. Only the swish-swish noise of

344

the slowly twirling blades gave it away. If you couldn't hear where it was you wouldn't be able to point it out.

The stars and the crescent moon lit the path in front of us. Was I mad to hope?

Soon we were halfway back to where we'd left the car. The rocks and bushes were shadows and ridges.

I was fearful about what might have happened to Mark and Ariel and Xena. Faces, snatches of conversations were playing through my mind, over and over. A surge of emotion gripped me. Anger mixed with sadness mixed with fear at what might have already happened to Isabel.

I had a sudden urge to go back in time. It seemed so close, that moment at the border when Mark had said goodbye, when none of this had happened, and almost reachable because of that.

I remembered what Xena had said about the symbol, how she'd drawn it in the earth. Would I be able to find it? Had it really been put there as a marker to show where someone was being kept? I walked faster, moving ahead of the others, uncaring that I was leaving them behind.

Suddenly, a shout echoed from a cluster of shadows ahead.

'Waqf!' was the shout. Then the gravelly voice shouted, 'Stop!'

I stood still, my eyes probing the shadows. Then I glanced over my shoulder. The Israelis had taken cover behind some large rocks. I saw a glint from a machine pistol. 'Walk back to us,' hissed the Israeli officer. 'We'll cover you.'

Was he going to suggest going back to the helicopters, pulling out, that I wait for a ground team to come in? I couldn't blame him. The Israeli army's presence here would only inflame things with the local Palestinians.

Instead of going back though, I raised my hands and took a step forward.

Isabel was near. I knew it.

I wasn't giving up. I didn't care what happened to me. Not for one second.

I felt the air from the bullet pass my cheek. I heard the sound of it being fired too, which meant one important thing. I was still alive. Whoever had fired in my direction was either a very good shot, missing me deliberately, or just getting his aim right.

My foot shook as I lifted it.

I spoke loudly as I put it down firmly in front of me, I had to go on. My hands were in painful fists. I could smell a faint whiff of gunpowder. In the distance the whoosh of the helicopter blades turning could still be heard.

I heard a rustle up ahead. The taste of smoke was still in my mouth, like poison.

'I am looking for my friend. Don't stop me.'

The next bullet buried itself into the rough ground at my feet, throwing dust into the air. I could feel the dust splatter my cheek.

'Go back,' came a shout.

An insistent voice inside me said, *do what he says, don't be stupid.*

I took another step forward. As I did a cold sensation, as if death was near me, settled inside my chest.

'Help me and I will help you find the man you are looking for!' I shouted into the darkness.

My voice sounded hoarse, dry. I stood still. Clinking noises sounded from up ahead, to my right.

I shouted again.

'You can kill me, go on, but it won't help you or your people. I am the only witness as to who set the fire in the Church of the Holy Sepulchre.'

I coughed, put my hand over my mouth. There was a horrible acidy burnt taste in my throat now. My hand was trembling. Shock most likely. I didn't care. I was beyond caring. I pressed my hand tight to my mouth. A smell of antiseptic cream filed my nostrils. My breathing was coming fast. A tremble passed through me, then died away. I had done my best.

I heard the breathing of a horse. The Palestinian I'd met when they first showed up was looking down at me again.

'Who set the fire in the great church?'

'Will you help me?'

'How many of our people are dead?' he said it fast.

'Two, at least. The Israeli helicopter will take one of your women to hospital.'

'Ayeeeeeee.' An angry sound escaped his lips. He turned his head to the sky as if saying a prayer. After a few seconds he looked back down at me.

'You saw the planes in the sky?'

'Yes.'

'They are claiming us Palestinians tried to destroy Jesus's tomb.'

I stepped forward. The horse was inches from me. I could smell its sweat.

'The world must know who set that fire. Do you want your people to be blamed for something they didn't do?' I paused. My throat was sore. I spoke slowly as I continued.

'Help me.'

'Who set the fire?' His gun, it looked old-fashioned compared to the machine pistols the Israelis had, was balanced on his knees. I was sure he could pick it up and fire it in seconds though. And that it would work well enough to kill me. Occasionally his gaze drifted behind me. He was well aware of where the Israelis were.

I was standing directly below him. The horse's presence above me, its muscles shifting, was intimidating. Its breathing was loud.

'You want to know?'

'Yes,' he said.

'Escort us back to where you found me. My friend's being held somewhere over there. She was taken by the madman you're looking for. That is why he came back here. He needed somewhere to hide her.' Was I telling him too much? I didn't care.

He waved at the air behind me. 'They will not come with you.' He shook his head, as if there was no question of him shifting on that.

To ask for them to come was probably too much. And if they went back to the helicopter, Xena and the Palestinian woman might get to hospital quicker too.

'Okay, just take me.'

'Tell me who set that fire.'

'Don't tell him anything,' said a voice behind me. It was the older Israeli soldier.

'I'll tell you when we get there.'

'Tell me now,' said the rider.

I studied him. Pale moonlight glinted on his skin, gave him a hard look, but there was something trustworthy about him too. Something in his eyes.

I hesitated, not sure what to do. Should I show him that I trusted him? Surely if he'd wanted me dead, he could have shot me already?

'Come back,' said the older Israeli, loudly. 'Forget this. You will not find your friend this way. We will send a team here in the morning.'

I looked up at the Palestinian. 'The man who set the church on fire is the man you are looking for in this valley.'

'Then we will find him together.'

The Palestinian reached down to pull me onto his horse. It turned as he did so, its feet stamping. I reached up. It took two tries to get up, but a minute later we were riding slowly through the darkness.

Other riders joined us from behind rocks as we passed them. Two minutes later the helicopter roared as it passed over us, flying low. The men with me might have wanted to loose a few bullets at it, but it was gone from the sky in seconds.

Soon all I could hear was the clip-clop of horseshoes on the track. Had I done the right thing?

Was there still a chance to save Isabel?

60

Isabel had given up. She'd spent a long time banging on the wall of the cave, on the floor too. It echoed, she'd found.

She was hoping someone would hear her, come for her. But they didn't. And now she was sitting with her back against the cold rock wall again.

Her mouth was as dry as the stone around her. Her tongue felt huge, rough. And her throat seemed about to close.

She'd drifted into a fitful sleep and had woken with a blinding headache. Susan's lifeless body was still beside her.

She knew that Susan was near death. And guiltily she dreaded what would happen after she died. One of the courses she'd done for her degree in biology had gone into a little too much detail about what happened to you after death.

The air was rancid already. But within twenty-four hours of a person dying the bacteria inside the intestines would start to eat their host. And then they would spread through the body. Isabel wasn't going to be able to see the big green and purple patches break out on Susan's skin, as the bacteria reached it. But the overwhelming smell of rancid gas emanating from the body would tell its tale.

And the darkness would be evil then. The tiniest insects in the area, and their bigger and bigger cousins, would all burrow their way to the cave. And then they would feast. And as their numbers grew, and more of their eggs hatched, they would look around for more food.

She didn't want to be alive when that happened.

It had been an easy decision to make, in the end. There was no hope. To believe anything else would be just fooling herself. If she couldn't build a way up to the opening, and she couldn't attract attention, and a horde of insects were on their way, there was no other answer.

But it was one thing making a decision, and another carrying it out.

Though she had a good weapon to do it with. She lifted the rock, feeling it in her hand. It was six inches long, four wide, and jagged at each end. It would take a mighty blow to ensure she died from a single self-inflicted wound. But at least she knew the best place to strike; the recess just above the eyes.

The frontal cortex was right behind it and a proper blow would knock her out. And kill her.

But it had to be done with all her strength. Because what would happen if she didn't die? Would she lie awake and brain damaged as the insects found her?

She weighed the stone in her hand, tapped it on the rock floor, then tapped it harder checking it wouldn't break too easily. If only he hadn't taken the belt from her jeans. She could have pulled it tight quickly, then knocked herself out. Asphyxia would have finished her off for sure.

But there was no point in thinking about what-ifs, about Sean, about the life they could have had.

She could hear a rustling.

It was the insects. The smell must have brought them. It was drawing them quickly.

She stood quickly, stumbling sideways. There was something on her foot. Revulsion made her shake her legs. Salty tears welled. Then she heard another noise. Were they on the roof? She looked up, saw red eyes.

Lots of them.

Her breath came in stuttered gasps as a cold trembling passed through her. She put her hands out, turned, kicked. The darkness was the worst thing. At least if you can see your enemy you have a chance.

She had to do it. She had to act. She wasn't going to listen as they ate her.

Was it ever right to kill yourself?

She could roll, spin, kill lots of them.

But more would come.

And they would bite her, poison her. Scorpion hordes in these parts enmesh any larger prey in cobwebs after disabling it to keep it warm and alive. Then they lay their eggs inside it. In the softest parts of the tissue.

She had thought about not coming to Jerusalem after she'd read about that.

She should have listened to her instincts.

She held the rock tight, stroking the rough edges as if she loved them.

What was that? Was her mind playing tricks?

No.

A weight lifted from her. The rock covering the entrance hole was being moved. A saviour was coming! The wound-tight ball of anxiety inside her exploded. Tears rolled fast down her face. A trembling cascade of relief poured into every part of her.

Even when he shouted down at her she couldn't stop crying with it.

Though she bowed her head with disappointment as he

roared and the hope inside her dimmed like a candle extinguishing.

When she opened her eyes again she could make out Susan Hunter in front of her, on the saucer-shaped floor of the cave. Her body looked swollen.

'Stand in the middle, where I can see you,' came his voice, hard as ever.

'I will throw down some water.'

She stood still. The thought of water had made her throat open, as if it was already in her mouth. But she knew there was a good chance he was lying.

'Throw it down,' she croaked. 'I cannot move.'

'Come forward,' he said.

She still had the stone in her hand. She leaned forward.

She could see him now, silhouetted against the stars, a jagged-edged curtain of spangled light, a purple shadow set against the subterranean blackness of the cave roof.

He was holding something. What was it?

She leaned forward. It glinted, darkly. It was a gun! She threw the rock. It didn't even reach the hole.

The flash from the muzzle was an orange explosion.

61

I heard the gunshot. It was coming from somewhere up ahead.

'We have no guns that make a noise like that.' He kicked the horse under us. It set off at a faster pace. But still it kept its nose down, as if it was sniffing the dark ground as we moved forward.

The sound of another gunshot reached us. Then two more.

'Can't we go faster?' I said.

We weren't even cantering. We were walking.

'Do you want my horse to break a leg?'

'I'll buy you a new horse.'

'You cannot buy a new horse in the middle of a ride.'

I wanted to shout at him, but I restrained myself. We bounced on. It was an agonising journey. The gunshots could be about Isabel. That evil bastard was shooting at someone. Or had he been spotted by someone else? Was he in a fire fight? The next minutes felt like wading through treacle.

'Get down. Your car is over there. This is where you wanted to go.'

I slid from the horse. Its leg muscles were trembling.

The rider who'd taken me looked over his shoulder, first

one way, then the other. His horse must have picked up on something too. It was moving restlessly, stomping.

Then there were three other riders beside us. All men. Two were wearing white Arab headdresses. The sky was darker now, heavy clouds had rolled over. The moon was low, visible in the south, where the clouds hadn't reached. Details, especially those at ground level, were hard to make out. Shadows ruled.

I could see our car. It was a dark shadow. I walked towards it.

A shot rang out.

The rider, the man who'd kept his word, who'd taken me here, slumped forward, fell almost soundlessly to the ground. The other riders were down from their horses and among the rocks before the body had settled.

I crouched.

I was watching for the next gun flash.

And my heart was thudding. He was near.

62

Lord Bidoner was packing. He had ordered a limousine to take him to Heathrow airport. The fact that an airstrike had been launched against Egyptian air bases would be enough to start a stock market panic. And that conspiracy video going viral would create international outrage.

The attack on Egypt would lead to a demand in the new Egyptian parliament for the total renunciation of the peace treaty with Israel, public support for Palestinian resistance, and free passage for shipments to Gaza from Iran.

The speeches were already in the right people's pockets. Outrage would be easy to whip up. That had been proved over and over. One or two popular media supporters was all it took to stir things up properly.

The long predicted great Middle Eastern war was on its way.

And hopefully, after its bases across the region were attacked and as casualties mounted, the US military would take off the kid gloves, do something symbolic, perhaps even destroy Islam's holiest sites.

The reaction to that would be like kicking a hornet's nest.

Both sides would suffer then. And the world's population

would be reduced in a fitting way – through the sacrifice of war.

It was unfortunate that he had no idea if Arap would make it out of Israel. The man was useful, if a little hot-headed. But there were others who would do his bidding now. He had friends in New York who were appreciative of his abilities and contacts. And if Arap ended up being a loose end, he would take care of that too.

And there were other reasons to go to New York.

There were flies buzzing him here, members of the UK Security Service who had been annoying him for a while. And now they had leaked stories about financiers profiting from war scares. Stories that would be published in the UK media in the coming hours.

An official investigation would be called for. Ministers from Her Majesty's Government would express their outrage.

Now that he had cracked the meaning of the square and arrow symbol the United States would be the best place to direct the search he had commenced.

63

One of the Palestinians let off a round. More gunshots rang out. And I knew where he was. The orange flash had been unmistakable.

And then it was raining, pouring down as if a deluge had been delivered according to some pre-ordained instructions.

In that moment I knew what I had to do.

What I could do.

His chance of seeing me, hearing me, would be minimal in the rain and the dark, if I crouched, kept low.

The real danger would come when I got up close.

My hands brushed the rocks and spiny bushes as I moved forward, towards where I'd seen the flash.

A volley of shots rang out.

My brain was fighting a deep-seated urge to dive for cover, to survive. But I couldn't.

I had to keep going. This was my chance. Him still being here meant that Isabel was here. Possibly alive too. And he was likely to want her dead. And Susan too, if they were together. I couldn't hide.

I had to find them.

My ankle rubbed stone. I stifled the pain, kept going. There was a row of pale rocks, a trail of leftover lava, in front of me.

And that was when I walked past the acacia bush. Its thorns stabbed my arm through the jumpsuit. I stopped, dripping from the rain, half crouching. Not a sound came out of my mouth, though I wanted to groan. The needles had plunged deep.

The unmistakable noise of a gun being loaded echoed faintly in the air.

He was near.

I pulled my arm from the bush. It didn't want to come out. Some of the needles were stuck fast. My skin tore as I pulled away. It took an effort not to make a noise or to move too suddenly. My eyes were slits as rain poured over me. I could smell damp earth, and feel the water seeping fast down my neck. The rain was beating strongly on my shoulders now, great waves of it washing over the valley and everything in it.

One of my hands was resting on a rough stone, the other was hanging beside me, after extracting it from the bush. My leg muscles were in pain. My throat was tight. I felt a cough on its way. Something itchy was in my chest.

And then a shot split the air.

He was firing at something! The bullet pinged off a rock far in the distance.

I turned my head, slowly. He was behind a rock to my left, about six feet away. Part of the shadow at the back of the rock was him. It had to be. And then the shadow moved and I noticed the sky behind him was lighter.

The moon was coming back into a break in the clouds.

He would see me.

I had a second, maybe two, to decide what to do. My head was at waist height. It was not a good position to launch an attack from. And I knew how strong he was.

I wasn't going to be able to overpower him easily.

I brushed my hand achingly slowly around the stones at my feet. I felt for the biggest one as the rain bounced over them. I held the hard wet rock like a stubby knife and inched slowly forward.

One step. Another.

My calf muscles were aching.

The shadow was just beyond a low bush.

I sprang, like a cat launching towards him, covering the three paces between us in an adrenaline-filled second.

I hit him, slammed my stone into the side of his head.

He grunted, 'Uuuuhhh', but swung at me as if he'd heard me coming. Something hit my cheek with a jarring metallic slap.

I swung again with the rock towards his head.

I missed. His arms were flailing. He grunted again. 'Aaaahhh.'

Then his gun went off.

A rush of burning wind passed my arm. We were grappling. It was frantic. I didn't know which side of him I was holding. His arms were flailing wildly. His body was jerking. A numbing blow hit the side of my head. I saw stars, yellow and orange, but I still held him. Then I heard a voice. As if from heaven.

'Help, help, I'm down here!' It was Isabel's voice!

She was alive! My grip on him tightened fast.

We rolled over, both of us frantically grappling, twisting, using every muscle not to be overpowered.

And then my feet were in the air. There was a hole in the ground under them!

A shuddering blow hit the side of my head. My vision blurred. Dust was in my mouth. My skull thumped, creaked, as if parts of it might come loose. I twisted, grabbing him as a rush of pain fogged my mind.

He was going to hit me again. My legs were dangling over the hole. His hands pushed my shoulders. He was going to push me in. I slipped back. He grunted in triumph.

'I'm down here,' came Isabel's voice.

I jerked back, yanking him towards me.

My legs were well over the edge of the hole. I had no idea how deep it was. I didn't care. I had to pull him in! Even if it killed us both.

Isabel's chances of being alive tomorrow would be a lot greater if he was dead. We fell back, down into darkness, grabbing wildly at the air. Then we hit something together, in a cracking shower of dust.

Billows of sand filled my vision. I was on my side, lying awkwardly, something sticking into me.

I was on a broken lattice of dust and sticks. No, not sticks, they were bones; tibulas, fibulas, hip bones, skulls! And there were thick pieces around me of what looked like a hard crust that had been put over the bones.

'Sean, Sean,' Isabel shouted. 'Get up! Get up!'

I rose, holding one of the sticks. It was thick, smooth, knobbly at the end. I heard grunting, and saw a shadow rising in front of me.

She'd been kept in a charnel hole, where bones were stored.

Was that why the local Arabs hadn't searched these holes? Were they off-limits?

My head was spinning. Pains were shooting through me. Pale moonlight was streaming in with the rain.

'Watch out!' shouted Isabel.

He was swinging something, as if clearing a path between us. I took a step towards him, crunching awkwardly through a knee-high crust of bones.

Isabel was behind him.

I saw her face, pale as a sheet of paper, lit faintly by the stream of moonlit rain. She was moving.

361

She smashed into him at speed as he turned. For a second I thought he was going to hold steady. Then, like a tree falling, he came towards me.

I held the thick end of the bone high. It wasn't much of a weapon, but it would do. As soon as his head came near me, his arms swinging, trying to defend himself, I smashed the bone into his skull, slamming it down with all my remaining energy.

His body jerked. I smashed the bone down again. There was a loud crack. The bone in my hand broke, cracking into jagged pieces. His skull had to have been broken too.

He fell, twitching, spasms jerking his body through the dust and smell and particles and a wave of pale bones scattering, the flotsam of an uncovered boneyard rubbish tip shifting all around us.

My breathing was ragged, my lungs hurting, my head aching, reverberating with pain in banging waves.

And then a euphoric surge of relief poured through me. I was shaking all over from the effort of the fight, my body unable to stay still.

But we'd won. We'd won!

The bastard was dead.

And Isabel was alive!

We hugged in the centre of the pit. I had one eye on his body, but it was still. I closed my eyes for a second.

I heard a faint crunch.

I pushed Isabel away.

He was rushing us, a jagged piece of skull in his hand. He swung it at my face. I leaned back.

I heard it pass with a whistling noise, saw its edge glisten an inch from my eyeball.

He howled like some wounded wolf, an animal in pain preparing to deliver his revenge.

Blood was seeping from his eyes. His face was half slick

with it. His mouth was open, his bulging lips were bloody purple.

I stepped forward fast, ramming my fist straight into his nose. A jack hammer of pain flowed up my arm.

'Finish him, Sean,' Isabel screamed.

A spurt of blood showered towards me. His eyes filled with it. His mouth opened impossibly wide as if he wanted to bite me. I swung again, smashed my fist into his nose, pushing it back into his brain, and felt something splinter. He tottered like a felled oak, crashing back onto the bones. I watched, waited, my heart thumping, as blood poured out of the hole of bone and gristle where his nose had been. It seeped across his face.

This time he wouldn't get up.

A shout came from above in Arabic. I looked up. I could see an Arab headdress against the stars. There was another shout.

I waved. The head disappeared.

Isabel was hugging me now, tighter and tighter. Thudding pains rose then fell inside my skull and down my side. I stood on one leg. The other one felt bruised. She held me, as if she never wanted to let me go.

We didn't speak.

Moonlight was filtering into the cave. I could see Dr Susan Hunter laid out where the floor wasn't broken. It looked as if that had been the real floor of the cave before we'd fallen in and crashed through it.

We broke apart. I went over to the bastard I'd just fought for my life with. He didn't appear to be breathing. His head was at an odd angle and he was staring up at the sky. A big spider was walking over him. It stopped at his open bloody eye, then walked across his eyeball. He didn't blink. 'Is Susan alive?' I asked, softly.

'Yes, just. Can we get an ambulance for her?'

'As soon as we get out of here.'

'Let's leave that bastard down here for the scorpions,' she said.

A rope came curling down from the hole. The Arab at the top motioned for us to come up. He made a gesture, as if we should tie the rope around ourselves.

The shaking in my body was still there, but it was subsiding, as was the thumping of blood in my ears.

I looked around. The rain was easing. I wanted out of there. The hole in the centre of the roof looked like the pupil of an eye.

There was thick dust in the air. The bones around us seemed odd, too densely meshed in places, strangely lined up in others, as if some demented artist, obsessed with death, had arranged them for an exhibition. I saw spiders crawling. Not many, just two or three, but enough to make me leery.

Isabel was hauled up first. Then they hauled Dr Hunter up. She was unconscious the whole time. I put the rope around her, held her as she started to go up.

After we were all pulled out I took one last look into the hole before I hobbled away. The pain in my head was circling and thumping at the back now as if it was going to burst.

I don't know whether it was a trick of the light, but it seemed his head moved as I watched. Had he woken up?

Then I saw the scorpions on his face. There had to be a dozen of them. Their tails were flexing. They were eating. And then his head moved again, as if he was trying to throw them off.

But they were still there when it settled back. And then I saw more scorpions moving up towards his face. A fitting end.

The Palestinians who had pulled us up were carrying Dr Hunter away between them. I heard shouting. It sounded like an argument someone was having on a mobile phone.

Then, in the distance, I saw the lights of a vehicle approaching slowly.

Isabel was beside me. And then we were standing near Ariel's car, waiting. It was locked. We had no way to get into it. The rain was coming down softly. I didn't care.

I held Isabel in my arms. I was trembling. She was too, her body fluttering as if she was ill. She didn't feel soft though. She felt wiry, like steel.

And I was ecstatic that it was all over.

And we were both alive.

64

The head of the local clan arrived a few minutes later in a fifteen-year-old mud brown Mercedes 220. He was a giant of a man wearing a red keffiyeh and a dusty suit. He had a suspicious expression when he got out of his car, but as soon as he saw Dr Hunter lying nearby, sheltered from the rain by the jacket and body of one of the Palestinians who had carried her, he changed.

He waved at his driver to turn their vehicle around.

'We have a good hospital in Bethlehem,' he shouted, as he came up to us. 'But the road is blocked because of this stupid Zionist air raid.' He gestured to the sky.

Then he put his hand on Isabel's arm. 'My driver will take you to the hospital in Jerusalem.' He turned to me.

'And you will tell me everything that happened here.' He poked a finger into my chest.

The fact that I was holding my head where I'd been hit repeatedly didn't seem to concern him at all.

'I'm going with them,' I said. I pointed at his face. I didn't want to be separated from Isabel for a moment.

Two Palestinians who were standing nearby raised their guns as soon as I pointed my finger. The man in the red keffiyeh waved at them to lower their guns. Then he took a step towards me. He pointed his finger at my face.

'My driver can get through the checkpoints easily with two injured women. You will stay here to explain what has been going on out here in our valley, my friend. Unless you think all of your injured friends should be delayed until the authorities are finished with you?' He looked quizzically at me.

The men behind him had lowered their guns, but they were still in their hands.

If Isabel and Susan would get to the hospital quicker, this had to be done.

'Okay. But I'll hold you personally responsible for getting them both to hospital fast.' I was shouting. My finger was shaking, jabbing at him.

'Sean, follow us as quickly as you can.' Isabel gripped my arm, as if she wanted to take a piece of me with her.

We hugged as they put Susan into the car. It was the longest hug I'd ever had. I whispered the news that Mark was dead. She squeezed me even tighter but didn't say a word. Our hug was interrupted by the driver tapping my shoulder.

'We have to go, yes, yes. Your friend is sick, very sick, very sick,' he said, in an accent that sounded part French. His face had a pleading expression.

I let Isabel go.

As the car drove away in the rain my friend with the red keffiyeh said, 'Show me this cave.'

I went with him back to the hole. There was a little more light now and I noticed the hole was in a saucer-like depression and that around it there were rocks that were large enough to push over the hole if you wanted to cover it.

I pointed down into it, saw the dust still rising down there. I didn't want to look anymore. He growled as he peered in.

'He is the man who killed your people,' I said.

'His body will have to be checked by the police,' he said. 'If no one claims him we will throw him back in here and cover this hole over. Evil ghosts must stay buried. This valley has seen many things before.' He waved at the steep hills around us. 'That hill there is called Ravenge, and that long one there is called Jalous.' He pointed at the spiny ridge circling around. 'This valley is cursed. Evil spirits live here. The ones who kill for pleasure No one comes here unless they have to.'

'That man murdered people like he was sacrificing them,' I said. How had he got so twisted, I wondered? Was it all about revenge on a world that had treated him badly, or was real evil, something ancient, at work here?

'Ibrahim tried to put a stop to human sacrifice when he spared his son,' he said. 'Let us hope it never returns.' Then he turned to his men, and spoke for a minute in Arabic.

The rain had stopped. We walked back to where Ariel's car was parked. Another car had arrived, this one was a rusty red Mazda. We sat in it as the sun came up. He quizzed me for at least an hour, as other vehicles turned up, including a battered looking ambulance and a jeep with three Palestinian policemen in navy blue fatigues in it. He got out when they arrived. Then a policeman sat in the car and I had to tell the whole story again.

My head felt as if it was going to fall off by the time I was finished. My side was painful too. It seemed as if every joint and muscle had been strained to its endurance point, I had so many aches.

I told them who Mark was, who Ariel was, why we were in their valley. And I told them what the evil bastard had done in Jerusalem, and here. Their questions veered a lot of the time to the role that Ariel had played, and what the Israeli commandos had done.

368

I got the impression that finding out if the Israelis had killed anyone was a vital part of what they wanted to know.

I couldn't help them on that one. All through the interrogation, memories of what had happened in the past few hours played over and over in my mind. I saw scorpions feeding, Ariel falling onto his face, Mark's skull fragments on his jacket. And images of flames and smoke from the fire I was nearly incinerated in swirled like a bad horror movie in my brain.

At times my words were jumbled as I spoke, and my answers sounded stupid to me. As if such things as I was speaking about couldn't have happened.

Pains in my arms and legs made them feel as if they weren't mine. I started thinking at one point that Ariel and Mark's death had been my fault as I answered another question. If I hadn't come here they would still be alive.

But it wasn't me that had murdered them.

If we hadn't come to Israel, that bastard's plan to blame the Palestinians for the burning of the Church of the Holy Sepulchre could well have succeeded.

Finally, I was told I could leave. I shook hands with all the Palestinians. Then I was put in the rickety looking ambulance. I reckoned, from the way the police had been talking to me, that the two men who had sneaked forward after the shooting, who had pulled us out of the hole, had told them everything they'd seen, and had confirmed that what I'd done had been in self-defence, that I'd been looking for Isabel, to rescue her.

The drive to the Israeli military checkpoint on the road to Jerusalem was, without doubt, the worst journey of my life. The side of my head was booming with pain at this point. It felt swollen too. The ambulance attendant had given me an injection, a painkiller I think, but it didn't seem to work.

Luckily, the Israelis let us through without many questions. An Israeli soldier looked in the back and when he saw me, he waved us on. As the back of the ambulance was being closed at the checkpoint I saw a Palestinian with his trousers down and his shirt up, showing he had no explosive suicide belt on, about twenty feet from us.

Isabel was in the same emergency ward at the hospital. It was the same hospital I'd been in the evening before, but all the staff were different.

I got moved to a bed beside Isabel as soon as I saw it become free. We were able to talk.

Susan had been taken away for surgery. Apparently her eyelids had suffered burns and she was as close to death as you could be without actually dying.

I spent the next few minutes thanking God that Isabel was alive. She was dehydrated, badly bruised – he'd hit her when she'd struggled – and she was in shock, but none of her injuries were life-threatening.

She stared into space a lot of the time, but she was sitting up in her bed, though she was very distant, as if she was somewhere else in her mind. I started talking in a low voice, telling her everything we had done to find her, everything that had happened. After a while she turned to me and reached out her hand.

I leaned out of the bed, and reached out mine. Our fingers touched. I could feel her warmth.

'We made a good team,' she said. We stared into each other's eyes. She smiled.

'I called the Foreign Office,' she said. 'Someone's coming here soon.'

She was wrong about that. It took them another hour to arrive. We told them, briefly and quietly, what had happened.

They disappeared when a nurse came to take me away for an X-ray, but they were waiting when I came back. Twenty minutes later, after a doctor had reviewed my X-ray and had told me I was lucky to just be bruised, one of the British Embassy staff, the older man, asked me whether I would address a press conference at the King David Hotel the next day, Monday.

I agreed. Apparently the Israeli media and other Western news media had been blaming a Palestinian terror cell for the fire and also blaming the Egyptians for providing the materials to enable the attack.

After being kept in the hospital overnight for observation, we took a taxi to the King David. I was amazed they didn't insist on keeping Isabel for longer. But she made it clear to them she was going to leave the hospital as soon as possible. She'd lost weight, had bruises and scratch marks, and the doctor had warned her that the psychological effects of being kidnapped would last a lot longer than the physical, but none of that seemed to bother her. She was advised, in the end, to see a trauma counsellor in London.

I had a bandage on the side of my head, another on my ribs and I was spaced out from the painkillers they'd given me. Half my teeth felt loose, on the left side. And I could still taste soot in my mouth.

But I was alive and so was Isabel.

We held each other for a long time after we walked out of the hospital. I didn't want to release her. People walked by us and we just stood there, holding tight. I knew then, without an atom of doubt, that I loved her.

'All I want now is a soothing bath,' said Isabel, as we got into a taxi.

After we got to our room at the King David, I called Simon Marcus. The Foreign Office man had told us we had nothing to worry about regarding our deportation. An official request to rescind it had been approved at a senior level in the Israeli Government.

I told Simon we were okay, that I'd found Isabel. He was delighted. I invited him to come to London.

I told him that Susan had survived too. He was delighted. He told me his wife and daughter had returned. We promised to meet again. As I showered, carefully, I saw scorch marks and bruises in places I hadn't realised had been damaged. My chest felt tight from inhaling smoke. Only the thickness of the wooden cart I'd been laid out on had saved me from being properly burnt. I felt deeply energised at having my life still in front of me after being so close to death.

Isabel could have taken an air ambulance back to London, as she was borderline for such priority treatment, but she decided to fly back with me.

Before we did that, I attended the press conference. A man from the British Embassy was waiting for me at the door to the meeting room. He advised me simply to tell the truth.

'It will be better if you do this on your own,' he said. 'Just keep to what you saw and went through. Don't speculate. What people want is the truth.'

I think the thin bandages on my face and hands were probably enough to convince viewers I was telling the truth.

There were only two TV crews in the room and three other journalists. I started by explaining who I was to the almost empty room. Isabel hadn't come to the press conference. She didn't want to be on TV. And I didn't expect her to after what she'd been through. But she'd agreed it was good that someone would dispel the rumours that had been circulating.

I told them why I'd come to Jerusalem, to look for Dr Susan Hunter.

'Then my girlfriend, Isabel, went missing. I thought she would end up like Max Kaiser.' I paused.

'Why did you think that?' asked one of the journalists.

I remembered my fear at the time. 'We knew Max. I was

372

scared Isabel had been taken because we were investigating his death. And I was right. The man I found in the Church of the Holy Sepulchre is the man who murdered Max.'

'You broke into the church,' said one of reporters.

'Please, let me tell you what happened.'

I told them what I'd done, that the man I'd found was a European, that he'd been responsible for the fire and the murders in the church.

There was a hush after that.

'Why did he do all that?' said the same journalist.

'I'm not going to speculate about his motives, but what I do know is that Dr Susan Hunter created a video while she was kidnapped by him, claiming that Jerusalem belongs to Islam. Isabel was kidnapped and she would, I believe, have been murdered like Kaiser was, and for the same reason, to stop anyone who might reveal what he was up to. I don't know how he found out we were poking around, but he did. And I am sure I was next on his list.'

I spoke then about how a group of Palestinians had helped us rescue Susan and Isabel.

A YouTube video of the press conference, ended up trending on Twitter. I was glad. People needed to know the truth.

It was also on the six o'clock news that Monday night in the US, the UK and most other countries, so I read on the web later.

I won't say we stopped a war, but we certainly stopped a round of escalation. The Israeli bombing the morning before had resulted in the destruction of eight Egyptian F-16 fighters and the retaliatory destruction of a new Israeli border post in the Sinai. But further Israeli bombing raids expected that Monday night never took place.

Later that day, according to the TV news, an Iranian submarine that had been in the Red Sea went home without incident.

373

I have no idea if a coordinated attack on Israel had been planned, to allow someone in the Egyptian military to seize power in the aftermath, as was rumoured, but it was certainly a possibility. I read later that investigations had taken place into share price fluctuations in advance of that weekend, and I wondered who else had been involved in that bastard's schemes and if they might have profited. I don't know if anything that happened helped engender any goodwill, but I doubt it.

It was early Monday evening when we flew back to London.

Two mornings later, when Isabel started a series of post-traumatic stress sessions, I went with her. As we waited in an empty all-white waiting room Isabel turned to me. She had a serious expression on her face.

'The doctor in Jerusalem told me I might not be able to have babies, because of what I've been through,' she said.

My mouth opened. I blinked. I felt hollow, as if something had been taken from me. I knew she'd been punched a few times, once in the stomach, and slapped, and that not eating properly or drinking had left her traumatised, but I hadn't realised how serious the long term effects of what she'd been through might be.

Then, weirdly, I remembered that early on in our trip she'd promised to tell me something when we got back to London. I asked her what it was. If I thought it would be a distraction, but I was wrong.

'I was going to tell you I wanted to have a baby,' she said quickly. 'It was the first time in my life I'd really wanted one. I felt such a strong urge.' The door of the room opened and a male nurse beckoned her. She stood. Her head was down as she went. I was sure I heard her crying. I went after her, but she turned, pushed her hand out, shook her head.

I waited an hour and a half for her to come back. We went home in silence.

Mark's death affected Isabel deeply too. She felt guilty, that it was her fault he was dead. Over the next few days we talked about it all.

'Someone you loved dying early seems like such a terrible waste,' I told her, as we had breakfast one morning.

'Life isn't as easy as you read in novels,' she replied.

Those were not good days.

I found out the following week that Xena had been released from hospital. She had recovered quickly. A friend of Mark's came around to tell us about his funeral, and that Ariel's had already been held. His name was Henry Mowlam. He seemed to know a lot about what had happened to us.

He didn't say much, but his questions were very interesting. He asked about what we made of the symbol in the book. I told him about finding it in Cairo, that I thought it was important, but that we still didn't know what it meant.

He asked me if I'd seen anything in Cairo about its use in funeral services.

I told him I hadn't.

Mark's funeral was in Maidenhead. We didn't go to the grave as some of his family were looking at us sideways and Isabel didn't want to be tempted to set them straight on how he'd treated her.

He was a hero who had died for his country was all she said about him, when we were asked about what had happened. She told people she'd been advised by the Foreign Office not to give away any details of his work.

But I had no problem saying he'd played a big role in Dr Susan Hunter being rescued. He deserved that.

Dr Hunter was badly injured. We'd visited her in hospital in Israel, but she'd been unconscious, and we'd called the hospital every day from London until she woke up.

She would probably regain her sight, although her eyes had suffered burn trauma, but it would be another two weeks before that good news was confirmed. A week after that we visited her in Chelsea and Westminster Hospital, where she'd been transferred.

Isabel gave her the rose and pistachio chocolates we'd bought for her and we made small talk for a few minutes. Susan was sitting up and looking almost back-to-normal in the small private room. When the conversation flagged, I asked her what had happened to the translation and analysis of the manuscript we'd found in Istanbul.

'I've passed that project onto a colleague,' she said. She looked disappointed.

'I couldn't justify holding onto it. There's pressure to get the work finished. But I will still be an advisor to the team who are taking over.'

Isabel moved in her chair, as if she was uncomfortable. 'I told Sean everything we discussed in that horrible hole in the Judean Hills,' she said. 'I don't think he believes half of it.' She smiled at me.

'Can you tell him what you told me?'

Dr Hunter didn't even look at me.

'It'll all be in the report,' she replied.

I knew that Susan had said that a few pages in the manuscript were the original written record of Jesus Christ's trial, in the hand of the official scribe who was present, and that it had been sewn into the manuscript we'd found in Istanbul at a later date.

Isabel had told me Susan had been convinced it was all for real.

I stared at Susan Hunter.

'It could be a forgery,' I said. Being in that hole would have reduced anyone's scepticism, but I wasn't going to say that.

Dr Hunter kept staring at Isabel.

'Findings like that should take years to verify,' I said.

She didn't answer. I shrugged. I felt relieved. Discovering something of global significance, the verification of the existence of Jesus and of his death by crucifiction, would put a spotlight on us forever. The record of his trial might end up being hotly disputed and our story as to how we found it made into lies.

I looked at Dr Hunter. Was she embarrassed that we'd come to ask her about all this?

'We should go,' I said, leaning towards Isabel.

As I turned away Dr Hunter spoke. 'I am the person who verifies such documents, young man,' she said.

I turned back to her. Her face was pale, but she looked determined.

'And I will verify it again when I am asked. The manuscript you found, without doubt, contains a first-hand record of Jesus's trial. The papyrus is verifiably from the correct period, that's proven by the papyrus Kaiser found in Jerusalem, and the text is in the right cursive style. Even the ink has the right chemical composition.'

'How long before the official report on the manuscript comes out then?' I said.

'It could be years,' she said. 'There will be a serious amount of academic interest in all this. The description of the events of his trial are different to what's in the Bible.'

My mouth opened. 'Significantly?' I said.

She nodded. 'Suggesting a slight variation from what's in the Bible could have got you burnt at the stake a few hundred years ago. And there are still people out there who get violent if you try to disprove what they believe.'

'Why would it have been in Istanbul?' said Isabel.

'A record of Jesus's trial could have been sent from Jerusalem to Constantinople before Jerusalem fell to Islam. Constantinople ruled the empire Jerusalem was part of for hundreds of years,' said Dr Hunter.

'I must ask you not to repeat what I have told you to anyone,' she went on, shifting in her bed so she could lean forward. 'And be aware that I will not confirm any of this to anyone who contacts me. People will simply have to wait for the report.'

'Why all the secrecy?' asked Isabel.

Susan sucked her breath in sharply. 'There will be consequences from all this, my dear. There's a lot of money and power in Christianity these days, and among its enemies too. I am simply being careful.'

I understood then why Susan had been reluctant to talk. She was scared.

'We won't tell anyone,' said Isabel.

'People deserve to know what's been found,' I said. 'Don't they?'

Susan looked pensive. 'If you reveal anything, please do not mention my name, or my college, please.'

We both nodded.

Isabel and I sat in the bright busy coffee shop of the hospital for a long time talking about it all.

I wanted the world to know everything, in case the academics tried to hide it all.

'If this gets publicity, they won't be able to hide the truth,' I said.

'You have a suggestion?' she said.

I leaned towards her, began talking. My head was aching. I hadn't got past all the injuries. My skin was tight and still painful in places, but the relief at both of us having escaped, from what we'd got caught up in, was what I thought of first when I woke up each morning.

'The important thing is that our names don't get associated with it all,' I said.

'I'm happy you're going to write down everything that

happened,' she said, 'but promise me not to release any of it until you're proved wrong?'

'I promise.'

'Okay.' Isabel nodded her agreement. She looked pale, and not that concerned about what I was suggesting.

I was worried about her.

You see, I had a question for her.

EPILOGUE

Dr Beresford-Ellis called me a few days after we met Susan. It had already been agreed that I would take some more of the holiday time I'd built up over the last few years.

He was surprisingly pleasant on this new call. When I was feeling better, he asked, would I assist him with a new security project for a bank, a project that one of his old colleagues had passed onto the institute?

My name had specifically come up in relation to it.

I asked him the name of the bank. As he talked I looked it up on the web. I was interested immediately.

I agreed to manage the project. Even if what I'd seen, the bank's logo, was a coincidence, it would be good to have something different to sink my time into. Now I needed to sort something else out.

When I put the phone down, Isabel appeared at the door of the kitchen. I think she must have been listening.

'You're going to work on another project?' she said. She sat opposite me at the white kitchen table.

'I can't mope around here forever. You'll get sick of me.'

'I won't.' She smiled.

I stood, then bent down on one knee to pick something

off the floor. As I was there I looked up at her, then reached a hand towards her. There was a buzzing noise in my ears. My heart was picking up speed.

'I've been plucking up the courage to do this for days,' I said.

'Do what?' She looked at me oddly, her eyes wide, as if she was shocked.

'Will you marry me?' I said.

The words came naturally now that the moment was here. I couldn't stop them. And suddenly I had no idea how she was going to reply.

Then she smiled, as if she knew all along what was going to happen, and had just been waiting for me to get on with it.

And as that second tumbled forward into the next, the last remnants of the ghosts of my past fled.

An Interview with Laurence O'Bryan

What items couldn't you live without?
My family, of course, then my laptop! Then books. Maybe books before laptop! Then movies and great TV and music that makes you want to get up and dance.

Which authors inspire you?
Kathy Reichs, Wilbur Smith, Enid Blyton, J.R.R. Tolkien, Robert Graves, Arthur Conan Doyle and Charles Dickens are my favourite authors. I like stories with strong themes, a great plot and lively characters.

Do you spend a lot of time researching your novels?
I love research. I love reading about the history of every city my stories are set in and visiting each one. It's a small indulgence and it allows me to smell what a place is like, and to see the look in the eyes of the inhabitants.

What is a typical working day like for you?
I write from about 8 a.m. until noon. Sometimes I'll start earlier, but often I am reading or doing research on the

internet before that. I also read history and interesting novels at night. In the afternoon I do some other editing or write posts for my blogs.

Have you ever had writer's block? If so, how did you cope with it?
I've had writer's block only once. Luckily that was seven years ago, so I seem to have conquered it. I'm self-disciplined and focused on writing these days so I don't really have a problem with this.

Do your characters ever surprise you?
Yes, ideas flow sometimes and you can't always be sure what a character will say next! That's part of the fun of writing.

Which five people, living or dead, would you invite to a dinner party?
I would start with a few of the writers above! Any who could make it. After that I would love to know what happened to the last Byzantine Emperor Constantine XI, and to ask along the Prophet Jeremiah, to see if he might spill the beans on what he did with the Ark of the Covenant. If the Queen of Sheeba could make it she could sit at the top of the table!

What's the strangest job you've ever had?
I cleaned the plates at a gentleman's club opposite the Bank of England in the 1980s. The room was beautiful, but I had to stay hidden behind a screen in the corner. I was the lowest of the kitchen staff, but it was a pleasure to even see the inside of that beautiful club.

And what can you tell us about your next novel?
The next novel in the series is called *The New York Puzzle*.

In it we finally find out what the square and arrow symbol means. We see Sean and Isabel in New York and get to find out some of the strange secrets of the oldest bank in the United States of America.

When did you start writing?
I started writing fiction on a daily basis in 2000. I had started a few stories before that, but after I lost a job in London and had to move house I decided it was time to start working on my dreams, to start creating something for myself. I miss days now and again, getting ill or suffering from a hangover are all that stops me now, but I have been working almost every day since then.

How did you decide what sort of books you wanted to write?
I always liked adventure stories. *The Lord of the Rings* is the only book I ever read three times. I loved *King Solomon's Mines* by Rider Haggard and *I Claudius* by Robert Graves. I always wanted to create modern adventure storied with real characters about important things that are happening in the world around us.

Do you belong to a writers' group?
I am in three live writers groups in Dublin. As I work from home these groups get me out of the house and help me understand what others think of my writing. They also provide real friendships. I am very grateful for that. I have also been in a number of online writer's groups, such as authonomy, which were very useful to me.

Paperback or e-book . . . what do you prefer?
Paperback feels more permanent to me. I do read e-books sometimes, but I expect the main advantage of e-books would be if I were commuting and wanted to read on the train or

in my lunch break. I am sure they are wonderful if you travel a lot. There is a place for both.

Does someone read over your books before you submit them?
No, some bits are read out at writing groups, but I do the plotting and create the main structure myself. The Avon team help a lot with editorial advice too.

What's your favourite part of the writing process?
Getting lost in the writing. When I get a good idea as to where the novel is going I can find myself totally involved in the creative process. I picture where the story is going and love that creative moment when all else slips away and there is only you and the words pouring out.

And what's the hardest?
The hardest is the fast rewrite where you have two weeks to make changes and have to work seven days a week to get it done. Don't let anyone fool you, writing is hard work. Very hard work.

What's the best piece of writing advice you've ever been given?
Never give up.

No matter what you write, if you keep going, if you keep learning, working on your craft, being open to feedback, you will succeed in some way. My middle initial is P. I like to think it stands for persistence.

Do you have a daily writing routine?
I get up at five most days, do some research, then start at either seven or a bit later. I revise what I wrote the day before, then write for about three hours, depending on what I have to do. Then I do some more research. I rarely write in the afternoon. The routine started when I had a full time

job and had to stop writing by nine a.m. Now I can go on longer.

Do you plan a book from start to finish before you start writing?
I do now. I submit an outline of the book and stick to it, except where new ideas will add significantly to the story. I like to have a plan, but to be open to twists and turns that emerge while I write.

Visiting Jerusalem

In Jerusalem you can go to hell or heaven in streets just wide enough for two handcarts to pass.

In the Old City of Jerusalem

Hell is the Valley of Gahenna, the rocky valley just to the south of the city walls, where the entrance to the underworld was traditionally placed. Heaven is the Temple Mount, the Wailing Wall or the Tomb of Jesus, depending on your religion.

'They won't shoot you,' the pretty Israeli girl on the bus from Ben Gurion Airport had said. I'd just explained that I was staying for a week in East Jerusalem.

It was late February 2012. The sky was blue and the bus was winding up through the hills. I was the last to be left off. The narrow car-choked streets of East Jerusalem were busy with electrical shops, restaurants and apartment buildings. The view from my Spartan hotel room was of a building site. It looked as if it had been abandoned.

I was reminded of the girl's words the following morning when I was walking through the Islamic quarter to the Church of the Holy Sepulchre, where Jesus' tomb is and where Golgotha is, where he was crucified. My hotel was near Herod's Gate. It seemed like a good idea to walk through the Old City, a walled medieval looking city with a Biblical core. Its walls were built by Suleiman I in the late sixteenth century when Jerusalem was part of the Ottoman Empire. They are massive, thick as a sand dune ridge at their base and still completely intact.

I decided to take a short cut by sticking close to the walls. I veered off the main alleyway and found myself on a winding lane that skirted sand coloured buildings like prison walls on each side. I rounded a corner and saw a stretch of empty lane ahead with steps and no humans anywhere to be seen.

My feet echoed as I moved fast in what I hoped was the right direction. I heard a shout and turned. But there was no one behind me. Which way now? Empty alleys led off to the right and left. Some of them were stairways. There was another shout behind me.

Two boys were racing down the street with satchels

dangling. I hurried on. Soon I was at the great church mingling with the tourists, and glad to be there.

The Church of the Holy Sepulchre, a pilgrimage destination since the early 4th century, was reconstructed a thousand years ago thanks mainly to donations by a Byzantine Emperor, Constantine IX. The previous church had been razed to the ground.

I went to Jerusalem in February, at the same time that The Jerusalem Puzzle is set, to ensure I experienced the weather, the smells and the feeling on the streets, and to get a good understanding of the daily life of the city at that time of the year.

I also travelled far south to near Taba, the border crossing with Egypt, and through the Palestinian territories via Hebron and Bethlehem, near where scenes in the book are set. I passed through military checkpoints, saw guns drawn and crowds demonstrating.

A demonstration outside Herod's Gate, East Jerusalem

This is not a political book. I am neither qualified nor inclined to write such a book. But in Jerusalem I found a powerful and evocative city. What surprised me most about it was:

- The small size of the Old City. The Old City is encircled with medieval walls and is where the main historical and religious sites are. You can walk across it in twenty minutes. At its heart it is a warren of narrow alleys.
- The fact that the people are so visibly devoted to religion. Coming from a superficially secular country this is striking. Much closes on the Sabbath in Jerusalem, but not only that, it is obvious that all sides there, Jewish, Muslim, Christian, are devoted to following the daily paths of their religion. Prayers are a focus and lives appear devout.
- The similarities between the modest dress of the Muslim women, mostly headscarfed, and the Jewish women, headscarfed too, but in different colours.
- The numbers of pilgrims from each faith visiting the city despite it not being a time of any great significance for any of the major religions.

I went to the Wailing Wall and saw the devotion that people have for this site. I experienced the wonders of the Dome of the Rock and went around and around and deep under the Church of the Holy Sepulchre. Each of these sites has its own special feeling. Each has its wonders. I will not attempt to list them.

The entrance to Lady Tunshuq's Palace is on the left

My background led me to spend more time at the Church of the Holy Sepulchre. It is also where some important scenes in the book are set. I was there early in the morning and as it closed at night with a special ceremony, one that is carried on and watched by Christian pilgrims each night of the year since the time of Saladin.

*Inside the Church of the Holy Sepulchre, with the
Tomb of Jesus on the left*

I found the interior of the Church beautiful and intriguing,
although the number of Christian denominations in control
of the site leaves much to be desired, for me, and illustrates
the fractious nature of the descendants of those who follow
Jesus.

For me Mount Zion, just outside the city walls, was the
most spiritual place I visited. As I went down a stone spiral
staircase to the chapel commemorating where Mary died I
listened to Polish people singing hymns.

Dormition Abbey, Mount Zion, Jerusalem

The Negev Desert, the Judean Hills and the Dead Sea were all on my itinerary too. I visited villages off the beaten track and an old house with a palm tree drive that could easily be a model for the villa described in the book.

I wish to pay tribute to the people of all faiths and none who welcomed me to Israel and the Palestinian territories and who let me eat with them and who showed such compassion and faith in an outsider, despite the terrible things that have happened to so many from all sides there and the fact that the conflict in this land is not over.

Finally, I hope for an enduring peace and an end to all the suffering in these lands. Hasn't there been enough?